False Fire

Helen York

Published by Helen York, 2024.

This is a work of fiction. Similarities to real people, places, or events are entirely coincidental.

FALSE FIRE

First edition. November 13, 2024.

ISBN: 979-8230775652

Written by Helen York.

Chapter 1: Into the Flames

The sirens wailed in the distance, growing louder, a warning that only added to the cacophony of chaos in the air. The heat pressed against me, suffocating, a constant reminder of what we were up against. I had no time to think, only to act—pulling a trembling child close to my chest, pressing her small form against my soot-covered uniform. She was crying, her sobs muffled by the thick smoke that choked the air, but the terror in her eyes was unmistakable. She clung to me like a lifeline, though I could offer her nothing more than a fleeting sense of safety in a world consumed by fire.

And then I saw him.

At first, I didn't believe it. The heat distorted everything, blurring the edges of reality, making things seem unreal. But there he was, emerging from the fire like a figure carved from the flames themselves. His silhouette cut through the smoke, hard and unyielding, and for a moment, I thought I might be imagining it. The man who'd been my rival, my thorn in every side I had, standing there with the same wild determination that had always been his hallmark.

Finn.

My heart stuttered in my chest, not with excitement, but with something far more complicated—resentment, perhaps, or maybe something darker. He had always been the one to push my buttons, to challenge my every move, whether it was in training or during the countless drills that tested our endurance and skill. We'd never seen eye to eye, but now, as he closed the distance between us with purposeful strides, I couldn't deny that there was a strange, magnetic pull toward him. It was an attraction I couldn't afford to indulge—not here, not now. Not with everything around us crumbling in flames.

He reached me in seconds, his arms extending out like a lifeline, not to save me, but to take the child from my arms. I didn't even protest, though I felt a surge of something—anger? Frustration?—flicker within me. It was just like him to take charge without asking, to move with the arrogance of someone who believed he knew best. But even I had to admit, the child's cries softened as he hoisted her up with practiced ease, cradling her against his chest. He shot me a look, eyes narrowed, lips pressed into a thin line.

"You coming or not?" His voice was low, a rasping growl that only added to the rawness of the scene around us. His hands were steady, even as the smoke swirled, the heat radiating off his body like a furnace. He didn't wait for my answer. Instead, he turned on his heel, his every movement sharp and deliberate, pushing through the inferno with a certainty that seemed absurdly confident.

I followed, not because I wanted to, but because I had no choice. The flames were closing in, licking at the edges of the building with a hunger that was almost tangible. The heat made my eyes water, and my lungs burned with every inhale, each breath like swallowing broken glass. The air was thick with ash, and yet, I couldn't tear my gaze from Finn's back as he led the way.

He didn't look back, not once. His focus was entirely on getting us out, as if he were oblivious to the tension crackling between us, to the years of animosity that had built up like a wall we could never climb. But I wasn't so quick to forget. Even now, with the fire threatening to swallow us whole, I couldn't dismiss the past.

We'd met years ago, during the fire academy, when I was still green, still trying to prove myself. I remember the first time we clashed—his cocky grin, the arrogance in his eyes, like he was born with the knowledge of how to do everything right. He'd always been the golden boy of the department, the one everyone admired for his flawless technique and unshakable confidence. And me? I was the wildcard. I didn't play by the rules. I didn't follow the protocols. I did things my way, even when it meant stepping on toes or challenging authority. That's why Finn and I had always been at odds. We couldn't have been more different if we'd tried.

I remembered the way his eyes had sparked in that first drill, the way his challenge hung in the air like smoke. We had butted heads more times than I cared to count, each confrontation more heated than the last. But in the fire, in the chaos, I'd always respected him. As much as I hated to admit it, he was good—damn good—at what he did. It was why he was standing here now, leading the charge to save a scared child from the jaws of death.

We reached the front of the building, and Finn didn't even slow. He made a quick turn, heading straight for the emergency vehicles parked across the street, where the medics were already tending to the injured. He didn't speak, but I could see the grim set of his jaw. His eyes were narrowed in concentration, focused entirely on the task at hand, and I almost wondered if he'd even noticed me still trailing behind him.

I had to hand it to him—Finn might have been my rival, my frustration wrapped in human form, but when it came to saving lives, there was no one better. I hated him for it, and yet, I couldn't help but admire him.

The medics swarmed around us as Finn handed the child off to a team member, their gentle hands taking her into their care, but I couldn't shake the feeling that my world had somehow shifted. The child was safe. That was all that mattered. Or so I told myself, though my mind kept lingering on Finn—his broad shoulders, the way his movements were so precise, as if he was born to navigate through chaos. A firefighter through and through. I'd never been one to buy into the hero worship surrounding him, but it was hard not to notice. Not now. Not when his presence felt like an electric charge, a pull I was unwilling to acknowledge but couldn't quite ignore.

"You're still here?" His voice broke through the haze in my head, laced with a mixture of disbelief and something else—something too close to the irritation I was familiar with. His brow furrowed as he adjusted the gear on his shoulders, his fingers moving with familiar ease, and I bristled, suddenly aware of how much time had passed since we'd last shared a conversation.

"Did you think I'd run off?" I couldn't help the sharp edge in my tone. What did he expect? That I'd vanish into the smoke, a coward in the face of danger? "I've been doing this longer than you think, Finn."

His gaze flickered over me, assessing, calculating. For a moment, I thought he might say something else, but instead, he exhaled and walked away, leaving me to stand there, heart pounding, breath shallow. My mind raced, and for the first time in years, I couldn't decide if I was annoyed or, quite frankly, a little intrigued.

"You've been doing it for how long again?" His voice floated back over his shoulder, thick with that sarcastic bite I recognized all too well. "Long enough to get yourself singed?"

I glared at his back, my fists clenched at my sides. I wasn't here for this. I wasn't here for him.

But there he was, not even trying to hide the challenge in his voice, his posture radiating that same damn arrogance that had always grated on my nerves. Maybe it was the heat, or maybe it was the fact that he'd pulled me from the flames once more—literally and metaphorically—but I found myself unable to let it go. Not this time.

"Maybe I like to play with fire." The words slipped out before I could stop them, and I hated myself for it the second they left my mouth. The last thing I needed was to get caught up in another verbal sparring match. But Finn—Finn had this way of making everything feel like a game. A dangerous one.

He stopped mid-stride, turning to face me with that familiar smirk, one eyebrow raised, the kind that made him look utterly infuriating and way too handsome for his own good. "Well, it's about time you stopped pretending you're too good for it."

Before I could fire back, I noticed something—something that had been lurking in the back of my mind, like an itch I couldn't scratch. The weight of his words, the challenge buried beneath them, wasn't just professional. No, there was something personal there, a history we'd never really dealt with. I knew it. He knew it. And yet, neither of us was ready to face it head-on. Not yet.

I shifted on my feet, suddenly uncomfortable in my own skin. The fire was still raging in the distance, but the heat in my chest had nothing to do with the flames. "What's your point, Finn?" My voice had softened, despite my best efforts. I hated that, too—how easily he could turn me into someone I didn't want to be. Someone who cared.

He eyed me carefully, his lips curling in a smile that was as wicked as it was unsettling. "No point. Just didn't think you'd stick around long enough to find out what happens when the fire burns out." His gaze flicked down to my hand, which was still clenched into a fist, probably from trying to contain whatever was bubbling up inside me.

"Funny," I muttered, finally managing to unclench my fingers, "I didn't think you'd care."

For a brief moment, the expression on his face faltered, and I thought—just for a second—that I'd caught him off guard. But then, just as quickly, the mask slid back into place.

"I don't," he said, his tone colder now. "I just don't like to see people get burned for no reason."

The air around us grew thick with the unspoken words we both knew had no place here. But we both held our ground, silently daring each other to break the tension, to shatter the brittle shell of professionalism we had constructed over the years. It wasn't just the fire we were dealing with now, but the heat of a history neither of us was willing to face.

I exhaled slowly, forcing myself to look away from his piercing gaze. The night was closing in, and the damage from the fire was becoming evident. The buildings around us were charred husks of their former selves, their skeletons jutting into the sky like reminders of the devastation that had just passed. But it was the faces of the people—those who had lost everything—who haunted me. They were scattered across the lawn, some still in shock, others already wrapped in blankets, their eyes hollow with grief.

I turned back to Finn, who was standing a few feet away, his face lit by the glow of the fire trucks. The line between us had always been drawn, and yet, in this moment, it felt so flimsy, as if it might shatter any second. Something was different, and I wasn't sure whether that was a blessing or a curse.

"I guess you're right," I said, the words coming out softer than I intended. "Maybe I do like to play with fire."

His gaze softened, but only for a split second. It was gone before I could pinpoint it, replaced by that familiar mask of indifference. "Just don't let it burn you, okay?"

And just like that, he was gone again, swallowed by the night and the smoke that still clung to the air, leaving me standing there—alone, and unsure of whether I wanted to thank him or punch him in the face. Or maybe, if I was being honest, both.

I hated that I couldn't shake the feeling. It wasn't the kind of thing I could wave away with a few deep breaths or a swift change of focus. The heat from the fire had long since subsided, but the smoldering tension between Finn and me had only intensified. His touch, fleeting as it had been, left a mark. The way his fingers brushed against my arm, almost possessive, as though he had a claim on me, a claim that neither of us had ever acknowledged. It was unnerving.

I'd spent years burying my feelings, burying everything that might distract me from the work. But Finn had always known how to draw me out. He was the kind of person who made it impossible to pretend that nothing was happening between us, even when we were supposed to be rivals. It was a game for him, I knew that much. But for me, it was something else. Something deeper. Something I couldn't quite grasp.

We didn't speak after he walked off, leaving me standing in the shadow of the ruins, feeling like the smoke had followed me, clinging to my skin. I was suddenly all too aware of the distance between us—the emotional gap that I had spent so long pretending didn't exist.

As I made my way back to the station, the chill of the night air only made the fire's aftermath more apparent. The smell of smoke still hung in the streets, clinging to the walls of the buildings, weaving through the cracks in my uniform. I had no intention of sitting idly in the station tonight. Not after everything that had happened. There was still so much work to be done, so many aftershocks to deal with in the wake of a disaster. People who had lost everything. People who would need more than just a warm bed. They would need hope.

But as I rounded the corner to the station, the flicker of a cigarette caught my eye. Finn was sitting against the wall, his back to me, his face obscured by the plume of smoke curling into the air. Of course, he was out here. Of course, it was him.

"Should've figured you'd be the one sulking outside," I muttered, already bracing myself for whatever sharp retort would come my way. He didn't respond at first, and I almost wondered if he was pretending not to hear me, but then he flicked the cigarette to the ground and crushed it under his heel.

"Sulking?" he asked, his voice low, even, as though nothing had happened earlier. As though nothing had changed. "It's called thinking, actually."

"Thinking," I repeated, nodding slowly, "Right. Because that's what you do best. Pretend you're always right while everyone else picks up the pieces."

He turned, finally making eye contact. There was a flash of something in his gaze—something dark, maybe even regretful—but it was gone too quickly for me to place it.

"You're right, I am always right. That's why they keep me around," Finn said with a half-smile, but there was an edge to his tone, something almost brittle beneath the bravado.

I crossed my arms, taking a step forward. "I didn't ask for you to come back, you know."

His eyes hardened. "You didn't have a choice. Neither did I."

For a moment, the night felt oppressive. Thick. Silent, save for the distant hum of traffic and the occasional cough from the next block. I wasn't sure where to take this conversation. Where to go next. All I knew was that standing here, talking to him, felt like trying to build a bridge out of smoke. We couldn't talk about what was really between us—not now, not here. But the more we ignored it, the more it threatened to crack open, splitting the surface of our professional facades.

Finn straightened up, stepping closer, his presence filling the narrow space between us. "You should go inside. You've had a long night." The words were curt, but there was an unmistakable thread of something in his voice—something softer, buried underneath his usual layers of irritation and arrogance.

"And you?" I asked, almost too quickly, catching myself before I let any more of my own vulnerability slip out. "You're just going to sit out here all night?"

He exhaled slowly, glancing up at the moon, the edges of his face shadowed, unreadable. "I'm not ready to be inside," he muttered, almost too quietly. "Not yet."

I frowned, unsure how to interpret his response, but something in my chest clenched at the thought of him alone out here, isolated by his own stubbornness. By his silence.

"I don't get it, Finn," I said, frustration creeping into my voice. "You can't just keep pretending everything's fine. You can't keep running from everything just because it's easier."

He shot me a glance, his eyes hardening once more, shutting down the vulnerability I'd glimpsed earlier. "Maybe you're the one who doesn't get it."

His words stung, but I refused to let him see it. "Maybe I don't need to get it," I said, the words barely coming out. "Maybe I just need to get through this—without you."

The silence that followed was thick, oppressive, the weight of all the unsaid words between us pressing down on me. He didn't move. Didn't speak. Just stood there, watching me like he was waiting for something—waiting for me to say something, do something. But I didn't know what he wanted. I didn't even know what I wanted.

"Maybe," he said finally, his voice lower than before, almost soft, "but I'm not sure you can."

I opened my mouth to respond, but the shrill blare of a radio cut through the tension, and without another word, Finn turned, his eyes darkening with determination. "Let's go," he said, already moving toward the truck. "We've got more work to do."

I stood there, still caught in the undertow of the moment, a thousand unspoken words suspended between us. As I turned to follow him, my hand reached for the radio clipped to my vest, but the static that crackled through the channel stopped me cold.

There was something in the air now, something far worse than smoke. And it had nothing to do with the fire.

"All units, report to—" The voice on the radio cut off abruptly, replaced by nothing but a chilling silence.

Finn's face darkened, and he didn't have to say a word. He knew. I knew. Something was coming.

And we were running out of time.

Chapter 2: Unwanted Rescue

The air that morning was thick with the kind of dampness that only comes with a summer storm brewing in the distance. The kind that clings to your skin, making you feel sticky and out of sorts before the rain even hits. I drove to the firehouse with the windows cracked, hoping for a bit of a breeze, but all that came through was the stench of wet asphalt and gasoline, an olfactory cocktail of something that belonged only to places like this. Fire stations had their own smells, and for all the crisp uniform shirts and polished boots, there was always a lingering musk of sweat, smoke, and history.

I pulled into the parking lot with my eyes scanning the familiar metal doors and the faded red trucks lined up like soldiers waiting for a battle. But today wasn't going to be like the other mornings. Not with him here. Not with Finn "The Hero" Sullivan, that infuriatingly charming thorn in my side, leaning against the truck like he'd just solved world peace. He didn't even bother hiding his smirk as I walked past him, pretending he wasn't watching me like some predator stalking its prey.

"Morning, Riley," he called, his voice so damn smooth that it almost sounded like a challenge. It was the same voice that had once coaxed me into doing things I should have never done. And it worked every time. God, I hated him.

I didn't stop to acknowledge him—let alone respond. That would have been far too easy. Instead, I marched into the firehouse with a firm step, trying my best to ignore the heat rising in my chest, the irritation simmering like a pot on the verge of boiling over. I could hear him follow me, his boots tapping lightly against the concrete as he walked behind me.

"You know," Finn's voice came again, closer this time, and I could feel the weight of his gaze on the back of my neck. "You never were one for small talk, were you?"

I gritted my teeth. If only he knew how much I wanted to spin around and say something sharp, something that would wipe that stupid grin off his face. But I didn't. I just kept walking, taking the sharp left into the supplies room where the boxes of medical equipment were stacked high. This was my sanctuary—my refuge from all the noise that was Finn Sullivan.

But of course, nothing could ever be that simple. Chief Davis appeared from behind the corner, his usual serious expression giving nothing away. I tensed, knowing exactly what was coming. The way he stood, arms folded, his heavy boots planted firmly on the floor, he looked like a man who had just made up his mind about something. And when Chief Davis made up his mind, you didn't argue.

"Riley," he said, the sharpness in his tone pulling me back into reality. "Got a minute?"

I raised an eyebrow. "For you, Chief, I've got more than one."

Finn cleared his throat from the doorway, making me want to roll my eyes. Was he really trying to insert himself into this conversation? Of course, he was. He always did.

"Good," the Chief said, motioning for me to follow him. "I've got something I need to discuss. You, too, Sullivan."

I didn't need to ask to know what was coming. I could already feel the trap closing in around me.

"We've got some new paramedic runs starting up," Chief Davis continued, turning to face me with a somber expression. "And I'm assigning you a new partner, Riley. Sullivan's your guy now. You two will be on all the emergency calls for the next month."

I stopped dead in my tracks. The world went silent for a second, as if I was floating in some bubble where time had paused just to let the absurdity of the situation settle in.

I couldn't believe this.

"Wait, what?" My voice came out far sharper than I intended. "You're assigning me to him?"

I jabbed a finger in Finn's direction, but he just stood there, looking smug as ever, like he hadn't just dropped a grenade into my perfectly organized life. It was the kind of grin that made me want to punch him in the arm, and in that moment, I might have considered it.

"Got a problem with it?" Finn asked, crossing his arms over his chest in that annoyingly confident way.

I didn't answer him. There was no point. If I didn't want to lose my job, I had to make nice with the man who had once betrayed me in the worst way possible.

Chief Davis didn't seem to notice the tension building between us. He was already scribbling something on a clipboard, looking like he had more important things to do than to deal with my impending meltdown.

"Not a problem," I bit out, because what else could I say? "I'll make it work."

It wasn't like I had any choice. This was the Chief's decision, and if I didn't want to end up on the next round of layoffs, I'd have to suck it up and deal with it.

But that didn't mean I had to like it.

As the Chief moved off, I found myself standing there, eyeing Finn like he was some kind of rabid animal I had to carefully avoid. We were partners now. We were supposed to work together, save lives, be the team that everyone depended on. And yet, the mere thought of it made my stomach twist.

Finn broke the silence first, his voice low and a little too knowing. "You know, I'm not such a bad guy to work with, Riley. I might surprise you."

I gave him a flat look. "I'm sure you're a great guy when you're not being an overbearing pain in my ass."

He chuckled, the sound as familiar to me as my own heartbeat. "Guess we'll find out, won't we?"

As much as I wanted to retort, to shove him out of my head, something flickered in my chest—a strange flutter of curiosity. What had he meant by that? Was there something more to this new arrangement than I could see? Or was I just reading too much into it?

I pushed the thought aside. No need to get tangled up in something I didn't need to understand. Yet, as I turned and grabbed the medical supplies, I felt the unmistakable sting of something I couldn't ignore. Finn Sullivan was back in my life, and this time, he wasn't going anywhere.

The day dragged on like an old, cracked record, each moment repeating the next in a loop that felt both tedious and unavoidable. I couldn't shake the strange tension that hung between me and Finn, the air around us charged, as if we were two magnets—constantly repelling, yet inexorably drawn together. My hands moved mechanically as I prepared for the first emergency call of the day, checking supplies and arranging everything with a precision that bordered on obsessive. I needed control—something to grasp onto in the face of this sudden shift in my routine, this terrible partnership.

Finn leaned against the wall near the equipment bay, watching me with that infuriatingly laid-back demeanor, like he had all the time in the world to wait for me to get my act together. His uniform clung to his broad shoulders, the sleeves rolled up to expose forearms that looked like they could bend steel if he tried.

He had the kind of physical presence that made a room feel smaller, but his energy was a strange mix of easy confidence and something that could have been boredom if it weren't for the amusement dancing in his eyes.

"Need help?" he asked, the question laced with more than a hint of sarcasm. "I'm sure I could grab a few things for you."

I paused mid-step, narrowing my eyes at him. "I'm good, thanks. I don't need to be rescued, Finn."

His lips twitched, the corner of his mouth curling upward just enough to show that he found my irritation more amusing than he probably should have. "It's not about rescue, Riley. It's about teamwork. You know, working together."

I shot him a look, the kind that was supposed to communicate exactly how much I didn't want to hear his version of teamwork. Finn and I had danced around this concept in the past. We'd been part of the same crew before, and while our skills were undoubtedly complementary, our personalities had never meshed. In fact, if I were being brutally honest, we were a lot like oil and water. He was too carefree, too comfortable with breaking the rules, while I had always preferred things in neat, tidy boxes. It was hard enough working with him before, but now? With everything that had happened? It was nearly impossible.

He didn't seem fazed by my silence. Instead, he walked over to the ambulance, his boots echoing softly in the cavernous space of the firehouse. "You know, we could at least try to make this fun. I hear the best teams have a little spark between them."

I wasn't sure whether to punch him or roll my eyes. The man had no concept of personal space—nor, apparently, of boundaries. But there was something about his casual bravado that pulled at the edges of my patience. I had to hand it to him; he was good at keeping the mood light, even if it was at my expense.

The sirens wailed before I could offer a retort, sharp and urgent, like a warning shot fired straight into my chest. My pulse kicked up immediately, adrenaline shooting through my veins. A call—this was the real reason we were here, after all. I shoved aside the irritation, focusing on the task at hand, the familiar routine settling over me like an old coat.

We climbed into the ambulance, the heavy metal doors shutting behind us with a decisive clang. Finn was in the driver's seat, and despite my best efforts to ignore him, I couldn't help but notice how naturally he slid into the role. His hands gripped the wheel with a steady precision, his posture relaxed but not lazy. It was the kind of confidence I secretly envied—an ease that I never seemed to have, no matter how many runs I'd been on.

The call was a standard one—a car accident just outside of town. Nothing too catastrophic, but enough to make the lights flash brighter and the stakes feel just a little higher. We were halfway there when Finn broke the silence, his voice steady but laced with an edge of something I couldn't quite place.

"You know," he began, glancing at me out of the corner of his eye, "I'm not just here to annoy you."

I scoffed, half in disbelief. "Really? Because that's exactly what you're doing."

He grinned, unfazed. "Fair enough. But seriously, Riley, I don't want to be your problem. I'm here to help. If you need to vent about the past, I'm all ears. But I'm not here to fight with you."

I blinked at him, taken aback by his unexpected bluntness. I had assumed Finn would be more like the Finn I'd known—a charmer with a grin that made your head spin, the kind of guy who talked a good game but never actually dealt with the real issues. But this—this was different.

"I don't need a therapist, Finn," I muttered, though I could feel a flicker of something softening inside me, something I didn't want to acknowledge.

"I didn't mean it like that," he replied, the tone of his voice no longer playful. "What I meant is, I don't want you to feel like you have to do this alone. Not when I'm right here."

I could feel the tension in my shoulders, the subtle shift from frustration to something else, something warmer. Something I didn't have time to explore, not when we were speeding through the town, lights flashing and the world outside blurring into streaks of color.

We pulled up to the scene, the familiar cacophony of chaos greeting us—the paramedics, the police, the gathering crowd. As we unloaded the supplies and rushed toward the injured, I pushed all the thoughts of Finn out of my mind. I wasn't here for that. I was here to do the job, to save lives. Nothing more, nothing less.

And yet, as I moved through the motions, working alongside him in the heat of the moment, something about this felt... easier. He wasn't in my way. He didn't hover. He just worked. And somehow, despite everything, it was almost like we were a team again.

It was strange, that feeling. And it unsettled me more than I cared to admit.

The call came in just as the sun began its slow descent, casting a soft golden hue over the town. The firehouse was quieter than usual, the kind of eerie silence that only happens when everyone knows a shift is about to get busy. I could feel the tension creeping into my bones, the anticipation of a real emergency, the kind that pushes everything else to the back of your mind. This was what we trained for—this was where all the preparation, all the sweat, all the late-night study sessions finally paid off.

Finn stood next to me, his usual smirk replaced by something more focused, more serious. He hadn't said much since the last run, but I could feel him watching me, his presence like a shadow lingering just out of sight. It was strange, the way we fell into this rhythm. We barely spoke, but the communication was there in the way we moved, in the way we seemed to anticipate each other's actions. He was good at what he did. That much I couldn't deny.

"Ready for this?" he asked, his voice a little quieter than before, though the usual hint of mischief still clung to his words.

I shot him a glance, trying to ignore the strange, unfamiliar flutter in my chest. "Always. It's not like I've got a choice, right?"

He chuckled under his breath, but I could hear the edge to it now, the tension in the air between us thicker than it had been earlier. It was the kind of laugh that said he didn't know what was coming either—but he was ready for it. He was ready for anything.

We climbed into the ambulance, the vehicle rocking slightly as Finn shifted into gear and pulled out of the lot. His driving was fluid, confident, and despite my best efforts to stay detached, I found myself watching him a little too closely. The way he navigated the streets, the way his jaw clenched when he focused, the small movements of his hands as they gripped the wheel—everything about him exuded this quiet command, as if nothing could rattle him.

I shook my head, trying to clear my thoughts. I didn't need to get caught up in the Finn Sullivan web again. I couldn't afford to. He was a distraction, nothing more.

The call was a fire—an old house out on the edge of town, one of those dilapidated structures that had seen better days but still held memories in its walls. By the time we arrived, the house was already engulfed in flames, the orange glow lighting up the night sky. The sirens from the other trucks wailed in the distance, a haunting chorus that matched the urgency of the scene.

"Looks like we're not the first ones here," Finn muttered, already unstrapping his seatbelt and preparing to jump out of the vehicle.

"Good," I replied, trying to mask the unease in my voice. "That means they're on top of it. We just have to do our job."

We grabbed the medical bags and rushed toward the scene, the heat from the fire radiating in waves that made it feel like the air itself was alive. There were already a few paramedics tending to the victims, but there was no mistaking the chaos in the air. The fire was unpredictable, as if it had a mind of its own, devouring everything in its path without mercy.

A woman staggered toward us, her clothes singed and her face streaked with soot and tears. She was shaking, her eyes wide with panic as she reached out for help. My heart raced as I moved toward her, instincts taking over as I knelt down and assessed her injuries.

"Ma'am, are you hurt?" I asked, my voice firm, calm, despite the pounding of my heart in my chest.

She nodded, choking back a sob. "My daughter... she's still inside. I couldn't... I couldn't get her out."

I felt the air in my lungs freeze for a moment, the weight of her words settling on my chest like a lead anchor. No one ever wanted to hear that. The house was a wreck, the flames licking at the edges of the windows, the structure groaning under the strain of the fire. We couldn't waste time. Not now.

"Finn!" I called, looking over my shoulder.

He was already there, his gaze locked on the burning house, his expression serious in a way that was almost foreign to me. This wasn't the Finn who liked to joke around. This was the Finn who knew what needed to be done.

"I'm going in," he said, his voice low, not a hint of hesitation in it.

"What?" I snapped, pushing forward until we were face to face. "Are you out of your mind? It's too dangerous!"

"I can get to her," Finn replied, his jaw clenched. "You stay with her. Keep her calm."

I opened my mouth to argue, but the words caught in my throat. I didn't have time for this. I didn't have time for any of it. He was right, in a way. There was no time to waste, no time to debate the risks.

Finn looked at me one last time, his eyes intense but with something else in them—something I couldn't quite place. And then, without another word, he disappeared into the inferno.

The heat from the flames was suffocating, like a physical thing pressing down on my chest. I forced myself to focus on the woman in front of me, talking to her, keeping her as calm as possible, though my heart was pounding with every passing second.

But as the seconds stretched on, my stomach twisted in knots. Finn had gone in. He hadn't come back out.

My mind raced. He couldn't be...

A scream tore through the night, high-pitched and desperate. It wasn't the woman I was tending to, but I knew immediately where it was coming from.

It was Finn.

Without thinking, without waiting for any kind of sign, I bolted toward the flames, my feet pounding against the earth, my pulse roaring in my ears. I couldn't let him be in there alone. Not again. Not after everything.

But as I reached the edge of the house, the structure gave a terrifying groan. The walls shook, and I saw the faintest flash of movement—Finn, stumbling toward the door.

And then, everything went black.

Chapter 3: Smoke and Mirrors

The crackling of fire had long faded from my ears, but its scent clung to the air like a lover unwilling to leave. I stood in the ruins of the old building, eyes tracing the jagged lines of what used to be an archway, now reduced to brittle skeletons of stone and ash. The building had stood for over a century, a relic of a forgotten time. Now, it was just another casualty of a fire that felt... off. Finn, standing next to me, crouched beside a blackened beam. His face was unreadable as he sifted through the debris, but I could see the twitch of his jaw that told me he wasn't satisfied with the story the fire was telling us.

"Another one," he muttered, lifting a piece of metal with gloved hands. "Doesn't it seem a little too... perfect?"

The way he phrased it—casual, like we were discussing the weather—made my skin prickle. Finn had a way of asking questions that never quite seemed like questions. More like accusations. I turned away, ignoring the spark of irritation that bubbled up. I wasn't about to admit that something didn't sit right with me, not to him. Not after the way he'd looked at me when I first suggested something strange was going on.

"Perfect?" I repeated, my voice flat. "It's just a fire. These things happen. Buildings burn."

"Do they?" Finn's gaze didn't leave me, but I felt the pressure of it, steady and unblinking. He was waiting for me to slip, to give him a reason to drag me into his web of suspicion, and I wasn't about to oblige him. The last time I let my guard down, it had cost me.

"You're looking for patterns where there aren't any," I said, forcing my tone to remain level. "It's just a fire."

Finn snorted, the sound like gravel scraping underfoot. "You don't believe that, do you?"

I ignored him and bent down to sift through a pile of charred books, their pages curling like brittle leaves. The acrid smoke still stung my throat, but the familiar burn was no comfort. The fire here had been too controlled, too specific. Like whoever set it knew exactly what they were doing. And, god help me, I had a sinking feeling that the fire was more than just a random act of destruction.

"It's just a fire," I said again, louder this time. The words tasted like nails in my mouth, but I had to say them. I had to make them true.

Finn's silence was louder than any argument. It stretched between us like a taut wire, waiting for one of us to snap. Finally, he stood up and brushed his hands off, a signal that his search was over for now. But I could feel him watching me, measuring me with every step I took.

That night, the air felt thicker. Maybe it was the smoke still hanging in the streets, or maybe it was the weight of Finn's silent suspicion. Either way, I couldn't shake the feeling that I was being followed. I checked the locks on my apartment door twice before I finally felt the bitter sting of exhaustion settle in. But even as I lay in bed, trying to force sleep, I kept hearing that distant sound—the faintest rustle of footsteps in the hallway outside my door.

I didn't sleep much, and when I did, it was fitful. My dreams were clouded by a looming shadow I couldn't quite make out, a figure I felt more than saw. They weren't normal dreams, not the kind where you float along and wake up with the soft disorientation of a peaceful slumber. These dreams were sharp, jagged, filled with cracks and sudden bursts of light. I woke more than once with my heart pounding in my chest, the cold sweat clinging to my skin.

The following morning, I left for work early, the need to get out of the house pressing on me like a weight. The streets felt different—too quiet, like everyone was holding their breath. I tried to shake off the feeling, but it stuck to me, a dull ache that wouldn't go away.

And then, when I got to my car, there it was. A folded piece of paper tucked under the windshield wiper. At first, I thought it was a fluke—maybe a flyer or some junk mail. But when I reached for it, the ink smudged beneath my fingertips, darkening the paper in a way that didn't look like anything I'd seen before. A warning, perhaps. A message. I unfolded it slowly, trying to calm the jitter in my hands.

I see you.

The words were simple, but the ink was smeared, as if the person who had written it had been in a rush. I turned it over, but there was nothing else. No signature. No explanation. Just those three words that made the hairs on the back of my neck stand on end.

Someone was watching me.

I stood frozen for a moment, my breath coming in shallow bursts. It wasn't just paranoia. Someone had been close. Close enough to leave me a note. And whoever it was knew more about what was going on than they were letting on.

I slipped the note into my pocket, the weight of it suddenly heavy against my side. I didn't want to think about it, didn't want to acknowledge the dark knot tightening in my stomach. But I couldn't ignore it. Not when it was clear that whatever had started this fire wasn't over. And I wasn't about to let it end with me as the next victim.

Finn's voice echoed in my mind, the one thing I hadn't been able to escape: You don't believe that, do you?

But maybe, just maybe, I was starting to believe him.

The scent of burnt wood still clung to my clothes as I sat in my car, the weight of the day's ashes in my lungs. The night air was cool but thick with tension, and every creak of the old building behind me seemed to echo ominously in the silence. Finn had gone back to the precinct hours ago, his questions lingering in the air between us like smoke. He didn't believe in coincidence, and neither did I, but the reality of what we were dealing with was unraveling too quickly, too dangerously.

I glanced at the note again, its jagged edges crumpled in my hand, its message clear and chilling despite the smudged ink. The words were rushed, as though the person responsible had written them in a panic, unsure of how much time they had before someone noticed. "Stay out of it, or it'll be your last fire," it said. A simple threat, yes, but I could feel the weight of it pressing against my chest, like a warning shot across the bow. Whoever wrote it knew me—knew my patterns, my vulnerabilities—and that thought made my skin crawl.

The car engine hummed quietly under me, but my mind raced, spinning on its axis as I tried to put the pieces together. Two fires in as many days, both suspiciously close together, and now a threat. It wasn't just coincidence anymore, and it sure as hell wasn't an accident. Someone was out there, orchestrating this, pulling the strings from the shadows. But why? And why now?

I tossed the note into the passenger seat, my hands gripping the wheel as I forced myself to think. What could I do? The fire had been contained, the damage, while severe, was contained. Yet the sense of urgency gnawed at me, the instinct to dig deeper, to get to the heart of it. I couldn't let it go. Not when there were so many unanswered questions, so many loose ends left hanging in the smoke.

My phone buzzed in the cupholder, pulling me out of my thoughts. Finn's name flashed on the screen, his message a simple question: Are you okay?

I rolled my eyes, the frustration bubbling up again. Finn always had to check in, always had to be the hero. It was endearing and irritating all at once. Part of me wanted to throw my phone out the window, to ignore him and focus on solving this myself. But another part of me— a much smaller part— knew he was right to be concerned. The last thing I needed was for this to get more complicated because I refused to let anyone in.

Instead of texting back immediately, I typed out a quick reply and hit send, then let the phone sit there, buzzing intermittently as I wrestled with my next move. The truth was, I didn't want to tell Finn what I really thought— that I was starting to fear for my life. That I was beginning to believe the fires were no accident, and that whoever was behind them wasn't just playing games.

I looked up, staring at the dark streets ahead, each one cloaked in an eerie calm that made my pulse quicken. That's when I saw it. A figure in the shadows, barely visible against the fading light of the streetlamps. My heart skipped a beat as my mind raced through possibilities. Was it him? The person who had sent the note? Or was I just being paranoid?

I gripped the door handle, my breath shallow as I waited. The figure didn't move, but I could feel his gaze on me—heavy, calculating. He knew I had seen him, but he didn't flinch. Just stood there, in the dark, as if waiting for me to make the next move.

My instincts kicked in. I didn't wait for him to approach. I threw the car into reverse and backed out of the parking spot quickly, my eyes never leaving the shadowed corner. I didn't know what I was hoping for, but the longer I watched, the more convinced I became that something was terribly wrong.

I drove, fast but careful, heading toward the only place I could think of: the station. If Finn wasn't in the mood to hear my suspicions, maybe his superior, Deputy Chief Walker, would be. I could already hear his deep voice in my mind, stern but pragmatic, telling me to stay focused, to trust the process. It was exactly the kind of advice I didn't want to hear, but it was the kind I might need if I was going to get through this alive.

The drive felt endless, the weight of my thoughts dragging me down. By the time I reached the precinct, my phone had buzzed at least a dozen times. Finn. Again. I ignored it. I had no answers for him yet, no real plan except to see if I could squeeze anything out of Walker. Maybe he knew something I didn't, or maybe he could put me in touch with someone who could help me make sense of this.

I parked in the back lot, the sound of my tires on the gravel sharper than usual. It was a strange feeling, one I couldn't quite explain. Like walking into a trap that had already been set, waiting for me to take the bait.

As I made my way to the back door, I caught a glimpse of something in the corner of my eye. A shadow, just like before. But this time, it wasn't moving. It was still. Dead still.

I froze, the hairs on my neck prickling as the adrenaline surged through me. Someone was watching me. And they had been for far longer than I realized.

Chapter 4: The First Threat

The day was too warm for autumn, the kind of heat that made the air sticky, settling between my skin and my clothes like a too-tight hug. The office felt even hotter, thick with the mingling scent of old paper, stale coffee, and the faintest hint of motor oil. I hated the heat. But not nearly as much as I hated the note that had found its way into my hands earlier that morning.

It had come without warning, left in my inbox like a ticking bomb. The neat handwriting, the kind that could belong to anyone yet felt so personal, made my stomach twist. It wasn't much—just a few lines. But those few lines had enough weight to crack open the carefully constructed walls around my mind. "You're being watched. The sooner you realize it, the better."

My fingers had lingered over the paper, skin grazing the delicate edges, but I'd crumpled it up, trying to dismiss it. I wasn't some paranoid amateur detective. This wasn't a conspiracy theory to unravel. The city was full of enough oddities, but this... this wasn't worth my time. Not when there were fires to investigate and lives to save.

I threw myself into the work, pushing the paper into a drawer and telling myself I didn't care. As if that would work.

Finn knew. I could feel it—the way his eyes tracked me just a moment longer than necessary, the way his jaw clenched when he thought I wasn't looking. I didn't blame him. It was impossible to keep things from him for long. Finn had a way of getting to the heart of the matter, whether you wanted him to or not.

The tension between us was palpable now, the air around us charged in ways I couldn't explain. I wasn't good at hiding things, not anymore. The last year, spent side by side with Finn on case after case, had cracked something in me wide open. He had a way of breaking past the defenses I'd built—using charm when it was needed, but more often than not, just by being impossible to ignore. I'd tried. God, how I'd tried to stay professional. But the truth of it was, I hated him a little less than I did before. Just a little. And that was the problem.

I focused on the screen in front of me, pretending the world outside didn't matter, trying to ignore the weight of his stare. If I could just get through this day—get through the next few hours without saying anything, without even acknowledging that this was an issue, then I'd be fine. But I wasn't fine. Not by a long shot.

"Coming?" Finn's voice broke through my concentration, rough and easy like it always was. His lips curled into that half-smile of his, the one that made my chest tighten and my thoughts scatter. It was the kind of smile that made you want to believe he was the good guy, the hero who'd always show up at the right moment. The kind of smile that didn't make you think about how much he risked just by being who he was.

I swallowed hard, gathering myself before looking up. "Where to this time?" I asked, already standing, though I'd been working for hours and my legs felt as if they were made of stone.

"Apartment fire. The one on West Main. You in or not?"

His challenge was soft, like a dare, and I hated how easy it was to fall into the rhythm of his commands. But that wasn't what bothered me. What bothered me was how I immediately felt that familiar sense of dread in my gut—an instinct, a warning that didn't come from anywhere logical, but from something deeper.

"Yeah, I'm in," I replied, pushing my chair back with more force than necessary.

We moved together through the cramped office, past the cluttered desks and papers strewn about like the remnants of some forgotten battle. I tried to push everything aside, but it all felt too much, too overwhelming.

Finn was already halfway to the elevator by the time I caught up, the sound of his boots echoing across the floor. I didn't know why it bothered me. He wasn't my responsibility. I didn't owe him anything.

But as we made our way outside into the crisp autumn air, I couldn't shake the feeling that something was off. The streets were as loud and chaotic as usual, but there was an edge to everything, a sharpness I couldn't put my finger on.

We arrived at the building just as the fire trucks were pulling up. The smell of burning wood and charred drywall was thick in the air, and the glow of the flames bled out of the windows, casting eerie shadows onto the street. I didn't know what it was about fires that always made everything feel surreal, like you were watching it unfold in slow motion. Maybe it was the way the heat pushed against you, like the building itself was trying to keep you out.

Finn didn't waste any time. He was already moving before anyone had a chance to stop him, charging toward the building with an energy that made everything else seem like a distant hum. I followed, feeling my heart race despite myself.

Inside, the heat hit me in waves, stinging my skin as I pushed forward. Smoke curled in thick tendrils, making it nearly impossible to see beyond a few feet. But Finn didn't hesitate. He was everywhere at once, shouting orders, pulling people out of harm's way. His movements were fluid, like he was made for this—always one step ahead, always ready to save anyone who needed it.

I stood back for a moment, taking in the chaos, but I couldn't just watch. The family trapped inside was scared, the father clutching his youngest daughter, her face streaked with soot and terror. It took everything I had not to rush in and pull them out myself, but Finn had already beaten me to it. His voice was calm, reassuring as he pulled the father out first, then the daughter, all the while ensuring no one got left behind.

I watched as he moved, saw the way his face tightened when a piece of debris fell dangerously close to them, and something in me shifted. This man, who I hated for reasons I still didn't understand, was saving lives, risking his own in the process. For a moment, I hated him a little less. Not much. But enough. Enough for it to sting.

And just like that, the doubt crept in.

The fire's heat clung to the air long after we'd made it out. The entire block seemed to pulse with the aftershock, the scent of burning wood still hanging, sharp and acrid, in the nostrils. I could feel the sweat trickling down my back, but it wasn't just the temperature; something else had settled over me, cold and heavy.

Finn stood a few feet away, leaning against the side of the fire truck as if he hadn't just been in the thick of it, pulling people from the jaws of a beast that could swallow you whole in seconds. He ran a hand through his hair, the action a little too casual, a little too practiced. His shoulders were still taut, even though the adrenaline from the rescue had faded. His eyes found mine again, like he had some kind of map to my soul, and I hated it.

"See?" he said, almost as if he could read my mind. "I told you I had it covered."

I bristled, but only for a second. "You always have it covered, don't you?" I wasn't sure where the words were coming from, but there they were, tumbling out like an uninvited guest at a dinner party. "You charge in, take risks, and then walk away like it's nothing. Like the rest of us don't even matter."

He cocked an eyebrow, and for a second, I thought he might laugh. "You think I don't care? That I don't notice the risk?"

The rawness in his voice caught me off guard. For a brief, breathless moment, I wanted to apologize. Wanted to take back the words I hadn't thought through, but the words that had already made their way out, taking root in the space between us.

But there was no time for that. Not in this life, not when the city was constantly holding its breath, waiting for the next disaster to unfold.

"You think I don't see it, too?" I countered, trying to dig in my heels. But the ground felt too slippery. "You think I don't notice the way you throw yourself into danger, knowing the odds are stacked against you?"

He leaned forward, his eyes narrowing slightly, and I wondered if he could see the cracks in my own defenses, too. "I'm not doing it for me, you know. I do it for them," he said, gesturing toward the family he'd pulled out of the building. The father was now talking to one of the officers, his hands shaking as he clutched his daughter, who still looked dazed but unharmed.

I nodded stiffly, but my insides felt raw. This wasn't about the fire, or even about the danger. This was about something else—something deeper that neither of us wanted to face. "Right," I said quietly. "For them."

Finn studied me for a moment longer, but his expression softened, just the slightest bit. Maybe he understood. Maybe he didn't. Either way, I wasn't ready to have that conversation.

"You can go back to the office," he said after a beat, breaking the silence. "I'll take care of the paperwork."

I didn't want to leave, but I also didn't want to stay. This—whatever it was—wasn't something I was prepared to unpack. "Fine," I said, turning on my heel, the words more clipped than I intended.

I walked away without another glance back, my steps fast and deliberate, not giving myself a chance to second-guess. But I could still feel his presence lingering, as though he were walking beside me, the weight of his gaze pressing against my back like a shadow.

The office felt like a suffocating box when I returned, the air stale with the remnants of a dozen different conversations that had already come and gone, all of them blending into one. I needed to focus, to drown myself in work to keep the chaos at bay. But even as I sat down at my desk, the note I'd tried so hard to bury at the bottom of my mind crept back into the forefront.

It wasn't like me to ignore warnings. It wasn't like me to let something like that go. And yet, I had.

My hands hovered over the keyboard, but the screen in front of me blurred as I found myself staring off into the distance. Maybe it was paranoia. Maybe it was nothing. But the gnawing feeling at the back of my mind wouldn't leave.

I tried to shake it off, diving into reports, numbers, anything to keep my mind occupied. But the message wouldn't stay buried, and I kept coming back to it: You're being watched.

It shouldn't have been a big deal, not in a city where everyone was always on the move, always caught up in the next emergency, the next crisis. People were always watching, whether they were the ones in charge or just random passersby. But there was something about the way the note had been phrased, the fact that it came without warning, that set my nerves on edge.

I couldn't explain it, and I didn't want to. But it was like trying to ignore a storm cloud on the horizon, pretending it was just a bit of fog.

I leaned back in my chair, staring at the ceiling as if I could find some answer in the chipped white paint. The sensation of being watched grew heavier, more suffocating, like a hand pressed gently against my chest. Every little noise in the office seemed louder now, the rustling of papers, the tapping of keys, even the hum of the fluorescent lights above me, each one a signal, a whisper, a sign that something was about to change.

The door swung open without warning, pulling me out of my thoughts. Finn stood in the doorway, his posture relaxed, but there was something in the air that made the tension between us snap tight again. I hadn't expected him to walk in, hadn't expected to feel that same twist in my stomach, but here he was, looking like he had all the answers, like he had control over everything—except the things that mattered.

"Everything okay?" he asked, and there it was again, that knowing look. The one that said he saw more than I let on, more than I was willing to admit.

I swallowed, trying to gather myself. "Yeah, everything's fine," I said, even though I knew I was lying.

And Finn knew it too. But neither of us said a word. Not yet.

The office felt like it was closing in on me. The walls, usually a neutral backdrop to the daily grind, now seemed to pulse with an oppressive heat that had nothing to do with the temperature outside. The note, that damn note, still hung in the air like a bad smell I couldn't escape. My desk, once a safe haven, now felt like the last place I should be, the hum of the fluorescent lights overhead pressing in on my skull. I hated how easily my mind wandered back to it.

"You sure you're okay?" Finn's voice sliced through the haze of my thoughts like a knife. He'd leaned against the doorframe, arms crossed, watching me with that same penetrating gaze I hadn't been able to shake all day.

I didn't look up. I couldn't. "Yeah," I said quickly, maybe too quickly. "I'm fine."

A lie, of course. But that was how this worked, wasn't it? Lie enough, and the truth becomes a memory instead of a living, breathing thing. Finn must have seen through it. He always did.

"Yeah, sure," he muttered under his breath, but I caught the edge in his tone. He knew. Or maybe he was just getting better at reading me. Either way, I was done with the conversation before it started.

I shifted in my seat, pushing the files in front of me away and grabbing for my jacket instead. "I'm going for a walk. I need to clear my head."

Finn didn't stop me, didn't even try to follow. He let me go, and for that, I was almost grateful. Some days, you needed to walk away from the noise, to pretend like the world was still simple. That the only things that mattered were the mundane, the daily tasks, not the things that made your chest tighten and your mind race with questions you didn't have answers to.

The streets outside were as chaotic as always, the mix of sounds—from car horns to street vendors to people arguing on corners—felt like white noise against the simmering tension in my chest. I let my feet carry me without thinking, weaving through crowds, half-listening to the snippets of conversation that flew by, feeling the weight of the city settling around me. There was something about being out in the open, where the buildings towered over me, the sky a sliver of gray above that made everything feel both small and huge at the same time.

It was a few blocks before I even realized how far I'd walked, how lost in my thoughts I'd become. A sharp wind cut through the streets, making me pull my jacket tighter around me. I stopped at the corner of a street, my gaze following the steady stream of traffic, but then something caught my attention—an alleyway to the left, hidden between two towering buildings. Something about it seemed different, like it didn't belong, like it was a part of the city that no one wanted to see. I should've kept walking. I should've turned around and gone back to the office. But my feet betrayed me, pulling me toward the alley without any logical reason.

My pulse quickened as I moved closer, the hairs on the back of my neck prickling with unease. The alley was dark, the only light coming from the distant glow of streetlights behind me. My eyes flicked to the shadows, expecting to see someone, anyone. But there was nothing. Just the whisper of the wind and the distant noise of the city.

I was being paranoid, I told myself. But it didn't stop the knot of anxiety tightening in my gut. I turned back, but before I could take a step, the sound of footsteps behind me froze me in place.

I didn't need to look over my shoulder to know someone was there. The hairs on the back of my neck stood on end. My pulse hammered in my throat as I slowly pivoted, my eyes scanning the street. A figure emerged from the shadows, tall and imposing, but masked by the dim light. I didn't recognize him, but something about his stance—his silence—told me he wasn't just a passerby.

"Can I help you?" My voice was steady, but only just. I was aware of how my hand had instinctively moved toward my bag, my fingers brushing against the cool metal of my phone.

He didn't answer, his gaze locked onto mine with an intensity that made my heart skip a beat. "You're being watched," he said, his voice low, almost a whisper. But there was no mistaking it—he wasn't making small talk.

My heart did a funny little flip in my chest. The note.

Before I could respond, he stepped back into the shadows, vanishing into the alley as quickly as he had appeared. I was left standing there, the words echoing in my head, the sensation of being watched growing heavier by the second. My breath caught, and the noise of the city seemed to swell around me, louder, more frantic, like the streets themselves were trying to drown me.

I didn't know whether to run or stay, but I didn't have time to decide. The sharp ring of my phone broke through the tension. It was Finn.

"Where are you?" His voice was clipped, concerned, but there was something else beneath it. Something urgent.

"I—" I started to respond, but I didn't know what to say. Should I tell him about the stranger? Should I mention the note again, or the overwhelming feeling that someone was watching my every move?

"Listen to me," Finn cut in, his voice tight. "I need you to get back here. Now. Something's going on. You're not safe."

The words hung in the air between us, more chilling than anything I'd heard all day. "What do you mean?" I managed to say, my pulse racing again.

"I don't know yet, but trust me. Get back to the office. Now."

I didn't hesitate this time. I turned on my heel and started walking, faster this time, feeling the weight of Finn's words sinking in, the shadows of the city pressing closer around me. But just as I neared the street corner, a shadow detached itself from the darkness ahead, blocking my path.

And then I heard it—the click of a gun being cocked.

Chapter 5: Secrets in the Ashes

The air smelled like smoke, thick and acrid, clinging to my lungs like an old memory I couldn't shake. As I leaned against the cool metal of the fire truck, I watched Finn sift through the charred remnants of what had once been a barn. His movements were quick, methodical, as if he could read the ashes like someone else might read a book. His sharp eyes caught every detail, even the things most people would have missed—like the faint shimmer of something oily where the fire had burned hottest.

I could feel the heat of the day still pressing down, even as the sun dipped lower, casting long shadows across the scorched earth. The fire had taken everything in its wake: timber, tools, memories. Nothing had been left untouched. Yet Finn's focus remained laser-sharp, his brow furrowed in a way that made me wonder what exactly he was seeing that I couldn't.

"What did you find?" I asked, my voice quieter than I intended, almost cautious.

He didn't look at me right away, his hands still working the debris. The silence between us stretched long, thick with unspoken words. Finally, his eyes flicked to mine, his gaze steady but unreadable. He held up a small vial, the kind we used for evidence. It shimmered darkly in the fading light.

"Accelerant," he said simply, but his voice lacked the usual confidence. It was a little too tight, as though the word had tasted sour in his mouth.

I swallowed, trying to process the implications. The fire hadn't been an accident. Someone had set it intentionally. The thought hit me harder than I'd expected. For a moment, I was back at the station, sitting in the break room, the hum of the coffee machine a distant sound as we reviewed reports. Fires were often random, chaotic. But this? This felt deliberate, calculated.

Finn stuffed the vial into his bag with a snap, and for the first time since we'd arrived, he seemed distracted, his posture stiff, like a man suddenly burdened by something he couldn't share.

"Why would anyone burn down an empty barn?" I asked, my voice barely more than a whisper. My heart thudded in my chest, an echo of the fire's violence. But Finn didn't answer right away. Instead, he pulled his gloves off with quick, sharp motions and turned back toward the truck.

I followed him, trying to keep my distance but unable to stop myself from closing the gap between us. The silence between us now felt heavier, more charged, like an electric current just waiting to snap. I wanted answers. I needed them.

"Finn." I stepped in front of him before he could climb into the truck. My voice was firm this time, steady. "What aren't you telling me?"

For a long beat, he didn't speak. His eyes flicked to mine—long, intense, as if he were weighing whether to speak the words that had clearly been haunting him. Finally, he let out a short breath, his lips pressing into a thin line.

"I'll tell you," he said, the words low, almost a promise, but then he hesitated. "But not now."

"Not now?" I repeated, incredulous. "You're telling me you have something, something huge, and you're going to sit on it? After all we've been through?"

He didn't answer. Instead, he climbed into the truck, his hands gripping the wheel with an intensity that made the muscles in his forearms bulge. I slid into the passenger seat, the door slamming shut behind me. The engine roared to life, and we were off, the tires kicking up dust as we left the burned-out barn behind.

The road stretched out before us, empty and endless. The silence between us wasn't comfortable, not this time. It was full of unsaid things, of secrets I could feel pressing in on me, suffocating me, even as the landscape passed in a blur of browns and greens.

I crossed my arms, looking out the window, trying to keep my thoughts from spiraling. But it was impossible. What did Finn know? What was so damn important that he couldn't even trust me enough to tell me? He was always so confident, so in control. This side of him—the side that was closed off, distant—was unfamiliar. And it wasn't just the fire. I could feel it in the way he'd spoken earlier, the way he held himself, like he was on the edge of something dangerous, something he didn't want me to see.

I couldn't stand it. I had to know.

"Finn," I said, forcing my voice to be calm, measured. "If you know something, you need to tell me now. I can't just pretend like everything's fine when I know you're holding back."

He flinched, and for a brief second, I thought I saw something—regret? Fear?—flicker in his eyes. But then it was gone, replaced by that familiar, guarded expression.

"Drop it, Chloe," he said, the warning in his voice unmistakable.

I felt my jaw tighten. "No. I won't drop it."

His knuckles turned white around the wheel, the only sign that he was feeling the pressure. "I can't tell you," he muttered under his breath. "Not yet. It's not the right time."

"Not the right time?" My voice cracked, the frustration seeping through. "You don't get to decide that. If there's something going on, you owe me the truth. You owe me that."

He was quiet again, but this time it wasn't just the silence of avoidance. It was the silence of someone holding something back, something that, once revealed, might change everything. The weight of his words—or lack of them—hung in the air between us, heavy and suffocating, as the miles stretched on.

The truck hummed along the road, and in that moment, I realized that no matter how far we drove, no matter how many quiet moments passed between us, Finn's secrets were not going to let me go. And neither would I let him.

The truck's tires hummed over the uneven road, the sound oddly soothing, like the rhythm of a heart beating just a little too fast. The steady vibration beneath me did nothing to calm the agitation swirling in my chest. Finn sat beside me, the engine's low growl an echo of the tension thickening between us.

I wanted to scream at him. I wanted to throw open the door, bolt into the woods, and demand that he tell me everything—everything he knew, everything he was hiding. But there was this small, insidious part of me that wanted to know more, too. I wasn't sure if it was the firefighter in me, trained to assess and react, or something else, something deeper, more unsettling. Whatever it was, it made me press my hands tighter together, the nails biting into my palms, trying to keep myself from unraveling.

The silence was a strange thing between us. It was one thing to work side by side, the easy camaraderie built over hours of fighting fires, cracking jokes, and working together as though we'd known each other for years. But now? Now it was like walking on the edge of a cliff, with only the slightest misstep threatening to send everything tumbling into chaos.

"Look, I get it," I said finally, breaking the silence with a sharpness that even surprised me. "You're not ready to talk about it. But if you think I'm just going to sit back and pretend like nothing's wrong, you're wrong."

Finn's hands tightened on the wheel, his jaw clenching. I caught a brief flicker of something in his eyes, something dark and conflicted, before he glanced at me.

"You don't get it," he muttered, almost to himself. "You don't understand what this is, Chloe. It's bigger than you think. It's bigger than both of us."

His voice dropped to a level I could barely hear, but the words cut through the tension like a knife. There was something cold in his tone, something that made me shiver despite the warmth in the cab.

"Bigger than us?" I echoed, my voice rising in pitch. "What does that mean? Is there something I'm missing here? Are we talking about some—" I stopped myself, unsure of how to finish the thought. "Some conspiracy? Some crime syndicate, maybe?"

Finn snorted, his lips twisting into a grim smile that didn't quite reach his eyes. "No," he said, his voice softer now, but with a weight that still made my heart race. "Nothing that glamorous. It's... more complicated than that."

The weight of his words hung in the air, pressing down on me, but before I could ask him to clarify, we crested a hill and saw the distant flicker of lights—a small town, nestled at the edge of the woods. My gut tightened. Something in the air was different, more charged. It wasn't just the fire, or Finn's strange behavior. There was a palpable shift, an unspoken unease that I couldn't shake.

"Where are we going?" I asked, my voice slipping into cautious curiosity.

Finn didn't answer right away, his gaze locked on the horizon. He was still driving with that determined precision, as though the destination was the only thing that mattered.

"Finn," I prodded again, less demanding this time, more of a gentle push. "Talk to me."

He exhaled through his nose, as though weighing whether to share whatever it was that gnawed at him. Then, his fingers drummed lightly on the steering wheel, the beat slow and deliberate.

"We're going to see someone," he said finally, his voice flat.

"Someone?" I repeated, unsure of what he meant.

Finn didn't elaborate, but the name of the town on the sign caught my eye: Riverton. It was small—nothing more than a handful of streets winding around a few blocks of shops, homes, and an old diner. The kind of place where everyone knew everyone's business, where the air smelled faintly of fresh bread and the occasional bonfire.

I didn't know what to expect, but I was starting to feel that gnawing curiosity again. Finn's evasiveness wasn't helping. If anything, it only deepened the mystery, the urgency. Something was unraveling just out of my reach, and no matter how much I prodded, it was slipping through my fingers like sand.

The truck slowed as we passed the town's welcome sign, the dim glow of streetlights casting a soft glow over the streets. Finn pulled into a quiet, tucked-away side road, the asphalt cracked and uneven. The houses here were older, the kind with sagging porches and peeling paint, but they had charm in a way that felt like a different era.

He parked in front of a house at the end of the street. It was smaller than the others, tucked beneath a blanket of thick trees, their branches reaching out like gnarled hands. The front porch light flickered intermittently, casting eerie shadows over the darkened yard.

"What is this?" I asked, my voice barely above a whisper, as though speaking too loudly would disturb whatever secrets lay behind that door.

Finn didn't answer. Instead, he cut the engine and climbed out of the truck, moving with an ease that suggested he had been here before. I hesitated, the hairs on the back of my neck standing on end.

"I don't like this," I muttered under my breath, but I followed him anyway, my boots crunching softly against the gravel.

When I reached the door, Finn knocked twice—quick, sharp raps that echoed in the stillness. We waited for what felt like an eternity.

Then the door creaked open, revealing a figure in the dim light.

It was a woman, her features partially obscured by shadows, but her eyes were clear—too clear. The kind of eyes that saw everything and nothing at the same time.

"Finn," she said, her voice quiet, like the rustling of leaves in a storm.

He nodded, his expression unreadable. "We need to talk."

The door creaked open, and the woman stepped back, just enough to let us inside. The dim light from the porch lamp barely reached her face, leaving her features half hidden in shadow. But there was something about the way she stood—relaxed, as if waiting for us—something that unsettled me more than I cared to admit.

Finn stepped forward without a word, his shoulders tense, but there was an unspoken agreement between them, a quiet familiarity that felt out of place for a town this small, this... secluded. I followed, taking a slow step behind him, my boots scraping the old wooden floor as we entered.

The house was a hodgepodge of mismatched furniture, the kind you only find in places untouched by time. The air was thick with the smell of herbs, a faint hint of something earthy and medicinal. There was a fire crackling in the hearth, casting flickering light across the room, but it couldn't cut through the palpable tension that clung to the space like smoke.

"You've brought her," the woman said, her voice surprisingly soft, almost a whisper. Her eyes flicked over to me, and I felt the weight of her gaze like a shiver crawling up my spine. "Interesting."

Finn didn't answer right away. Instead, he pulled a chair out from the small wooden table, dragging it across the floor with a screech that made me wince. He sat down, running a hand through his hair, eyes still fixed on the woman, his jaw tight.

"We need your help," Finn said, the words clipped, almost reluctant.

The woman's eyes softened slightly, but her mouth remained tight. "I know," she said simply, as if the need for help was as natural as breathing.

I stayed standing, unsure if I should make myself comfortable, unsure if I wanted to. The flickering firelight painted strange shadows on the walls, turning the room into a dance of eerie shapes. It didn't help that I had no idea who this woman was or why she seemed to hold so much power over Finn. The way he was looking at her—almost pleadingly—was unfamiliar. It was a vulnerability I hadn't seen from him before, not in the years we'd worked together.

I took a breath, trying to steady myself, my frustration bubbling up again. "Help with what?" I asked, crossing my arms. "What is going on, Finn? And who is this?"

Finn's eyes darted to mine, and I saw the familiar walls come up, that look that said, I don't want to talk about it right now. But I wasn't backing down. Not this time.

"Her name's Lila," Finn said, his voice low but firm. "And she knows more than we do."

Lila smiled, but there was no warmth in it. Instead, it was a sharp, knowing curve of her lips, the kind of smile that made me feel like I was missing some key piece of the puzzle.

"More about the fire?" I asked, trying to keep the suspicion out of my voice, though I was sure it bled through.

She nodded. "Yes. And more about the person who set it."

The air in the room seemed to thin at her words. I wasn't sure whether to feel relieved or even more uneasy. If she knew who was behind it, why hadn't she said anything sooner? Why was Finn bringing me here now, at this hour, with nothing but vague promises and an unsettling sense that we were being drawn into something much larger than any of us had anticipated?

Finn shifted in his seat, looking at Lila. "What do we need to know?" His tone was more clipped now, impatient. The walls weren't just up—they were steel.

Lila's eyes flicked between the two of us, like she was weighing something in her mind, deciding how much to reveal. Finally, she spoke, her voice barely above a murmur, but the words were clear enough to send a chill down my spine.

"There's a network," she said. "Not just here in Riverton, but across the county. People who think they can play god, decide who gets to live, who gets to die. They've been operating in the shadows for years."

I felt the floor shift beneath me, though I knew it wasn't the ground that had moved. It was the sudden, terrifying weight of her words. A network? People deciding who lived and died? It sounded like something out of a bad crime novel, not the sleepy town I'd grown up in.

"Wait, hold on," I said, stepping forward, unable to contain the disbelief in my voice. "You're telling me this fire wasn't random? That someone—what, some group—set it on purpose?"

Lila nodded slowly, her expression distant, as though she were speaking not just to us but to a memory, a vision of something far older and darker than we could understand. "The fire was meant to send a message," she said, each word deliberate. "A warning."

"A warning for what?" I asked, my stomach clenching. The hairs on my neck were standing at attention, and I wasn't sure whether to be angry or terrified. Or both.

"To stay out of their way," Lila replied simply, her gaze never leaving mine. "To stop digging into things you don't understand."

I felt the floor beneath my feet shift again, but this time it wasn't the weight of her words. It was the sudden realization that Finn was involved in something much deeper than I had ever imagined. He'd known about this—he had to have. How could he not have? And if he had known, why hadn't he told me?

I opened my mouth to confront him, to demand the truth, but the words caught in my throat. There was something in the way Lila was watching us—something in the air that made it clear we were being drawn into a storm, one that might destroy everything in its path.

Before I could speak, Lila stood up, her movements fluid, graceful, like a dancer. She walked to a small cabinet at the side of the room, and without a word, pulled out a small box, handing it to Finn.

"I'm giving you this," she said, her voice soft but firm. "But you have to understand—this will change everything."

Finn took the box, his expression unreadable, and for the first time, I saw something in his eyes that I hadn't seen before. Fear.

"I'll handle it," he said, his voice tight.

Lila turned toward me, her gaze piercing. "I hope you're ready for what's coming," she said quietly.

And with that, she turned and walked out of the room, leaving the three of us alone in the thick silence, the weight of the unknown pressing down on us like a hand around our throats.

Chapter 6: Close Quarters

The elevator doors slid open with their usual groan, and I stepped out into the dim hallway of my building, fumbling with the keys in my hand. The corridor felt eerily still, its beige walls and the faint smell of dust clinging to the air. I'd gotten used to the quiet, solitary hum of apartment life. Or at least I thought I had—until Finn moved in.

His presence was like a foreign object in a world that had otherwise settled comfortably into routine. Every time he brushed past me in the hallway or casually leaned against the doorframe, I was reminded of how small my world had been before his arrival. He had an easy way of filling spaces—too easy, too loud. He'd start with some offhand remark, his voice rumbling low, and the next thing I knew, I'd be laughing. Or worse, enjoying myself. Something about his brashness made me feel like I was peeling back a layer of my own skin I hadn't known existed.

I was just reaching for the door when I heard his laugh—a low, surprisingly warm sound that resonated from behind me. "You know," he said, "you don't have to look so put out every time you see me. It's not like I'm a fire-breathing dragon."

I turned, half-expecting him to be leaning against the wall with that smirk of his, the one that made me want to throw a pillow at his head every time I saw it. Instead, he was standing there, in the middle of the hallway, holding a half-empty beer in his hand. The light from the overhead bulb caught the edges of his jaw, casting shadows that made him look a little too... magnetic.

I narrowed my eyes at him. "You're right. You're more like a charming little housecat. A lion, but, you know, the kind that likes to nap on the windowsill and occasionally knock over a glass of water for fun."

He grinned, taking a swig of his beer. "I could live with that."

I didn't know if I was supposed to be offended or flattered, but somehow, the tension that always hung between us seemed to evaporate in that moment. I opened the door to my apartment and stepped inside, but not before I heard Finn's voice follow me.

"You're not getting away from me that easily. We've got a date with the couch and your world-class sarcasm."

I stopped short. "Excuse me?"

"You heard me," he said, voice muffled now as he stepped into my apartment. "I brought beer, snacks, and my brilliant conversation skills. You can't possibly refuse."

I couldn't even remember when I'd started thinking of Finn as more than just an annoying fixture of my everyday life. There was a quiet force about him—like a storm waiting to break. In the months since he'd been assigned to the building, I'd found myself waiting for the moments when we'd cross paths, almost wishing for the inevitable snarky comment he'd deliver like an offering.

As he walked into the living room and tossed himself onto the couch, I couldn't help but notice how easily he fit into the space—like he belonged here, as if the room had always been waiting for him to claim it.

I stood in the doorway for a second, unsure of what to do with the absurd situation. Finn was the kind of person you either liked immediately or couldn't stand at all. There was no in-between, no casual acquaintance. And for reasons I still couldn't explain, I found myself hoping for more of the former.

"Are you going to stand there all night, or are you going to join me?" he asked, that ever-present smile tugging at the corner of his mouth.

I sighed, fighting the urge to smile back, before sinking into the armchair across from him. It was a habit now, one that had started with simple exchanges, but lately, those exchanges had shifted into something more... complicated. He wasn't supposed to make me feel this way. And yet, as I glanced over at him, a wave of frustration washed over me, followed by something that felt dangerously close to affection.

"So," he started, cracking open another beer. "You've been awfully quiet lately. Are you sure you're not secretly plotting my demise? I've heard that's your thing."

I scoffed, folding my arms across my chest. "You wish. You're not worth the trouble."

"Is that so?" His eyes gleamed, and for a split second, something between us shifted, a glint of understanding passing through the air. It was there and gone in an instant, but it left an imprint on the space between us that I couldn't ignore.

"I'm just trying to figure out why I'm still letting you hang around," I muttered under my breath, more to myself than to him.

Finn didn't respond right away. Instead, he placed his beer on the coffee table and leaned back against the cushions, his eyes settling on me with a kind of openness I hadn't expected. "You don't have to figure it out all at once, you know. Sometimes it's okay to just... be. No pressure."

I shifted uncomfortably in my seat, not sure how to respond. I wanted to laugh, to brush off his words as some kind of absurd attempt at sounding profound. But there was something in his voice—something raw—that made my chest tighten.

I didn't trust it, didn't trust him. Not yet. But I couldn't ignore it either. Something was changing, something I wasn't ready for, and yet—stupidly—was already getting used to.

I watched as Finn casually draped his arm across the back of the couch, his fingers lightly tapping on the fabric. It was a familiar gesture, one that seemed to settle him into the space, making everything around him feel... less like a place I lived and more like a space he occupied. I had never been one to let people take up too much room in my life, but Finn was an exception. And I hated how easily he'd slipped under my skin.

There was something about the way he existed in the world—big, loud, unapologetic—that made my usual world of quiet routines feel like it had been shaken out of its carefully arranged place. He had a way of making everything feel a little less predictable, like the world had somehow tilted in his direction and I was left trying to catch up.

I took a long sip from my glass, wishing I had something stronger in it than wine. Finn's eyes flicked to me, a half-smile playing at the corner of his mouth. I wondered if he could sense how much I was fighting to keep my distance, how much I didn't want to feel what I was feeling.

"You're awfully quiet tonight," he said, his voice low, as if trying to crack some secret I was keeping.

I put the glass down and met his gaze, steeling myself for whatever came next. "Maybe I'm just getting better at pretending I don't hate your face."

He chuckled softly, but there was something else in his expression that made me pause—something darker, something less certain. I couldn't put my finger on it, but it felt like he was testing the limits of our strange little truce. The one where we bantered and sparred but never got too close.

"You don't hate my face," he said, the words almost a challenge. "You're just trying to convince yourself you do."

I frowned. "Is that what you think?"

He shrugged, but his eyes didn't leave mine. "I think you like to make everything harder than it needs to be."

I wanted to argue, to throw some sarcastic remark back at him, but for some reason, the words got caught in my throat. It was like I could hear the edge of vulnerability in his voice, the subtle shift in his tone that betrayed the confidence he always wore like armor.

The air between us felt heavier now, charged with something I couldn't name but didn't want to acknowledge. I wanted to reach for the safety of sarcasm, of dismissing him, but something about the way he was looking at me made that impossible. For the first time in weeks, I felt like I was being seen—not the version of myself I wanted the world to see, but the one I kept hidden. The one that wasn't quite so sure, so in control.

"Why do you do that?" I asked before I could stop myself, my voice quieter than I intended.

"Do what?" Finn's gaze softened, the usual teasing gone, replaced by something warmer.

"Act like you know me," I said, shifting uncomfortably in my seat. "Like you can just... figure me out."

His lips twitched, but there was no mockery in it. "I don't know you," he replied honestly, leaning forward slightly, his elbows resting on his knees. "I just like to see where your walls are, so I can watch you tear them down."

I had to laugh at that. It wasn't a mocking laugh, but a sharp exhale of disbelief. "You think you can break down my walls?"

"I think I already have," he said, a glint of mischief returning to his eyes.

I raised an eyebrow, determined to hold onto the last shred of my dignity. "What makes you think you're so special?"

"I'm not," he said, leaning back again with a lazy smile. "But I am persistent."

There was something about that word—persistent—that struck a chord deep inside me. It wasn't the first time someone had accused me of being difficult to read, of being closed off, but the way Finn said it made me wonder if I was starting to believe it myself. What had started as a nuisance—his constant presence, his loud, unapologetic personality—was beginning to feel like something I might not be able to ignore for much longer.

I had spent so much time telling myself I didn't need anyone, convincing myself that the quiet, simple life I led was all I needed. But then Finn had waltzed in, disrupting everything with his infectious grin and his willingness to push against my walls. And now I was starting to wonder whether I had made those walls to protect myself, or because I was afraid of the kind of person who might break them down.

The conversation lulled between us, a silence settling in that felt less awkward than I expected. It wasn't uncomfortable. In fact, it was strangely... comfortable.

"I don't get you, Finn," I muttered, leaning back in my chair and looking away. "You're like a walking contradiction. You're so damn stubborn, but when you finally let your guard down—just a little—you're... different."

Finn was silent for a moment, and I felt the weight of his gaze even before he spoke.

"You think I'm different?" he asked, his voice soft but with an undercurrent of something more serious.

I nodded, my eyes not meeting his. "Yeah. You're like this big, loud... thing. But sometimes, you look like you're carrying the weight of the world. And then you act like you don't care."

Finn didn't laugh this time, didn't make some sarcastic remark to deflect. Instead, he seemed to consider my words carefully, his expression momentarily distant. For once, there was no bravado, no shield. Just a quiet, raw honesty in his eyes that I hadn't expected—and it made my chest tighten.

"I guess that's the thing with pretending," he said, his voice barely above a whisper. "It's exhausting."

The words hung in the air like smoke, filling the space between us with a kind of unspoken understanding. For the first time, I didn't feel like I was fighting him. I didn't feel like I needed to keep my distance, to hold onto my safe little world of control and detachment.

Instead, I felt something that was even more terrifying. Something close to hope.

The air in my apartment felt different after that night—charged, like a storm was gathering on the horizon and I was too foolish to see it coming. I hadn't expected the shift. I hadn't even known I was on the edge of something until I found myself standing in my kitchen the next morning, staring blankly at a cup of coffee that had gone cold. The quiet between Finn and me felt unfamiliar now, like two people on the edge of something they couldn't name but were somehow afraid to explore.

I poured the coffee down the sink and braced myself for the inevitable awkwardness that was sure to follow. There was no way to go back to how things had been, no way to unsee the vulnerability in Finn's eyes when he let his guard slip. It was disorienting, almost disloyal to the version of myself that had always kept the world at arm's length. The version that never, ever let anyone get too close.

Finn, as always, found his way into my space without warning. His presence was like a shadow, a reminder that my solitude was no longer mine alone. The sound of the door opening and closing behind him startled me from my thoughts. I turned to see him leaning casually against the doorway, an almost mischievous grin on his face. It was the same grin he always wore, but today it seemed... different. More knowing. As if he was waiting for me to catch up.

"Hey," he said, tossing his keys onto the counter as though this were his apartment, too. "You busy?"

I rolled my eyes, trying to muster up the usual irritation, but it came out softer than I meant it to. "Isn't it a little early to be barging in?"

He shrugged, that devil-may-care attitude of his still firmly in place. "You say that like you mind."

I didn't reply immediately, my eyes scanning his face for some hint of the Finn I thought I knew. The confident one, the one who would make fun of me and laugh it off. But underneath the teasing, there was something else—something quieter and more subdued. He wasn't just here for the usual banter; there was something else in his eyes, something I didn't have a name for.

"I wasn't expecting you," I said, my tone still carrying the remnants of that defensive edge I couldn't quite shed. "What's up?"

"Nothing," he said, and then he hesitated, which was enough to make my heart thud a little faster. "I was just... thinking we could do something today. You know, take a break from all the usual arguing."

A beat of silence passed between us, hanging in the air like an unspoken question. I wasn't sure what he was asking. Was he offering an olive branch, or just trying to force a truce for the sake of not being bored?

I met his gaze, but this time, the words felt too heavy, too real. "You mean you want to hang out?"

"I mean," he said, his voice softer now, "I think you might need a reminder that there's more to life than your own walls."

I swallowed hard, feeling a strange mixture of irritation and something else—something I couldn't place. A flicker of something more than just the casual annoyance I'd always felt when he was around. Something I wasn't ready to face.

"I'm not sure I want to let you in on that secret," I said, my voice betraying me. I tried to keep it light, but it came out quieter than I intended, like I was giving away something I didn't want to.

Finn stepped into the kitchen with an almost absurd level of confidence, as though he had permission to be there, even though I had never given him any. He didn't even wait for me to respond before he grabbed a bottle of wine from the counter and popped the cork, the sound of it echoing in the small space.

"Come on, just one drink. It'll be like... old times," he said, flashing that grin that made my heart do a strange little flip in my chest.

I watched him for a moment, then glanced at the door, considering the possibility of retreating, of shutting myself off again. I didn't want to let him get to me. But Finn was persistent, and for reasons I couldn't explain, I wasn't sure I wanted him to stop.

"Old times, huh?" I said, my voice more brittle than I meant it to be. "When was that? Before you decided to camp out on my couch for an indefinite amount of time?"

"Hey, it's not like I chose to be here," he shot back. "But since I'm stuck with you, we might as well make the best of it."

I watched as he poured the wine, his movements easy, familiar. There was something about the way he moved through my space, like he had every right to be there, that made my stomach tighten. It was like he was already inside my head, making himself a permanent resident without asking permission.

I grabbed the glass he handed me, taking a cautious sip, still trying to push away the weird, tight feeling in my chest. But no matter how much I tried to stay detached, no matter how much I told myself I wasn't ready to deal with whatever was between us, Finn seemed determined to crack the walls I'd built up. And I was starting to wonder if I might be too tired to stop him.

"So, tell me something," Finn said after a beat, leaning back against the counter and staring at me with that characteristic gleam in his eyes. "What's your deal? Why the walls? You can't tell me it's just because of your... charming personality."

I felt a sharp pang in my chest at the question, and I didn't answer immediately. Instead, I took another drink, trying to quiet the voice in my head that was urging me to keep my distance, to shut him out like I always had.

"You really want to know?" I said, my voice quieter now. Finn nodded, his gaze never leaving me.

For a moment, I considered telling him. I almost did. But just as the words formed on my lips, there was a loud crash from the hallway—a sudden, jarring sound that made both of us jump. The door to my apartment swung open before I could react, and the last person I expected to see stepped into the room, face flushed and eyes wild.

"Get out!" she screamed. "It's happening again!"

Chapter 7: The First Kiss

The fire crackled in the distance, a furious, living thing, as if it had a mind of its own. My heart pounded harder, drowning out everything but the sound of it. The night air was thick with the stench of smoke, and my skin felt raw, coated with a layer of ash I knew would be impossible to scrub off. The adrenaline was a heavy, burning buzz, thumping through my veins as we worked in chaotic unison, dragging people away from the encroaching flames, the world around us shrinking into a haze of orange and red.

Finn moved beside me, his body a steady force, his presence like an anchor in the midst of all the chaos. We didn't speak. There was no time for words when the smoke was thick enough to choke on and the fire was so close you could feel its heat eating away at the edges of the earth. We communicated in gestures—hands pointing, eyes meeting, understanding in the swift exchange. His movements were sharp and sure, each one honed by years of doing this. I was still learning, my hands trembling as I pulled a woman out of her house, feeling her ragged breaths against my cheek.

The flames twisted higher, licking the night sky like a mad beast wanting to swallow everything whole. I could taste the smoke in my mouth, gritty and foul. And then, a momentary pause. A shift in the madness. Finn was there, his arm around my waist, his voice a low shout above the din.

"Get the children out of the second house," he ordered, already moving toward the next emergency. The sharpness of his tone was all business, but there was something in the way he said it, the way his eyes lingered just a second too long on me, that made my pulse flutter.

I nodded, barely hearing him as my gaze was drawn back to the burning inferno. But something shifted again, a weight in the air, like a breath we'd all been holding. Finn was there again, closer this time, his face inches from mine. His eyes, dark with intensity, flickered with something more than just the firelight.

"Now," he said, pulling me along with him, his voice barely above a whisper, but the urgency in it sent a jolt through me.

The smoke was choking, and the flames seemed to move faster than we could fight them, but we pushed forward, each movement a deliberate step toward safety. The world outside of this was fading. There was only the next rescue, the next life to save. And then, just as quickly as it had come, the fire seemed to relent. The wind shifted, and the roar of it diminished, leaving only the crackling remnants of what had been.

We stumbled back, our bodies covered in soot, sweat running down our faces. My lungs were tight from the smoke, my hands shaking from the effort, but I couldn't let it show. Not yet. Not in front of Finn. We had a job to do, and nothing could stop that. Nothing except maybe the way his hand brushed against mine as he reached for a water bottle, his fingers warm and steady against my skin.

It was that small touch that unraveled me. It was so simple, so unassuming, yet it felt like a spark. For a split second, I could have sworn I felt something shift between us, something palpable in the air that neither of us had anticipated. I looked at him, but his gaze was focused on something far off, distant, like he was already somewhere else, thinking ahead.

"Thanks," I said, my voice rough, hoarse from the smoke and the strain.

He nodded, but there was something different in the way he looked at me now. Something deeper. I felt my heart flutter uncomfortably in my chest, like it was unsure whether to slow down or speed up, unsure of what to do with the sudden tension that seemed to fill the space between us.

Finn didn't say anything, but there was something in the way he stood—close enough that I could feel his warmth, the weight of his presence—something that made me feel like I might burst from the inside out.

And then, without warning, his hand was at my face. It wasn't a gesture of comfort or a soft reassurance. It was rough and sudden, like he needed to touch me, to make sure I was real, as real as the fire that had just raged through the night. His thumb brushed over my cheek, tracing the line of it with an intensity that made my breath catch. I could see the way his gaze lingered on me, his eyes flicking from my lips to my eyes in a way that made everything feel too close, too intimate.

I knew I should pull away. I knew I should step back, regain my composure, keep the distance between us that we both needed. But when his lips finally pressed to mine, I didn't want to fight it.

It wasn't gentle, not at first. It was urgent, almost desperate, as if the moment itself demanded it. His mouth was hot and firm, a brand of fire all its own, and for a split second, I forgot everything—forgot the chaos of the fire, the heat that still burned my skin, the people we'd just saved. There was only him. Only the feel of him against me, like he was trying to drink me in, like he might disappear if he didn't. I wanted to pull back, to stop, to reason with myself, but I couldn't. And neither could he.

The kiss deepened, our bodies pressing closer, and I let myself be consumed by it. For a moment, nothing else mattered—no dangers, no consequences. There was only this.

And then, just as quickly as it had started, it was over.

I pulled back first, my chest heaving, my body humming with something I couldn't name. Finn stood there, a step away, his eyes still fixed on me, his breath just as ragged as mine. Neither of us spoke. We didn't need to. I could feel it—like the world had shifted on its axis, tilting toward something I couldn't define, but something that felt far too big to ignore.

Reality came crashing in around us like a wall of sound, but I couldn't shake the weight of his gaze. It was too much. Too intense. And I wasn't sure I was ready for whatever came next.

I stood there, my breath still shaky, and fought the urge to look at Finn again. His presence seemed to fill every corner of the air around us, heavy and impossible to ignore. The flames had long since died down, the night air now cool, the smell of smoke slowly giving way to the damp scent of earth and the remnants of fire. It should have been over, right? Just another night in the line of duty. But it wasn't. Not anymore.

I tried to shake it off, to focus on anything else, but my mind kept drifting back to that moment—the feel of his lips, the heat of his hands, the way everything had melted away in the space between us. It wasn't like anything I'd expected, not the kind of kiss that came after a long flirtation or a careful build-up of emotion. It had been raw, impulsive, born of something I hadn't fully understood. But what terrified me was how much I had wanted it, how much I had needed it in that moment.

"Are you alright?" Finn's voice broke through my haze, low and concerned, though his words didn't quite match the storm in his eyes. His brow was furrowed, lips pressed tightly together, as if he were trying to figure something out.

I swallowed, trying to gather the scattered pieces of myself, and nodded. "Yeah. Fine. Just... I think I swallowed half of the smoke back there." I forced a laugh, but it came out too sharp, too high-pitched.

"Right." He didn't buy it. I saw the way his gaze lingered on me, as though he was seeing right through the cracks I was trying to hide. His eyes flicked to my mouth, just for a second, but it was enough to send another jolt through me. Then, just as quickly, he turned away, his back to me as he paced a few steps before stopping with his hands on his hips, facing the remnants of the fire.

The silence between us stretched, thick and uncomfortable, as if neither of us knew what to say next. We were too close now, too tangled in something neither of us had signed up for. I wanted to speak, to say anything, to break the tension, but I found myself frozen, caught in the storm of my own thoughts. I was a firefighter, for heaven's sake. I should have been thinking about the aftermath, about the people we saved, about what needed to be done. But all I could think about was the kiss.

"Listen, I didn't—" Finn began, turning toward me again, his expression soft but guarded. "That wasn't... I didn't mean to make things weird."

"I'm not... it's not weird," I found myself saying, the words spilling out before I could stop them. "It was just..." I trailed off, searching for something—anything—that could make sense of the mess swirling inside me. "It was just a moment. I get it. We were both caught up in the adrenaline."

Finn's eyes darkened, a flash of something—anger? Frustration?—flashing across his face before he exhaled sharply. "Right. Adrenaline."

And that was the crux of it, wasn't it? The kiss hadn't been born out of something sweet or tender. It had been born out of heat, out of the raw need to feel something—anything—after everything we'd just been through. And I wasn't sure which part of it had been more dangerous. The fire or the kiss.

"Look, I'm sorry," I said, rubbing my temples in frustration. "That kiss shouldn't have happened. I—"

"Stop." Finn cut me off, his voice quiet but firm, and it took me by surprise. "It wasn't just you." He met my gaze, his expression hard to read, but there was something there—something deeper, something that made my pulse quicken again. "I... I don't know what it was. But it happened. And it doesn't matter now."

Of course it mattered. It mattered more than anything. But I couldn't find the right words to say it, couldn't figure out how to explain the mess of emotions I felt—confusion, desire, guilt—all tangled together in one impossible knot.

"Doesn't matter?" I echoed, finally finding my voice, though it was too sharp, too defensive. "How can you say that? It matters. It has to matter. Because if it doesn't... then what the hell was that?"

Finn opened his mouth, but no words came out. He shut it again, his jaw clenching tightly. The weight of his silence pressed down on me. I felt myself unraveling, just a little more with every passing second. There was no way to go back, no way to pretend that kiss had never happened. It was too late for that.

"We can't..." I began, but I didn't finish. My heart was pounding too loudly in my chest, and the words caught in my throat. What were we supposed to do with this? How were we supposed to be now that this tension was between us, hanging in the air like smoke from the fire we'd just fought?

Finn's shoulders dropped, and he took a deep breath. "You're right. We can't just pretend it didn't happen. But it doesn't change anything. We can't let it."

"Let it?" I repeated, stepping closer to him now, frustration seeping into my words. "How am I supposed to not let it change things? It's already changed everything."

Finn didn't respond. His gaze flickered to the ground, his expression unreadable, before he shook his head, almost imperceptibly. Then he took a step back, putting a few feet of distance between us, as if to create space, as if that would somehow help us both breathe again.

“I think we need to figure this out. On our own. We can’t keep dancing around this,” he muttered, voice low, his eyes still avoiding mine.

I wanted to argue, to demand that we face it head-on, but something in the way he said it, the weariness in his tone, made me hesitate. Maybe he was right. Maybe time, or distance, or both, was what we needed.

The night stretched on, full of unsaid words, and neither of us moved to fill the silence. It wasn’t comfortable, not in the least. But it was the kind of silence that pressed on you from every direction, forcing you to acknowledge what had been left unspoken.

The morning after was a betrayal. The kind of betrayal that leaves you standing in front of a mirror, wondering what you’ve done to deserve this odd, sticky mess of emotions. The adrenaline was gone, the fire was out, and the world seemed to have returned to its rightful place. But I wasn’t the same. I could feel it in the way my hands trembled just slightly when I reached for my coffee, in the way my mind refused to let go of that kiss. And the worst part? Finn seemed completely unaffected. It was like the night had been a blip on his radar—a fleeting, reckless moment he could forget as easily as the smoke from the fire.

But for me? It lingered, clinging to the edges of everything I did, everything I saw.

I busied myself with my morning routine, trying to force my thoughts into a box and shove them out of sight. The air was crisp for a November morning, and the familiar hum of the station filled the background, the chatter and noise of everyone getting ready for another day. Still, I couldn’t escape the feeling that something was wrong, like I had misplaced a puzzle piece and didn’t know which one it was or where it went.

When Finn walked in, I wasn't prepared. I should've been, should've expected him to show up at some point, but I wasn't ready for the way he looked at me.

He didn't speak immediately. Instead, he stood there, arms crossed, eyes narrowed as though he were trying to solve a problem that didn't quite make sense.

I could feel the weight of it, that unspoken thing between us, hanging in the air like an electric charge. I hadn't known until that moment how much I wanted him to say something, anything. The silence was unbearable, and I was about to break it when he finally spoke.

"I need to talk to you," he said, voice low, but his eyes didn't meet mine.

"Yeah, okay." I set my mug down, suddenly aware of the way my hands shook. "About what?"

He glanced at me then, sharp and intense, before he shifted his weight from one foot to the other. "About last night."

The knot in my stomach tightened. The words were exactly what I'd expected, and yet, they were worse than anything I could've imagined.

"I think we both know what that was," I said, trying to keep my voice even, trying to convince myself that it didn't matter. "Just... one of those things. A weird moment in the middle of a crisis."

Finn's gaze flickered toward the door, then back to me, but this time, there was no hesitation. "It wasn't just that. Not for me."

I froze, the breath I was holding slipping out of me in a slow, reluctant exhale. "What do you mean?" I asked, voice quieter than I intended.

He ran a hand through his hair, frustration flickering in his eyes. "I mean... it wasn't just a kiss. I don't know what it was, but it wasn't nothing."

The weight of his words settled around us like a fog, and for a second, I couldn't think. I didn't know how to respond to that, how to unpack the mess of emotions that immediately started flooding in.

"I didn't mean to make things complicated," Finn said, his tone gentler now, more measured. "But I think I did. And that's not fair to you."

I stood there, staring at him, as though trying to make sense of it all. My mind was whirling, spinning like a tornado, but I couldn't seem to catch my breath. What did that even mean? What was he trying to tell me?

"I don't know what you want me to say," I finally muttered, shaking my head. "I don't know what any of this means, Finn."

For a moment, he was quiet, eyes flicking over my face as if searching for something in me. I didn't know what he was looking for, but I knew what I was feeling. Confusion. Fear. A desire to run and hide, but also something else. Something that burned, something that made my stomach tighten in a way I wasn't sure I could name.

"I don't know either," he said, his voice raw. "But I do know that I don't want to pretend nothing happened. I can't do that. Can you?"

The question hung in the air between us, suspended in time.

I felt it. That pull. That undeniable magnetism that had started with the fire, with the chaos, and now, here it was, stretching between us, waiting to snap. The silence stretched, and I knew that the moment I spoke, it would either break or make everything worse.

"I don't know," I whispered finally. "I don't know if I can handle it."

His jaw clenched, his eyes hardening just a little. I could see him wrestling with something—whether it was his own emotions or the situation, I couldn't tell. I didn't have the answers either, but I hated this feeling, this uncertainty gnawing at the edges of everything.

"You don't have to figure it out right now," Finn said, as though reading my thoughts. "But we need to talk. Soon."

I nodded stiffly, my chest tight with a mixture of relief and anxiety. He was giving me space, but not a lot of it. There was an urgency in his tone, a pressing need to resolve whatever this was, but the more he said, the less I understood. Was it just a fire-induced frenzy? A bad decision in a moment of desperation? Or was it something more?

"I'll be around," Finn added, turning toward the door, his shoulders taut. "Just... don't shut me out. Please."

He walked away, his footsteps heavy and deliberate, leaving me standing there, feeling like I was on the edge of a cliff, one foot already dangling over the side.

The door swung shut behind him, and I was alone.

For a few seconds, I stood there, hands gripping the edge of the counter, my heart beating faster now, as if trying to tell me something. Something I didn't want to hear. Something I didn't know if I was ready for.

Then, the door swung open again. And before I could even react, Finn stepped back in. His eyes were wide, and his voice caught in his throat as he said, "There's something I need to tell you. Something important."

And that was when everything—everything—changed.

Chapter 8: Cold Reality

The morning broke with a sharpness I didn't expect—like a glass of cold water poured straight down my back. It wasn't just the weather. The air had a crispness to it, a bite that reminded me of a forgotten argument or a piece of a past I'd tried to ignore. I had no intention of chasing the chill away, not when the one thing that had kept me warm, at least for a fleeting moment, was now a stone wall in front of me.

Cole wasn't here.

No surprise there. In the past 24 hours, he'd turned from a burning ember to an icy stone, and there was nothing I could do to melt him back. His silence had become an impenetrable fortress, his eyes glazed over like the sharp edge of a broken mirror. I'd spent the better part of the morning replaying our last conversation in my mind—wondering if I'd said something wrong, if the closeness between us had been nothing more than a fleeting spark to him. I should've known better. He wasn't the type to let anyone in, and I was too naïve to realize that until it was too late.

The heavy smell of charred wood brought me back to reality. It had been the unmistakable scent of something smoldering—a fire that had started up in the warehouse district. I had to focus, to work, or else I'd risk losing my grip on what little sense I had left. The fire department had been called in, and I had my gear on before the sirens even hit a peak. I walked to the trucks, mind preoccupied with how I was going to avoid Cole, who, no doubt, would be on the front lines, eager to prove something that had nothing to do with saving lives.

I knew the moment I saw him. The dark circles under his eyes, the set of his jaw, the way his shoulders tensed as though he was bracing for an impact. Cole didn't just fight fires; he threw himself into them like they were personal battles. There was something in the way he looked at flames, as though they were the only thing he understood, the only thing he could control. It was almost as though he was punishing himself with each breath of smoke he inhaled, daring the flames to consume him.

I swallowed the bitter lump in my throat. I didn't know what I was expecting—some sign that maybe he cared about me. Or at the very least, that he was still the man who had held me in the quiet spaces between chaos. But no. Today, he was all fire and no warmth.

"Let's get moving," he barked at the crew, his voice clipped, commanding. He didn't spare a glance in my direction. His eyes stayed on the building, on the smoke that was rising like a dark ghost. I wanted to say something, but the words felt like stones lodged in my throat. Instead, I nodded and followed him, the sound of my boots on the gravel the only noise between us.

The heat from the fire hit us before we even reached the building. It was a wall of intensity, a wave of heat that stung my skin and pulled at my breath. The air was thick with smoke, swirling in the gusts like some phantom, twisting and turning around us. I could taste it—tangy, bitter, acrid. My mask went on, the world suddenly narrowing to the small space between me and the fire, between the task at hand and the raging inferno I had no choice but to face.

Cole was already in the thick of it, moving with a purpose, a relentless drive to get as close to the flames as possible. I hated it. Hated the way he seemed so at home, so comfortable in a place where everything else burned. It made my chest tighten. I'd seen it before—this almost obsessive compulsion to save everything, to rescue anyone and everyone, like if he could save enough people, maybe he could save himself too. I didn't understand it. But I couldn't stop watching.

We worked in silence, our movements synchronized, two parts of a whole, like gears clicking into place. My hand brushed against his a few times—accidental, but there was something unmistakably charged in the contact. His eyes flicked to me, but only for a second, a mere flash of something that might've been recognition. Maybe. Maybe not.

He was a puzzle, an enigma wrapped in a uniform that smelled like smoke and sweat, a man of few words but many secrets. And I hated him for it. Not because I didn't care, but because I cared more than I should have. I cared too much to let him keep shutting me out, to keep pretending like I didn't notice the way he pulled away every time I tried to get close.

I wanted to ask him, to scream at him, but I knew it wouldn't matter. His eyes would shut, his walls would rise higher, and nothing would get through. I wasn't sure what I wanted from him anymore—answers, clarity, maybe just an admission that I hadn't been a passing distraction, that I hadn't just been another person he could forget once the smoke cleared.

And then, as we worked our way deeper into the building, the world seemed to stop for a second. The fire roared louder, threatening to engulf us both, but in that moment, I found myself staring at him—really staring at him—for the first time in hours.

"What are you running from?" The question slipped from my lips before I could stop it, and even though I knew it wouldn't make a difference, I couldn't keep the words in. They hung between us, suspended in the charged air like a dare.

His hand paused on the nozzle, and for a moment, he didn't speak. The sound of the fire filled the gap between us, growing louder, but it wasn't until I saw the briefest flicker of something in his eyes—something deep and heavy—that I realized how dangerous it was to ask him.

"I'm not running from anything," he said quietly, his voice hoarse. But I could hear the lie in it. And in that moment, I wondered how long it would take before the fire burned through everything, everything we were pretending to be.

The fire was always a brutal truth, and in moments like this, it was the only thing that made sense. The crackling heat, the roar of the blaze, the sharp stench of charred wood—it all had a way of drowning out everything else. It didn't care about the lies, the misunderstandings, or the fractured conversations that echoed in the back of my mind. The fire didn't ask why, or what we wanted, or why we couldn't have what we craved. It simply was.

Cole and I moved as if we'd done this dance a thousand times before, each step instinctual, though neither of us was fool enough to trust it. Not anymore. My hand brushed his as I passed the hose, and it was like a spark hit the air. There was something in the way his fingers gripped the nozzle, in the steady rhythm of his breath, as if everything around him was chaos, but his body was locked in the familiar, controlled panic of saving what could still be saved.

"Watch your step," he warned, voice rough from the smoke. There was no room for softness, no time for anything except the harsh reality that this fire was relentless. But even with the urgency, even with the life-threatening intensity of the heat that swirled around us, I couldn't help but notice the brief flicker in his eyes when our gazes met—something raw and untamed that he quickly buried beneath the surface, just as he always did.

I didn't respond. What could I say? That I wasn't some green rookie who needed constant reminders to stay sharp? That I wasn't in this just for the adrenaline, for the rush of saving people, of playing hero? I didn't need to prove anything to him. But somehow, the sting of his indifference cut deeper than any burn from the fire.

We worked in silence, moving through the wreckage with precise steps, too close to each other for comfort yet far enough to keep our boundaries intact. The smoke clouded everything, my vision dimmed by the thick haze, but I felt it—the heat that rippled through my skin, the pressure that pushed me forward, step by step, until it felt like we might never leave the flames behind. I could've stayed like that forever, working in this strange, lonely proximity to him, if only to avoid confronting what was happening between us.

I'd been trying to figure out what exactly it was that kept me tangled in his web. Maybe it was the way he never asked for help, the way he shouldered the world's burdens alone and kept on moving forward, like it was his job to save everyone and everything, even when he was the one who needed saving most. Or maybe it was the quiet moments, when I would catch him glancing at me from across the room, only for him to pull away as if he were suddenly reminded of a distance neither of us had the courage to cross.

"Need some help over there?" I called out, more out of a need to fill the silence than anything else. But as soon as I spoke, I regretted it. It sounded too casual, too innocent, like I hadn't been spending the last few hours staring at him, wondering what the hell was wrong, wondering why I couldn't shake the feeling that there was more to his storm than just smoke and mirrors.

Cole didn't look at me when he answered. His voice was low, almost detached. "I've got it."

And I did the one thing I told myself I wouldn't: I tried to dig deeper. "You sure? You've been at this for hours. You need a break?"

His eyes flicked to mine, just a flicker, before he returned his attention to the blaze. "I don't need breaks."

It wasn't what he said, but how he said it. His jaw tightened, his shoulders set in that familiar, stubborn stance that had become all too familiar. I could almost hear the warning in his voice, the silent message: Don't push me. I wasn't stupid enough to ignore it. And yet, there was this thread inside me, stubborn and foolish, that refused to let go.

He was breaking, piece by piece, and he didn't even know it.

I wanted to reach out, to grab his arm and stop him, make him face whatever it was he was running from. But I knew it wouldn't work. It would only make him pull further away, retreat back to whatever dark place he had locked up inside. The fire was his escape, and I couldn't blame him for that.

The moment passed, and I forced myself to focus on the task at hand. The fire was relentless, but so were we.

We worked for what felt like hours, the heat consuming us, but we didn't stop. Not for the pain, not for the exhaustion. Not for the memories that clawed at the edges of my mind, trying to bring me back to reality. Every time I thought about stepping away from the blaze, to give myself a moment to breathe, to think, to regain my bearings, something kept me tethered to the flames, tethered to him.

And then, as if by some unspoken agreement, the fire began to wane. The smoke started to clear, and we found ourselves standing in the wreckage of what was once a building, now reduced to smoldering debris. The air was thick with the scent of burning wood and ash, and the distant wail of sirens still echoed in the distance, a reminder that the battle was far from over.

I wiped my brow with the back of my gloved hand, the sweat mixing with the soot. My muscles screamed in protest, but I couldn't focus on that. Not yet. Not when the real battle was just beginning.

Cole stood a few feet away, breathing heavily, his chest rising and falling in a steady rhythm. He wasn't looking at me, his face still a mask of cold determination. But beneath the surface, I saw the flicker of something else—something almost vulnerable, as if he were waiting for something, anything, to knock him off balance.

I should've walked away. I should've kept my distance, let the tension die down. But the words left my mouth before I could stop them.

"Are you ever going to let anyone in?" It was quiet, almost a whisper. But in the thick silence of the aftermath, it was loud enough to shatter everything.

He didn't answer right away. And when he finally did, his voice was rough, like gravel grinding against bone.

"You wouldn't like what you'd find." His gaze met mine, cold, unreadable.

And for the first time in a long while, I wasn't sure whether I wanted to know.

The tension between us thickened as the days dragged on, and I couldn't escape it. Not when every shift seemed to drag me back to him, his presence an inescapable weight that hung in the air like the smoke from a fire that never quite went out. Cole and I hadn't spoken about the things that mattered—not the things that festered beneath the surface of his stoic exterior. The small glances, the moments when our hands brushed too closely, the way he still managed to haunt my thoughts when I least expected it, told me that the quiet wasn't just for show. There was something more—something I wasn't sure I wanted to know, but needed to.

It was late one night when I found myself standing in the hallway of the station, staring at the door that separated me from the man who had become both my obsession and my undoing. The station was quiet, save for the muffled hum of distant conversations, the thud of boots against the concrete floor, and the occasional crash of a door swinging open. I'd been pacing, mostly, trying to keep myself busy, trying to ignore the gnawing feeling that if I didn't do something now, I'd regret it.

There had been a fire earlier in the day—another one of those stubborn, unpredictable blazes that refused to go down easily—and Cole had worked through it with the same cold, focused intensity he always did. He was an expert at keeping everything locked up tight, never letting the cracks show. And yet, every time we crossed paths, I could see them—those small, almost imperceptible fissures in his armor.

My fingers drummed against the edge of the door, my heart pounding against my ribs. I knew I should leave, that walking away would be the safer choice. I wasn't sure how many more times I could stand in front of him and pretend that I didn't want to reach out, that I didn't want to know what he was hiding. But there it was—this pull, this maddening desire to understand him. To see the parts of him that he refused to show anyone.

I was tired of pretending I didn't care. The ache in my chest had grown too strong to ignore. I'd told myself over and over that it wasn't my problem, that I wasn't the one who could fix him. But deep down, I knew I wanted to. I wanted to be the one who reached inside that fortress he'd built around himself and tore it all down, piece by piece.

I knocked lightly on the door, the sound almost drowned out by the silence that followed. I waited. No answer. My breath hitched in my throat, but I didn't back away. Instead, I turned the knob and stepped inside.

Cole was sitting at the small, cluttered desk, his face illuminated by the faint glow of a desk lamp. He didn't look up as I entered, didn't acknowledge me in any way. His gaze was focused on something on the desk—probably paperwork, though he wasn't exactly the type to obsess over small details like that. His posture was stiff, but it was the stillness of someone waiting for the world to catch up with them, someone who had already resigned themselves to the idea that nothing would ever be enough.

"Did you need something?" His voice was low, almost too calm, as if he was trying to mask the underlying tension. I could tell he wasn't thrilled by my presence. But then again, when had he ever been?

"I think we need to talk." The words felt foreign on my tongue, but they slipped out before I could stop them. I hadn't planned on being so direct. Hell, I hadn't planned on walking into his space at all. But here I was, facing him, trying to find the courage to push past whatever wall he'd built between us.

Cole didn't look up. Instead, he leaned back in his chair and exhaled slowly, almost as if he were bracing himself. "I don't have anything to say."

My heart twisted at the flatness in his tone. It was like a slap to the face. But I wasn't about to let him shut me out—not this time. Not when I could feel the weight of everything left unsaid between us, all the things that were slowly eating away at me.

"You don't have to say anything, but I'm tired of this. Of pretending that there's nothing between us when it's clear there's something." I took a step closer, my voice growing more insistent with each word. "Whatever it is that's going on with you, I need you to stop shutting me out. I can't keep doing this."

His eyes flicked up, meeting mine for the first time in what felt like forever. The look he gave me was a mixture of disbelief and something darker, something that made my stomach flip. But there was no anger, no defensiveness. Instead, there was an empty resignation, like he'd already given up on whatever it was we could've been.

"You don't get it," he said quietly, his gaze flickering to the papers on the desk. "I'm not the guy you think I am. And it's not worth the effort."

I opened my mouth to argue, but the words caught in my throat. Something about the way he said it, something about the finality in his voice, made me pause. My chest tightened, and I suddenly found it hard to breathe. Was it really that simple for him? Did he really think I would just walk away?

I took another step forward, ignoring the sudden surge of fear in my veins. "You're wrong. You think you know how this is going to end, but you don't. You've built all these walls around yourself, but they won't protect you forever. Eventually, something's going to break through."

His eyes narrowed, his lips curling into something that wasn't quite a smile, but wasn't exactly a sneer, either. "You don't understand the first thing about me, do you?"

The words hit me like a slap in the face, but I stood my ground. "No, maybe I don't. But I'm willing to learn. If you'd let me."

For a long moment, there was nothing but silence between us—thick, heavy silence that felt suffocating. His eyes bored into mine, his expression unreadable, and I could feel my pulse racing in my ears. Then, slowly, he stood up, pushing his chair back with a screech that made my skin crawl. He stepped toward me, closing the distance until I could feel the heat of his body, could almost taste the tension that vibrated between us.

"I warned you," he said, his voice dangerously low, almost a whisper.

And before I could respond, before I could even think, his lips were on mine—rough, insistent, as if he were trying to claim something he'd long since lost.

Chapter 9: The Message

The night air was unusually warm for a late September evening, thick and stifling, clinging to my skin like an unwanted lover. My fingers were cold as they fumbled with the lock, my mind miles away from the task at hand. I was preoccupied, haunted by a sense that something was watching me, lingering just out of sight. It had been that way for days—since the first note had arrived. No matter how much I told myself it was nothing, that it was just some twisted prank or a misdirected threat meant for someone else, the nagging voice in the back of my head refused to be silenced. It was always there, sharp and persistent, like a splinter I couldn't dislodge.

I hadn't told Finn about the first letter. Not because I didn't trust him—no, it was far more complicated than that. I trusted him with my life, but I wasn't ready to trust him with this part of me. The part that had been fractured for years, piecing itself back together in shaky fragments. My life had never been the neat little picture people seemed to think it was. And Finn, for all his charm and easy smile, wasn't the kind of person I wanted to drag into my mess.

I finally pushed the door open, the familiar squeak of hinges greeting me like an old friend. The house was still, too still. The silence settled around me, thick and uncomfortable, like it was waiting for something—waiting for me to breathe. I stepped inside, toeing off my shoes, and caught sight of the envelope resting on the welcome mat. It wasn't there when I'd left for work. Not a chance.

My heart skipped, then settled into a steady, uncomfortable beat as I approached. It was different from the last one. The paper was heavier, the handwriting more deliberate, and the words... chilling. "You think you're safe with him, but you're not. I'm always watching."

A cold dread curled around my spine. It wasn't just a threat—it was a promise. Someone was in my life, someone who knew more than they should. They knew about Finn. They knew about the quiet moments I'd shared with him, the unspoken things that had been passing between us, things I hadn't even been able to fully admit to myself yet. And they didn't like it.

I crumpled the note in my hand, the paper crinkling as if it were laughing at my fear. My thoughts swirled, the edges of my mind fraying, pulling at each other. Who would want to hurt me? Or worse, hurt Finn?

No, that was the part that terrified me most. Whoever this was didn't just want to scare me; they wanted to tear at the fragile thread of something that had barely begun to form between Finn and me. And I had no idea how far they were willing to go.

I shoved the note into my pocket, my breath catching in my throat as I turned back to the door. I couldn't stay here tonight. Not like this, not with that message lingering in the back of my mind. I needed to see him, to hear his voice. Just once, I needed the assurance that I hadn't imagined it all—that the world outside wasn't quite as dark and dangerous as it felt in this moment.

My phone buzzed on the kitchen counter, its sharp tone slicing through the silence like a knife. My heart stuttered as I reached for it, praying for a moment of calm. A text message from Finn.

"How about dinner tomorrow? I'll cook."

Just the thought of his hands moving over a cutting board, the soft rustling of vegetables, the way his eyes focused on whatever he was making... It made me ache. I didn't deserve him, not with the way my life was. But maybe, just maybe, I could let myself have him for one more night.

I started to type, then paused, my fingers hovering over the keys. What was I supposed to say? "I'm afraid someone is threatening me"? No. That would be ridiculous. He'd be furious, and I didn't want that. Not yet.

Instead, I typed, "I'd love that." I hit send before I could second-guess myself.

The seconds ticked by like hours. And then, finally, the reply came: "Great. I'll pick you up at six?"

I smiled to myself, a small, fleeting thing that felt out of place with the weight of the night pressing down on me. But still, there it was—a glimmer of something that felt real. I didn't want to lose it. I wasn't sure how much time I had before everything unraveled. But for now, I wanted to hold on.

The phone buzzed again, but this time, I was already halfway to the door, my mind spinning with what I needed to do. I needed to go to him. I needed to be near him. And whatever shadow was hanging over me, I'd deal with it later.

But as I grabbed my keys, a thought stopped me cold. What if the person who left that note already knew where I was going?

I drove to Finn's house with my knuckles tight around the steering wheel, the weight of the letter still heavy in my pocket like an unwanted guest I couldn't shake. My mind raced in frantic circles, each thought colliding with the next, none of them making any sense. I couldn't even focus on the road. My eyes kept drifting back to the rearview mirror, searching for something—anything—that would offer an explanation, a clue, a shadow in the distance that would put me at ease. But there was nothing. Just the quiet hum of my car cutting through the night air, the gentle flicker of streetlights casting long, eerie shadows across the empty road.

When I pulled into Finn's driveway, the house seemed almost too perfect, too serene. There was something about it that made everything feel... wrong. His house was the kind you saw in movies—neat, tidy, the kind of place where nothing bad could ever happen. Inside, the smell of freshly baked bread and simmering garlic drifted from the kitchen, luring me forward, but even that warmth couldn't thaw the icy knot in my chest. Finn's presence had always been a balm, a kind of comfort I could never quite explain, but tonight, it felt like a mask I couldn't quite wear.

The door swung open before I could even knock. Finn stood there, his dark hair slightly tousled, his shirt wrinkled in that endearing, effortless way. His smile was the first thing I saw, and it was all wrong. He was too damn good at being happy. Like his entire existence revolved around making people feel at ease, as if nothing could possibly trouble him. I envied it. I wanted that smile to pull me in and make everything else fade away.

"You're late," he teased, stepping aside to let me in. "But you're forgiven. I'm cooking. And I'm a genius in the kitchen."

I hesitated at the threshold, unsure of how to move forward, of how to fit into the space that felt suddenly too small, too constricted. "I didn't mean to be," I muttered, forcing a smile.

Finn's gaze softened as he led me into the kitchen. "Don't worry about it. You look like you've been running through a storm. Everything okay?"

I nodded, too quickly. "I'm fine." The lie tasted bitter on my tongue, but I had no choice. I couldn't tell him—not yet.

The kitchen was warm, almost impossibly so, like a cocoon of comfort and familiarity. The soft sizzle of vegetables in a pan filled the room as Finn moved about with practiced ease. I watched him, a tiny part of me aching for this normalcy, for this moment where the world hadn't yet come crashing down. But I knew it was only a matter of time before I had to face the truth—before the darkness would reach its fingers into this little slice of peace.

"You're quiet tonight," Finn remarked, his back to me as he stirred something in a pot. He didn't look up, but I could tell from the tension in his shoulders that he was waiting for me to say something more.

I toyed with the edge of my sleeve, stalling. What could I say? Could I tell him about the note? Could I explain how I felt like a target? That someone was watching us, waiting for something to break, something to unravel?

"I'm just tired," I finally said. "Long day at work. You know how it is."

Finn's voice was gentle but insistent. "Yeah, I get it. But you can talk to me, you know. If something's on your mind."

I swallowed, my throat dry. I wanted to tell him, wanted to lean into him and let him take this burden away from me. But the words wouldn't come. Not yet. Maybe never.

I forced myself to focus on the present, on the small details—the way the steam curled from the pot, the clink of utensils against glass, the soft hum of the refrigerator. Finn moved effortlessly in his space, like he was born to make dinner, to create something from nothing. He was so comfortable, so at home, and I was... not. I was an outsider in my own life.

Finn finally turned, and for a moment, he studied me with a curious tilt to his head. "You know, I thought you'd like this. I've been trying out some new recipes. Something to get your mind off things."

"I'm sure it's great," I said, my voice sounding hollow even to my own ears.

He raised an eyebrow. "What's really going on? You're not this distant, even on your worst days."

I exhaled slowly, feeling the weight of the night press down on me. There was a part of me—just a small, vulnerable part—that wanted to tell him everything. That wanted to be honest, to let him in and hope that he would fix it, or at least help me carry it. But I couldn't. The letter, the fear gnawing at me, it all felt too... raw. Too close to the surface.

I didn't trust myself to speak. Instead, I walked over to the table, gently pushing the letter further into the depths of my bag, hoping it would disappear if I just ignored it long enough.

"You know," Finn continued, his tone light but tinged with concern, "you don't have to carry everything by yourself. You're not alone, you know?"

I could feel the heat rise in my chest, a mix of guilt and frustration. I wanted to tell him that it wasn't his burden to bear. But the words were tangled, like a knot I couldn't quite untie.

"I know," I said, finally meeting his gaze. "I'm just... not used to asking for help."

Finn's smile softened, but there was an intensity behind his eyes. "You don't have to ask," he said, his voice low and steady. "I'm here. Whenever you need me."

The sincerity in his words made my chest tighten, and for a moment, I wished I could let him take everything from me. But instead, I only nodded, unable to say anything more.

The smell of dinner filled the air, but it didn't settle the storm in my mind. It only made it worse, reminding me that the quiet moments I so desperately craved were slipping through my fingers like sand.

Dinner was awkward. Not in the clumsy, easy way where you can laugh about spilled wine or a crooked napkin, but in the slow, creeping tension that slid between us, curling its fingers around everything we said and did. Finn, ever the charmer, had tried to lighten the mood with a few off-hand comments about his disastrous attempts at cooking in his younger years, but I was barely listening. My mind was still circling back to the letter, to the creeping sense of being watched, and how impossible it was to just let it go.

We ate in silence, or at least, that's what it felt like to me. The occasional clink of forks against plates was the only sound, as if even the air had decided it could no longer pretend everything was normal. Finn was too quiet too, his eyes flicking to me with a frequency that suggested he knew something was wrong. I caught him looking more than once, his lips pursed like he was chewing over something, debating whether to ask me about the distance he sensed. He didn't, of course. He never did. Finn had a gift for patience, even when it was clear I didn't deserve it. I almost hated him for it, the way he made it so easy to pretend I could keep everything buried.

I shoved the remnants of my meal around the plate, the fork scraping noisily. "I'm sorry," I blurted, the words too sharp. Finn stopped, his brow furrowing, but he didn't say anything right away. He just looked at me with those soft, too-kind eyes, and it made me feel like I was the one who'd done something wrong. It made me feel like I was the one ruining everything.

"What for?" he asked, his voice too gentle.

"Just... being like this. I'm sorry I'm not..." I trailed off, my throat tight, the words choking me. I wasn't even sure what I was apologizing for. For pulling away, for being a stranger in my own life, for letting someone else dictate the way I felt? The list could've gone on forever.

"You don't owe me an apology," Finn said, his voice firm now, pulling my attention back to him. "But you do owe yourself one. Whatever's going on in that head of yours, you need to stop pretending it's not happening."

I shook my head, a bitter laugh slipping out before I could stop it. "It's not that simple."

He leaned forward, placing his elbows on the table, eyes never leaving mine. "I don't want to push you. But I'm not going to pretend I don't see you falling apart. You don't have to tell me everything, but you've got to start telling someone."

I held his gaze, the weight of his words pressing down on me like a physical force. For a moment, I thought I might crack open and spill everything—the note, the feeling of being watched, the irrational fear that had taken root in me like poison. I opened my mouth to speak, to tell him what had been eating at me, but then the house creaked.

The sound wasn't loud, just a low, subtle groan of wood, but it was enough to freeze both of us in place. I looked up, my heart skipping a beat. There it was again—the sensation that something wasn't right.

"Did you hear that?" I asked, my voice betraying the unease swirling in my stomach.

Finn was already standing, moving toward the kitchen door. His hand brushed the side of his neck in that way he did when he was trying to mask his own anxiety. "Probably just the house settling," he said, but I could see the tension in his jaw. He didn't believe it either.

I couldn't explain it, but there was something in the air, something thick and oppressive that wasn't just the normal creaks of an old house. The hair on the back of my neck stood on end.

Before I could say anything more, a sharp knock echoed from the front door, loud enough to make us both jump. I didn't move. Finn's gaze snapped to me, his expression unreadable. "Stay here," he whispered, the command as much for himself as for me.

I nodded without thinking, my heart hammering in my chest. Finn approached the door cautiously, the familiar creak of the floorboards beneath his feet sending a shiver down my spine. When he reached the door, he hesitated for just a moment, a flicker of doubt passing over his face, before he reached for the handle.

"Who is it?" Finn called out, his voice steady but laced with a tension that echoed my own.

No answer. Just the soft sound of breathing, shallow and quick.

I stood, my hands trembling as I gripped the edge of the table. I didn't want to be the one to ruin the moment by jumping to conclusions, but it was impossible to ignore the growing sense of dread.

Finn didn't open the door right away. Instead, he pressed his ear against it, his body tense, like he was listening for something beyond the surface. After a few agonizing seconds, he pulled back, looking at me with a frown that deepened when I didn't say anything.

"Something's wrong," he said, his voice low. "Stay here. I'll check it out."

I opened my mouth to protest, to tell him that I wasn't going to let him face whatever was outside alone, but before I could speak, the door creaked open.

It was only a crack, just enough to peek through. But that's when I saw it. The edge of something—a hand, pale and trembling, holding another envelope.

My heart stopped. The letter.

It was addressed to me.

Before Finn could react, the hand slid the envelope under the door, the action swift and smooth, almost too practiced. It wasn't the first time. It wasn't even the second.

And now, there was no turning back.

Chapter 10: Investigating the Blaze

The sharp scent of paper and ink filled the air as I sifted through the pile of fire reports on the old oak table, the papers curling slightly at the edges, worn from years of use. I didn't know what I was looking for, but I knew I had to find something. Each file seemed to bleed into the next—names, dates, addresses—all too similar, all too vague. But there was a rhythm to the chaos, like the frenzied tapping of a distant drum, always in the background, just out of reach.

My fingers ached from flipping through so many pages. Every fire seemed like a call for attention, a cry for help buried beneath charred remnants. Yet, no one was stepping forward to answer. Not the authorities, not the fire department, not even the residents themselves. It was as if the town had resigned itself to the flames, each scorch mark a quiet admission that something was terribly wrong. But what?

I ran my hand across the top of the last report, my fingertips catching on the jagged corner of a paper that had been folded too many times. Unfolding it carefully, I scanned the report again, even though I had already read it twice. The words on the page were all too familiar: "Unexplained cause. No suspects." It was always the same. A fire started—no one knew how. Or worse, they just didn't care enough to find out.

The door creaked open behind me, and I didn't have to look up to know who it was. Finn's presence was as unmistakable as his silence. I hadn't heard him approach, but there he stood, just inside the doorframe, his expression unreadable. For a moment, the weight of his gaze was like a physical thing, settling over me like a heavy blanket. The air between us felt thick, charged. I tried to ignore the tight knot of anxiety that curled in my stomach, but it wouldn't go away.

"What are you doing?" he asked, his voice low and cautious, like he was walking on a thin layer of ice.

I didn't answer immediately. Instead, I focused on the report in front of me, the words blurring slightly as I realized how long I had been staring at them. The fire reports were more than just reports. They were the echoes of something darker, something that had been growing silently in the background, waiting. I was trying to make sense of it, but the pieces just wouldn't fit.

"I'm looking for something," I said finally, my voice betraying more frustration than I intended. Finn moved closer, and I could feel the tension in the air like a palpable force, winding tighter with every step he took. He didn't touch me, didn't even come close enough for that, but the space between us felt small, too small.

His eyes flicked to the scattered papers on the table, then back to me. "What's this about, Liv? You're digging into things that... don't need to be dug into."

I didn't know why I did it, but I couldn't stop myself. "You didn't answer my question," I said, my voice a little sharper than I meant. "About the letters. You know about them. You're the one who found them, right?"

Finn's jaw tightened, and for a moment, I thought he might turn and walk away, like he usually did when something hit too close to home. But he didn't. Instead, he walked around the table, settling down in the chair opposite me, his gaze never leaving mine. He leaned forward, his hands resting on the table, palms flat against the wood. His eyes were dark, full of something I couldn't quite name, and in that moment, I saw the man who had been hiding beneath the surface—someone far more complex than the guarded, stoic firefighter I had come to know.

"I didn't want you involved in this," he said, his voice low, just above a whisper. "This is bigger than you think, Liv. And it's not just about the fires anymore."

I raised an eyebrow, unimpressed by his secrecy. "And what is it about then, Finn? Because right now, all I see are a bunch of smoke signals that no one's bothering to decipher. You think I'm going to sit here and pretend I don't notice something's off?"

He exhaled sharply, running a hand through his hair in that way he always did when he was frustrated. I had seen it a dozen times before, but this time, it felt different, like there was a battle raging inside him—one he was losing. "You're not the only one trying to put the pieces together," he muttered. "But not everything's meant to be uncovered. There are things in this town—things in my past—that need to stay buried. For your sake, for everyone's."

I swallowed hard. His words felt like a warning, but it wasn't the first time I had heard something like that. He was always looking out for me, always trying to protect me from something, but the walls he had built around himself were too high for me to scale. And, frankly, I was getting tired of trying.

"So, you think if you just keep me in the dark, everything will be fine?" I shot back, my tone sharp, almost biting. "I'm already in the dark, Finn. I've been in the dark. You think I don't see what's going on? You think I don't know that you're hiding something?"

His eyes flickered with something like guilt, but he quickly masked it with a steely calm. "I'm trying to keep you safe, Liv. Don't you get that? I don't want you involved in this mess. I don't want you hurt."

I clenched my fists, trying to hold back the frustration bubbling inside me. "I'm already hurt, Finn. Every day I sit here, doing nothing while fires burn and people suffer, I'm hurt. This isn't about safety anymore. This is about justice. And you're not going to stop me from finding it."

He stared at me, his gaze unwavering, and for a moment, I wondered if he saw me at all—really saw me—or if I was just a problem to be fixed in his eyes. But before either of us could say another word, the shrill sound of my phone ringing broke the tension between us. I snatched it up, trying to shake off the last remnants of the argument.

It was a number I didn't recognize, but there was something in the back of my mind that told me I had to answer. I hit the green button, pressing it to my ear. Finn was still watching me, his posture stiff, waiting.

"Hello?"

A voice—low, gravelly, and far too familiar—came through the receiver.

"You're getting too close, Liv," it said, the words laced with a chill that made my blood run cold. "You won't like what you find."

The chill in the air seemed to press harder on my skin, a subtle reminder of how close we were to something dangerous, something no one wanted to confront. Finn's words had landed heavy, lingering like smoke in a room long after the fire had been put out. I knew he didn't want me involved—hell, I could see it in the way his jaw clenched, the way he fought to keep his emotions buried beneath layers of control. But I wasn't the type to stand by and wait for someone else to fix things. Not this time.

The phone call had only added fuel to the fire, and though the voice on the other end was an echo of a past I didn't understand, its warning was crystal clear. The tension between Finn and me deepened, each word hanging like a crack in the ice just waiting to break. I lowered the phone slowly, still not quite sure what to make of the threat, the warning that felt too personal. A chill crept up my spine, creeping like the fingers of doubt I refused to acknowledge.

Finn leaned forward, his expression unreadable, but I could see the storm behind his eyes. He was a man on the edge of breaking, and I was standing too close to the precipice. He didn't need to say anything for me to know what he was thinking. He wanted me out of this. He didn't want me to get caught up in whatever was spiraling out of control, but there was no way I could just walk away now. Not after everything.

"Liv, this isn't your fight," he said, his voice tight but still trying to hold that calm, authoritative edge. It was the same tone he used on the job, the one that made people listen, even if they didn't want to. But I wasn't about to be one of those people.

I crossed my arms, staring him down. "Maybe it's not just your fight either," I shot back, unable to keep the bite from my voice. "And you don't get to make that call. Not this time."

There was a beat of silence, the kind that stretched long enough to make the air heavy with words unsaid. He didn't argue, but I could see the frustration tightening his features, the way his hands fidgeted at his sides like they were itching to do something—anything—besides stand there, staring at me with that unreadable expression.

"I don't want you involved, Liv," he repeated, softer this time, though the warning was still there, hanging between us like a guillotine's blade.

I met his gaze head-on, unflinching. "You think I'm going to sit on my hands and let someone burn this town down? Let them threaten me into silence?" I felt the words slip from my mouth before I could stop them, each one more final than the last.

His eyes darkened, but this time, there was a flicker of something else—something I couldn't quite place. "You don't know what you're asking, Liv. Some things aren't meant to be found."

I almost laughed. It was bitter, sharp. "You can't keep secrets forever, Finn. I've already found enough to know this is bigger than you're willing to admit."

Finn's lips pressed into a thin line, and I knew that look. It was the look of a man who had made up his mind, who was trying to decide whether to walk away or take another step deeper into a world that wasn't supposed to be his to enter. The moment stretched, both of us locked in a silent tug-of-war over control, neither of us willing to give ground.

The phone rang again, this time cutting through the tension like a knife. I grabbed it without thinking, my heart hammering in my chest as I answered. The voice on the other end was different this time—this wasn't the low, gravelly tone of the previous caller, but a sharp, clipped voice that was all business.

"This is Detective Harper," the voice said, and for a moment, I froze. The name hit me like a ton of bricks, memories rushing back to me. Detective Harper had been the one to write me off, to tell me that my suspicions about the fire were nothing more than a coincidence.

"You need to stop," Harper continued, her tone colder than I remembered. "We know what you're doing, and if you keep digging, you won't just be putting yourself at risk."

I stood there, the phone pressed to my ear, staring at Finn, who was now watching me with a look I couldn't decipher. He was waiting for me to hang up, to back down, to let someone else take control of this mess. But I wasn't about to listen. Not now. Not when I was this close.

"Who are you?" I asked, my voice steady even though my insides were a whirlwind. "What do you want?"

The line went silent for a moment, as if Harper were considering her words carefully, weighing whether or not to answer. When she spoke again, it was with a new sharpness, as if she had finally decided that enough was enough.

"Just know this, Liv," she said, the warning in her voice palpable, "some people are not meant to be protected. And you're one of them. Stay out of this."

The line clicked dead before I could say another word. My grip on the phone tightened, and for a brief moment, I wondered if I had just made a mistake. But I couldn't think about that now—not with Finn still standing there, his face shadowed by something far more dangerous than any threat I'd received.

I dropped the phone to the table with a little more force than necessary, my breath shallow as I looked at him. He didn't move, didn't speak for a long moment, but the weight of his gaze was enough to leave me feeling stripped bare.

"You should listen to them, Liv," Finn said quietly, his voice softer now, almost like he was trying to coax me into understanding. "I'm not trying to keep you safe because I want to control you. I'm trying to keep you safe because if you keep pushing, it won't end well. You don't know who you're dealing with."

His words hung in the air, a cold promise I couldn't quite ignore. But I wasn't ready to back down. Not yet.

"I can handle myself, Finn," I said, my voice steady, though there was a tremor running through me that I couldn't quite suppress. "But what I can't handle is standing by while this town burns, while people like you—people who know something—keep it all locked up."

For the first time since I'd met him, Finn's eyes softened, and in that brief moment, I saw a flicker of something I hadn't expected—guilt. He looked away, his jaw tightening again, and when he spoke, his voice was thick with something far heavier than concern.

"I'm not trying to hurt you, Liv. But you need to understand that this is bigger than you think. This isn't just about fires. It's about everything. And some things... some things are better left buried."

The quiet hum of the house surrounded me like a muted background to the whirlwind of thoughts spinning through my mind. I paced the floor, unable to settle, unable to shake the feeling that the truth was just beyond my reach. Finn's words had been like a weight tied around my chest, but I wasn't about to let them stop me. Not now. Not when I was so close to something, something that felt like it could unravel everything. My fingers hovered over the stack of fire reports, but this time, it wasn't the papers I was after—it was something deeper, something beneath the surface.

I'd seen enough fires to know how they worked. But this—this was something different. The fires weren't random. No, there was a pattern, hidden in plain sight, and I was the only one willing to search for it.

I moved to the wall where I had pinned up the photos, each one a snapshot of a life burned to the ground. A fire at the old bookstore. Another at the mechanic's shop. A small, forgotten cabin on the edge of town. The charred remnants of these places didn't just speak of destruction; they whispered secrets, ones I was determined to hear. As I studied the images, something caught my eye. A small detail, almost too insignificant to matter: a faint streak of black smoke rising from the same direction in each photo, like a signature left behind. I leaned in closer, the hairs on the back of my neck prickling as the realization hit me. These weren't isolated incidents. They were connected.

"Liv," Finn's voice broke through the quiet, low and tense, pulling me back to the present. He had been watching me for longer than I'd realized, standing in the doorway with that unshakeable air of authority he wore like a second skin. The way he said my name—almost like a warning, almost like a plea—stopped me dead in my tracks. "What are you doing?"

I didn't answer right away. I couldn't. Because the truth was, I wasn't sure what I was doing anymore. My heart was racing, my thoughts tangled in a web of fear and determination. I turned slowly to face him, trying to steady my breath, but my hands betrayed me, trembling as I pushed the hair out of my face.

"I'm trying to put this together," I said, my voice quiet, though the urgency behind it was unmistakable. "Trying to see the connection. To understand why this is happening."

Finn's gaze softened, and for a moment, I saw a flicker of something that almost looked like regret. "You need to stop, Liv. This is too dangerous. You don't know what you're getting into."

I crossed my arms, my frustration rising like a wave crashing against a cliff. "I'm not going to sit here while everything burns. I can't. You said it yourself—this is bigger than just fires. If there's something else going on, I need to find out what it is."

He exhaled sharply, stepping into the room with a resigned look on his face. "You're not thinking straight. People have died, Liv. And there's no way you can fix this. You need to let the authorities handle it."

"The authorities?" I laughed, the sound bitter in my throat. "The authorities haven't done anything. They've been sitting on their hands while everything burns. I can't just wait for someone else to take care of it." I shook my head, frustration bubbling up inside me like an untapped geyser. "I can't."

Finn moved closer, his eyes narrowing as if trying to read me, trying to understand why I was so stubborn. "What's driving you, Liv? Why are you so hell-bent on solving this?"

I swallowed hard, the answer sitting heavy on my chest. "Because I'm tired of being afraid. I'm tired of letting fear dictate my life. I won't hide anymore." I held his gaze, willing him to understand, but he only looked more troubled. "You don't get it. This isn't just about the fires anymore. It's about taking back control."

Finn didn't respond right away, his gaze flicking to the photographs pinned on the wall, then back to me. The tension between us grew thicker, the air crackling with the weight of unspoken words. But finally, he spoke, his voice barely above a whisper.

"You don't know what you're dealing with, Liv. This isn't some simple arson case. You're in way over your head."

I felt a surge of anger flare inside me, my pulse quickening as the words left my mouth before I could stop them. "And you think I care? You think I'm going to just let it slide? I know what you're hiding, Finn. I've known for a long time. So don't stand there like you're the only one who understands how dangerous this is."

His jaw tightened, his fists clenching at his sides. "You have no idea what you're getting into," he repeated, his voice low and dangerous now, the warning finally breaking through the barrier of his calm demeanor.

I took a step closer, refusing to back down. "Then tell me. Tell me everything, Finn. Because I don't think I can walk away from this until I know the truth."

For a long moment, neither of us moved. The tension in the room was so thick, I could almost taste it, bitter and metallic on the tip of my tongue. Then, as if he had made a decision, Finn took a slow, deliberate step back, his eyes never leaving mine.

"You're right," he said, the words heavy, as if he had just made a decision that would change everything. "There's something I haven't told you. Something I should've told you a long time ago."

My heart skipped a beat, a flash of hope cutting through the fog of uncertainty. "What?" I asked, my voice barely above a whisper.

Finn looked away for a moment, his face clouded with something I couldn't name. Then he turned back to me, his eyes darker than I had ever seen them.

“The fires aren’t just about money, or revenge,” he said slowly, his voice strained, like he was holding back something dangerous. “It’s about something... someone. And if you keep digging, if you keep pushing, you won’t just be putting yourself in danger. You’ll be walking straight into the eye of a storm you can’t control.”

I opened my mouth to respond, but the words died on my lips as the sound of shuffling footsteps came from the hallway. Someone was at the door. My heart skipped in my chest, the tension between Finn and me suddenly forgotten.

I glanced at Finn, but he was already moving toward the door, his expression unreadable. Without thinking, I grabbed the closest object—one of the fire reports—and stuffed it into my bag, my pulse hammering in my ears. Whoever it was, they weren’t supposed to be here. Not now.

Finn’s hand was already on the door, but before he could open it, the unmistakable sound of a key turning in the lock froze us both in place. The door creaked open. And the last thing I heard before everything went dark was a voice—low, menacing—saying, “You’ve been asking the wrong questions, Liv.”

Chapter 11: Dangerous Confessions

The rain pounded against the windows, a steady drumbeat that seemed to vibrate through every bone in my body. Outside, the storm was unforgiving, thrashing the world with sheets of silver. Inside the engine compartment, it felt like the air itself was being pressed down, stifling the small space we shared. The engine rumbled with all the power of a machine fighting to stay alive, but even it seemed to struggle against the fury of the storm. It wasn't just the wind or the rain that pressed on me, but the silence between Finn and me, thick as a fog and equally suffocating.

He sat across from me, his brow furrowed in that way he always did when he was trying to hide something. His hands, usually so steady, were now gripping the armrests of the seat, knuckles white with tension. It wasn't just the storm that had him on edge. I could see it now, the tremor in his fingers, the tightness in his jaw, the way his gaze kept darting to the small window as if looking for something or someone to rescue him from whatever was threatening to unravel him.

I should have said something to break the silence, to offer him comfort, but I couldn't. Every word felt too heavy, too wrong. I had spent so many months building walls between us—had spent so long convincing myself I didn't care about the reckless, sarcastic man who seemed to live his life with one foot in the fire—that hearing the way his breath caught as he tried to steady himself made my chest tighten.

The storm outside roared louder, almost drowning out the strained rasp of his voice when it finally broke the silence.

"I don't know why I'm telling you this," Finn muttered, his eyes avoiding mine. "Hell, I shouldn't. You're probably the last person I should—"

"I'm here," I interrupted gently, though I wasn't sure what I was offering him. Comfort? Protection? Or just a distraction from whatever demons were stirring behind his usually impenetrable walls?

He shook his head, almost as if trying to shake off the moment, but it was too late. The words were already spilling out of him, ragged and raw. "When I was seventeen," he began, the sound of the storm outside suddenly taking a backseat to the sound of his voice, "I... I made a mistake. A big one. One that I've carried with me for so long that sometimes I can't even remember what it feels like to not have it hanging over my head."

My breath caught in my throat, and I leaned forward without thinking, drawn in by the brokenness in his voice. He never let his guard down. Never. So why was he now? Why now, of all times?

"I—I hurt someone," he continued, the words trembling between us. "Someone I cared about. And I can't take it back. Can't undo it. And that's... that's the thing, you know? I don't even know if I would. If I'm being honest, part of me wishes I could, but the other part—God, I don't even know how to say this without sounding like a monster—part of me feels like it was... deserved."

I could feel my chest tightening, the shock of his confession rattling me. I wanted to pull away. To retreat. But something in the way he said it—the way he was looking at me now, a raw desperation in his eyes—kept me tethered to the spot. I couldn't look away, couldn't breathe for a second.

I'd always thought of Finn as brash, careless. The kind of person who made you question everything you thought you knew about yourself. But now, sitting in that cramped, shaking space with him, it felt like I was seeing him for the first time, really seeing him, and what I saw scared me more than anything.

"I wasn't—I wasn't the same then," he added, voice strained. "I was angry. So angry. At the world. At my family. At myself. And

I took it out on her. I pushed her away. And I ruined everything. Everything."

I could hear the pain in his voice, feel the weight of it pressing down on both of us. The storm outside seemed to howl louder, but nothing could drown out the torment I could see etched into his face. I didn't know what to say, how to comfort him, because the truth was that nothing could take that back. Nothing could undo the years he'd spent living with it.

"Finn," I whispered, uncertain of how to approach the depth of the confession, but my voice caught, betraying the flood of emotions crashing over me. "You don't—"

But he cut me off, his hand reaching for mine, gripping it with such urgency that it startled me. "Don't say it wasn't your fault," he said, his voice raw, laced with a pain that dug deep into my chest. "Don't give me that. I did it. I... I hurt her."

And there it was—the thing that hung between us, more dangerous than any storm outside. I could feel the weight of it, the danger of it, like a dark shadow clinging to him, refusing to let go. A mistake. A confession. But it wasn't just the confession that shook me. It was the way he was unraveling before me, and the way I found myself reaching out, not in pity, but in a desperate attempt to understand, to make sense of the man who had always been a puzzle I couldn't quite solve.

In that moment, I realized just how dangerous Finn really was. Not because of the past he couldn't outrun, but because in spite of it all, in spite of the mistakes and the wreckage, he was still the person I found myself falling for. The one person I couldn't pull myself away from, no matter how hard I tried.

I squeezed his hand, my fingers trembling as I spoke, though the words felt too small for everything between us. "Finn, I... I don't know what to say."

He didn't answer. He didn't have to. We both knew that there were no words that could make this okay.

The storm raged on outside, relentless, a fury I couldn't escape. It had already shredded the calm night, and now, as the seconds dragged by, I felt it tear at something inside me, too. Finn's confession hung in the air like smoke from a fire, curling and twisting, impossible to ignore. My hand was still held tight in his, and though I could feel the slight tremor of his touch, it grounded me in ways I didn't expect.

I wanted to say something to make it better, but nothing came to mind. I hadn't exactly been a beacon of emotional insight in my own life, and yet here I was, trying to navigate the jagged edges of Finn's darkness. He was still staring out the window, his jaw tight, his profile hardened against the storm, but I knew—somehow—that he wasn't seeing anything outside. He was still locked in that moment, in the pain he'd confessed, and I was just a shadow, offering nothing but my presence in the space between us.

"Why are you telling me this?" I asked finally, my voice quiet, unsure. It wasn't the most profound thing I could have said, but it was the question that had been gnawing at me since he'd opened up. I wasn't angry. Not at him, at least. But there was something unsettling about hearing him say it, like a door had opened to a part of him that wasn't just filled with bad decisions, but with regret that he couldn't undo.

Finn exhaled sharply, and for the first time, he looked at me, his eyes unguarded, vulnerable in a way I hadn't seen before. "Because I don't know how to keep it locked away anymore," he said, the weight of the words heavier than the storm. "I've spent years carrying it, pretending like it didn't eat at me. But every time I push someone away, every time I screw up, it's like I'm running from the same damn thing. And I can't outrun it."

I didn't know what to say. How do you respond to that? I wasn't some trained therapist, some saint with answers. I didn't have the skills to fix him or tell him the right thing to make it all feel better. Hell, I was still trying to figure out how to keep my own life from collapsing in on itself. But here he was, this storm of a man, and somehow, I was part of his chaos now.

"So, what do you want from me?" I asked before I could stop myself, my tone sharper than I intended, as if I could push the weight of his confession back where it belonged—away from me.

Finn's laugh was bitter, more out of frustration than humor. "I don't want anything. I'm not asking for anything. I just—shit. I don't know." He leaned back in his seat, his hand still clinging to mine, but there was something raw about his grasp now. "I guess I just don't want to be this anymore. But I don't know how to stop being this."

There was a heavy silence, the kind that seeps in like cold air through a cracked window, until finally, I spoke.

"You're not just your mistakes," I said, my voice more steady now, as if I could actually believe the words that left my lips. "You can't be. None of us are just the worst thing we've ever done."

Finn didn't respond right away, and for a moment, I thought he might dismiss my words like he had everything else in the past, but instead, his eyes softened, just for a second. It was fleeting, but it was enough to make me wonder if I was starting to see him for who he truly was, and not just the version I had built in my head—the reckless, defiant Finn who pushed people away without a second thought.

"What if it's too late to be anything else?" he asked, his voice barely above a whisper.

The question hung between us like a storm cloud. I could feel the weight of it, pressing against my chest, demanding an answer. But how could I answer him when I didn't have the slightest idea of what I was doing with my own life? I didn't have the wisdom to reassure him, to fix him, but something inside me, something I hadn't expected, wanted to try.

"I don't think it's ever too late," I said, the words coming out quieter this time, more fragile. I wasn't so sure anymore, but it was the only thing I could offer. "Maybe it's just... hard to see the light when you're stuck in the dark."

Finn let out a low breath, and for a moment, I thought he might say something more. But he didn't. Instead, he pulled my hand closer to his chest, and I felt his heart beat beneath my palm, the rhythm steady but laced with tension. His thumb traced circles over my skin, as if grounding himself in something real, something that didn't feel like a past he couldn't escape.

The world outside was a blur of rain and lightning, but in that small compartment, with Finn's warmth seeping into me, I didn't feel quite so alone. He had confessed the worst of himself, and here I was, still sitting beside him, despite everything. I wasn't sure why. Maybe it was because I saw something in him that nobody else did. Or maybe it was because I had my own demons to fight, and for the first time, I didn't feel like I had to do it alone.

The storm outside screamed louder, a fierce wind howling in protest, but inside, things were different. In that moment, I could feel the smallest shift between us, as if the air had changed, charged with something neither of us could name. I wasn't sure what came next. What we would do with all these confessions, these half-formed promises that neither of us had the courage to voice.

But for the first time, I didn't need to know. All I knew was that I was still here, still with him, and that was more than enough.

The storm outside seemed to stretch endlessly, an unrelenting howl that echoed in the corners of my mind. The rhythmic tapping of rain against the metal walls of the engine compartment had become white noise, a distant reminder that the world beyond us was still turning, still storming. But here, inside this little metal box, it felt as though time had slowed, suspended in that charged space between Finn's confession and the silence that followed.

He hadn't said much after that. The confession hung in the air like an unfinished sentence, and for the first time, I wasn't sure whether to push him for more or leave him to settle into the uncomfortable quiet. His hand had tightened around mine, but it was no longer the desperate grasp of a man on the edge. It was something else—a tentative connection, like two broken puzzle pieces that had, somehow, found their place.

I couldn't look away from him. There was a flicker of something in his eyes—something dark, but vulnerable, too. He was a labyrinth, and I was starting to get lost in him.

"I'm not that person anymore," he murmured, almost as if he was convincing himself. "At least, I don't want to be."

I squeezed his hand, the warmth of his skin grounding me in a way that felt both comforting and unsettling. "But you're still you," I said softly, knowing it was the only truth that mattered right now. "You don't have to erase what happened to move forward."

Finn's lips pressed into a thin line, and for a moment, I thought he might pull away, retreat into the carefully constructed walls he'd built around himself. But he didn't. Instead, he shifted, his body closer now, the air between us charged with a tension I couldn't ignore.

"I don't know how to move forward," he admitted, his voice barely above a whisper. "I keep trying, but every time I think I've got a grip on it, it slips away."

I wanted to say something to ease his burden, to tell him that it wasn't as complicated as he made it seem. But I didn't know how. How do you tell someone who has carried around so much weight for so long that the road ahead isn't as hard as it feels? I could offer no grand gestures or words of wisdom. I had nothing but the quiet solidarity of my presence.

And then, unexpectedly, the storm seemed to quiet. The howling wind softened, the crackling thunder retreating into the distance. The sudden calm felt like a lie, as if nature itself were trying to lull us into a false sense of safety.

"I don't want to be afraid anymore," Finn said, his voice trembling in a way that mirrored the rawness of the storm's fading rage.

I couldn't help myself. I reached up and cupped his face, the roughness of his stubble scraping my palm. His eyes closed for a moment, and I could feel the soft exhale of breath he took, as though he had forgotten how to breathe without the weight of his past suffocating him.

"You don't have to be afraid," I murmured. "You just have to keep going."

His lips twitched, a ghost of a smile, something between gratitude and resignation. And for the briefest moment, I saw him—really saw him. Not the reckless, sarcastic Finn who made sarcastic jokes to shield himself, not the angry, brooding version of himself who lashed out in his own pain—but the man underneath it all, the one who had learned to survive despite everything.

I couldn't deny it any longer. I was in deeper than I had intended, tangled up in the storm of him. And I was afraid it was too late to find my way out.

"You make it sound so simple," he said, the corner of his mouth lifting in a teasing smile that didn't quite reach his eyes. "But you don't know what it's like to have all that guilt eating you alive."

I wanted to laugh, but the ache in my chest kept it lodged there, a weight I didn't know how to shift. He was right. I didn't know. But that didn't stop me from wanting to help him. I couldn't be the answer, couldn't carry his burden for him. But maybe, just maybe, I could help him find a way to carry it without it breaking him.

"Well, maybe I don't," I said, my voice catching for just a second. "But I know what it's like to feel like you're suffocating. To feel like you're drowning in things you can't control."

He didn't say anything. He didn't need to. His eyes spoke the words I knew he couldn't bring himself to say, a silent understanding between us. There was no grand resolution, no perfect promise that everything would be okay. We were both still grappling with our own demons, still too close to the edge to see clearly.

But in that moment, there was something unspoken, something raw and real, that held us together. It wasn't a fix, but it was enough.

I took a deep breath and let it out slowly. The storm outside was still raging, but I couldn't focus on it anymore. All I could think about was the man beside me, his face illuminated by the soft flickering light of the engine, the tension in his shoulders, the silent plea for something I wasn't sure he even understood.

"I'm not going anywhere, Finn," I said softly, my words sincere, even though the uncertainty twisted my insides. "You don't have to carry this alone."

He didn't reply, but the way he looked at me, with those heavy eyes, made my heart beat faster, made me wonder if, despite everything, this was what he needed—this strange, delicate bond we were forming.

But before I could process the weight of my own confession, before I could think through the implications of what I had just said, the engine stuttered, and the lights flickered out, plunging us into total darkness.

I froze, my heart leaping into my throat. "What the hell was that?"

Finn's hand shot out in the dark, grasping mine once again, his grip tighter now, almost frantic. "We're not alone," he murmured, his voice low, urgent.

And then the sound came—a heavy thump, followed by a crackling noise. It wasn't the storm. It wasn't the wind. It was something else. Something we hadn't expected.

The silence that followed was thick with tension, and as I strained to hear the next sound, I could feel the storm inside of me mirror the one outside.

Then, from the darkness, a voice—low, menacing, and all too familiar—whispered.

"You're not going anywhere."

Chapter 12: Sparks in the Night

The morning was shrouded in an eerie haze, the kind that blankets a city after a fire, when the air itself feels scorched. I could still taste the remnants of smoke in the back of my throat, its bitterness clinging to the inside of my mouth. The sirens had died down, but the low hum of the aftermath lingered, as though the world itself was still trying to shake off the memory of the flames. Outside the window, the sky had a strange, fiery hue—like a bruise spreading slowly across the horizon. The sun, too shy to make an appearance, had been swallowed whole by the heavy clouds.

I rubbed my eyes, trying to dispel the lingering weight of dreams—dreams that were only fragments now, slippery and fading. But it wasn't the nightmares that had woken me, nor the half-formed remnants of sleep that clung to my mind. No, it was the steady beep of my phone, relentless and demanding, as if reminding me of what the day would hold. A message from Finn, the last person I wanted to hear from but the one I knew would pull me back into the storm I had tried so desperately to escape.

"Are you okay?" was all it said. Simple. Direct. No question of my whereabouts, no plea for reassurance. Just that.

I pressed my thumb into the screen, reading it again, trying to find the meaning hidden between the words. Maybe it was the early hour, or maybe the remnants of adrenaline still running through my veins, but I didn't feel like answering.

I didn't feel like doing anything but burying myself under the blankets and pretending the world didn't exist for a while.

But that was never an option when it came to Finn.

I glanced at the clock—6:30 a.m. The same time we had been at the scene of the fire. It felt like hours had passed, but I knew it had only been a few short minutes since the last siren had faded into the distance. I sighed, turning the phone over in my hand. The air in the room felt dense, like a thick fog had settled in the corners of my mind. The smell of charred wood and gasoline still clung to my clothes, my hair—everything felt sticky with the memories of the night before.

It was strange how easily the ordinary things could slip away when faced with something as violent as a fire. It was as though the blaze had burned everything to the ground—every plan, every expectation, every feeling I thought I had control over. And in the midst of that destruction, Finn had been there, reckless, unhinged, and wild. The way his eyes had burned with intensity, the way he had thrown himself into the flames without a second thought, it had scared me more than I cared to admit.

But in the end, it wasn't the fire that had nearly consumed us—it was the silence afterward. The words we didn't say to each other, the accusations that hung heavy in the space between us. I had thought I could keep my distance, keep my heart safe from him, but I was wrong. He had crawled under my skin, finding his way into places I thought were buried, untouched.

When I finally picked up the phone, I hesitated for only a moment before responding.

"I'm fine. Just tired." The words felt empty even as I typed them. But it was what he needed to hear. It was what I needed to say.

The message came back almost instantly. "Meet me at the diner?"

I didn't have to think about it. I had been expecting it. I knew this was where we would end up. Some things were inevitable, like the way a storm builds on the horizon, no matter how much you try to ignore it.

I swung my legs off the bed, feeling the cold floor beneath my feet. The room felt small, suffocating in the way it always did when my mind was racing. I wasn't ready to face him, but I knew I couldn't stay here, pretending the world hadn't just torn itself apart. Not again.

The diner wasn't far. It had been our spot once—a place we used to retreat to when the world felt too heavy, when the weight of our lives threatened to crush us. But that was before. Before the distance. Before the silence. Now, it felt like a reminder of everything we had lost—and maybe a little of what was left between us.

I pulled on jeans and a sweater, the same one I had worn the night before. It smelled faintly of smoke, the scent following me as I stepped into the cool morning air. The streets were quiet, save for the occasional car passing by. There was something surreal about this hour, when the city hadn't yet fully woken up, when everything seemed on the verge of being both too much and too little at the same time.

As I walked, I couldn't shake the feeling that something was about to shift. That whatever was left between Finn and me was teetering on the edge of something bigger. I wasn't sure if it was something I wanted to fall into or something I needed to escape.

When I reached the diner, I spotted him through the window before I even pushed open the door. Finn sat in his usual booth, elbows resting on the table, staring into his cup of coffee as if it held the answers to every question he couldn't ask. I hesitated in the doorway, unsure if I was ready for this conversation. But the doorbell chimed behind me, and I knew there was no turning back.

"Hey," I said, slipping into the seat across from him.

He didn't look up immediately, his fingers curling around the mug like it was the only thing holding him together. But then, finally, his gaze met mine, sharp and intense. It always hit me like a punch to the gut, the way he could see straight through me, like nothing was hidden.

"Are you okay?" he asked, his voice low, rough.

I nodded, though I wasn't sure if I believed it myself. "Yeah. You?"

He scoffed, pushing the mug aside. "Don't lie to me, Grace." His voice was rougher now, his eyes narrowing. "You weren't the one playing hero last night."

I wasn't sure if he meant it as an accusation or a confession. But I couldn't ignore the tremor in his voice, the way his anger was barely a cover for the hurt underneath.

"I didn't think you'd actually do it," I admitted, my own voice softer than I intended. "I didn't think you'd throw yourself into that fire, not after everything."

He leaned back in the booth, shaking his head slowly. "You think I want to be reckless? You think I enjoy this?"

"I think you're running from something. Something you're not telling me."

The diner was the kind of place that felt eternal. The faded red vinyl seats, the chipped coffee mugs, the hum of a jukebox in the corner that no one ever bothered to fix—it was everything I'd tried to avoid for the past few months, yet it had somehow become the one place I couldn't escape. Finn was still staring at me, his expression unreadable, as if he were trying to decide whether to speak or leave it all unsaid. The tension between us was thick, almost tangible, and I could feel it crawling under my skin, like something was just about to break wide open.

"You really think I'm running from something, Grace?" He repeated the words slowly, as though testing their weight, letting them hang between us like the smoke from the fire still clung to my clothes. His eyes darkened, and I felt the shift in the air, the way it stilled when the storm was coming.

"I think you're avoiding what's right in front of you," I said, not backing down. The words were out before I could stop them, sharp and biting. And yet, somehow, the silence in the booth deepened.

"You're wrong." His voice was barely above a whisper, but there was an edge to it, a rawness that told me there was more beneath the surface. "I'm not the one running."

It wasn't what I expected him to say. Not by a long shot. I thought he'd double down on his deflection, on his anger. But instead, there was something in his voice—an honesty, a vulnerability—that rattled me.

I leaned back in my seat, suddenly unsure of everything I thought I knew about him. My hands wrapped around the chipped mug in front of me, the warmth of it a strange comfort. "Then what is it, Finn? What's going on with you?"

He pushed the mug aside, the motion swift and decisive. The steely calm I'd come to associate with him cracked then, just for a moment, and I saw something else—something that scared me more than the fire itself.

"It's not just about the fire," he muttered, his fingers tapping out a rhythm on the edge of the table, like he was trying to hold himself together, piece by piece. "It's everything. It's everything I've been trying to outrun. The things I can't fix."

His eyes met mine, and in them, I saw something flicker—desperation, maybe, or fear, but it was gone so quickly I wasn't sure if I imagined it. Finn had never been the type to show weakness. He wore his scars like armor, and I'd always respected that. But now, sitting across from him, I wondered just how much that armor had cost him. How much of himself he'd buried to keep everyone else at arm's length.

"You're not the only one with scars, you know," I said softly. I wasn't trying to sound accusing; I didn't want to fight anymore. But there was a bitter edge to my words I couldn't quite tame. "I didn't ask for this, either."

He flinched, just barely, but it was enough to make me pause. Finn didn't flinch. Not for anyone.

"I didn't mean to—" He started, but his words trailed off, swallowed by the awkwardness that filled the space between us. His jaw tightened, and for a moment, I thought he might get up and walk out.

But he didn't. Instead, he sat there, shoulders slumped slightly, his gaze not meeting mine anymore. It was the first time I saw him like this—vulnerable, fragile in a way I couldn't quite understand.

"Why are you so scared of letting me in?" I asked, my voice quiet but insistent.

He stared at his hands, the veins in his wrist standing out in stark relief. "Because I don't know how to fix it, Grace," he whispered, his voice so raw I barely recognized it. "I don't know how to fix me. And I sure as hell don't know how to fix you."

The truth of it hit me like a slap, sharp and stinging. For so long, I'd thought we were on opposite sides of some invisible line, that he was the one who couldn't see me. But in that moment, I realized I hadn't been able to see him either. Not really.

I wanted to say something, anything to fill the silence, but the words stuck in my throat. I wasn't sure what he needed to hear. I wasn't even sure what I needed to hear.

It wasn't until the waitress arrived, refilling our coffee cups with a loud clink, that I realized how heavy the quiet had become. She didn't ask if we were okay, didn't try to make small talk. She just moved around the booth like we were invisible to her, which, in that moment, was kind of a relief.

Finn took a deep breath, as if gathering himself before he spoke again. When he finally did, his words were slower, more deliberate, like he was choosing them carefully. "I didn't think I'd survive it, you know? The fire. It wasn't just about saving people—it was about saving me. I didn't think I'd make it out of there, Grace. Not the way it felt in that moment."

There it was—the truth of it. His words hit me harder than anything else, deeper than I could have prepared for. The idea that Finn, of all people, had felt so desperate, so close to losing everything—it shook me.

"I'm sorry," I said before I could stop myself. It wasn't enough, but it was all I had to offer. "I didn't know."

He looked up then, his gaze meeting mine, and for the first time in what felt like forever, there was a flicker of understanding between us. He reached across the table, his hand brushing over mine. It wasn't a declaration, not a promise, but something more subtle—a silent truce, maybe, or the quiet recognition that we had both been carrying too much for too long.

"I never wanted to drag you into this," he said softly. "But it's been so damn hard not to, Grace. I don't know how to let you go."

I swallowed hard, my throat suddenly tight. "Then don't."

It wasn't the answer I'd expected to give. I wasn't sure it was even the right one. But as his hand closed over mine, I realized that sometimes, there were no easy answers. Only moments like this—fragile, fleeting, but real in a way I couldn't explain.

The waitress came back to clear our plates, and for a moment, neither of us moved. We stayed there, hands still entwined, caught between the past and whatever future we hadn't yet figured out. There was no grand gesture, no words that could make everything better. But in that silence, I knew we had found something we'd both been too afraid to admit.

I left the diner with Finn still beside me, the weight of our unspoken words hanging between us like a storm cloud. The daylight seemed wrong, bright and unforgiving, like it didn't belong in a world so steeped in ash. I could still feel the lingering warmth of his hand on mine, an imprint I wasn't sure how to erase, even if I wanted to. But I didn't want to erase it. Not anymore.

We walked in silence, each step more laden than the last, as though the city itself was holding its breath, waiting for something to happen. I glanced at Finn, watching him from the corner of my eye as we passed the rows of buildings, the hum of traffic dull in my ears. His jaw was clenched, but I could tell his mind was somewhere else—somewhere dark. He wasn't the same man who had stood at the fire line last night, his face set in grim determination, a mask I couldn't read. Now, the cracks were visible, and it was like I was looking at a stranger. A stranger who'd been shattered and then put back together, all the pieces still jagged.

I had thought that by now I would've figured him out—how he worked, what made him tick. But every time I thought I had him, he slipped through my fingers, like sand, or smoke. I didn't know if it was because he was running from something—or if it was me who had been running all along.

"Why didn't you just let me handle it?" Finn's voice broke the silence, low and tight with frustration. He didn't look at me as he spoke, his gaze fixed straight ahead. "The fire, I mean. You could've walked away. You shouldn't have been there."

I felt my stomach twist at the mention of it. It wasn't the fire that had bothered me, not really. It was the way he had looked at me afterward, like I was the one who didn't understand. The anger that had bled out of him—raw and uncontained—had been a reflection of something deeper, something I wasn't sure I could reach.

"Don't you get it?" I stopped in my tracks, forcing him to stop too, turning to face him. "I wasn't just there for the fire. I was there for you. I'm not just going to watch you burn yourself alive while you play hero. I'm not going to stand on the sidelines, Finn. Not anymore."

He met my eyes then, his expression hard to read. But there was something there—something that had been absent the night before, when everything had been flames and chaos. The walls were still up, but maybe... just maybe... they were starting to crack.

"Grace, I—" His voice faltered, and for a moment, I thought he might say something that would make it all clearer. Something that would unlock the door we both had been keeping closed. But the moment slipped away, just like the others.

Instead, he looked away, the muscles in his neck tightening as if he were trying to hold back a storm. "I didn't ask for any of this. You think I wanted to drag you into my mess? You think I wanted to turn my life into something you couldn't even look at?"

"I'm already looking," I said quietly, stepping closer, my voice firm despite the way my heart was racing. "You're not as invisible as you think, Finn."

For the briefest second, his guard dropped, and I saw a flash of something unspoken pass across his face. Regret? Longing? I couldn't tell. But it was gone before I could analyze it, as he stepped back, hands shoved in his pockets, his gaze now firmly on the cracked sidewalk beneath our feet. "I'm not asking you to fix me," he muttered, voice rough. "I'm asking you to stay away. You can't help me."

The words stung more than I'd expected. A reflexive part of me wanted to argue, to tell him that I didn't need him to ask, that I was already in it. But the words got stuck, caught in the back of my throat. Maybe it was because I knew he was right. Maybe it was because I had been trying to fix him for so long that I'd forgotten why I'd stayed in the first place.

"I'm not going anywhere, Finn," I said finally, my voice softer. "I'm not running. You don't get to decide that for me."

His lips pressed into a tight line, his entire body radiating frustration, as though every word I said was only making things harder for him. I wanted to reach out, to ease the tension that had grown between us, but I didn't know how. It felt like standing at the edge of something, waiting for the fall, but too afraid to jump.

And then, just when I thought the silence might swallow us whole, my phone buzzed in my pocket.

I pulled it out, trying to pretend the interruption wasn't a relief. But the moment I saw the message, the relief evaporated, replaced by a cold knot in my stomach.

It was from my sister.

"Grace, you need to come home. It's Mom. Something's wrong."

The world tilted beneath me, the sidewalk suddenly seeming too hard, too unsteady. My breath caught in my throat as my heart skipped a beat. I looked up at Finn, my mind a whirl of confusion, panic, and guilt. How could I go to her now, when this—whatever this was between us—felt like it was on the verge of breaking wide open?

Finn was staring at me, his face unreadable, but there was a shift in his eyes, a flicker of something darker. "What is it?" he asked, his voice quieter now, but with an edge to it I couldn't ignore.

I shook my head, unable to form the words, my hands suddenly trembling as I typed a quick reply to my sister. The world was spinning again, the fire still burning in the background, but now, something else—something more personal—was demanding my attention.

"I have to go," I whispered, almost to myself, as I looked at Finn. "It's Mom."

He didn't say anything, just nodded, his expression a mask of unreadable calm. But the look in his eyes—something flickering there, something that mirrored my own turmoil—told me everything I needed to know.

"You'll be okay?" he asked, his voice low.

I nodded, though I wasn't sure if I meant it. "Yeah. I'll be okay."

But as I turned to leave, a cold gust of wind swept past us, and I felt it—something was about to shift. Something neither of us could control. And for the first time, I wasn't sure if I was ready for what was coming next.

The phone buzzed again.

Chapter 13: Under Lock and Key

The dim light of early morning filtered through the half-drawn curtains, casting jagged shadows across Finn's apartment. I stretched beneath the heavy quilt, still half asleep, tangled in a nest of sheets that smelled faintly of him. His scent—woody, sharp—lingered on the pillows where his head had been just hours before. We had spent the night tangled in each other's arms, but now, in the soft quiet of dawn, the tension seemed to hang in the air like smoke, thick and ever-present.

I rolled over, feeling the coolness of the sheets where his body had been, and let my gaze wander across the room. The walls, a muted gray, felt strangely claustrophobic despite the generous amount of space. The windows, tall and narrow, only let in the smallest amount of sunlight, casting everything in a subdued, somber hue. His apartment was tidy, but not in a sterile way—more like someone who didn't want to leave traces of their soul behind, but couldn't quite help it. There was a bookshelf that held a mix of classic novels and textbooks, evidence of his never-ending quest for knowledge. His couch was worn, the leather softened by time and use. A half-finished mug of coffee sat abandoned on the coffee table, the steam long since vanished.

I swung my legs over the edge of the bed, my feet hitting the cool floor. The soft thud of my feet meeting the ground felt jarring in the stillness. I had gotten used to waking up in the apartment every day for the past week. Finn had insisted I stay, argued that it was safer here, that I would be better off under his watchful eye than wandering the city alone. His protectiveness had initially grated on me, but it had softened over the days, and now, I couldn't deny the comfort of knowing he was nearby. Still, something gnawed at the back of my mind, something I couldn't quite place.

I moved toward the window, lifting the corner of the curtain slightly to peek outside. The city was waking up, the hum of traffic faint in the distance, but something else hung in the air—an unspoken tension, a feeling I couldn't shake. I wasn't sure if it was the constant fear of someone lurking just outside of sight, or if it was the looming dread of whatever waited for me on the other side of this fractured relationship with Finn.

He had been distant at times, pulling away when I'd try to ask him about his past, about who he was before he became the man who lived in this apartment, who guarded secrets like they were precious gems. But there had been moments, little cracks in his armor, when he let something slip—a look, a half-remembered name, the trace of something buried deep in his eyes. And every time, it made me want to push harder, to find the answers I knew he was hiding, but I also feared that doing so might break whatever fragile connection we had managed to build.

I was jolted from my thoughts by the sound of Finn's footsteps approaching. I turned toward the door just as he stepped into the room, his dark hair messy, his shirt wrinkled from sleep. He looked impossibly handsome in the way that people who had seen too much in their lives often did—like they carried the weight of the world, but wore it like an old coat, faded and comfortable.

"You're up early," he said, his voice rough from sleep, though he tried to mask it with a half-hearted smile. He didn't move any closer, keeping a careful distance, as if my mere presence in the room made him cautious, like I could somehow slip away if he wasn't careful enough.

"I couldn't sleep," I replied, shrugging, though the truth was much darker. I hadn't been able to shake the feeling that someone was watching, waiting for the perfect moment to strike. I could feel their eyes on me, though I had no evidence, no concrete proof. It was just a gut feeling, one that gnawed at me every time I left the safety of Finn's apartment.

"You're still worried," Finn said, stepping closer, his expression softening. He reached for me, his fingers brushing my arm as he moved to stand next to me by the window. His touch sent a wave of warmth through me, but it didn't entirely banish the feeling of dread that lurked just beneath the surface.

"I can't help it," I muttered, staring out at the city below. "It feels like they're getting closer, like someone's closing in, and no matter how much you try to protect me, it doesn't feel like enough."

He didn't say anything at first, just stood there, the weight of his silence hanging heavy between us. When he finally spoke, his voice was low, almost a whisper.

"You don't know what it's like, living in constant fear, never knowing if you're safe or if you've just bought yourself a little more time before everything unravels."

I turned to face him, his eyes shadowed by something darker, something I hadn't seen before. The man who stood before me was not the confident, somewhat cocky Finn I had come to know, but someone raw and unguarded, someone who had been through things I couldn't even begin to imagine.

"You think I don't understand fear?" I asked, raising an eyebrow. "You think I don't know what it feels like to constantly look over your shoulder, to wonder if today's the day it all comes crashing down?"

Finn stiffened, his jaw tightening. "I didn't mean it like that."

But I wasn't finished. "Maybe you don't know what it's like to have your life upended, to have everything you thought you knew stripped away. To live like a shadow, always a step behind, never really sure if you're living or just waiting for the moment when everything will fall apart."

His eyes softened, and for a brief moment, I saw the man I had been trying to reach—the one who wasn't hiding behind his walls. But it was fleeting, and soon enough, the walls came up again, stronger than before.

"I'm trying to protect you," he said, his voice a little more strained now, like he was trying to convince both me and himself.

"I know you are," I replied, my voice quiet. "But sometimes, I wonder if you're trying to protect me... or just trying to keep me close enough so that I don't slip away."

The words hung between us, sharp and undeniable. Neither of us spoke for a long time, the silence stretching out until it felt like it might swallow us whole. And still, despite everything—the tension, the uncertainty, the unresolved feelings—I couldn't help but feel drawn to him, as if the connection between us was a force of nature I couldn't escape, even if I wanted to.

I could hear the muffled hum of the city even with the windows closed, the pulse of life beyond the apartment walls—distant, unrelenting. It wasn't exactly comforting. I wanted to get lost in the normalcy of the everyday, the way people simply existed without fear, without paranoia creeping into every glance, every quiet moment. But that wasn't my reality. It never had been. And for all Finn's quiet reassurances, I knew deep down that nothing would make me feel truly safe again until the storm passed, until the silence I could almost taste in the air no longer felt like a ticking clock.

"You're brooding again." Finn's voice was light, but there was an edge to it that suggested he was tired of seeing me lost in my thoughts.

I glanced over at him, sitting on the couch, his broad shoulders slumped slightly as he worked through some paperwork spread across the coffee table. He was good at pretending he wasn't noticing me, pretending that nothing weighed on him, even though I knew better. There was always something beneath the surface with Finn, a current of tension running through him, like he was just waiting for the other shoe to drop.

"I'm not brooding," I muttered, a half-smile tugging at the corners of my lips despite my best efforts to maintain a serious face. I grabbed my coffee cup from the table and took a slow sip, avoiding his gaze. "I'm thinking."

He raised an eyebrow, clearly unconvinced. "Thinking, huh? About what? How we're all about to be murdered by a crazy stalker?"

I couldn't help the laugh that escaped. "You're a real charmer, you know that?"

He leaned back into the couch, stretching out his long legs with a sigh. "Just trying to make sure you don't spend the entire day contemplating your inevitable demise, sweetheart."

I rolled my eyes, but my chest tightened at the word. Sweetheart. It was both a comfort and a reminder of everything I was afraid of losing—of everything I wasn't sure I could handle.

"I'm fine," I said, my voice firmer than I felt. "You're overestimating my existential crisis."

"Sure," he said, his voice laced with skepticism. He reached over and flicked the corner of a paper in front of him, the subtle movement drawing my attention to the details scattered across the table. He was piecing together something—papers, photographs, notes. I could tell it was important, but he hadn't let me see much of it. The fragments of information he'd let slip so far had been vague, riddled with gaps. I had the sense that Finn was only half in this with me, that there was a part of him holding back, unwilling to trust fully.

It was frustrating, this dance we were doing—me trying to close the distance, him pulling away just as quickly. But today, I wasn't going to let it slide. I pushed the cup aside, crossing the room to stand at the edge of the table, letting my eyes fall on the disorganized mess of papers he was working through.

"What's all this?" I asked, glancing up at him.

He stiffened for a second before covering the papers with his hand. The movement was subtle, but it was there. "Nothing you need to worry about."

I raised an eyebrow, unimpressed. "Nothing I need to worry about? Right. Because that's what I do best—ignore everything."

He didn't say anything for a long moment. The silence stretched, thick and awkward, and I almost expected him to shut down completely. But then he pushed his chair back, his face softening just slightly as he leaned forward, dragging a couple of the papers out from under his hand.

"Look, I know you don't like being kept in the dark. But it's not that simple. I can't just tell you everything all at once."

"Why not?"

"Because you wouldn't believe me," he muttered, almost under his breath.

I studied him for a beat. "Try me."

He hesitated, but only for a second, before reaching into the stack and pulling out a few photographs. They were black and white, the kind of images you only saw in old, worn-out files. I leaned over to look at them, my heart skipping a beat as I caught sight of one.

It was a picture of a man—tall, dark hair, intense eyes. He looked familiar, but I couldn't place him. His features were sharp, his posture rigid in a way that made him seem untouchable, dangerous even. I stared at the photo, my mind trying to piece it together, but nothing clicked.

"This is him," Finn said, his voice low. "The man behind it all."

My blood went cold. I had known something was wrong, had sensed the danger that loomed in the background. But this? This was another level entirely.

"You're telling me this guy is the one who's been making my life hell?" I asked, my voice barely above a whisper.

Finn nodded, his jaw set tight. "He's not just some random creep. He's tied to everything. To me, to you, to...everything."

Everything. The word echoed in my head, and a sick feeling settled in the pit of my stomach. I had no idea what Finn meant by that, but I wasn't sure I wanted to know. There were things he wasn't telling me, things he was too afraid to even hint at, and I had the growing suspicion that no matter how much I wanted to press him for answers, I wouldn't be ready for the truth when it finally came.

"So, what now?" I asked, trying to keep my voice steady, though I could feel my hands shaking slightly as I folded my arms across my chest.

Finn sat back in his chair, his gaze distant as he stared at the papers before him. "Now, we figure out how to take him down. Without anyone else getting hurt."

The weight of his words hung in the air, thick and heavy. I couldn't shake the feeling that no matter how carefully we moved, no matter how much Finn tried to protect me, we were already too deep in this. There was no easy way out now.

The air in Finn's apartment felt heavier that evening, as if it had absorbed every unspoken word, every unacknowledged fear, until it was thick with the weight of things we had yet to confront. He had been quieter than usual, his eyes flickering to the door every time there was a noise in the hallway, as if expecting someone to burst through at any moment. I had noticed the way his hand would hover near the lock on the door whenever we were alone—always within reach, always ready.

I'd thought I was the one who couldn't relax, but Finn was just as trapped by the tension that hung over us. The man who had seemed so sure of himself in the beginning now seemed just as lost as I felt, wrapped up in something that neither of us could fully grasp. There was no telling how far this would go, how deep we would sink into this mess before we found solid ground. Or if we ever would.

"You're doing it again," Finn's voice broke through my thoughts, his tone more playful than serious, but there was a sharpness to it that let me know he wasn't entirely amused.

I turned from where I had been standing by the kitchen counter, idly stirring a cup of tea I didn't even want. He was sitting on the couch, elbows resting on his knees, his face cast in shadows from the low lighting. The image of him like that—vulnerable in a way I hadn't seen before—made my heart clench. He wasn't a man accustomed to showing weakness, but lately, that's all he'd been giving me: little fragments of himself, raw and unguarded.

"Doing what?" I asked, trying to feign innocence.

"You're brooding." He grinned, but it didn't reach his eyes. He was trying to lighten the mood, but there was a crack in his smile that betrayed how much he was actually struggling.

"I'm not brooding," I said, my voice a little too defensive. I set the mug down, moving to the couch and sitting beside him. The space between us felt like it had grown with each passing day. "Just thinking."

He raised an eyebrow, clearly unconvinced. "About what? How we're all going to end up in witness protection by the end of next week?"

I snorted at the thought, but it came out too harsh, too forced. "I'm not that dramatic."

Finn didn't respond right away, and I could feel the distance between us lengthening. A silence fell, one of those heavy silences that only seemed to make things worse. My eyes dropped to the floor, my mind working in circles. We were both too tangled in this mess to make any progress, but I couldn't seem to find a way out.

"You should talk to me," Finn said after a beat, his voice quieter this time, tinged with something I couldn't quite identify. Was it concern? Or was it frustration? Either way, it had me turning toward him, unsure of how to navigate the moment.

"I don't even know what to say anymore," I admitted, the words slipping out before I could stop them. "Every time I think I understand what's going on, everything changes. I feel like I'm losing my grip."

"Join the club," he muttered, his lips curling in a grim smile. "But we'll figure this out. You just need to trust me."

Trust him. I had trusted him before, but the more I learned, the more his walls grew higher. What was he hiding? What had he been through that made him so damn elusive? There was a part of me—one I couldn't deny—that felt like I was finally beginning to see the cracks, the chinks in his armor, but at what cost?

"And if we can't?" The question was out before I even realized I'd said it. I didn't want to know the answer, but now that it was out, I needed to hear it.

Finn turned toward me, his eyes dark with something unreadable. "Then we fight until we can. Until we take this guy down."

I felt a shiver run through me at the intensity of his words. Finn was never one to back down, but something in the way he said it—so final, so sure—made me wonder if he was more afraid of losing this fight than he was letting on.

I swallowed, my heart pounding a little faster. "And if we fail?"

He looked at me, really looked at me for the first time that evening, his expression hardening with an emotion I couldn't place. "Failure isn't an option."

I opened my mouth to respond, but before I could, the sound of a sharp knock on the door froze me in place. It wasn't a casual tap; it was heavy, deliberate, and it set off an alarm bell deep in my gut.

Finn was on his feet in a flash, his hand instinctively reaching for the small gun he kept hidden in the drawer. My pulse raced, the sudden surge of adrenaline pumping through me with alarming speed.

"You didn't hear that," I whispered, but it came out more like a plea than a statement.

Finn shot me a look, his jaw clenched as he moved toward the door, his steps quiet but calculated. "Stay here," he murmured, but it wasn't a suggestion. His voice held that dangerous edge that told me not to argue, even though every fiber of my being screamed to follow him, to see who was on the other side of that door.

I stood frozen for a moment, the silence of the apartment almost suffocating as I waited for something to break it. My heart hammered in my chest as I slowly backed away, moving toward the far corner of the room where I could get a better view of the door.

Finn reached for the handle slowly, his body tensed, like he was bracing himself for whatever was about to come. He glanced back at me once, his eyes hard, but there was a flicker of something in them—something that made me feel like I might not be the only one on the edge of losing control.

He opened the door just a crack, peering out through the small gap. I couldn't see who was on the other side, but I could hear their voice. It was low, gravelly, but unmistakably familiar.

"Finn," the voice said, cool and calm, like it had all the time in the world. "We need to talk."

Chapter 14: A Shattered Heart

The sun had barely set, and the soft orange glow of twilight spilled through the office windows. I watched it stretch lazily across the cluttered desk before me, a reminder of how little time had passed since everything changed. Finn's face, more familiar to me now than my own reflection, hovered in my mind—its shadows darker than I'd ever seen them. There was something about his silence, the way he wasn't looking at me, that made my pulse quicken. A subtle tremor rippled through my fingers as I clutched the edge of the desk.

"Finn," I said, my voice a mere whisper. It felt like I was testing it, unsure whether the words would break apart before they could even form. "Tell me the truth."

He was still, like a storm waiting to hit. I'd seen him this way before, quiet and calculating, but this time, the weight of his secrets seemed heavier. He stood by the window, his back to me, his jaw set tight. In the reflection, his shoulders were hunched, and for the first time, I noticed the strain in the muscles of his neck. He wasn't just keeping things from me—he was holding back a storm that threatened to unravel us both.

I took a deep breath, trying to steady myself. I wanted to reach out to him, to hold onto the version of him I thought I knew. The man I'd shared late-night conversations with, the one whose laughter still echoed in the corners of my heart. But there was something more, something jagged under his skin. I could feel it now—like a presence in the room, just waiting to break free.

His voice cut through the silence, low and strained. "I didn't want to drag you into this, but it's too late now."

I let out a shaky breath, my heart beating so loud in my chest that it drowned out his words for a moment. "Drag me into what, Finn?"

He turned slowly, his eyes meeting mine, but they didn't look the same. The warmth I'd once seen in them was gone, replaced by something cold and unreadable. "The fires," he said, as if that explained everything.

I blinked, a flash of confusion flickering across my face. "The fires? What are you talking about?"

His hands, once so steady, clenched at his sides. "They're not random, Delilah. They're a message. A warning."

I felt my stomach drop. "A warning from who?"

The words seemed to hang in the air for a long, terrible beat before he spoke again, each syllable coming slower, like he was trying to convince himself more than me. "From someone I used to know. Someone I thought I'd left behind."

A chill washed over me, creeping up my spine, tightening my chest. My mouth went dry. "Who?"

He hesitated, his gaze drifting to the window as if he could find the answers in the fading light. "It's a man named Gabriel. He's—" Finn's words faltered. He was holding back again, and it stung like a slap across my face. I reached for him instinctively, my hand brushing his arm, urging him to open up.

"Finn," I said, my voice trembling. "Please. Tell me what's going on."

His eyes met mine, and for a brief moment, there was a flicker of regret. "You don't want to know this, Delilah."

But I was already drowning in it, the weight of his secret crushing me with every passing second. "I do," I whispered. "I need to know."

Finn exhaled sharply, and the air between us seemed to thicken, heavy with something unsaid. "I wasn't always... who you think I am," he began, his voice barely audible. "Before I came here, before I found you, I was tangled up in things I can't undo.

Gabriel was part of that life. And now he's threatening everything I've worked for—the people I care about."

I felt the world tilt beneath me, my vision blurring as my heart skipped a beat. "You—" I stopped myself, swallowing the lump that had formed in my throat. "You've been hiding all this time because of him? All this time, Finn?"

He nodded, the weight of his past settling heavily on his shoulders. "I thought it was over, that I'd escaped. But when the fires started, I realized I couldn't outrun it anymore. Gabriel's back, and he's made it clear that he's not done with me."

I could feel the room shrinking around us, the walls closing in as I tried to process his words. I wanted to scream, to shake him and demand that he make it stop. But I couldn't. The man standing in front of me was a stranger, someone I thought I knew but had never truly understood. My heart ached with the realization that I didn't know who he was anymore, and worse, that I didn't know who I was in all of this.

"Why didn't you tell me?" My voice cracked, the question coming out weaker than I intended.

"I didn't want to drag you into it," he repeated, the words falling like stones between us. "I didn't want you to get hurt."

But I was already hurt. In ways that I hadn't even begun to understand. The weight of his betrayal, the coldness of his silence, it all shattered something inside me. I'd been so sure that our connection was something real, something that could survive anything. But this? This was more than I was prepared for.

Finn stepped toward me, his hands reaching for mine, but I couldn't bring myself to meet him halfway. "Delilah, please," he pleaded, his voice raw with regret. "I never wanted this for you."

I pulled my hands away, my heart breaking with each inch of distance that grew between us. "You should have told me, Finn.

You should have trusted me enough to let me decide if I wanted to be part of this."

He flinched, the words hitting him harder than I'd anticipated. I saw it then, the way the weight of his choices settled on him, like he was suffocating under the burden of everything he had tried to hide. But it was too late. The truth had already burned me, and there was no coming back from that kind of fire.

The quiet that followed was suffocating. It wasn't the kind of silence you could sink into like a warm blanket, the kind that comes when you're content and comfortable. No, this was the kind of silence that wrapped itself around you like a straitjacket, tight and restrictive. I stood there, frozen, my heart thudding so loudly in my chest that I wondered if Finn could hear it too. It felt like I was drowning, my lungs full of air that refused to be breathed in.

"You don't have to do this," Finn said, his voice low, the edges of it fraying as he tried to find a way to undo what he had just confessed. "You don't have to be a part of this mess."

I wanted to laugh at how absurd that sounded. I was already a part of this mess. I had been for a while now, whether I liked it or not. The whole thing had crept up on me in such a slow, insidious way that I didn't even realize how far I'd fallen until the walls came crashing down.

"Don't you think I've already been dragged into this?" I bit out, the words sharp and brittle. "You think you're protecting me by keeping secrets? By burying things that should've been out in the open from the start? You're not protecting me, Finn. You're suffocating me."

The words hung there for a moment, heavy between us. I could see him flinch, a fraction of a movement, but enough to betray the fact that my words had cut deeper than he expected. His eyes flickered, a mixture of guilt and something else—a sharp, unspoken desperation—as though he were looking for an escape, a way to undo the damage.

"I didn't want to lie to you," he said, his voice quieter now, as though he was speaking to the version of me that wasn't here yet—the one who hadn't learned the truth, the one who hadn't been broken by it. "But I couldn't tell you everything. Not before. Not when I was still trying to figure it all out myself."

I narrowed my eyes at him, the anger boiling just beneath the surface. "That's convenient, isn't it? You couldn't tell me. But you sure as hell let me get tangled up in your mess. You let me fall for you, didn't you? You let me believe in us, in something real."

His jaw tightened, and for a moment, I wondered if he would walk away—if he would pull his usual trick of retreating into the shadows to avoid facing the truth. But this time, he didn't. This time, he stayed right where he was, standing at the edge of the abyss he had created, unsure whether to jump or to pull me down with him.

"I'm not a good man, Delilah," he said, almost pleading. "I never was. I don't deserve your trust, your love."

The words stung. He didn't know how badly they hurt until they were already out, slipping between us like an echo. I had known, on some level, that he had his demons, that there were parts of his past he couldn't—or wouldn't—share with me. But this? This was a whole new level of betrayal. I had fallen for the illusion, the version of him he'd allowed me to see, the charming, clever man who made me laugh and made me feel safe, the man who kissed me like he would never let me go.

But now, in the face of the truth, I wondered how much of him was ever real at all.

"Then why did you let me in?" I asked, my voice softer now, not because I had softened, but because the weight of his admission was starting to crush me from the inside out. "Why did you make me feel like I was the one thing you could count on?"

Finn's eyes darkened, the storm inside him swirling again, more violent than before. "Because I wanted you," he said, his voice rough, as though the admission itself hurt him. "But wanting something doesn't always mean it's good for you."

I shook my head, stepping back from him, as if his words were physical things, pieces of glass I couldn't bear to touch. "And now you want me to just walk away, right? That's what this is. You're telling me everything so I can run in the opposite direction, so I don't get caught in the wreckage."

His face contorted, and for the first time, I saw the crack in his carefully constructed mask. "I'm trying to save you from the wreckage, Delilah."

"Save me?" I scoffed, my hands trembling at my sides. "By making me part of it?"

Finn's lips parted as if he were going to say something more, but then he stopped, as if realizing that nothing could undo what had already been set in motion. There was a long moment where neither of us spoke, just stood there, the tension between us so thick it was suffocating.

I wanted to run. I wanted to scream, to tell him he had no right to ask this of me. But then I thought about the fires—the ones that had been popping up, one after another, sending waves of destruction across our town. And Gabriel. I hadn't missed the way Finn's voice had tightened when he spoke the name, as though it were a curse he couldn't quite shake. He was scared—genuinely scared, in a way that made the entire situation even worse. Because I knew, deep down, that his past had come back to haunt him, and it was dragging me down with it.

"You don't get it, do you?" I asked softly, the anger giving way to something else—something much worse. "You don't get that I have a choice too. You can't decide everything for me, Finn. You can't just make me the victim of your past because it's convenient for you."

His expression faltered, and I saw the panic flash behind his eyes. "Delilah, please—"

But I turned away before he could finish. I couldn't listen to any more of his excuses, his pleas. Not when every word felt like a knife being twisted deeper into the very heart of everything we had built together.

The door slammed behind me, and the sound echoed in the empty space, leaving nothing but the hollow ring of a heart that had already begun to break.

The walk to my car felt like an eternity, each step heavy with the weight of everything I couldn't untangle. I could still feel the echo of Finn's words in my mind, each one sharper than the last, each one digging deeper into the fragile shell of what we'd been. The streetlights above flickered, casting long, wavering shadows across the cracked pavement. The cool night air hit my face with a bite, but it couldn't numb the ache in my chest.

I was halfway to the car when I heard the footsteps.

At first, I thought it was just my mind playing tricks—maybe it was the adrenaline, the aftermath of too many emotions colliding at once. But then I heard the second step, deliberate and too close for comfort. My hand instinctively reached for the door handle, but before I could touch it, a voice stopped me.

"Delilah."

His voice, ragged, raw, sent a chill up my spine. Finn.

I didn't turn around. I couldn't. I wasn't sure I trusted myself enough to face him. What was left to say anyway? He'd laid it all out there, his confession hanging in the air like a noose. The man I loved—no, thought I loved—had dragged me into his mess, and now he was asking for more. For me to be more.

"I know you're angry," he said, stepping closer, his voice now steady, but the tension beneath it was unmistakable. "I know you want to run. But just listen to me, okay? Please."

I took a deep breath, gripping the car door as if it were the only solid thing in my life. "Why should I, Finn? You lied to me. You kept all of this from me, and now you want me to believe that you're still the person I thought you were?"

The words felt like sandpaper against my tongue, rough and painful. I could hear the soft rustle of his clothes as he shifted closer, the heat of his body inching toward mine, even though the space between us felt like an ocean. He was still close enough for me to feel the pull of him—his presence, the gravity of his apology hanging in the air.

"I didn't want this for you, Delilah," he said again, but this time there was a certain finality to it, as though he knew there was no going back from here. "I thought if I kept you away from this part of my life, if I kept it buried, we could have something... real. Something that didn't involve the chaos."

"You're right," I shot back, bitterness creeping into my voice. "We had something real. I thought we did. But that wasn't enough for you, was it? You thought you could keep this life separate, like it wouldn't spill over, like it wouldn't destroy everything we were building."

I could hear him take a slow breath, as if he were steeling himself for the words to come. When he spoke again, it was barely a whisper, but it cut through me like a blade.

"I never wanted to hurt you, Delilah. You've got to believe me."

I didn't want to believe him. Not anymore. My heart was already shattered, already in too many pieces to even attempt to put it back together. I needed distance. I needed to escape, to stop the rapid spinning of my thoughts before they made me dizzy. So

I opened the car door, not looking at him as I slid into the driver's seat.

"Delilah," he said once more, and this time, his hand landed on the frame of the door, just as I was about to close it.

My breath caught, but I didn't pull away. I stayed still, my hands clenched tightly around the steering wheel, as if I could somehow hold myself together with just that grip.

"What do you want from me, Finn?" I finally asked, the question spilling out before I could stop it. I hadn't meant to sound so defeated, but there it was, the raw, open truth. "What do you want me to do?"

There was a long pause. I could hear the hitch in his breath, the hesitation. And then, finally, he said, "I want you to stay."

The simplicity of his request stunned me. As if I could just push everything aside—the lies, the fires, the shadows—and step back into his world like it was all still real. Like it was still safe.

I wanted to scream at him, tell him that I couldn't do that anymore, that I couldn't pretend to be okay with the fact that his past had a hold on him in ways I couldn't even begin to understand. But as I looked at him, standing there, that tortured look on his face—so much like a man trapped in his own mistakes—I couldn't bring myself to do it. I couldn't hate him. Not even now.

But I couldn't stay either.

"Finn," I said, the word shaky, my resolve slipping like sand through my fingers. "I don't know if I can trust you anymore."

He nodded slowly, as if he had expected me to say those words, and maybe part of me had expected to say them too. But the ache that followed wasn't any less painful.

"I understand," he murmured, his voice thick with emotion, his hand pulling away from the door. "I'm sorry. For everything."

I closed the door then, unable to look at him anymore. My fingers trembled as I started the engine, the sound of it filling the silence that hung between us. The headlights illuminated the road ahead, but all I could see was darkness. I wasn't sure where I was going, or what I was going to do when I got there, but I couldn't stay with him. Not now. Not with everything that had been uncovered.

I pulled out onto the street, my heart heavy, my mind swirling with a thousand unanswered questions. And then, just as I passed the corner, the lights ahead flickered, and the screech of tires echoed in the distance. I slammed my foot on the brake, the world around me coming to a screeching halt.

And that was when I saw him—standing in the middle of the road, his face pale and drenched in sweat.

Gabriel.

Chapter 15: Beneath the Surface

I ran my fingers over the edge of the file, the paper crisp under my touch, the weight of it pressing on my chest like a secret too heavy to carry alone. Finn hadn't said a word, just stood there, his hands shoved into the pockets of his jacket as if he were waiting for something—a confirmation, perhaps, that I was willing to dive deeper into this mess with him. The truth seemed to hover between us, teasing, pulling, begging to be exposed. The fire reports—each one a story, a moment where someone's world had been engulfed by flames—were like a trail of breadcrumbs leading into the dark. I couldn't ignore it. I wouldn't.

"Do you think this is intentional?" I asked, my voice tight, reluctant to fully accept what the evidence pointed to.

Finn's eyes never left mine as he answered, his words measured, deliberate. "I don't believe in coincidences anymore, not with this. This has been building for months, maybe longer. Someone is behind it. And if we don't stop them, it won't end with just arson."

The cold air of the station pressed against my skin, but it was nothing compared to the chill in his voice. He had seen too much, known too much, and still, there was that part of him—undeniable, raw—that clung to the idea of justice, even if it came with a price. And I had a sinking feeling that we were about to pay it.

I skimmed through the reports again, trying to make sense of the overlapping patterns: the exact type of accelerant, the precise way the fires had been set—deliberate, meticulous. Whoever was behind it wasn't just starting fires for the thrill of it. There was a method to their madness. They were sending a message. The question was, who were they sending it to, and why?

"I need to know what happened at that last fire," I said, finally lifting my gaze to meet Finn's. "The one you mentioned yesterday. The one with the... the child."

He stiffened, his jaw tightening, a flicker of something darker crossing his features. "It wasn't supposed to happen that way. That's all I'll say."

The unsaid words hung between us, thick with the weight of guilt, of responsibility, of something far worse than either of us were ready to confront. But I could feel the pull—this was bigger than any of us. And as much as I wanted to pull back, to leave it for someone else to solve, I couldn't. I was in this now. Whether I liked it or not.

"Finn," I said, my voice softer, more insistent this time. "What aren't you telling me?"

He exhaled, a shaky breath that sounded far too close to a sob, though I knew better than to read too much into it. His hands clenched at his sides, and for a brief moment, I saw something in his eyes that mirrored my own fear—fear of facing what was coming. He wasn't ready to speak the truth. Not yet.

"I'll tell you," he said, his words quiet, hesitant. "But not here. We need to get out of sight. Someone's watching."

I didn't question him. I knew the kind of danger that followed people like us. I knew what it felt like to be hunted, to have eyes on you even when you couldn't see them. We couldn't afford to be careless.

We made our way through the back alleys behind the station, my boots clicking against the pavement in sharp contrast to the quiet that surrounded us. The tension between us was palpable, as if we were walking a tightrope and any wrong move would send us crashing down. Finn kept glancing over his shoulder, scanning the shadows, his senses sharp, alert.

Finally, when we reached the little café that had become our unofficial headquarters, he led me inside. The warm scent of coffee and fresh pastries hit me immediately, a comfort in a world that had suddenly become far too uncertain. The barista, a woman with a bright smile and an ever-watchful eye, nodded at Finn, as if she understood without needing to ask.

We took our usual corner booth, the one hidden away from the main foot traffic, where no one could overhear. Finn placed the file down in front of me with a deliberate motion, the paper crackling under his fingertips.

"Do you remember the name of the family who lived in that house?" Finn asked, his voice barely above a whisper as he met my eyes.

I frowned, trying to recall. "The house fire from last month? The one that made the news?"

He nodded, his gaze never leaving mine. "The mother—she was a volunteer firefighter. And the kid... I had worked with her before, on a few cases. The boy was only five."

I felt a knot tighten in my stomach. That family had been part of the community I thought I knew, people whose faces I'd passed on the street, whose stories had been woven into the fabric of everyday life. And now they were gone, reduced to ash and memory.

"There's something about the way the fire was set..." Finn's voice faltered for a moment, and I could hear the raw edge of guilt in his words. "It wasn't random. It was too precise. Someone knew exactly where to hit them."

I leaned in, my fingers trembling slightly as I turned the pages of the file, my eyes scanning the photographs—burned remnants of the home, the charred skeleton of the roof, the blackened walls. In one of the photos, there was a small toy truck, its wheels melted but still recognizable. My heart lurched in my chest.

"You think it's connected to the other fires?" I asked, the words heavy in the air.

Finn didn't answer right away. Instead, he reached into his jacket pocket, pulling out a small, crumpled photograph. He slid it across the table, and as my eyes met the image, I felt a cold shiver run down my spine. It was a picture of a man I didn't recognize, his face partially obscured by shadows but with eyes that seemed to see right through me.

"This man," Finn said, his voice low, almost a whisper. "He's the one who set the fires. And I think I've seen him before."

The photo stared back at me, the man's half-hidden face a jagged puzzle piece I couldn't quite place. The shadows of the picture seemed to shift every time I blinked, the edges of his silhouette growing more familiar with each passing second. Finn, for all his quiet intensity, wasn't rushing me to make the connection. Instead, he waited—tension humming in the air between us—his hand resting lightly on the table, just far enough away from the photograph for me to feel the invisible weight of his unspoken question.

"Who is he?" I asked, finally, feeling the words scratch their way up from the pit of my stomach.

Finn's gaze flickered over the photo, his lips pressing into a thin line. "I wish I knew."

His voice dropped so low, I had to strain to hear the words, but the uncertainty there was unmistakable. "You've seen him before?" I pressed. It wasn't a question, but more of a push, a subtle demand that I hoped would get him to speak the truth I could feel lurking in the silence.

Finn's fingers drummed lightly against the table, a rhythm that almost matched the frantic beating of my heart. "I think he's connected to the first fire," he said. The words tumbled out, forced like he'd been holding them in too long. "There's a pattern, but it's not just about the fires. This man..." He trailed off, his eyes distant, lost in a memory I didn't have access to.

I leaned back, the coldness of the booth pressing against my spine, the small café around us oblivious to the storm building at the table. "You think it's personal?" I asked, my voice soft, trying to pull him back from whatever dark place he had gone.

Finn nodded, but it wasn't the firm, assured motion I'd come to expect from him. This was different, more tentative, as if he weren't entirely sure what he was saying. "Could be. It's like..." He paused, rubbing his forehead as if the words were stubborn, unwilling to cooperate. "It's like there's a message behind the flames. But I don't know who's supposed to get it."

The room felt suffocating all of a sudden, the flickering fluorescent lights above us buzzing like an ominous warning. I set the photo down, the image of the man's shadowy face lingering in my mind, curling around my thoughts like smoke. "Tell me about the first fire," I urged. I didn't need to ask twice. I could tell from the shift in his posture that he was going to give me something now.

"The first fire..." Finn muttered, his fingers curling around his coffee cup, his thumb tracing the rim. "It wasn't random. Not at all. It happened in a small warehouse just outside the city. An old building, just sitting there, collecting dust. They said it was an electrical fault. But when I showed up on the scene..." His voice trailed off, and I could see the memory hitting him hard, dragging him back into the chaos of that night.

I leaned forward, my elbows resting on the table. "What did you find?"

Finn's eyes flickered to mine, and for the briefest moment, there was something like regret in them. "The building was empty. No one inside. But the way the fire started—it wasn't electrical. The accelerant used? It was professional, controlled. Too precise. I knew it wasn't a typical arsonist." He swallowed, his voice lowering. "I thought about it for weeks after. Something about it nagged at me."

I felt it then—the same weight he was carrying. Something about that fire hadn't added up, and now I could see it: the threads, the connections, the strings of fate that had woven us into this tangled mess. The deeper we went, the harder it became to see the path forward. It was a maze of clues, each one leading us further into the unknown, where the answers wouldn't be what we expected. Where the answers might make us question everything.

"Do you think someone's targeting you?" I asked, the question slipping out before I could stop it.

Finn stiffened, his shoulders tight as if the very notion struck too close to the heart of whatever dark secret he was holding. "Could be. But it's not just me. Whoever's behind this—they're more organized than that. I've been looking into other cases. There are fires I never connected until now, patterns I missed. This..." He broke off, his eyes narrowing as if a thought had just clicked into place. "This is bigger than anything I've dealt with."

I could see it in his face then—the realization, the weight of the truth settling on his shoulders like a mantle he wasn't ready to bear. But I knew him well enough to understand that once he started down this road, there was no turning back.

"If we don't stop them, it's only going to escalate," I said, my words careful, deliberate. I didn't want to frighten him, but we both knew that this was the truth. Whatever this was, it wasn't going to burn itself out.

Finn's eyes met mine, and for a moment, something passed between us—an unspoken agreement. We were in this together, for better or worse. I felt the tension in my chest ease, just a fraction, but I knew that this was only the beginning.

"Do you trust me?" he asked, the question coming out of nowhere, sharp and raw, as though he had been holding it back for far longer than he should have.

I hesitated. The air between us was thick with unspoken words, with histories we hadn't shared, with all the unknowns that still loomed in front of us. But there was something in his eyes that I couldn't deny, something that grounded me, that pulled me closer to him.

"I don't know if I trust you," I said finally, my voice steady. "But I do know this—whatever's happening here, it's not just your fight anymore. It's ours."

For a long moment, Finn didn't speak. He simply looked at me, and I could feel the weight of his gaze, as if he were seeing me for the first time. Then, with a small, reluctant nod, he stood, pushing the photograph toward me.

"Then let's figure out who's behind it," he said, his voice low but steady, like the calm before a storm.

And just like that, the next step was clear. We were no longer just bystanders, no longer mere witnesses. We were players in a game we didn't fully understand, but there was no going back now.

We moved quickly, though the silence between us stretched tight, like the seconds before a storm. Finn's eyes darted between the door, the window, the corners of the café. It wasn't paranoia; it was instinct. There were too many unanswered questions hanging in the air. We weren't alone in this fight, not by a long shot, and whoever was watching—whoever was pulling the strings—wasn't going to give up easily.

I glanced down at the photo again, the man's face still blurry but now more imposing, like a shadow I couldn't outrun. "You really think this is about the warehouse fire?" I asked, my voice quieter than I intended, as if speaking louder might summon the figure in the photograph into reality.

Finn's lips twitched, a brief flash of something—frustration or maybe the beginnings of guilt. "I don't know. But when you start looking for connections, you find them whether you want to or not."

"And what about this guy?" I asked, setting the photo back on the table. "If he's the one responsible, why is he hiding behind shadows? Why not just go public?"

He rubbed the back of his neck, a nervous gesture I'd seen before, one that always signaled Finn was running out of answers. "Maybe he's got something to hide. Maybe he wants us to come after him. The thing is, when we start asking questions, it gets messier. This is bigger than just a couple of fires. There's more to it—people who don't want their names in the light."

I could feel the heat of frustration building in my chest. This wasn't what I signed up for, but then again, none of it ever was. "What are we really dealing with here, Finn? This doesn't feel like some random arsonist looking for attention. There's something... methodical about it."

He met my gaze then, his eyes flickering with something I couldn't quite place. Maybe it was regret, or maybe it was something darker. "You're right," he said, his voice low, almost hesitant. "This isn't random. It's all connected."

"What do you mean?" My heart rate picked up, my pulse hammering against the quiet tension in the room.

Finn's lips parted as if he was about to speak, but before the words could form, the café door swung open. The little bell above it jingled, the sound sharp and unwelcome. My body tensed, and Finn's eyes narrowed. He turned his head ever so slightly, his muscles coiling, preparing for something. We weren't alone anymore. I could feel the shift, the sudden presence of someone—or something—that wasn't supposed to be there.

A man stepped into the café, his movements smooth but calculated. His eyes scanned the room briefly, pausing just long enough to meet mine. I couldn't place him. He wasn't familiar, yet there was something about him that felt like a déjà vu—like a fragment of a memory I couldn't quite reach. He didn't glance at Finn, not once. Instead, he approached the counter, ordering his coffee with a voice that was too calm, too casual.

I looked back at Finn, who was watching the man with narrowed eyes, his posture rigid. He was holding something back, the tension in his body as tight as a bowstring ready to snap.

"Who is he?" I whispered, my voice barely audible, afraid the wrong question would set everything into motion.

Finn's lips pressed into a thin line, the kind of line that spoke volumes without saying anything. "Don't know," he said, his voice tight. "But I think he knows us."

I froze, the hair on the back of my neck standing up. "How do you know?"

"I don't," Finn replied quickly. "But I feel it."

The man ordered his coffee, paying in cash, never acknowledging anyone around him. He moved with the quiet confidence of someone who didn't need to make a scene to be noticed. He was exactly the kind of person you'd overlook if you weren't paying attention. The kind of person who blended in too well. I didn't like it.

Finn's hand, which had been resting on the table, slid beneath the edge of the booth. His fingers curled, not around a weapon—at least, not that I could see—but something else. He was preparing for something, for whatever move the man at the counter was going to make next.

I shifted in my seat, trying to play it cool, but I felt the blood rushing to my ears, the air thickening with each passing second.

Every instinct in my body screamed that something was about to happen, something big, and it was going to change everything.

The man took his coffee and turned toward the door. I exhaled a breath I didn't realize I'd been holding, but the relief was fleeting. Just as he reached the threshold, he paused. Slowly, deliberately, he turned back to face us.

For the first time, I saw the edge of a smile tug at the corner of his lips. It was subtle, barely noticeable, but it was there. And it was meant for Finn.

I saw Finn stiffen, his face hardening, his fingers gripping the edge of the table so tightly his knuckles turned white.

The man didn't speak. He didn't need to. His smile was enough of a message.

"I think he knows you," I said, the words coming out before I could stop them. My voice was tight, brittle, as if cracking under the pressure of what was unfolding before us.

Finn didn't respond right away. Instead, his eyes never left the man. The seconds stretched, the space between them becoming a void that neither of them seemed willing to cross. The stranger turned and walked out the door, the soft chime of the bell marking his exit, but that didn't bring relief.

In fact, it felt like the start of something much worse.

I reached for the photo on the table, my mind racing to connect the dots. The face of the man in the picture—the man Finn claimed he'd seen before—loomed in my thoughts like a shadow. The man who had just walked out of the café was too familiar now. It was as if he was playing a game I didn't understand, and worse, Finn was playing it too, whether he realized it or not.

I turned to him, but before I could speak, the café door opened again. This time, I wasn't prepared for the person who walked in.

And that's when everything changed.

Chapter 16: The Shadow Within

The sirens howled in the distance, a symphony of urgency that churned the air with an electric tension. Finn's hands gripped the wheel, knuckles stark white against the leather. His jaw was tight, the set of his mouth grim, and I could almost hear the grind of his teeth over the hum of the engine. I leaned forward, peering through the windshield as the flames danced higher, licking at the sky like a wild animal desperate to break free.

"Another one," I muttered under my breath, barely recognizing the words myself. The heat from the fire hit me even through the cracked window, a violent reminder of the damage we were racing to contain. We'd been to enough of these scenes over the past few months that I'd lost count. The pattern was impossible to ignore, yet Finn refused to acknowledge the most unsettling part of it—the fact that they were happening too close to home. Too close to us.

I glanced at Finn again, noting how the tautness in his posture seemed to have deepened, like a string pulled too tight, threatening to snap. He hadn't been the same since the first fire, the one that started a chain of events neither of us was prepared for. His gaze was fixed ahead, unfocused, distant, like he wasn't really there. The closer we got to the scene, the worse it became. His foot pushed harder against the gas pedal, eyes never leaving the road.

"You're pushing it," I said, my voice a little sharper than I intended. I wasn't sure if I was warning him or myself.

He didn't respond, and I let the silence stretch between us. My fingers drummed nervously against my leg. The tension between us had been building for days now, a quiet undercurrent to every conversation, every glance. Finn was slipping away from me, disappearing into some place I couldn't follow, and it was starting to eat at me from the inside.

By the time we arrived, the sky was an inferno. The building—already half-collapsed—was a monument to chaos, its bones splintering and cracking as the fire devoured what remained. Firefighters rushed around, their voices lost to the roar of the flames. Finn was out of the truck before I could even take a breath, striding forward with that same relentless energy that had drawn me to him in the first place. But now it felt different. It felt like he was running toward something, not away from it.

I followed close behind, catching up just as Finn reached the edge of the fire line. He stood there for a moment, his body stiff and unmoving, staring at the blaze as though it held all the answers he was searching for. His fists were clenched at his sides, his chest rising and falling in jagged breaths. The heat of the fire seemed to draw him in, pulling him toward it like an obsession.

"Finn!" I called, my voice rising over the crackling of the fire. "What are you—?"

But he didn't answer. Instead, he took a step forward, almost as if the fire was calling to him, coaxing him closer.

I grabbed his arm, pulling him back, my grip tight with the kind of desperation I couldn't even explain. "Stop. You're not thinking clearly."

His eyes snapped to mine then, wild and unfocused, like he wasn't quite seeing me. "I have to find it, Maddy," he said, his voice low and strained. "It's here. I know it's here."

His words hit me like a punch, and for a moment, I didn't know how to respond. What was he talking about? What was he looking for?

"I don't know what you're talking about." I tried to keep my voice steady, but there was a tremor in it that I couldn't hide. "You need to get away from this—"

Before I could finish, Finn yanked his arm out of my grip and turned toward the wreckage. The blood had drained from his face, his eyes fixed in that same haunted stare. His hands were shaking, the tremors subtle, but enough for me to see.

I took a step after him, but before I could get close, one of the firemen—barely visible in the haze of smoke and debris—shouted at us. "Get back! It's unstable!" His voice was muffled but urgent.

Finn didn't listen. He was moving forward, as though nothing could stop him.

"Finn!" I shouted again, my heart pounding, fear clawing at the back of my throat.

This time, he did turn, but only for a second. His gaze flickered over me, unreadable, before he returned to the fire. "I can't let it go," he muttered, more to himself than to me. "Not until I find it."

I was caught between his need to solve whatever it was haunting him and the sheer, overpowering danger of the situation. I had seen Finn like this before—fixated on a problem, to the point of obsession. But this was different. This wasn't about putting out a fire or saving a life. This was personal. He was searching for something. But what? And why was it pulling him into the heart of this inferno?

As Finn stepped closer to the edge of the building, I felt the ground beneath me shift. The heat from the fire seemed to pulse against my skin, a warning that I couldn't ignore. Every fiber of my being screamed at me to stop him, to drag him away, but I couldn't. Not without understanding. Not without knowing what he was fighting so desperately to find.

A crack echoed from the wreckage, louder than the fire, a sound like the breaking of a thousand bones. Finn froze. The air stilled for just a moment, and then the building seemed to groan, leaning dangerously toward collapse.

"Finn, get back!" I yelled, but my voice was swallowed by the roar of the fire, the heat pressing against me like a living thing.

Finn's gaze never wavered, his expression darkening, as though the flames were revealing something to him, something I couldn't see.

And then, with a suddenness that took my breath away, he charged forward, disappearing into the smoke. I stood there for a long second, frozen in place, unsure if I should follow or if I was about to lose him completely.

And then I realized—Finn wasn't just fighting the fire. He was fighting something else. Something inside him. Something that was just as dangerous as the flames around us.

I stood there, staring at the swirling smoke, my chest tight with a kind of quiet panic. The fire had claimed so much, but it was Finn's silence that truly unsettled me. The smoke curled up into the sky like some sort of grotesque offering, but it was Finn that I couldn't shake from my mind.

He hadn't come back out of the wreckage.

I told myself he was fine. I told myself he was probably just trying to get his bearings, standing in the charred remains like some kind of damn hero. The trouble was, that was exactly what Finn was—he never asked for help, never admitted when things were unraveling. He bore his demons like chains, as though struggling alone was the only way to keep them at bay. And I knew him well enough by now to recognize that he was drowning. Slowly, methodically, and yet... he still hadn't asked for a rope.

"Don't you dare," I muttered, pacing in place. I looked at the wreckage again, my heart leaping in my throat.

I took a step toward the inferno and immediately halted myself. I wasn't a firefighter. I wasn't trained for this. But I knew Finn. I knew him better than anyone. And right now, he was a mystery wrapped in torment, something I wasn't sure I could reach but something I couldn't leave behind either.

I wasn't sure how long I stood there, frozen in indecision. It felt like an eternity. The crackle of the fire echoed in my ears, the heat rising in waves that nearly scorched my skin. The air was thick with the smell of ash, burnt timber, and something metallic. Something sharp.

Suddenly, I heard it—a cough, faint and ragged, like a whisper trying to escape from the depths of a suffocating cave. My head snapped toward the sound, and there he was, emerging from the smoke.

Finn was crouched low, his hands bracing against the debris around him, his dark hair matted to his forehead, his face pale. His breathing was jagged, almost too loud for the stillness around him. And his eyes... I had never seen them look so haunted.

"Finn!" I rushed to him, my voice betraying the raw panic I'd tried so hard to suppress. I reached for him, but he recoiled, his gaze locking on mine with a fierce intensity, like a man who was terrified of what might happen if I came too close.

"I'm fine," he snapped, the words harsh, cutting into the heavy air between us.

I didn't buy it for a second. Not when the air reeked of something more than just smoke. Not when I could feel the weight of whatever battle he was fighting pressing down on him like the fires he'd just fought. This wasn't just about flames or destruction—it never had been. It was about something deeper, darker. Something I couldn't reach.

"Finn, you're not fine," I said, my voice soft but insistent. "You're covered in ash, your hands are shaking, and your face..." I hesitated. His face, or what I could see of it in the firelight, was too pale, too strained. It wasn't just exhaustion. It was something else.

His jaw tightened, but he didn't look away. The silence stretched between us again, as he stood there, half a man, half a ghost.

"I just need to find it," he muttered, more to himself than to me. "It's here. I can feel it."

I didn't understand. Not yet, anyway. But there was something in his tone, in the desperate, rasping way he spoke, that made my stomach twist. "What's here, Finn? What are you looking for?"

He hesitated, his eyes flicking over the wreckage as if the very structure of the crumbling building might offer him some kind of answer. His fists clenched again, the pain evident in the sharp way his knuckles whitened.

"It doesn't matter," he said through gritted teeth. "I'll find it. And then maybe—maybe then I can put it all behind me."

My heart squeezed painfully in my chest, the words landing with the force of a punch. I didn't understand what "it" was, but I knew it had nothing to do with fires or accidents. This was something personal. Something that lived in his past, buried so deep that he hadn't found the courage to dig it up until now.

"You don't have to do this alone," I said, my voice quiet but firm. "You don't have to carry whatever this is by yourself."

His eyes flickered with something—defiance, fear, regret, all tangled together in that one single moment. For a second, I thought he might open up, might let me in. But then, with a sharp exhale, he stepped back, shaking his head.

"I can't," he muttered. "You wouldn't understand."

"I don't need to understand, Finn," I replied, my voice barely above a whisper, but louder than the storm of his thoughts. "I just need you to trust me."

The tension in his shoulders seemed to snap at that. He turned away, his back stiff, but I could hear the words falling from his lips before he could stop himself.

"I'm not who you think I am."

My heart dropped, the words slicing through me like a blade. The distance between us stretched farther than ever, like some invisible force pulling him further away, a force I couldn't see but could feel. I knew he was broken, knew that the cracks in his soul ran deep. But this? This felt like a piece of him was already gone—already lost.

I reached for him, but he flinched away again, his hands shaking violently now, his breath coming in short, shallow bursts. "Finn—please, don't shut me out," I said, my voice cracking despite my best efforts to stay composed.

But there was no answer. Not from him. Only the howling wind and the fire's consuming roar.

And in that silence, I realized something: I wasn't just fighting for him anymore. I was fighting against whatever darkness was wrapping its claws around his heart, pulling him further into a place where I couldn't follow.

I just didn't know if I was too late.

The night felt heavier now, as though the earth itself was holding its breath. Finn hadn't said much since that night at the warehouse, and I wasn't sure whether to feel relieved or terrified by the silence that followed him. I wanted to believe that maybe he was finally processing whatever haunted him, that he would reach out when he was ready, but the quiet was growing unbearable. There was something about it, something ominous in the way he carried his sorrow like an invisible cloak, draped too tightly over his shoulders. I could see it in the way his eyes flicked to the side whenever I caught a glimpse of him, as though he was trying to outrun whatever shadow had taken root inside of him.

I wasn't sure how to fix this, how to break through the wall he'd built. I wasn't even sure if I could. Every word I tried to offer seemed to fall short. Every gesture, every offer of comfort, felt like I was trying to fill a hole too wide, too deep to reach the bottom. But I wasn't going to stop. Not now. Not when he needed someone—whether he believed it or not.

It was a few days later, when the city was covered in a thick, stifling fog that seemed to seep into everything, that I found Finn standing in front of the old brick building near the docks. His silhouette was barely visible, a shadow in the mist, his hands buried deep in his pockets, his posture stiff. He looked like he hadn't moved in hours.

I took a step forward, the chill of the fog nipping at my skin, but he still didn't acknowledge me. His eyes were fixed on the building, unblinking, as though it was the only thing that mattered in the world. Something about the intensity in his gaze made my chest tighten. I didn't know what it was about this particular building that had him so transfixed, but the air between us was thick with unspoken words.

"What are you looking for, Finn?" I asked softly, my voice barely rising above the sound of the mist swirling around us.

For a moment, there was no answer. Then, he shifted, turning his head just enough for me to see his face in the dull light. His eyes were darker than ever—darker, and... empty. It was like he wasn't there with me. He was somewhere else, trapped in some part of his mind that he couldn't escape.

"I don't know," he said finally, the words coming out in a hoarse whisper. "But I have to know. I can't leave until I do."

I nodded, my heart aching at the rawness in his voice. I didn't press him further, not yet. The way he spoke, like every word took something out of him, made me hesitate. I didn't want to push him too far. But I also couldn't stand by and watch him spiral further down into whatever hell he was fighting alone. I stepped closer, and he didn't move, didn't flinch. That alone was a small victory.

"I'm not going anywhere," I said, more firmly this time, more to myself than to him. "Whatever this is, whatever you're looking for, you don't have to do it alone."

He let out a short, bitter laugh that caught me off guard, and I could hear the edge of something brittle in it. "You don't know what you're asking. You don't know what you'd be walking into."

I felt a surge of something, a mixture of anger and frustration, and my own voice came out sharp. "I'm not scared of you, Finn. I'm scared for you. And if you're not going to trust me, then trust the fact that I'm here. I'm not going anywhere."

His gaze met mine then, and for a fleeting second, I saw a flicker of something in his eyes. Something soft. Something raw. But it was gone almost as quickly as it appeared, replaced by that same cold, impenetrable mask. He took a step back, pulling away, as though my words had burned him in ways I didn't understand.

"I'm not the man you think I am," he said, his voice low, his gaze drifting back to the building. "I've done things. Things that—" He broke off abruptly, like he'd hit a wall he couldn't scale.

I could feel the distance growing between us again, the gulf widening with every breath he took. "Finn," I said, my throat tight, but I couldn't find the words. How could I help him when he wouldn't let me?

"I didn't choose this," he continued, his voice barely above a whisper, like the words had been trapped in his chest for years. "But now it's too late to walk away. I can't walk away from this."

I didn't ask him what he meant. I didn't need to. The anguish in his voice, the deep well of regret and pain, told me everything I needed to know.

He wasn't just fighting the fires anymore. He was fighting himself. And I didn't know if he could win.

The silence stretched between us again, thick and uncomfortable, until Finn took a step toward the building. I didn't stop him this time, didn't say a word, just followed behind him as he walked through the fog like a man determined to face whatever lay beyond those walls.

The closer we got to the building, the more the air seemed to change. It wasn't just the fog. There was something in the atmosphere, something heavy, like the weight of old secrets pressing down on us. My pulse quickened as we neared the door, and I could feel the unease bubbling up in my chest, threatening to spill over.

Finn reached for the handle, but before he could turn it, a loud crash echoed from inside the building. I froze, my heart pounding in my chest. Something was in there—something that didn't belong.

"Finn," I whispered, but he was already moving. There was no hesitation, no second thought. He pushed the door open with a force that made the old hinges creak in protest. I followed him inside, my breath caught in my throat, my every instinct screaming at me to turn and run.

But I didn't. Because somewhere deep inside, I knew this wasn't just about Finn anymore.

It was about whatever waited for us in the darkness.

Chapter 17: The Heart's Confession

The night had folded itself into a hushed silence, the kind that seeps deep into your bones. The only sound that lingered in the air was the soft hum of the refrigerator, a lazy reminder that life continued on, even in the quietest moments. The city outside, with its persistent clamor, had become a distant memory, muffled by the thick curtains and the soft lighting of my living room. There was a certain intimacy in the stillness, something that made the world feel smaller, more confined, like it was just him and me—two strangers who'd become something far more complicated in the span of a few months.

I shifted on the couch, the fabric cool against my skin, as I stole a glance at him. He sat next to me, his shoulders tense, his eyes avoiding mine, as if the very weight of my question was too much to bear. I had always known there was something lurking beneath the surface of his easy smile, something he wasn't ready to share. But tonight—tonight I needed the truth.

His fingers drummed restlessly on his knee, a quiet rhythm that I knew was his way of grounding himself. "I told you everything," he murmured, the words barely making their way through the air. "There's nothing left to say."

I bit my lip, holding back the frustration bubbling inside me. "Don't lie to me. Not anymore. You're not fooling anyone."

He froze at my words, his face tightening, his jaw clenching. It was the first time I had ever seen him truly vulnerable, not the kind of vulnerability that comes from a moment of weakness, but the kind that seeps out in the most unexpected places. I could feel it, the crack in his composure, the raw edges of a past he wasn't ready to confront.

I leaned forward, my heart pounding against my ribcage as I reached for his hand. His skin was warm, the calluses from years of hard work rough against my fingertips. The touch seemed to ground both of us, the simple act of contact bridging the distance that had always lingered between us.

"Please," I said, my voice softer now, almost pleading. "You can't keep hiding from it. Whatever it is, it's eating you alive, and I can't stand to watch you suffer in silence. You don't have to carry it alone."

He pulled his hand away, rubbing the back of his neck, his eyes closing as if to shield himself from what was coming. For a moment, I wondered if he'd turn away entirely, if the door would close between us forever, and I'd be left sitting here with nothing but questions and unanswered hopes. But then he spoke, and his words cut through the tension like a knife.

"I've never told anyone this," he said, his voice barely audible. "Not my family. Not my friends. No one." His words hung in the air, heavy with years of guilt and regret. "I wasn't there when it mattered. I failed her."

The words echoed in my head, reverberating through my chest like a drumbeat. A sudden chill swept through the room, and I could see the flicker of something deep in his eyes—something jagged and broken. I wanted to reach out, to pull him close and tell him everything would be okay, but I knew the words would feel empty, meaningless in the face of what he had done—or what he believed he had done.

I waited, holding my breath, until he finally spoke again. "It was my sister. She... she died because I wasn't there when she needed me. I was too wrapped up in my own life, too busy with my own problems, and I couldn't get to her in time." His voice cracked on the last sentence, and I felt the weight of his grief settle between us like a third person in the room.

My heart ached for him, for the pain he had carried for so long, a burden that had slowly eaten away at the person he had become. I wanted to tell him it wasn't his fault, that no one could have known what would happen, but the words stuck in my throat. He needed to say them. He needed to believe them.

"How could I have known?" he asked, his eyes searching mine, as if looking for some kind of answer, some kind of solace that I didn't have the power to give. "How could I have known that she was... that she needed me?"

I didn't know what to say. There was nothing I could say to make it right, to undo the years of guilt he had piled upon himself. But in that moment, as his pain lay exposed before me, something shifted between us. It wasn't pity that I felt, nor was it sympathy. It was a deep, quiet longing to take his hurt, to carry it for him, if only for a moment. To make him understand that he wasn't alone, that there was still hope, even in the darkest places.

"I'm so sorry," I whispered, my voice barely a breath, as I reached out to touch his arm. "But you're not alone anymore. I'm here, and I'm not going anywhere. You don't have to carry this burden by yourself."

For the first time since I had known him, I saw the weight of his walls begin to crumble, piece by piece. The hard exterior, the guarded expressions, the bravado—it all fell away, revealing the man beneath. And in that moment, I understood him completely. All the anger I had felt earlier dissolved into something else—something softer, something deeper.

He turned to me then, his eyes raw and vulnerable, and in the space between us, a thousand unspoken words passed. Without thinking, I leaned in, closing the distance, and for the first time, our lips met—not out of passion, but out of understanding, out of a shared need to heal, to be whole again.

When we pulled away, his forehead rested against mine, and for a fleeting moment, the world outside ceased to exist. We were simply two souls, tethered together by the weight of the past and the promise of something better. And I knew, in the depths of my being, that whatever the future held, we would face it together.

There was something strangely tender in the way he held me after that kiss, as if the act itself had unraveled the tight, unspoken knot of pain he carried. He had given me a glimpse into the part of him that nobody saw—not his friends, not his family. Certainly not the easy smile he so often wore. And in exchange for that raw honesty, I felt something stir inside me, something deeper than sympathy, something that made the walls around my heart soften just enough for him to slip through.

The night stretched on, but no words were spoken as we sat there in the dim light. His fingers traced idle patterns on the back of my hand, the gesture simple yet intimate in its quiet certainty. He didn't ask for forgiveness, not in the way I thought he would. It wasn't like that. He simply allowed himself to be seen, stripped of any pretense, and for the first time, I realized how much he had buried beneath layers of charm and detachment.

The room felt like it had become a cocoon—soft, quiet, and impossibly still. A far cry from the chaos that had reigned before. I had always been a woman who prided herself on keeping things light, on laughing when things got heavy, on never letting the serious stuff settle too long before pulling myself free. But tonight, I didn't want to escape.

"You know," he said, his voice low, pulling me from my thoughts, "I never wanted anyone to feel sorry for me."

I glanced at him, finding that same guarded look in his eyes again, the one that hinted at unspoken histories, and yet, there was something vulnerable there now too. It was a disarming combination, and I wasn't sure if I wanted to kiss him again or ask him to tell me more about the person he used to be.

"Then why did you let me in?" I asked, my voice more vulnerable than I intended.

He sighed, glancing down at the floor before meeting my gaze again. "I don't know. Maybe I didn't want to be alone anymore. Maybe I wanted someone to know who I really am."

"And what happens if I don't like who you really are?" I teased lightly, trying to push back the weight of the moment. I wasn't ready to dive that deep just yet.

"Then I'll have to make you like me," he said with that signature smile—the one that was just a little too confident, too charming. But I noticed the way his fingers clenched around mine, as if he was bracing for some kind of rejection.

"Well," I said, arching an eyebrow, "I'm not sure you're my type."

He laughed, but it was a half-hearted sound, as if it wasn't quite reaching his eyes. The playful tone dropped, and I realized that maybe he wasn't used to being confronted with uncertainty.

"What if I told you that I wanted to be someone worth loving?" he asked, his voice rougher now, stripped of any bravado. There was an earnestness there, raw and unfiltered.

I swallowed hard, my chest tight at his words. It wasn't just the confession he had shared, but the weight of everything he hadn't yet said—the parts of himself he hadn't fully revealed. It was a challenge, an unspoken plea, and it was one I wasn't sure I was ready to accept.

"You are," I said, surprising myself as the words came out without hesitation. "You're already someone worth loving. But maybe you just have to believe it first."

He shook his head slowly, the small movement betraying the doubt that still gnawed at him. "I don't know if I can. I don't know if I can ever make peace with it all."

"Well, you're going to have to," I said, my voice gentle but firm. "Not for me. Not for anyone else. But for yourself."

The air between us grew heavier, the weight of his past clinging to the space like an invisible fog. I knew he wasn't there yet, not fully. The truth of his past was still fresh, the guilt still raw, but I also knew that tonight, something had shifted. Maybe it wasn't a dramatic transformation, but it was enough. Enough for me to see him—really see him—and enough for him to begin to let go of the chains he had wrapped around his own heart.

I stood up, breaking the moment of intimacy, and walked over to the window. The city lights below flickered like a thousand tiny stars, and for a brief second, I felt a strange sense of calm settle over me. The world outside seemed so vast, so full of possibilities. And yet, in that moment, all I wanted was to be here, with him.

"You've got a lot of work to do," I said, not turning to face him, my voice light again to break the tension. "But that doesn't mean it's impossible. Just... stop running from yourself."

I could feel his gaze on me, but I didn't look back. Instead, I focused on the stars. I wanted to be the one to light his way, not in a grand, dramatic sense, but in the quiet, persistent way that sometimes love does. A steady flame that doesn't burn out, even when the wind threatens to blow it away.

"Do you think it's worth it?" he asked, his voice uncertain, but there was a thread of hope in it now. It wasn't much, but it was there.

"I think everything worth having is worth fighting for," I said with a small smile, finally turning back to meet his gaze.

He smiled, and there was a softness in his expression that I hadn't seen before, the kind that hinted at the possibility of healing, of moving forward, of leaving behind what had broken him. I wanted to believe in that possibility, for both of us.

"Then maybe," he said quietly, "I'll fight for us."

And that, somehow, felt like the beginning of something I hadn't expected, something neither of us could have predicted. It wasn't just his past that was being healed tonight. It was mine too, in the quiet, steady rhythm of his words, in the shared silence that had no room for fear.

The weight of his confession lingered between us, an invisible force that held us in place, the silence wrapping around us like a blanket. The air felt heavy with unspoken things, the kind of thoughts that could drown a person if left unchecked. I could feel the tension in the space, but also something else—something quieter, gentler. Maybe it was the understanding that had settled between us, or the tenderness in his eyes that refused to look away from mine. Whatever it was, it wasn't like anything I had ever known. It was vulnerable, yes, but there was a raw honesty to it that made everything else feel trivial in comparison.

He finally broke the silence, his voice low, almost hesitant. "You don't have to be here, you know. You don't owe me anything."

I couldn't help but laugh, the sound escaping my lips before I could stop it. "Is that really what you think?" I asked, shaking my head as I looked at him, the soft glow of the lamps casting shadows across his face. "You've got it all wrong, you know. You've been pushing people away for so long, you've forgotten what it feels like to have someone stick around."

He sighed, the sound a mixture of frustration and regret. "I don't want to drag you into my mess."

"Well," I said, leaning forward, "I'm already in it. Might as well see it through."

There was a flicker of surprise in his eyes, and for a moment, I thought he might argue, might tell me I was making a mistake. But then he simply nodded, as if resigning himself to something that had already been decided for him.

"I'm not good at this," he admitted, his voice softer now, almost apologetic.

"Good at what? Letting people in?" I asked, raising an eyebrow. "You're not the only one. Believe me, it takes some getting used to."

He didn't respond at first, but I could see the wheels turning in his head. The truth was, I wasn't sure what I was doing either. I had no roadmap for this kind of thing—no guide to tell me when it was okay to give someone your heart, and when to hold it back. But there was something about him, something about the way he was trying so hard to move past the things that had haunted him, that made me want to take the leap with him.

I shifted my position, tucking my legs under me as I faced him more fully. "So what happens now?" I asked. "You tell me your tragic backstory, and I magically make everything better?"

He gave a small, rueful smile. "Wouldn't that be nice?"

"I mean, I can't promise a magic wand," I said, matching his tone. "But I can promise I won't run away just because you're not perfect. I've got my own stuff, you know."

He raised an eyebrow, clearly skeptical. "Stuff?"

I shrugged, unable to suppress a grin. "We all have it. Mine just happens to be messier than yours." I leaned in a little closer, my smile growing. "But you're not going to get away from me that easily. I'm stubborn."

His eyes softened, and for a moment, it felt like we were two people who had finally found something solid to stand on, even if it wasn't much. His hand reached for mine, and this time, I didn't pull away. I could feel the warmth of his touch, the quiet strength in it, and I realized that maybe—just maybe—this was the beginning of something different.

"Are you sure about this?" he asked, his voice almost a whisper.

I didn't have an answer. Not a clean one, anyway. But there was something about him, something in the way he looked at me like he wasn't sure whether he was ready to let go of his past, but was willing to try. That was enough for me.

"I'm sure," I said, and it felt true. "But don't think this means you get to escape all the hard stuff. I'm not going to let you off the hook."

He chuckled, the sound light and easy now. "I didn't expect to be."

The tension that had once filled the room seemed to evaporate, replaced by something quieter, more content. We sat there for a while, not saying anything, just existing in the same space. It was nice, really. For once, it felt like we were simply two people, neither of us perfect, neither of us whole, but somehow fitting together in a way that made everything else fall into place.

Eventually, I pulled back, breaking the silence. "We should probably get some sleep," I said, though I wasn't entirely ready to let go of the moment just yet.

He nodded, his hand still loosely holding mine. "Yeah, I guess we should."

But as we stood to head toward the bedroom, a sudden knock on the door shattered the fragile peace we had just begun to create. It was sharp, urgent—out of place in the otherwise quiet apartment.

I froze, my heart skipping a beat. I had no idea who would be at the door this late, but I already knew that the moment we opened it, everything would change again.

His face hardened, and I could see the muscles in his jaw tighten. "Stay here," he said, his voice sharp.

"No," I said, taking a step forward. "I'm not going anywhere."

He looked at me, his expression conflicted, but there was no time to argue. Another knock echoed through the room, this time more insistent, and I knew that whatever was on the other side of that door wasn't going to be good.

"Who the hell could that be?" I murmured.

He didn't answer, only stepped toward the door. With every step he took, I felt a rising sense of unease—a warning that the night had just taken a sharp turn. And when the door finally creaked open, I had no idea what we were about to face.

I only knew one thing for sure: it was about to get much more complicated.

Chapter 18: The Silent Threat

The sun had barely risen, casting a pale, watery light over the floorboards when I found the letter. At first, it was nothing but a crumpled piece of paper, innocuous in its appearance, left delicately on the pillow where I had been resting just moments before. The disheveled state of the room, the soft scent of freshly brewed coffee still lingering in the air, made the sight of it feel surreal, as though I were standing at the edge of a nightmare, watching it unfold in slow motion.

My fingers trembled when I reached for the letter, its edges curling as if it were alive, waiting to be unfolded by someone who knew all too well the weight of fear. I didn't want to open it. Not again. But I knew I had to.

The ink was smudged in places, as though the writer had hurried, or perhaps shaken with some frenzied emotion while writing. The words were short, sharp—punctuation like an afterthought, leaving the message cold and final.

"Stay away from him. There are consequences."

The room seemed to close in around me, the walls pressing tighter, suffocating the breath from my chest. The letter was silent but screamed louder than any sound could. The chill of it seeped into my bones, making the air feel heavy, suffused with something dark. It was a message, a warning, and I couldn't tell if it was one last plea or a threat to seal my fate.

I folded the letter with deliberate care, setting it aside. A moment later, Finn appeared, his footsteps heavy on the stairs, the door creaking open as he stepped into the room. He didn't need to see the letter to know what it meant. His eyes had that look—the one that said he could see straight through me, straight through the mask I had carefully crafted to hide my unease. His jaw tightened, and the muscles in his arms bunched, betraying the quiet fur simmered beneath the surface.

"What is it?" His voice was low, controlled, but there was no mistaking the tension there.

"It's nothing," I said, offering a smile that probably looked as shaky as I felt. "Just... a bad joke."

Finn's eyes narrowed. "A bad joke?" His gaze flicked to the letter on the bed. "You and I both know that isn't true."

I sat up straighter, resisting the urge to push the letter further under the pillow, to hide it like some childish attempt at denial. "It's nothing," I repeated, more firmly this time. But my words felt hollow. "Just some... some prank, you know? The sort of thing you get when people find out you're—"

"When people find out you're close to someone they don't like?" Finn finished for me, stepping toward the bed. The room seemed to contract further around his words, and the space between us felt charged with a current I didn't know how to navigate.

I nodded, trying to keep my composure, trying to ignore the fear that gripped my throat. "Exactly. It'll pass. It's just someone trying to scare me." I gave a small, uncertain laugh. "It's not like it's the first time."

He didn't laugh. His eyes were cold, too cold, and his lips pressed together in a hard line.

"You're not alone in this. You know that, right?" His voice softened, but it was a dangerous softness. It carried the weight of a promise, one I wasn't sure I wanted.

I swallowed hard, the sting of unshed tears pricking behind my eyelids. I didn't want his protection. Not like this. Not in the way that was becoming all too familiar.

"I'm fine, Finn," I said, my voice barely a whisper. "It's just a stupid letter."

He raised an eyebrow, skeptical. "A stupid letter? You sure about that?"

I wanted to argue, to tell him I could handle this on my own. But the words were stuck in my throat, tangled up with the knowledge that I couldn't. This wasn't a silly prank. This was something darker, something much more insidious. And Finn—he knew it too.

He sat beside me on the bed, the mattress shifting beneath his weight, and his arm brushed against mine. For a moment, the world outside felt still, as if the two of us were suspended in time, our breathing the only sound in the room. But the silence between us wasn't comforting. It was fraught, tense with an unspeakable truth neither of us was willing to voice.

"We'll find out who's behind this," he said, his voice firm with a resolve I couldn't shake. "And when we do, they won't be able to hide."

I wanted to believe him. Really, I did. But there was a sinking feeling deep in my gut, one that told me this was no simple game, no random act of vengeance. Whoever was sending these letters knew us—knew me. They knew exactly where to strike, what words to use. And they weren't going to stop.

"Finn," I began, the weight of the words pressing down on me, "this isn't just about me. This is about you too. Whoever this is, they know something. They know us."

He stiffened, his eyes darkening. "I'm not going anywhere. Neither are you."

I could have argued, could have said something to try and distance myself from it all, but the words never made it past my lips. Instead, I stayed silent, my gaze flicking to the window, to the trees outside swaying gently in the breeze, as though the world were unaware of the storm that was quietly gathering on the horizon.

But it was there. I could feel it. And I knew that no matter how tightly I tried to hold on to the illusion of safety, the truth was already seeping through the cracks.

I tried to laugh it off, telling myself that whoever was behind these letters was probably just some misguided fool who didn't know when to quit. But as I stood there, staring at Finn's clenched jaw and the fire burning in his eyes, I realized it wasn't that simple. I didn't know how deep this went, how far this person would go to break us. And somehow, despite all the fear and uncertainty clawing at my chest, I found myself standing even taller beside him.

"What's next?" I asked, my voice a bit more confident than I felt. Finn looked at me, his face a mask of determination, and then—just as quickly—softened into something gentler. His hand reached for mine, his fingers brushing over the scars on my palm like he could erase them with a touch.

"We dig deeper," he said. "I'm not letting anyone threaten you. Not now, not ever."

That should've made me feel safer. And on some level, it did. But there was something about the way he said it, the conviction behind his words, that made my stomach turn. The kind of protection he was offering was more than I'd ever asked for, more than I'd ever wanted.

But it was also the kind I couldn't push away.

Finn and I spent the next few days in a haze of urgency. The house felt different—quieter, more oppressive. Every creak of the floorboards felt like a footstep. Every knock at the door, a potential threat. It was as though the world had grown smaller, tighter, more dangerous. I had to remind myself to breathe sometimes, to stop and look around, to stay grounded in the present, and not lose myself in whatever it was that lurked just out of sight.

I'd never realized how much Finn's presence anchored me until now. He had this way of making the world feel less threatening, like nothing bad could happen as long as he was near. But now, with the weight of that letter hanging over us, I wasn't so sure.

Late one night, after we'd finished combing through every scrap of evidence we had—every torn envelope, every hastily written message—I sank into the worn armchair in the corner of the room, the fabric soft and familiar under me. Finn stood near the window, staring out at the horizon like he was hoping for an answer to fall from the sky.

"You know what's strange?" I said, breaking the silence, the sound of my voice almost jarring against the stillness. "We don't even know who we're dealing with. It's like they know everything about us, but we don't know a thing about them."

Finn didn't turn around, but I could see his reflection in the glass. His eyes narrowed, his lips a thin line. "I know. And it's not sitting well with me."

He moved then, crossing the room in two quick strides before dropping down next to me. His hand brushed against mine again, and I let out a breath I hadn't realized I was holding.

"Whoever this is, they want to hurt you," he said softly, the words falling between us like they were too heavy to be ignored. "And I won't let that happen."

I shook my head, though I knew he wasn't wrong. "I don't want you to fight my battles, Finn. You don't have to protect me."

But the corner of his mouth lifted in that half-smile that always made my heart skip a beat. "You don't get to decide that, not right now. If someone's threatening you, they're threatening me too. You think I'd just let that go?"

I met his gaze, my chest tightening as I saw the intensity in his eyes. "Finn, we don't know what we're up against. This person—they're smarter than we think."

His jaw clenched, and for a moment, I saw the storm behind his eyes. He didn't speak, didn't need to. He understood. And

I knew, deep down, that he would move mountains if it meant keeping me safe.

But I also knew that kind of protection came with a price.

The next few days blurred together in a mix of restless nights and tense mornings. Finn and I dug into every corner of our lives, trying to uncover something, anything, that could help us understand who was behind these threats. It wasn't just the letters anymore—there were other signs, too. A car parked across the street for hours, always just out of view, always vanishing the moment I looked. The feeling of being watched, the unsettling sense that someone was waiting for the perfect moment to strike.

Still, no matter how hard we looked, the trail grew colder the further we went.

One evening, after a long day of searching, Finn stood in front of the fireplace, the glow of the flames flickering in his eyes as he ran a hand through his hair. He looked exhausted, worn down in a way I hadn't seen before. But there was something else in his expression, something that pulled at me.

"I'm starting to think this person isn't just watching us," he said, voice low and intense. "They're getting closer. They know our every move—what we're doing, where we are. They've been planning this for a long time."

I took a deep breath, trying to steady myself. The realization hung in the air, sharp and unrelenting. It wasn't just a simple threat. It was an invasion. A game of cat and mouse where we were always a step behind.

"I know," I said, my voice barely above a whisper. "But it doesn't matter. We'll find them. And when we do, we won't stop until they've disappeared for good."

Finn didn't answer. Instead, he stepped toward me, his presence like a force that pulled me into his orbit, steady and sure. His hand cupped my cheek, his thumb brushing over my skin in a gesture that was both comforting and possessive.

And in that moment, with the weight of everything pressing in on us, I knew one thing for sure—I wasn't walking away from him. Not now. Not ever.

I woke in the dead of night to the sound of the wind rustling against the window, a sound so eerily quiet it almost felt like a warning. Finn's side of the bed was empty, the coolness of the sheets where his warmth had been just an hour ago a reminder of how much space this situation had begun to take up. I sat up, my pulse quickening for no reason I could put a name to. There was a sense of heaviness in the air tonight, thick and stifling, like something was waiting to happen.

The house felt too still. Even the usual creaks of the old floorboards seemed muted. I ran my fingers through my hair, pushing it back from my face, and swung my legs over the side of the bed. Barefoot, I padded softly toward the stairs, careful not to make a sound, though it felt like the walls themselves were listening.

The light in the kitchen was on, a low glow that flickered like a heartbeat. When I entered the room, Finn was standing by the counter, his hand gripping the edge like it was the only thing holding him upright. His broad back was to me, but I could feel the tension radiating from him, thick and tangible. It was always like this, wasn't it? The quiet before the storm. And it wasn't just the letter anymore—it was the things that followed it. The hushed whispers on the wind, the odd shadows that darted in the corners of my eyes, the way the hairs on the back of my neck prickled when I was alone.

"Finn?" I said softly, my voice catching in the stillness.

He turned slowly, his face shadowed, eyes dark. "You shouldn't be up."

I raised an eyebrow, fighting the familiar wave of frustration that rose in me. "I could say the same about you."

He didn't answer, his gaze flicking over me like he was searching for something. I wasn't sure what it was, but I knew the look. It was the same one he wore when he was trying to protect me—only now it felt like he was trying to keep me at arm's length, a distance I wasn't sure I wanted.

"We need to be careful," he said finally, his voice low and rough, as if he hadn't spoken in hours. "I think they're closer than we realize."

A chill ran down my spine at his words, though I tried not to let it show. "Who?"

His jaw clenched. "The person sending the letters. They're not just watching us anymore. They're in our lives. They know too much."

I could feel the pulse of my heart speeding up. The walls seemed to close in around us as if the very air was thick with this unspoken threat. I took a step toward him, but Finn held up a hand to stop me.

"You need to stay away from me," he said abruptly, his voice sharp, like he was trying to convince himself more than anything.

I froze, the words hitting me harder than I expected. "What do you mean, stay away from you? After everything? I'm not just going to—"

"I'm not asking, I'm telling you." His voice had an edge now, raw and desperate. He looked at me like I was something fragile, something he might break if he wasn't careful. But I wasn't glass, and I wasn't about to shatter that easily.

I stepped closer, not backing down. "Finn—"

"I can't lose you," he cut in, his voice breaking in a way that made my chest ache. He was silent for a long beat, his eyes softening before he said the words I wasn't ready to hear. "I'll keep you safe.

I don't care what it takes. But I need you to trust me—stay away from me. For now."

My heart dropped. Stay away? My thoughts spun, a hundred questions flooding my mind. I didn't want to feel the way I did, this dizzying pull between love and fear, between wanting to protect him and wanting to be the one standing beside him, facing whatever came next. But I couldn't do it. I couldn't step back and watch him fight this battle alone.

"I won't." I couldn't stop the words from tumbling out, couldn't stop the steady resolve in my voice. "I'm not leaving you."

For a moment, he said nothing. And then he dropped his gaze, his hands running through his hair in that frustrated, almost defeated gesture that had become too familiar. The silence between us stretched on, thick and heavy. There was so much unspoken in the air, so much left hanging between us like a blade waiting to fall.

"I can't do this," he muttered, half to himself, as though he was trying to sort through the chaos of everything that was happening. "I don't know how to keep you safe."

"You don't have to," I said softly. "We'll figure it out together."

The words felt like a promise, but they were heavy, laced with an undercurrent of uncertainty that neither of us could escape. I wanted so badly to believe them.

Just then, the sharp ring of the phone cut through the tension like a knife. Both of us froze. Finn's hand shot out before I could even think to move, grabbing the phone with a speed that almost startled me.

"Who is it?" I whispered, my heart thundering in my chest.

He didn't answer, his focus entirely on the line. He looked at me, his eyes narrowing. Something was wrong. My stomach dropped. Whatever he saw, whatever he was hearing, wasn't good.

I took a slow step toward him, reaching for his arm, but he shook his head, his finger pressed firmly to his lips, urging me to stay quiet.

"Hello?" His voice was taut, like a string about to snap. He listened for a moment, and then his face went pale, the color draining from his features. I didn't have to hear the other end of the conversation to know something had changed, something irrevocable.

His grip tightened around the phone.

"Where?" he asked, his voice hoarse. And then, "I'll be there."

He hung up, the silence that followed a deafening weight between us.

"What's happening?" I asked, my voice barely a whisper.

Finn didn't answer right away. He turned away from me, pacing toward the door. "Pack your things. Now."

I blinked, my pulse quickening. "What? Why?"

"I don't have time to explain. Just trust me. We have to go. Now."

I didn't hesitate, though my hands shook as I grabbed a bag. I had no idea what was going on—what Finn had just learned—but whatever it was, it was worse than I could have imagined. And as I grabbed the last of my things and followed him out the door, I realized one thing: we weren't safe anymore. Not even close.

The car was already running when we reached it. Finn slammed the door behind me, his hands gripping the steering wheel with a kind of urgency that made my chest tighten.

And then, just as we pulled out of the driveway, my phone buzzed in my pocket. The message was simple.

I know where you are.

Chapter 19: Fireline

The acrid smell of smoke hung in the air like a constant companion, a reminder that the world was burning just beyond our doorstep. I had gotten used to the crackle of flames in the distance, to the red-tinged sunsets that spoke of destruction. Each night, Finn and I would sit on the small balcony of my apartment, the city lights below blinking like stars caught in a twisted dream, while the fires raged just beyond the horizon.

I always knew when Finn's mind started to wander—his eyes would grow distant, his jaw tightening like he was chewing on a memory he couldn't quite spit out. I tried not to read too much into it, but I couldn't help it. I was beginning to understand the weight of the man I was becoming far too attached to.

Finn had this way of carrying himself, like the world couldn't possibly touch him, but I knew better. Underneath his tall, broad frame, beneath the meticulously groomed beard and the carefully unbothered demeanor, there was a storm. I'd seen it when the fires first started—how he bristled, how his gaze would flicker over each callous decision made by the authorities, as though he could hear the whispers behind their carefully scripted words.

"The fire's spreading." His voice cut through the hum of the night, low and gritty, a tone that made me clench my hands to keep from reaching for him. "Too close this time."

I didn't ask which fire he meant. It didn't matter. They were all the same, yet each one felt like a personal message to him, a challenge we couldn't avoid.

"What's the plan?" I asked, my voice steady despite the nervous flutter in my chest.

He didn't answer immediately, which only made the silence more excruciating. Instead, he leaned back against the wrought-iron railing, crossing his arms over his chest. I knew that posture. He was calculating, keeping his thoughts wrapped up tight. I wanted to push him, to ask what was really bothering him, but I knew it wouldn't do any good.

"We're not dealing with amateurs anymore," he said finally, his gaze flickering over the street below, as if the answer to all of this was hidden somewhere in the shadows. "This feels personal."

The words sent a cold chill down my spine, a chill I hadn't realized I'd been holding at bay until that very moment. I was beginning to feel it too. The fires had started as a series of random incidents, each one barely touching the surface of the city's concerns. But the way they had escalated, the precision, the pattern that emerged—it couldn't be coincidence. Someone knew what they were doing. Someone who had a score to settle.

I watched Finn's face, tracing the tense line of his jaw, the way his shoulders stiffened as though bracing for impact. The weight of this case had grown far too heavy for him to bear alone. I could see it in his eyes—the frustration, the helplessness. He hated being outsmarted, especially when it meant innocent people were getting hurt. And I knew, without a doubt, that the only way to make him stop was to walk away. But walking away wasn't an option. Not now. Not with the fires so close to everything we'd built.

"Who could it be?" My voice was quieter than I meant, almost lost in the stillness between us.

Finn's gaze snapped to mine, his expression unreadable. "Someone close."

The words hung there, unspoken and chilling. We had circled each other in this strange, delicate dance for months now, but the thought that one of our own might be responsible for these fires felt like a knife to the gut. Who in our circle would even think of such a thing?

And then it clicked—so obvious, so simple—that I almost laughed at how blind I had been. The town's firefighting crew, the very ones who were supposed to be stopping the flames, were all connected. Every fire, every shift, every suspicion tied back to one of them. And I'd seen them, all of them, in the shadows of my past—people I thought I knew, people I trusted.

Finn's voice broke through my reverie, a quiet murmur that didn't need to be loud to carry weight. "We have to find out who."

I nodded, my stomach twisting in knots. I had a terrible feeling that the truth was closer than either of us wanted to believe.

The problem wasn't just the fires. It was the silence that followed them. No one was talking. Not the authorities, not the local news. It was as though everyone was in on a secret we weren't privy to. It was clear the fire wasn't the only thing burning—it was everything that surrounded it. Every conversation, every glance that passed between Finn and I, had become loaded with unsaid words, unacknowledged fears.

As if on cue, Finn's phone buzzed, its vibration slicing through the heavy silence. His eyes narrowed as he checked the screen, and for a split second, I could see the shift in his expression—something had changed. Without a word, he stood, a quick motion that I could never hope to mirror, and headed for the door. I rose with him, more out of instinct than any real understanding of what was happening.

"Where are we going?" I asked, my voice betraying the urgency I felt in my chest.

"Somewhere that might have answers." He didn't look back as he grabbed his jacket from the chair and slipped it on, the fabric rustling like a whisper against the night air.

I wanted to argue, to ask why we couldn't just stay here and talk it through, but I knew better. When Finn was in this mode, no amount of talking would stop him. And I wasn't going to let him face this alone.

I grabbed my purse, hurrying to catch up as we both stepped into the hallway, the dim lights flickering overhead like a warning.

The streetlights flickered as we moved through the shadows, the city's pulse muffled beneath the weight of what was hanging between us. The fire had long since crept into the heart of everything, smoldering away at secrets and histories we'd thought we understood. Finn was quiet, too quiet, his eyes focused on the cracked pavement ahead, the lines in his face deepening as though the night itself had conspired to age him. I wanted to ask what he was thinking, but I knew he'd tell me nothing until he was ready. He never did.

I was starting to feel like a passenger in a story I didn't quite belong in. I had known Finn long enough to know he didn't need help solving problems; in fact, he hated it. Every time I'd tried to push him, to get him to open up, I was met with that same guarded expression, like he'd built an impenetrable wall around his thoughts, and no one was allowed to climb over. Still, it was hard to ignore the flicker of something else I saw in his eyes—the fear he was trying so desperately to bury.

"So, where are we going?" I asked, my words sharp in the cool air, hanging between us like a dare.

Finn's answer came without hesitation. "To find out who's been feeding the fire."

It was as blunt as it was cryptic, but I didn't question him. The city was too quiet tonight, too still for the unrest that had been steadily growing like an infection. I didn't know what answers he was hoping to find, but I suspected he was looking for something I wasn't meant to see. Maybe he wanted to prove something to himself. Maybe he wanted to make sure the arsonist wasn't someone we'd been trusting all along.

We turned a corner, the sharp sound of our footsteps echoing off the walls of buildings that seemed to shrink with every step we took. The city felt smaller now, more claustrophobic, as if the fires had reduced it to a tinderbox, ready to combust. The atmosphere hung heavy with tension, a low hum in the back of my mind telling me that we were walking deeper into a maze we might never escape.

Finn paused in front of a building—a long, low structure, tucked away from the main roads. It was nothing special, just another nondescript warehouse, its exterior coated in layers of grime and age. I didn't know what to expect, but I had learned not to ask too many questions when Finn had that look on his face.

"Stay close," he muttered, pushing open the rusted door with a creak that sounded far too loud for the quiet of the night.

I followed him inside, the smell of damp concrete and forgotten machinery hitting me immediately. The warehouse was filled with shadows, the corners thick with dust and neglect. Finn moved through the space with purpose, his silhouette cutting through the gloom as if he knew exactly where he was going.

"Do you know what this place is?" I asked, my voice too soft against the vastness of the room.

He didn't answer right away, instead pausing by a stack of crates near the back wall. There was something familiar about the way his hands rested on the wood, the subtle tension in his posture. The feeling that he was anticipating something—that he was waiting.

"Should I?" I pressed, the silence stretching longer than I liked. "I mean, you're the one with all the secrets, not me."

He looked over his shoulder, his expression unreadable. "You don't know half of it."

I could tell he was holding something back, but the more I probed, the more I realized I wasn't going to get anything out of him. Not yet. Instead, I followed his gaze, trying to make sense of the shadows, the smell of old machinery and gasoline that permeated the air. There was a sense of abandonment here, the kind that made me feel both uneasy and strangely at home. A place for things to be forgotten. A place for things to burn.

Finn crouched by a pile of old papers, his fingers sifting through them quickly, his brow furrowing. I could see the tension in his movements now, the edges of his calm slipping. He knew something. I could feel it in my bones.

"Who were you expecting to find?" I asked, keeping my voice casual, but my heart racing in my chest.

He didn't respond right away, but I didn't need him to. I could see the answer written in the way he studied the papers, the way his jaw clenched when he found the particular one he was looking for. The silence in the warehouse was so thick that it almost had weight, like we were intruding on something sacred.

"Arsonists don't leave evidence," he muttered, his voice tight. "But sometimes they're careless."

I walked over, glancing at the crumpled paper in his hand. At first, it didn't make sense—the blackened edges, the small marks that looked like fingerprints scorched into the paper. Then it hit me. The same pattern. The same marks I had seen in the aftermath of the fires. It was the evidence we had been looking for, but not in any way we'd expected.

"Do you think it's them?" I asked, my voice small as I stepped closer.

Finn stood up, his eyes meeting mine with a fierce intensity I hadn't seen before. "It's them. And they knew exactly what they were doing."

The realization hit me like a slap in the face, the pieces falling into place with terrifying speed. The fires weren't just random acts of destruction. They were messages. The arsonist wasn't just trying to burn the city down—they were trying to send us a warning. A warning that we had all been too blind to see until now.

I wanted to say something, to ask the questions swirling in my mind, but I knew it wouldn't change anything. Finn had already made up his mind, and I was in this with him, whether I was ready or not.

"Let's find out who they are," I said, surprising myself with the resolve in my voice.

Finn nodded, the familiar spark of determination flickering in his eyes. He wasn't alone in this anymore. And neither was I. The flames were coming closer, and we were about to walk straight into them.

The night stretched on, and with it, so did the tension. The warehouse was still, save for the occasional creak of its old bones. My eyes flickered back and forth between Finn and the papers scattered around us like discarded thoughts. It was clear now—this wasn't just a case anymore. It was personal. The fire wasn't a random force of nature; it was a deliberate act, a message from someone who knew the ropes. A message that Finn was desperate to decode before it burned through everything.

The stale air seemed to grow heavier with each passing second, as if the warehouse itself was holding its breath. Finn was silent, too silent, as he sifted through the papers. I couldn't shake the feeling that we weren't just dealing with an arsonist anymore. We were facing a shadow—someone who had been watching, planning, manipulating everything around us. The longer I stood there, the more I felt like I was being drawn into a game I didn't understand, and I hated that I was starting to play along.

"Do you recognize any of this?" I asked, trying to steady my voice, though the words came out strained, like they had been stuck in my throat for far too long.

Finn didn't look up. "I've seen the patterns before. In the reports. In the places where things don't add up."

My heart skipped a beat. There it was. The cracks. The things that didn't quite fit, but were hidden beneath layers of official reports and half-truths. The arson had escalated far beyond random acts of madness; it was strategic. Someone was setting a path, marking a trail for us to follow—and Finn, stubborn as ever, was doing his best to follow it to the end, no matter how dangerous the journey.

"I thought you were done with this," I said quietly, stepping closer, unsure if I was challenging him or trying to ground myself in something real. "You said you were done. Why keep going?"

Finn's jaw tightened at the reminder. "Because I know who's doing it. And it's someone we trust."

The words settled over me like a cold wave. Someone we trusted. I had known the fires had been deliberate, but I hadn't been prepared for this—this feeling that someone in our inner circle had turned against us. The people we had worked with, laughed with, confided in. The people we had allowed to get close, too close.

"I don't know if I can do this," I murmured, the reality of what we were about to uncover sinking in. I wasn't sure I had the strength to keep walking down this path.

"You don't have a choice," Finn said, his voice low but firm. "None of us do."

I wanted to argue, to tell him that there was always a choice, but I couldn't bring myself to say it. Because he was right. We didn't have a choice anymore. Not with the city on fire, not with the weight of the truth pressing down on us, threatening to smother every ounce of hope we had left.

I turned back to the papers, my fingers skimming over the documents, each one revealing a layer of desperation. The ink smudged with sweat, the edges of the paper singed as though someone had tried to destroy the evidence. And then I saw it. The address. My breath caught in my throat as I leaned in, eyes scanning the lines again, confirming what I thought I had seen.

"Finn," I whispered, almost afraid to say it aloud. "This... this is the address. The one the fire started near. It's not a coincidence, is it?"

He finally looked up, his eyes meeting mine with the kind of intensity I couldn't look away from. "No. It's no coincidence. It's where it all started."

My pulse quickened, and for a split second, the room felt too small, the air too thick. The walls seemed to close in around me as the weight of the revelation hit. The fires weren't random. They were connected. They were leading us to something. To someone. And we were walking straight into it.

Finn's phone buzzed in his pocket, the sound slicing through the silence with the precision of a warning bell. He pulled it out quickly, his eyes scanning the message, his face shifting with the kind of expression I had learned to dread—one that said things were about to take a turn for the worse.

"It's happening," he said, his voice flat, as though the words had no power left in them. "They're moving now."

Before I could respond, Finn was already heading toward the door, his steps quick, purposeful. I didn't hesitate. I followed him, my heart racing in my chest, the adrenaline already flooding my veins. We were both running on instinct now, the clarity of our mission fading into something darker, something we hadn't anticipated.

We didn't speak as we navigated through the winding streets, each one darker than the last, each shadow threatening to swallow us whole. The city had changed. The once familiar streets had morphed into something unrecognizable, a labyrinth where danger lurked behind every corner.

By the time we arrived at the address, the cold night air seemed to thicken, the tension hanging so heavily between us that it felt almost unbearable. The building was nothing more than a dilapidated shell, windows boarded up, the paint peeling in long strips. It was the kind of place you would ignore if you didn't know what to look for. But we did.

We didn't have to speak the words. We knew what was waiting inside. Whatever we were walking into, it wasn't going to be easy. We were about to face the truth, and that truth might be more dangerous than the fires themselves.

Finn stepped forward, his hand hovering over the door. For a moment, he paused, looking back at me, his gaze intense, almost apologetic.

"Are you ready for this?" he asked, his voice low.

I nodded, though every part of me screamed to turn around, to walk away and leave the chaos behind. But I couldn't. Not now. Not after everything we'd been through.

We entered the building together, and the moment the door creaked shut behind us, I knew we had crossed a line we couldn't uncross.

And then I heard it.

A sound. Soft at first. A whisper, like a breath against the wind. But then it grew louder, the unmistakable sound of something—someone—moving in the shadows.

The door slammed shut behind us, and the darkness swallowed us whole.

Chapter 20: Heat of Betrayal

The moment I saw Finn collapse into the worn leather chair across from me, I knew. It wasn't the sinking weight in his eyes that gave it away, though it should have. Nor was it the way his hand clenched and unclenched by his side like a man trying to outrun his own thoughts. It was the sudden, bone-deep silence that hung between us like a storm cloud, pregnant with something I couldn't yet name. A quiet fury, maybe. A hurt too jagged to touch. I'd seen that look before—felt it, too, in the pit of my stomach—and it never boded well. Not for the world around us. Not for anything that came next.

"Do you want to talk about it?" I asked, though I already knew the answer. The air in the room felt thick, almost sticky, as if the heat of the summer outside had wormed its way into the walls, turning everything to slow motion. The kind of heat that sits like a weight on your chest, reminding you that nothing good ever happens in such unbearable stillness.

Finn didn't respond right away. His gaze was fixed on the window, eyes tracing the scattered raindrops that hit the glass in an uneven rhythm. They seemed to dance, spinning in slow arcs, until they collided with each other and splattered into oblivion. I could almost hear the tap of his mind doing the same thing—scrambling to understand how the hell it had all gone wrong. How the plan we'd been constructing, brick by painstaking brick, had suddenly crumbled beneath us.

"It's not just the betrayal," he muttered under his breath, as though the words were thickened by the weight of every unspoken thing. "It's the feeling of being watched. Followed. The knowledge that someone I trusted has been sitting on the inside, playing me like a fool."

I didn't know what to say to that. I had never been on the inside of a team like his—no, I was too much of an outsider to understand the brotherhood of it all. How one man's betrayal could send ripples through everything, warping relationships, unraveling loyalties. But I could feel the sting, the rawness of his emotion. I'd been hurt before, though nothing quite like this.

"You never saw it coming, did you?" I asked, my voice quiet but heavy with the empathy I wasn't sure how to show.

Finn let out a bitter laugh. It was humorless, a rasping sound that seemed to echo too loud in the small space. He wiped a hand across his face, eyes squeezed shut for a moment as if he could somehow erase the image of betrayal from his mind.

"No," he said finally, dragging a shaky breath in as he opened his eyes. "I thought... I thought I knew who had my back. I was wrong."

The words hit harder than I expected. And yet, there was something else in his eyes now—something sharper, like the tip of a blade that had been sharpened too long in the dark. Anger. Resentment. The beginnings of a plan.

It wasn't my place to ask, but I did anyway. "Who?"

"Maxwell." The name fell from his lips like poison. "I should've known. It was always him. Always so damn eager to impress, to climb higher. And now—now he's feeding lies to the press, making sure the world sees me as the villain. He's orchestrating the whole damn thing."

I could feel the world around me tilt. Maxwell? The name meant nothing to me, but the way Finn said it—the way the venom slipped off his tongue like a curse—was enough to make my stomach twist. Maxwell had been one of the few men Finn confided in. A colleague who had shared not just office hours but also dinners and drinks and moments of vulnerability, all the small, unseen things that bind men together. To be betrayed by him, it was like losing a limb.

"What now?" I asked, though I already knew that was the wrong question. I'd seen this kind of tension before. It wasn't about what came next—it was about how long Finn would let the rage simmer before it boiled over.

"Now? I'm going to find out what he's got on me. What he's using to twist the narrative. And when I do, I'm going to make sure he regrets it."

The words sent a chill down my spine. It wasn't just the intensity in his voice, or the ice in his eyes that made my pulse stutter. It was the way he said it. Like it wasn't a threat—no, it was a certainty. Finn wasn't just angry. He was about to go to war.

I swallowed the lump in my throat, but it didn't help. "Finn, this isn't just about clearing your name. You need to think about what this could cost you."

"I've already lost," he said flatly, his gaze now locking onto mine, raw and unguarded. "It's just a matter of making sure Maxwell loses more."

The words rang in the air like the strike of a bell, so clear, so final, that I almost felt the sting of the chime in my chest. What was it about betrayal that made even the kindest men want to break something? Maybe it was the weight of it—the sick, hollow feeling of knowing that someone you had trusted was willing to destroy you for their own gain. Maybe it was the way the world became so small when you were betrayed, everyone else shrinking into blurred shadows while you stood alone in the center, fighting for your life.

I couldn't help but wonder if I was becoming one of those shadows.

The silence stretched longer than it should have, thick and suffocating, like the kind of quiet that happens when something unspeakable has been said, and no one knows where to go from there. Finn's eyes were still distant, lost in a world where betrayal wasn't a sudden slap to the face, but a slow, persistent ache, gnawing at the edges of everything he thought he knew. I wanted to reach out, to pull him back into the warmth of the moment we had shared just days ago, but the space between us felt vast now—too wide to bridge with any amount of comforting words.

I shifted in my seat, trying to give him some space, but also to keep him tethered here, grounded in the present, where the weight of Maxwell's betrayal hadn't fully crushed him yet. "You don't have to do this alone," I said, the words coming out softer than I intended. "We can figure it out together. You don't have to go to war, Finn. Not yet. Not until you have all the pieces."

He turned to me then, eyes finally locking on mine with a force that made my breath hitch. The corner of his mouth twitched, almost like he was trying to smile, but the effort was as weak as a dying candle flame. "It's already too late for that, Grace. He's out there, spreading lies, making sure everyone believes I'm guilty before I even have a chance to prove otherwise. The damage is done."

I was about to argue—tell him there was still time, still a way out—but then his gaze softened, as if some unspoken understanding passed between us. He didn't need me to remind him of the battle he was facing; he was well aware of it. It was the way his jaw set, the way the tension in his shoulders finally seemed to melt, that made me realize he had already decided. This wasn't a situation he would navigate with half-measures or cautious steps. Finn wasn't the kind of man who took things lying down. Not anymore.

"You've always had my back, haven't you?" he asked, his voice low, a shadow of vulnerability slipping through. He wasn't asking out of pity. It was more like he needed to confirm the unspoken bond we'd forged in those long, hard hours spent in the trenches together.

"Of course," I said, though it felt like I was answering not just for now, but for everything that had led us to this point. I wasn't sure whether it was the loyalty or the sense of being caught up in something much larger than either of us that made my chest tighten. But as I looked at him, I knew the stakes had changed. What had once been a partnership of convenience—two people thrown together by circumstances—had morphed into something else. Something dangerous, complicated, and undeniable.

He leaned forward, resting his elbows on his knees, staring at the floor like it had all the answers. "You don't get it, do you?" His voice was thick with something—disappointment, perhaps, or the shadow of a fear he hadn't quite acknowledged yet. "The people I've trusted are the ones turning on me. It's not just Maxwell. It's everyone. All the faces I thought I could count on—they're all just playing their part, acting like it's business as usual, while they're doing everything they can to bring me down."

The words stung, but not in the way I expected. Instead of anger, I felt something else rise in me—something I hadn't realized was there until that very moment. Sympathy. A deep, gnawing sympathy for the man sitting across from me, his world crumbling in slow motion, and the helplessness he was trying to hide behind his steely resolve.

"Finn," I said, my voice tentative, careful, "it doesn't have to be this way. You don't have to face this alone. You've got more allies than you think. You have me."

For the first time since the storm had hit, his eyes softened, the harsh edges of his anger and betrayal melting away, just a little. I saw the flicker of gratitude in his eyes before it was smothered by the weight of everything else. But that moment—that brief, fragile connection—was enough. Enough to remind me that even in the midst of this turmoil, there was still something between us worth saving.

"I don't know if that's enough," he muttered, running a hand through his hair, frustration turning his features into something fierce. "I don't know if I can trust anyone anymore. And when it's over, when I've made sure Maxwell pays for what he's done, I'm not sure I'll ever be able to look at anyone the same way again."

I felt the cold bite of that statement in my chest, a chill that made it hard to breathe. I wanted to argue, to tell him it wasn't true, but I couldn't. Not when the depth of his pain was so evident. How could I promise him the world wouldn't change? That people wouldn't disappoint him? I couldn't. Not yet, anyway.

Instead, I did the only thing I could think of. I reached across the space between us and placed my hand over his, letting the warmth of my touch settle over the clenched fist he had resting in his lap. Finn looked up at me, surprise flickering across his face, as though he hadn't expected me to do it. And maybe he hadn't. I wasn't sure if I had expected it myself.

"I know it feels like the whole world is against you," I said softly. "But you're not alone in this. And I'm not going anywhere."

He didn't say anything for a long time. I could feel the weight of his silence, the weight of all the things unsaid, pressing down on us. And then, just as I was about to pull away, his fingers curled around mine, firm but gentle. He didn't need to say anything more. The gesture—silent, simple—spoke volumes. We didn't have all the answers. But we had each other. And maybe, for now, that was enough.

The evening wore on in a quiet haze, as if the world outside had stopped spinning and left us suspended in this moment of raw, unrelenting tension. Finn's hand had stayed firmly locked around mine, a silent acknowledgment of the storm still raging inside him, though his silence was like a deep ocean, impenetrable, endless. The rain that had been falling so relentlessly now seemed like the softest of whispers, as if even nature knew to hold its breath, waiting for what would come next.

"You're right," he said eventually, his voice a low murmur that barely cut through the quiet, "I can't let Maxwell get away with this. But I can't just go in and tear everything apart without a plan."

His words were measured, calm, but I could hear the controlled fury underneath. Finn wasn't the kind of man to lash out blindly. No, he was always calculating, precise—everything with him was a slow burn, but the kind that consumed everything in its path when it finally ignited. And yet, I could feel him teetering on the edge, like a man standing at the precipice, unsure whether to jump or retreat.

I squeezed his hand tighter, trying to ground him, but it felt as if I were the one clinging to him, not the other way around. "What are you thinking?"

"I need to get ahead of this. I can't let Maxwell control the narrative any longer. If I don't, it's over before it even starts." His eyes were fierce now, the fire rekindling in their depths. "I'll track down the leaks. Find out what he's telling them. Then, when I have the proof, I'll make sure the truth comes out."

I wasn't naive enough to think that finding the truth would make everything right. The damage had already been done, and the press didn't care about facts—just the stories that sold papers. Finn could clear his name, but some stains didn't wash out, no matter how hard you scrubbed. Still, the way he was looking at me, the determination in his gaze, made my heart ache. He wasn't ready to give up, not yet, not while there was any chance of fighting back.

"Do you have a plan to handle Maxwell?" I asked, my voice softer this time, hesitant, because I knew how dangerous it could be to push someone like Finn into a corner. When a man like him was backed into a place where he had nothing left to lose, he could become the most dangerous kind of creature.

His lips twitched at the corner, like he was fighting back a smile, but it didn't quite make it. "I don't know if you could call it a plan. But I know where to start." His fingers tapped nervously against the edge of the table, a habit I had come to recognize as a sign that he was thinking, his mind running through a thousand scenarios at once.

"I've got a friend—someone who owes me a favor." He hesitated, as if weighing whether or not to go further. "He's got eyes on Maxwell's movements. Everything he's doing, who he's meeting, where he's going. I just need to get the right information before it's too late."

"And when you have it?" I asked, my heart thudding a little faster as the weight of his words sank in.

"When I have it, I'm going to make sure Maxwell knows exactly who he's messing with."

The cool air of the evening had begun to creep into the room, chilling the space between us, but it wasn't the temperature that made me shiver. It was the edge to Finn's voice. It wasn't just vengeance. It was something darker, more unsettling. As if the man sitting in front of me was already preparing himself for the worst, ready to lose everything in order to get back what had been taken from him.

I wasn't sure if I was ready for him to cross that line. I didn't want to see him go down a path where there was no return. But what choice did we have? Maxwell had already made it clear there would be no peaceful resolution. No friendly handshake and a promise to never do it again. This was going to get ugly, and there was no way around it.

Finn stood abruptly, his chair scraping against the hardwood floor as he paced toward the window, his figure silhouetted against the faint glow of the streetlights outside. "I hate this," he muttered, almost to himself, running a hand through his hair. "I hate that it's come to this. That I have to fight like this, with no one to trust but myself."

"You're not alone," I said, my voice steady even though I felt anything but. "You've got me."

He turned to face me, the rawness in his eyes catching me off guard. For a moment, it felt like he might say something more, but the words seemed stuck, tangled in his throat. Instead, he gave a nod, slow and deliberate. "I don't want to drag you into this, Grace. I don't want you to see the side of me that's..." He trailed off, his gaze shifting away as though he couldn't quite finish the thought.

"Too late," I said, a dry laugh escaping before I could stop it. "I'm already here. You're not getting rid of me that easily."

Finn's lips twitched upward at that, a brief flash of humor that vanished just as quickly as it appeared. He took a deep breath, his shoulders rising and falling with the motion, as though gathering the strength to face whatever came next.

The silence that followed was thick, charged with everything we weren't saying, everything hanging between us, unspoken but impossible to ignore. I could feel it—could feel him retreating even as he moved closer, closing himself off in ways he never had before. There was a part of him, I knew, that wanted to shield me from the mess he was about to dive into. But the other part—the part that was wrapped up in all this, tangled up in the anger, the hurt, the betrayal—needed me there, whether I liked it or not.

"Grace," Finn said, his voice barely more than a whisper, but there was something in it that made my blood run cold. "There's something I need to show you. Something you need to see before it's too late."

I took a step toward him, confusion tightening in my chest, but before I could speak, the sound of a sharp knock on the door cut through the stillness. We both froze.

I felt my heart leap into my throat. Finn's eyes narrowed, suspicion creeping into his expression. For a moment, neither of us moved.

Then the door creaked open.

Chapter 21: The Unseen Danger

The air smelled like charred metal and something sickly sweet, like burning sugar, as we approached the fire. It was already well past midnight, the moon low and sharp in the sky, its glow casting long shadows over the sprawling woods that lined the outskirts of town. The only light, besides the moon, was the dancing orange of the flames licking at the heavens, hungry and voracious. My boots crunched on the dry leaves as we made our way forward, the scent of smoke filling my lungs. I could feel the heat through the fabric of my jacket, though the cool night air fought to steady my pulse. Finn walked beside me, his eyes scanning the darkness, every nerve stretched tight, like he was waiting for something to jump out of the trees and tear us apart.

The fire wasn't just any fire—it was methodical. No wild spread here. Whoever had set it, knew exactly what they were doing. They'd chosen a location that was both isolated and close enough to draw us in. Like a predator laying its trap. And I could almost hear them—laughing, watching us stumble right into the snare. I tightened my grip on the fire extinguisher, though I knew the best we could do was keep it from spreading. We had no chance of putting it out without proper equipment, but that was never the point. The point was to keep us occupied, distracted, while they prepared for something worse.

Finn was already talking, his voice tight with controlled urgency. "Stay sharp. Watch your six. We don't know if this is the end of it or just a warm-up." His words were like a rope, pulling me back from the edge, but they also made my stomach churn. His protective nature had always been something I appreciated, but tonight, it felt like a tether holding me back, when all I wanted was to charge forward, find the person responsible, and make them regret ever starting this game.

I nodded, though my gaze never strayed from the fire. I could feel it—something was off. The crackling of the blaze should've been louder, more chaotic, but there was something strangely subdued about it. The flames weren't frantic; they were controlled, deliberate, like a work of art. I frowned, instinctively taking a step back, pulling Finn closer to me. "This isn't just a fire. It's a message."

Finn's eyes flickered to mine, a silent acknowledgment that we both felt it. "But what's the message?" he muttered, more to himself than to me, his gaze never leaving the shadows that seemed to stretch on forever. His hand rested on the small of my back, grounding me, but I could feel his muscles coiled tight with tension, waiting for something to move in the dark.

"That's the part I don't like," I said quietly. "They know we're going to respond to these fires. They're luring us out." My mind raced, trying to piece together the pattern. We'd been chasing these fires for weeks now, each one more targeted, more specific. But this? This felt different. Personal. Someone was watching, studying, learning our every move. And they were getting closer.

Finn exhaled sharply, his voice lowering to a murmur. "It's not just about the fires anymore, is it?"

I shook my head slowly. "No. This is something else. They're testing us." My words were punctuated by the sound of a distant crash, the unmistakable rattle of metal colliding with the ground. We both froze, our instincts kicking in as we scanned the area. Finn's hand was on the holster at his side, though I knew it wasn't a gun he was thinking about. We were firefighters, not soldiers, but that didn't mean we couldn't handle ourselves if the need arose.

Before I could open my mouth to suggest we move toward the source of the noise, the ground beneath us gave a violent shake. A split second later, a piece of burning debris shot toward us like a missile, trailing flames as it spun through the air. My heart jumped into my throat as Finn yanked me backwards, his arms like iron bands, pulling me out of harm's way. The debris whizzed past, missing us by mere inches, and crashed into the ground with a deafening thud, scattering embers in every direction.

I stumbled as I regained my balance, my heart racing. Finn's grip didn't loosen, his voice harsh as he muttered under his breath. "That was too close. Too damn close."

I nodded, chest heaving. "We're not dealing with an amateur anymore."

A cold chill crawled up my spine as I realized the full extent of what we were facing. Whoever was behind this had no intention of just scaring us. They were playing a deadly game, one where the stakes were higher than we could've imagined. The fire had been a distraction, a way to get us here. But now, I understood—they didn't just want to burn things down. They wanted to destroy us, piece by piece.

Finn's hand tightened around mine, and I could feel the pulse of his steady heartbeat against my skin. He was scared too, but he wasn't going to show it. He would never show it. "We need to get back to town," he said, voice tight but controlled. "This isn't over."

I nodded, not trusting myself to speak. The fire was no longer our biggest threat. The unseen danger—the one lurking in the shadows, waiting for the perfect moment—was. And the realization hit me hard, like a punch to the gut. Whoever was out there, was ready to take things to the next level. And it wasn't just about burning things down. It was about taking everything—everything I loved—and turning it to ash.

The drive back to town was a silent one. The hum of the engine was almost deafening in its emptiness, the dark road ahead stretching on endlessly, punctuated only by the occasional flicker of the headlights cutting through the shadows. Finn's fingers gripped the wheel tightly, his jaw clenched in that way I knew all too well—the way he got when he was thinking, processing, and doing his damned best not to let it show. His silence, though, said everything. The kind of silence that never bodes well for anyone involved.

I leaned my head against the cool glass of the window, staring out at the passing trees, their branches twisting in the wind like something trying to claw its way out of the earth. It was a peaceful sight, at first glance, until you remembered that in the quiet of the forest, something was hunting us. Watching. Waiting. And I couldn't shake the feeling that this wasn't just some random act of vengeance or rebellion. It was too precise. Too planned.

"You think it's just about the fires?" I asked, breaking the stillness between us, though my voice felt too loud in the silence. It wasn't a question that needed an answer, not really. But I needed to say it out loud. To let the words hang in the air, heavy with the unspoken truth. We both knew it. The arsonist, whoever they were, wasn't after a message alone. They wanted something more. They were playing us, testing us. And they were winning.

Finn's grip tightened on the wheel. "It's more than that, but I can't figure out the why." His words were clipped, controlled. "It's like they know everything. Every move we make."

I didn't have an answer, either. If I did, I would've blurted it out right then and there. I wanted to believe that this was just some twisted game—an unhinged mind out for a thrill—but it was too methodical for that. Whoever was doing this was watching us, waiting for the perfect opportunity to strike. And now, it felt personal. Too personal.

I shifted in my seat, glancing at him sideways. His face, bathed in the faint glow of the dashboard lights, was a study in focus, eyes darting between the road and the rearview mirror, as if he expected something—or someone—to appear from the dark. He was trying to keep it together, but the strain was starting to show. I could see it in the way his shoulders were hunched, the way his brow furrowed in a permanent scowl. Finn wasn't one to show fear, not when it counted, but the edges of his calm were beginning to fray.

"You ever get the feeling," I began, my voice quieter now, "that we're not just running toward the danger? That maybe... maybe we're running away from something worse?"

His eyes flickered to mine for a moment, but he didn't answer. He didn't need to. The look he gave me was enough—a mix of concern and uncertainty that was far too real to ignore. The truth was, neither of us knew what we were dealing with anymore.

I ran my fingers over the seatbelt across my chest, fidgeting with the metal clasp. "Maybe this isn't just about us, Finn. Maybe we're just pawns in a game we don't understand yet."

Finn let out a short laugh, but it was hollow, a sound that held no joy. "I don't like that idea."

"I don't like it either," I admitted, glancing out the window again. The moon, now fully visible, hung in the sky like a cold, indifferent witness to everything unfolding. The night was too quiet, too still, as if the world was holding its breath.

We arrived back at the station shortly after, the familiar sight of the fire trucks and the old brick building looming in the dark. The place should have been a sanctuary, a haven where we could regroup and plot our next move, but tonight, it felt like a trap—like stepping back into a cage, the bars closing around us, tighter with each passing hour.

As soon as I stepped out of the truck, I felt it—the weight of something pressing down on me. I wasn't sure if it was the fire still smoldering in my lungs or the unease crawling up my spine, but something about the air felt wrong.

"Finn..." I started, but I didn't finish the sentence. He was already walking ahead, his long strides carrying him toward the entrance without a word, as if he hadn't heard me at all.

I followed him, the sound of my boots echoing on the pavement as I tried to shake off the feeling of being watched. Every shadow seemed to flicker with life, every creak of the old building felt like a whisper in the dark. We entered the station, the door creaking as we stepped inside, and immediately, the lights flickered.

Great. Of course.

The silence was thick inside, the kind of silence that made the hairs on the back of my neck stand up. I could feel the weight of the night pressing against the walls, the air in here just as charged as it had been outside. But it wasn't the fire or the arsonist that unsettled me now. It was the sudden, chilling realization that something else was happening—something even more dangerous than the flames.

Finn had already disappeared down the hallway, heading toward the office where we kept our reports, our maps, and all the evidence of the fires we had been chasing. I didn't follow. Instead, I lingered by the door, watching the shadows twist and stretch, a faint, almost imperceptible hum filling the air. I stood there, holding my breath, trying to listen for anything out of place.

And that's when I heard it—a soft scrape against the floor, too quiet to be anything but deliberate. I wasn't imagining it. Someone else was here, and they were waiting for us to make the first move.

The scrape echoed again, louder this time, a deliberate drag of something heavy across the floor. My heartbeat stuttered as I froze, eyes darting across the room, but there was nothing—nothing except the oppressive silence pressing against the walls. The faint light from the hallway barely penetrated the darkness, casting long, creeping shadows across the station. I stepped back slowly, careful to make no sound. I knew what I was hearing. It wasn't just a rat or the creaking of old pipes. This was something else.

I turned toward the hallway where Finn had gone, but I couldn't bring myself to move any closer to that stillness. The sense of being watched had returned, stronger now, like fingers brushing against my neck. My breath caught in my throat as I fought the instinct to bolt, but I couldn't shake the feeling that if I turned around too fast, I would find someone right behind me.

The scrape came again, followed by a soft, almost imperceptible click. My mind raced, and a cold chill ran down my spine. Whoever was here was careful, too careful. Whoever it was, they weren't afraid of us. If anything, they seemed to be enjoying the game, savoring the tension, letting it stretch out between us like an elastic band waiting to snap.

I should have gone after Finn. I should have made sure he was okay, but I couldn't move. My legs felt heavy, like they were encased in concrete. The sound of my own breath was deafening in the silence, each exhale a slow, deliberate escape of air.

Suddenly, a light flickered in the far corner of the room. A dull glow from one of the old lamps, the kind that seemed to work only when they felt like it. I hadn't noticed it before. It blinked once, twice, and then stabilized, casting a sickly yellow light across the floor. And then—there it was again—the scrape. Closer this time. It was unmistakable.

I took a slow, cautious step toward the noise, my mind racing with the possibility of what I might find. A figure. Someone watching. Or worse, someone waiting. The scrape stopped. The room was still, eerily still. I hesitated, fighting the urge to call out, to break the silence. But what if that was exactly what they wanted? To hear me speak. To draw me into their trap. I wasn't stupid. I had been doing this long enough to know that people didn't play by the rules when they were this far gone.

I pressed my back against the nearest wall, feeling the rough surface dig into my skin. My pulse was a constant thrum in my ears now, every beat a reminder that I wasn't alone. And just when I thought I couldn't take the quiet any longer, the scrape came again, right behind me this time, close enough that I could almost feel it on my skin.

Before I could react, the floor beneath me groaned in protest, and the lights flickered once more, plunging us into darkness. Panic rose in my chest, but I swallowed it down, forcing myself to stay calm. I wasn't alone. Finn was still out there. He had to be.

I turned on my heel, determined to find him, but I didn't get far. A cold hand closed over my wrist, and I gasped, heart leaping into my throat. I wrenched myself free, spinning to face the attacker, but the room was empty. The cold lingered on my skin, the ghost of a touch that shouldn't have been there.

"Finn?" I whispered, my voice barely audible, but the sound of my own name seemed to hang in the air longer than it should have. I waited, breath held, straining to hear any sound. Any movement. But there was nothing.

The panic was rising again, clawing at my chest, but I pushed it down. I couldn't afford to lose control. Not now.

A light flickered again, this time brighter, illuminating the hallway. A shadow moved, just out of my line of sight, and I felt my breath catch in my throat. Whoever was in the building wasn't trying to hide. They were toying with me, like a cat batting at a mouse, slow and deliberate.

I stepped forward, my mind set on finding Finn, but as I did, I heard a noise—footsteps, soft and measured, coming from behind me. A figure stepped out from the shadows, and I froze. The person wasn't tall, but their presence was unmistakable, like a dark hole in the world. Their face was partially obscured, a hood drawn low, but the gleam of their eyes caught the dim light, cold and calculating.

"Looking for someone?" the voice was low, almost mocking, and it sent a shiver straight down my spine.

I didn't answer. Instead, I took a step back, hand reaching instinctively for the fire extinguisher at my side, but the figure raised a hand, a swift motion that stopped me cold. "I wouldn't. You might want to save your strength."

I swallowed hard, trying to keep my voice steady. "Who are you?"

The figure laughed softly, a sound that sent another chill running through me. "You don't know, do you? I guess you'll find out soon enough." They tilted their head, like they were studying me, weighing me like I was some kind of prize. "But first, let's see if you can find your friend."

I didn't need to be told twice. I spun on my heel and sprinted down the hallway, every step echoing in the silence. But as I turned the corner, I skidded to a halt.

Finn was standing there, eyes wide, his face pale. His jaw was set in that way he had when he was trying to hide his fear, but I could see it. Something was wrong. And I was sure that the worst was still to come.

Before I could ask him what was happening, the lights flickered again—and then went out completely, plunging us both into total darkness.

And I heard it—the sound of something else moving. Something not human.

Chapter 22: The Past Unearthed

I didn't realize I was holding my breath until the first phone call ended. My fingers drummed against the cool, worn surface of the desk, the hum of the city barely audible through the thick windowpane. The sunlight streaming in from the cracked blinds seemed too gentle, too innocent for the mess I was diving into. But the truth wasn't going to reveal itself gently, not after all these years.

The voice on the other end, a woman who'd worked with Finn years ago, had been reluctant at first, hesitant to dredge up old wounds. But after a few gentle prods and some promises of discretion, she'd told me what I needed to know: the fire. It wasn't just a tragedy; it was an inferno that had consumed everything. The way she spoke about it—quietly, as if the words themselves were fragile and could break apart under the weight of memory—was enough to make my heart tighten in my chest. Finn had been there, she said, not as a victim, but as someone who could've stopped it, if only he'd made different choices.

I set the receiver down, the weight of the revelation sinking deep into my bones. I hadn't been prepared for this. I wasn't prepared for Finn to be the type of person who could carry that kind of guilt around, burying it under layers of charm and wit, as if he could just shrug off the weight of it all. But it was there, lurking beneath the surface, and now it was mine to carry, too.

The next call was to his sister, who was far less reticent. Her voice was clipped, the edges sharp like broken glass. She didn't like talking about Finn's past, but she didn't mince words. "He blames himself," she said, a bluntness in her tone that made my stomach twist. "For everything. The fire, the people who didn't make it out, the fact that he wasn't the one to save them. He'll never forgive himself for that." Her words hung in the air, and I could almost feel them tightening around my chest. But she wasn't done. "You want to know why he's so distant now? Why he hides behind that mask of indifference? It's because he thinks he's worthless. Because in his mind, if he hadn't been there that night, maybe things would've turned out differently."

I stared at the phone in my hand, unsure of what to do with the information, the pain she'd just handed me. Was I supposed to comfort him, to make sense of it all, or was I doomed to be a witness to his unraveling?

I had a sinking feeling that whatever it was, it wasn't going to be easy. And it wasn't just the past that haunted him. No, there was something far darker creeping into the present—a person, a shadow from his history, who had somehow found a way to tie his past to our present.

The fire had been bad enough. But if Finn was right, if the arsonist who had been tormenting us knew about this... then it meant we were dealing with something far more dangerous than a simple revenge plot. It meant we were dealing with someone who had been watching, waiting for the perfect moment to strike. Someone who understood Finn in ways no one else could.

I couldn't ignore the feeling that settled deep in my gut. The past wasn't just lurking at the edges of Finn's life—it was closing in, wrapping itself around us like a vise. I had to find out who was behind this. I had to understand why they were targeting Finn now, why they seemed so intent on making him suffer.

That night, when Finn walked into the apartment, his usual smirk was absent. His eyes were shadowed, a little too tired, a little too strained, and for a moment, I wondered if he could see it in me—how much I knew, how much I'd uncovered. But if he did, he didn't say anything. Instead, he tossed his coat onto the back of a chair, running a hand through his hair with a quiet sigh.

"Busy day?" I asked, my voice too light, too casual for what was unfolding in my head. He looked at me with those intense, searching eyes, and for a second, I wondered if he could read me better than I thought.

"Yeah, something like that," he replied, his voice guarded, yet not entirely defensive.

I couldn't just blurt out everything. I had to tread carefully. I needed more time to piece things together, to understand the full extent of what had happened all those years ago, and why it mattered now.

He paused, looking over at me, his expression unreadable. "You look like you're thinking about something," he said, his tone soft, almost too soft for the usual Finn. He moved closer, and I could feel the heat of his presence, like a force that tried to draw me in. "What's on your mind?"

I opened my mouth to say something, anything, but the words stuck. The truth wasn't something you could just throw out there in casual conversation. And I wasn't sure I was ready to see what would happen when I did. Instead, I gave him a small smile, one that I hoped was convincing enough to let him think everything was fine, at least for the moment.

"Nothing," I said. "Just... thinking about dinner."

But it wasn't dinner that filled the space between us. It was the fire, the grief, and the tangled web of lies that had already begun to suffocate the life we were trying to build. And I wasn't sure if there was any way out of it now.

I spent hours combing through old records, making calls to people who hadn't heard from Finn in years, each conversation bringing me closer to a revelation I wasn't sure I was ready for. The fire. It wasn't just some tragic accident; it was a betrayal, a cruel twist of fate. I couldn't understand how anyone could live through that, let alone carry the weight of guilt Finn seemed to bear. Each new detail uncovered only deepened the mystery of what had truly happened that night.

The fire had been set in a small, rundown building on the edge of town, a place Finn had once frequented. I'd spoken to his sister, Emily, whose voice had faltered when I mentioned it. "Finn won't talk about it," she'd said, her words clipped with an edge of concern. "He was the one who found them, you know. The bodies. I don't think he ever got over it." Her words echoed in my mind, a faint warning bell ringing in my ears. Someone had been close to him—close enough to make sure he was the one who would have to live with the aftermath.

But what truly sent a shiver down my spine was when I spoke to one of Finn's old colleagues, a man named Rick who had been there that night. "You don't know the whole story," he said, his voice low and tight. "Finn didn't just lose someone that night. He lost everything."

Everything. What did that mean? I could feel a dark pit opening up inside me, as though the world itself was suddenly tilting on its axis. Finn had always been so guarded, so careful with the details of his past. But now I understood why. The weight of whatever had happened that night was something I could only begin to comprehend.

I pressed Rick further, my curiosity pushing me past any hesitation I had left. "Tell me. Please," I urged. "What exactly happened?"

Rick sighed, the sound so heavy I almost expected it to come through the phone. "It wasn't just an accident," he said finally. "It was deliberate. And Finn... Finn thought he was the one who'd started it." The words hit me like a slap to the face, but they made too much sense. The guilt. The distance. The self-imposed isolation.

"Why does he think that?" I managed, my heart pounding in my chest.

There was a long pause before Rick answered, his voice dropping to a near whisper. "He was there, you know. Right in the middle of it. He had the matches."

The revelation hit me like a ton of bricks. Finn had been the one with the matches? But why? Why would he do something so reckless, so inexplicable? There had to be more to this story, more than guilt and blame. But the truth was elusive, slipping through my fingers like water. I couldn't let go. Not now. Not when I was so close.

I wasn't sure how much time had passed when I finally found myself standing outside Finn's apartment, staring up at the darkened windows. I had to see him. I needed to hear it from him—straight from his lips. But as I reached for my phone to text him, the screen flashed with an alert: an anonymous message. My heart skipped a beat as I opened it.

"The truth is buried in the ashes. You don't know what he's capable of."

I stared at the words, a sickening chill spreading through me. Who was sending these messages? How did they know about Finn's past? I felt a sudden urgency, a need to act before things spiraled out of control. I was already in too deep, but the thought of walking away now—of leaving Finn to face whatever demons he was hiding—was unbearable. There was something sinister at work, something that wanted to expose him for the world to see, to rip open the wound he had buried so deeply.

I didn't know what to do. Part of me wanted to confront him, to demand answers. But another part of me feared what the truth might mean. What if it wasn't just the past that was haunting him? What if the fire wasn't the only thing he had to answer for?

I took a deep breath and rang his doorbell, my finger hovering over the button for what felt like an eternity. When the door swung open, I barely recognized the man standing before me. Finn's face was drawn, his eyes haunted, as though the weight of every secret he carried had finally caught up with him.

"I know," I said, the words tumbling out before I could stop them. "I know about the fire."

For a moment, he didn't say anything. He just stared at me, as though trying to decide whether to slam the door in my face or pull me inside. Finally, he spoke, his voice barely a whisper.

"I never wanted you to know."

But it was too late for that. We were already on the edge, standing on the precipice of something I didn't fully understand but was desperate to uncover. And then, just as I was about to press him for more, something shifted in his gaze—something dark and uncertain.

"I didn't start it," he said suddenly, his eyes flashing with a mixture of pain and anger. "But I might have been the one who finished it."

The words hung in the air between us, each one carrying the weight of a thousand unspoken truths. Before I could respond, a loud crash echoed from inside his apartment, followed by the sound of footsteps. Someone was in there—someone else.

And in that moment, I realized just how little I knew about the man standing before me.

Chapter 23: A Dangerous Plan

I'd never been one for grand plans. I'd learned early in life that careful, quiet observation often yielded better results than charging in like a bull in a china shop. But in that moment, as Finn and I huddled together, the faint scent of smoke still lingering in my hair from the last fire, I realized that my usual method wasn't going to cut it. The arsonist we were chasing was too clever, too elusive. We needed to think outside the box, even if that meant stepping into dangerous territory.

The room smelled faintly of coffee and something sharper, like burnt toast. Finn stood by the window, his eyes scanning the street below, arms folded tightly across his chest. He always had that stance when he was deep in thought—tense, closed off, as though his mind were a fortress and he had the keys to every locked door within it.

"You're sure about this?" I asked, trying to keep my voice steady, even though the nerves were bubbling under my skin like a pot about to boil over.

"Sure as I am about anything in this mess," he said, turning to face me with a smirk that didn't quite reach his eyes. "It's the only way. We have to make the arsonist believe we're an easy target."

His eyes—usually so soft and warm—were hard now, sharp. I couldn't quite get a read on him, which only made me more anxious. Finn had been through more than most people in a lifetime, and yet I still found myself questioning if I knew him well enough to trust him with this. The stakes had escalated so quickly. What had started as a simple investigation had morphed into something dark, something far more dangerous. The fires weren't just random; they were personal, deliberate.

I felt the weight of that responsibility settle over me like a heavy coat. It was on both of us now. He wouldn't say it, but I could see it in the line of his shoulders, in the way he clenched his jaw, as though everything rested on this one decision.

"You'll be okay," I said, though my words felt hollow, even to me.

Finn raised an eyebrow, and the faintest hint of a smile tugged at the corner of his mouth. "You're not so convincing when you try to be reassuring."

I half-laughed, half-sighed, glancing down at my hands. "It's just... I can't help but think there's something we're missing. It's too neat. Too calculated." I couldn't shake the feeling that this arsonist was watching us, studying us, just as we were doing to him. We were pieces on a chessboard, and neither of us knew if we were the pawn or the queen.

He stepped closer, his presence warm and solid beside me. "I know. But we don't have time to overthink this. If we want to catch them, we need to make a move. Take a risk."

I swallowed, trying to shake off the unease that clung to me like a shadow. "And if it's too much of a risk?"

Finn didn't answer at first, his eyes scanning my face as if weighing his words. "Then I'll be careful. But we have to make it look real. Like I'm vulnerable."

"I hate that I'm agreeing to this." My voice was quiet, but there was an edge of determination beneath it. The kind that came when you had no other choice.

He let out a slow breath, the tension in his posture easing just a fraction. "I don't like it either, but it's the only way. You've got to trust me on this."

It wasn't trust that was the problem. I trusted him with my life—always had. But in this game, trust felt like a flimsy thing. Like a breath in the wind that could disappear without a trace.

We had a plan, but even the best-laid plans were like fragile glass. One wrong move, and everything could shatter.

It felt as though we had been preparing for this moment for days, weeks even, but I knew deep down that the real challenge was just beginning. The fake fire drill, the rumors spread by a select few who could be trusted to keep their mouths shut, would only serve as bait. A calculated risk. We were essentially feeding the arsonist the very information he wanted—Finn acting alone, vulnerable, an easy target. And once the fire was set, we'd be waiting.

It wasn't just about catching him anymore. It was about stopping something far worse. Every fire had left behind more than just destruction; it had left fear. Fear that a killer was walking among us, a predator with a burning hunger for chaos. And it wasn't just the flames that threatened to consume us—it was the knowledge that we were dealing with someone who had no boundaries.

Finn moved to the door, pausing to glance back at me. "Stay safe, okay?"

I nodded, though my heart was already miles ahead of me, tangled in the web of this plan. "I'll be here when it's over."

The sound of the door clicking shut behind him was the last thing I heard before the silence filled the room, pressing down on me with the weight of everything we were about to face. I couldn't let myself be distracted. Not now.

I stood there for a moment, fighting the urge to pace, to run after him, to call it all off. But I knew I couldn't. Not if I wanted to stop this madness. Finn and I were in this together, even if the world was on the edge of falling apart.

The air outside was heavy with the promise of rain, thick with the scent of damp earth and the faintest trace of smoke. The sky had that gray, bruised look to it, as though it were holding its breath, waiting for something to happen. I felt it too—the weight of the unknown pressing in on all sides.

And then, as if the world had decided it had waited long enough, the storm broke.

The storm arrived as if on cue, its first crack of thunder slicing through the night like a blade. I stood by the window, watching the rain hit the pavement in sheets, each drop a tiny flash of lightning before it disappeared into the ground. The world outside felt too calm, too still for what was happening just a few blocks away. I told myself Finn was fine. He had to be. But even the logical part of my brain—the part that knew everything had been carefully planned—couldn't stop the adrenaline from kicking in.

I hadn't expected the waiting to be so excruciating. I paced back and forth in the cramped room, the sound of my shoes on the hardwood a steady reminder that time was slipping through my fingers. Every few minutes, I glanced out the window again, hoping to catch sight of Finn, or at least some sign that the plan was unfolding as we had hoped. But the street was empty. It always was when the storm hit.

I caught myself pulling at the hem of my shirt, a nervous habit I hadn't noticed until now. The tension was almost unbearable, my stomach tied in knots. I hadn't realized just how much I depended on the quiet moments of our partnership—the way we worked together, how we'd gotten to know each other's instincts so well. The space between us had always been comfortable, natural. But now? It felt too wide. Too empty.

A crash of thunder jolted me from my thoughts, and I snapped my gaze toward the door. The sound was different, though. Not the typical rumble of thunder, but something... closer. My heart skipped a beat. I reached for my phone, only to find it vibrating in my hand. Finn.

I answered without hesitation, my breath already catching in my chest. "Finn?"

"Just checking in," his voice was quiet, but there was an edge to it that sent a cold shiver down my spine. "Everything good on your end?"

I exhaled, realizing I'd been holding my breath. "Yeah. All quiet here. What about you?"

There was a long pause, so long that I felt the unease begin to knot in my chest again. "I'm... I'm not sure. Something doesn't feel right."

My pulse quickened. "What's going on?"

Another pause. Then, "I think they know I'm here. I'm going to have to move soon."

"Finn, no. Don't—"

But he was already gone, the line cutting off sharply.

My feet moved before my brain could catch up, my hand reaching for my jacket and the door already swinging open before I could think to stop myself. I wasn't sure what I intended to do—run after him, shout at him to come back—but I knew the moment I stepped into the hallway, it was too late.

The air in the building felt thick, as though it was holding its breath. I could hear my heartbeat echoing in my ears, louder than any of the usual background sounds. The halls stretched before me like a maze, the low hum of fluorescent lights above doing nothing to calm my nerves. The ground floor was silent, but I couldn't shake the feeling that someone was watching me. Every shadow seemed to flicker and shift, every corner holding something I couldn't see.

I made it to the stairs just as the front door swung open.

"Hey!" The voice was low, too calm. Too controlled.

I froze, my heart leaping into my throat. I knew that voice.

"Looking for someone?" The man stepped into view, his silhouette framed by the light from the streetlamps outside. The hood pulled low over his face did little to conceal his identity.

The arsonist.

I should've run. I knew that. Every instinct screamed for me to turn around and bolt, but my feet felt rooted to the floor, as though the fear had taken over completely. He took a step toward me, and then another, his movements smooth, calculated. Like he knew exactly how this would end.

"You really thought I'd fall for that trick?" he asked, his voice dripping with mockery.

"I didn't think you'd fall for it," I replied, forcing the words out, my voice steadier than I felt. "I thought you'd think it was too obvious."

He chuckled, low and rich, as if he were indulging a child. "You're far too clever for your own good. But cleverness won't save you now, sweetheart."

I swallowed, trying to stay calm, to think past the panic that was beginning to bubble up. "You don't know where he is, do you?"

For a moment, the arsonist's eyes flashed with something—something cold and deadly. But then he shrugged. "I don't need to. He's walking right into my trap."

My stomach twisted into a knot so tight I could hardly breathe. It was too late. Finn hadn't realized that the trap had already been set, that every step he'd taken had been planned in advance.

"You're not going to stop him," I said, my voice a whisper now. "You'll have to kill me first."

His lips twisted into a smile, but it wasn't a smile at all. It was a grimace, something far more dangerous than any grin could be. He took another step forward, but I wasn't about to let him get closer. I darted toward the nearest exit, my legs moving faster than my brain could process, the sound of my own feet pounding against the floor almost drowned out by the thudding of my heart in my chest.

I wasn't sure what I was hoping for, but I knew one thing for certain: I was running out of time.

The sound of my own footsteps echoed down the dimly lit hallway, a steady rhythm I tried to synchronize with my thudding heart. The adrenaline that had been coursing through my veins only moments before now felt like a roaring tide, washing away any sense of clarity. The arsonist's mocking words—his confident stride—still lingered in my ears, but they did nothing to comfort me. His trap was closing, and Finn was walking right into it.

I reached the building's back entrance and didn't hesitate. The door groaned in protest as I pushed it open, the scent of wet asphalt and rain-soaked earth filling my lungs. Outside, the storm was a torrent, the rain lashing against the ground as if trying to drown out the world. I could barely see through the sheets of water, but I wasn't waiting for clarity. I needed to find Finn before it was too late.

The streets were practically empty, save for the occasional flash of headlights slicing through the night like a warning. But the silence—god, the silence—was suffocating. Every shadow seemed to hide something darker, something waiting to pounce. I kept moving, my shoes slapping against the slick pavement, praying that I was going the right way.

I didn't know what had made me think that I could pull this off. The more I thought about it, the more ridiculous it seemed. Pretending to be an easy target? Letting Finn take the risk on his own? It was insanity. I should've been there, should've been with him. But now, as I sprinted down the street, it was clear I had no choice but to trust him. To believe that he could handle himself, even when the odds were stacked against him.

A sharp, sudden noise behind me—like the sound of a heavy footstep crushing glass—shattered my thoughts. I spun around, every muscle in my body tense, every instinct screaming that I wasn't alone. But the street remained empty.

My breath was coming in shallow bursts now, my legs burning from the strain of running, and my mind racing faster than my feet. I couldn't shake the sense that I was being watched, that someone was lurking just beyond my reach, waiting for the perfect moment to strike. The night was alive with danger, and I was too far out of my depth to pretend otherwise.

Then, I saw it.

A flash of movement at the far end of the street, a silhouette too deliberate, too calculated.

I froze, my gaze locking onto the figure as it stepped into the light.

Finn.

I couldn't believe it. My heart leapt in my chest, and for a moment, all the fear that had been gnawing at me disappeared, replaced by a surge of relief so strong it almost knocked me off balance.

But then the figure moved again. Not Finn.

It was the arsonist.

My stomach dropped. I knew that walk. The same confident swagger, the same deliberate pace. And in that instant, I realized the horrible truth: he was leading me away from Finn.

I ran toward him, ignoring the scream of caution in my head, ignoring the sting of rain as it whipped against my skin. If I had any hope of stopping this madness, I had to stay one step ahead. I had to—

A hand closed around my wrist, pulling me into the alley before I even had time to react.

"Not so fast, sweetheart." The voice was low, smooth, and entirely too familiar.

The arsonist.

I twisted in his grip, but his fingers tightened, like iron wrapped around my skin. "What do you want?" I managed to rasp, my throat tight with fear.

He smiled, though there was no humor in it. "I want to make sure you're paying attention. Your little plan was clever, but not clever enough."

"You—" I started, but the words faltered as he shoved me harder against the brick wall of the building, the cold stone biting through my clothes.

"I thought I'd give you a front-row seat to the real show," he said, his lips curling into a slow grin. "After all, you've been such a good little distraction."

Before I could respond, he released me, stepping back to admire his work as though we were sharing some sort of twisted performance.

My breath came fast and shallow, every nerve in my body screaming at me to do something—anything—but I couldn't move, couldn't think past the terrifying realization that he had outmaneuvered us. I had walked right into his trap.

"What—what do you mean?" I demanded, though the question tasted like ash in my mouth.

The arsonist gave a short laugh, dark and knowing. "Oh, don't play coy with me, darling. You thought I didn't know about your little fire drill? Thought I wouldn't be aware of your dear friend, your brave hero?" His eyes darkened, and the sharp edge to his smile twisted even further. "No. I've been one step ahead from the start. And now... now you get to watch as it all burns."

A sound, soft at first but growing, echoed in the distance.

My pulse quickened.

A fire alarm.

I glanced at the arsonist, suddenly understanding the malicious intent behind his words. He hadn't just been setting fires. He'd been setting a stage. The alarm was a signal, a countdown.

I couldn't feel my legs, couldn't breathe through the suffocating weight of the dread crashing over me.

"No!" I gasped, the word breaking free as I pushed myself off the wall, only to find that my limbs were betraying me.

"You really think you can stop me?" The arsonist was closer now, his presence towering. "You've already lost."

Before I could form another thought, a sudden burst of light filled the alley, and the world went white.

The blast hit with the force of a freight train, throwing me back against the wall like a ragdoll. The sound was deafening, the heat searing even as I slammed into the ground, and then... darkness.

Chapter 24: Confrontation in the Flames

The smoke thickened, swirling like a living thing, each breath a jagged, bitter bite in my lungs. The heat pressed down from all sides, a suffocating presence that clung to the skin, making everything feel too close, too urgent. Finn's silhouette was just ahead of me, the faint outline of his broad shoulders barely visible through the haze. My heart was pounding in my ears, drowning out the world, yet somehow, I knew the moment he moved—smooth, controlled, predatory. He had that way about him, like a wolf among sheep, though tonight, there would be no sheep.

I could feel the sharp edge of my own resolve cutting through my fear, propelling me forward with each step. Finn had been by my side through everything. There was no way in hell I was letting him face this alone. Not when the shadows around us felt alive, pressing in with every flicker of flame that licked at the edges of the building. And when the figure emerged from the smoke, standing tall, almost smug in the crackling orange glow, my stomach dropped. I didn't know why I was surprised. I should have known it would be him.

Leo Daniels. A face I'd once trusted, once called a friend. The bastard who, just a few weeks ago, had been on the other side of the law, but now stood before us with flames dancing in his eyes. The man who had once helped me through dark days now stood as an embodiment of every nightmare I'd tried to outrun.

The first thing I noticed was the smirk. It was arrogant, like he already knew the game was over before it even began. His dark jacket hung loose around his shoulders, the fabric still warm from the blaze that burned behind him. His eyes, those same green eyes I had once thought were full of kindness, were now cold, distant, like a predator watching its prey. And I was the prey, wasn't I? The realization hit me like a punch to the gut, the world tipping dangerously on its axis. This wasn't just a confrontation. This was a reckoning.

"Did you think you could stop me, Finn?" Leo's voice was low, taunting, as if they were just two old friends meeting in a bar, not two men facing off in the ruins of a building set on fire by his own hand. "You were always too good for your own good. Always trying to save people who never asked for it."

Finn stepped forward, his jaw clenched, his eyes never leaving Leo. "You're a damn fool, Leo. You're playing with fire, and you're going to burn."

The tension between them was so thick I could almost touch it, the air crackling with an energy that felt like it could snap at any moment. I moved in closer, my pulse echoing louder with each step. Finn had always been the protector, always the one who stepped into the fray, but I wasn't going to be the one standing on the sidelines tonight. Not this time. If Leo wanted to finish this, he'd have to deal with both of us.

Leo's laugh echoed through the smoke, a sharp, biting sound that made my skin crawl. "You think you're going to stop me? You're nothing but a shadow of what you used to be. A relic."

He stepped closer, the flames behind him casting a hellish light on his face. I saw the flicker of his weapon then, the glint of steel in the firelight—a knife. My hand instinctively moved to the small gun I kept tucked in my waistband. There was no way I was letting Leo get the upper hand, not when he was so close. Finn's hand shot out, stopping me before I could draw it.

"Don't," Finn murmured, the command soft but firm. "He's not worth it."

I wanted to argue, wanted to snap back that Leo was worth it. That we couldn't let him walk away from this. But there was something in Finn's eyes, something I hadn't seen in a long time. A quiet desperation, an understanding of just how far this could go. He wasn't just trying to stop Leo. He was trying to stop me from crossing a line we couldn't come back from.

Leo seemed to take Finn's silence as a victory, his smile widening. "Always the martyr, huh?" He raised the knife, the blade reflecting the flames, and for a split second, I saw the man I once knew in the way he held it—not in anger, but in calm certainty, as though he was going to slice through everything that had ever mattered to us.

But I wasn't going to let him.

"Leo," I said, my voice cutting through the smoke like a shard of glass. "You were never the hero you thought you were. You were just another person hiding behind a mask. And now, look at you. You're nothing."

His eyes snapped to mine, anger flickering in the depths of them. He wasn't used to being challenged, especially not by me. I could see it in the way his fingers tightened around the hilt of the knife, the small muscle in his jaw twitching as if he could crush the words I'd just spoken with sheer force.

"You think you can talk to me like that?" He spat the words out, but the anger in his voice didn't sound as solid as it had before. "You don't know what I've sacrificed. What I've done."

I met his gaze, unflinching. "I know exactly what you've done, Leo. And I'm not afraid of you anymore."

There was a beat of silence, thick with the weight of unspoken things, before Finn moved. Quick, precise, like a man who had made his peace with the consequences. Before Leo could react, Finn had him by the arm, twisting him into an agonizing hold that left him breathless and stunned.

But it wasn't enough to end it. Not yet.

I stepped forward, my voice steady. "This ends tonight, Leo. No more games."

And for the first time in a long time, I felt that same certainty within me—that nothing, not even this, could break us.

Leo's grip tightened on the knife, his fingers trembling slightly, though whether from rage or something else, I couldn't tell. The fire raged behind him, a hungry beast devouring everything in its path, but Leo seemed oblivious to it. The heat of the blaze didn't reach him the way it should have. He was too wrapped up in the memory of his betrayal, in the bitterness of what he had become. His eyes flicked from Finn to me, settling on me with a contemptuous smile.

"You always did think you were better than me, didn't you?" His voice was as cold as the steel in his hand, and it sent a chill that had nothing to do with the smoke. "You and your perfect little world."

I squared my shoulders, stepping into the clearing between him and Finn. If he wanted to go through me, he was going to have to try a lot harder than that.

"I never thought I was better," I said, my tone flat, betraying none of the swirling anger inside me. "I just thought I was different. But you—" I paused, the words tasting bitter on my tongue, "you were always willing to burn it all down. And for what? A few coins? A twisted sense of revenge?"

Leo's lips curled into something more like a sneer than a smile. "You don't get it, do you? I didn't do it for revenge. I did it because there's no other way. I was pushed to this." His eyes flicked back to Finn. "You pushed me, Finn. You kept coming back with your damn lectures, your reminders about what's right and wrong, about what's worth fighting for. It was suffocating. So I had to burn it all down, to show you that you don't control me anymore."

Finn took a slow, deliberate step forward, his body still coiled with tension, but his voice was calm. Too calm, like he was trying to talk down a rabid dog. "No one controls you, Leo. You chose this path. You've been making these choices all along. Don't pretend like you were a victim here."

The smirk on Leo's face faltered for just a moment, like it was a mask teetering on the edge of shattering. "You think I'm the villain in your little story, Finn? You think I'm the one who lost my way?" His voice cracked, the underlying crackle of desperation breaking through for a second. "You've been so busy playing the hero, you never stopped to wonder who you were hurting along the way."

Finn didn't respond right away, his silence hanging in the air like a thick fog. I could see the wheels turning behind his eyes, the battle he was fighting. Leo wasn't wrong. Finn had his demons, too—he carried them in the quiet moments between words, in the way he held himself like he was bracing for something. But he wasn't about to let Leo twist this any further.

"I don't need to justify myself to you," Finn said, his voice tight with restraint. "You've made your choices. You've crossed a line you can't come back from. And I'm done trying to save you from yourself."

The air between us was alive with tension, the fire crackling, the night swallowing any sense of peace we might have once had. My throat tightened, the weight of it all pressing down on me. I thought I understood what Finn had gone through, but I hadn't seen this version of Leo—the desperate, self-righteous version of him who thought he could justify it all. The Leo who still thought he had control over this situation.

But Finn was right. He was done saving people who didn't want saving.

Leo's face twisted into something darker, something more dangerous. He raised the knife higher, his arm trembling with a kind of fury that was almost poetic in its intensity. "You're all the same. You think you can stand in judgment, throwing your moral high ground at me, but it doesn't mean anything. In the end, you'll all be ashes, just like this place."

His words hung in the air like poison, but they didn't have the weight they once would have. I could see it—the shift in Finn's posture, the hardening of his eyes, the steel that replaced the softness he used to have when dealing with people like Leo. He wasn't going to back down. And neither was I.

Leo lunged forward, the knife flashing through the air, but Finn was already moving, his body reacting instinctively. I didn't even register the movement until it was done—the swift, decisive way Finn had disarmed him. Leo's arm hung at his side, the knife clattering to the ground, his face twisted with shock more than pain.

"You're done, Leo," Finn said, his voice low and steady. "This ends now."

Leo stumbled back, his eyes wild, his chest heaving with the exertion of a man who had just realized his whole world was unraveling. "You think this is over? You think you've won?" His laughter was bitter, edged with panic now. "This is only the beginning, you fool. You've made a powerful enemy tonight."

"You're the one who made the mistake," Finn replied, stepping forward, his presence imposing. "You thought you could manipulate everyone into doing your bidding. But you never counted on the fact that people might stop being afraid of you."

The silence that followed was thick with the weight of unspoken things, the knowledge that Leo wasn't just defeated in that moment—he was broken. And for some reason, that felt like a victory. But it didn't feel as sweet as I imagined it would.

Leo didn't fight back, didn't even try to make another move. Instead, he dropped his shoulders, his face a mask of resignation as he turned, limping away into the smoke, the sound of his retreat the only victory we'd get tonight.

Finn's hand brushed against mine as I stepped up beside him, the heat of the flames washing over us, but the fire in the distance felt less like a threat now and more like the light at the end of a long tunnel. We didn't need to chase Leo anymore. He had already made his choice, and it had cost him everything.

"You good?" Finn asked, his voice quiet, the tension between us melting away.

I nodded, my heart still racing, but for a different reason now. "Yeah. I'm good."

The fight was over, but the truth had only just begun to sink in.

The flames danced, their orange tongues licking the sky, consuming the building in an eerie embrace. The heat was suffocating, the air thick with smoke that clung to my skin and burned in my throat. But despite the chaos, the world around me seemed strangely muted, the crackling fire nothing more than a backdrop to the confrontation that loomed in front of us. Finn stood tall, unyielding, his silhouette framed by the inferno behind him. His jaw was set, eyes narrowed with a determination I hadn't seen in him before. This wasn't just about saving a building or stopping a criminal. This was personal.

"You," the arsonist sneered, their voice cutting through the thick smoke like a knife. It was a voice I recognized. A voice I could never forget, though I had buried it in the deepest corners of my mind.

Finn's gaze flicked toward me, just for a moment, and I saw the question there. The same one I had, echoing in my chest with a cold, disbelieving thud. Could it really be? Was this the same person we had been hunting all this time?

"You're—" I began, but the words choked in my throat as the arsonist threw back their hood, revealing a face that sent a shock of disbelief straight through me.

It was her. Jessica.

I couldn't breathe. My pulse thudded in my ears as the world around me seemed to spin. Jessica had been a friend once, back when the world was simpler, before everything had fallen apart. She had been the one who encouraged me when I was too scared to step into the unknown. She had been the one I leaned on when I thought Finn might be lost to me forever. And now, here she was, standing before us, her eyes glinting with an unsettling mix of fury and satisfaction.

Her lips curled into a smile that was all teeth, no warmth. "You didn't really think I was just going to let you walk away, did you, Finn?"

Finn's hands clenched at his sides, his voice a low growl. "What the hell, Jessica? This... this isn't you. You've gone too far."

Her laugh echoed in the chaos, harsh and bitter. "Too far? You're one to talk. You don't get to lecture me about lines I've crossed, not after everything you've done. After everything you let happen."

I flinched as if her words were a slap, the accusation landing with brutal precision. Finn's past had always been a shadow, one he kept hidden, one I'd only heard whispers of. But hearing her spit it back at him with such venom made me realize just how deep those shadows ran. The guilt in his eyes was unmistakable, but so was the resolve. This wasn't about justifying the past anymore—it was about stopping the madness before it consumed us all.

"Stop playing games, Jessica," Finn said, his voice steely, the rage simmering beneath the surface. "This isn't a vendetta. This is a crime, and it ends here. Now."

But Jessica didn't move. Instead, she took a step closer, her feet barely making a sound on the cracked pavement. The fire behind her illuminated her face in stark contrast, casting shadows that made her look almost... ethereal. The flames made her look like something less than human, something twisted and corrupted. But her voice, when she spoke, was painfully clear, slicing through the smoke like a blade.

"You don't get it, do you? None of this is about you, Finn. This is about me—about what you took from me. You don't even remember, do you?"

Her words were heavy, laden with an accusation so fierce it took me a moment to process. Finn stiffened beside me, his eyes narrowing as though he was seeing her for the first time, as though her words were unraveling something he didn't want to face.

"You've lost your mind," he muttered, but I could hear the uncertainty creeping into his voice. Jessica's words had found their mark.

"No, Finn. You did," she shot back, her voice sharp. "You tore me apart. And now I'm just finishing what you started."

I looked at Finn, my heart racing in my chest. What had she meant? What had happened between them that could drive someone to this? Before Finn could respond, Jessica pulled something from behind her—something small, but unmistakable. A trigger. The sight of it froze my blood in my veins.

"Don't even think about it," I warned, taking a step forward, my own pulse pounding in my throat. "You don't want to do this."

But she didn't seem to hear me. She was staring at Finn, her lips trembling with a mix of fury and grief. Her eyes were wide with something unrecognizable, something that wasn't entirely anger. It was something darker.

"Do you know what it's like, Finn?" she asked, her voice softening, as if she were asking a question only he could answer. "To be left behind? To watch everything you cared about burn to the ground? You don't even realize what you've done, what you've cost me."

Finn's face tightened, the muscles in his jaw working overtime as he fought to keep his emotions in check. "I didn't leave you, Jessica. I didn't want this. You know that."

"You can say that," she spat, her eyes flashing with the fire of long-buried resentment. "But it's too late now. Too late to save me. Too late to fix anything."

Without warning, she pulled the trigger.

The sound of it echoed in the night, sharp and deafening, louder than the crackling fire that was quickly encircling us. But it wasn't the gunshot that made my heart stop. It was the figure that stumbled forward, just behind Jessica—someone I hadn't expected, someone I thought was lost to us.

And then, everything went black.

Chapter 25: The Ultimate Sacrifice

The flames licked at the ceiling, curling like hungry snakes. The heat, suffocating and intense, pressed against my skin as if the air itself had caught fire. I could feel it in my lungs—every breath was thick with smoke, the bitter, acrid sting of burning wood and scorched memories. My vision blurred in the haze, but I could still make out Finn, just a few feet away, his broad back turned toward me, shoulders tense, every muscle coiled with urgency.

"Move!" he shouted, his voice hoarse, raw from the smoke. But it was more than that—it was a command, an order, the kind of thing you don't argue with when someone's life is on the line. His words hit me like a splash of cold water, but it didn't stop the fear from rising up in my chest, threatening to choke me, too.

We'd known it would be risky. This wasn't some grand, clean-cut plan. It was a gamble, one that had depended on timing, stealth, and more than a little luck. But luck had deserted us the second the arsonist lit the match, sending us careening toward a hell that had no exit.

I stumbled, my heart hammering, the smoke thickening around us. Finn didn't even flinch. He reached for me, pulling me close, his arm a steel band around my waist, guiding me through the fire like a lifeline. I clung to him, my body betraying me, moving on instinct, not trusting my own legs. But the heat grew unbearable, the walls of the building groaning and cracking, and for a moment, I thought the whole place might just collapse around us.

"We need to go," Finn said again, his face drawn tight with concentration. But I could see the subtle tremor in his jaw. He wasn't just worried about the flames—he was worried about me.

I opened my mouth to argue, but the words died on my tongue as he gave me a sharp push toward the exit. My legs wobbled, and

I caught myself on the doorframe. The world outside had never seemed so far away, but that was nothing compared to the fear that gripped my chest. I could feel Finn's presence behind me, his body a shield against the fire that threatened to consume us both.

"Finn, you have to come with me," I gasped, my voice catching in my throat as I turned to face him. The heat seemed to intensify as I made eye contact with him. He didn't respond right away, his eyes scanning the room with a steely focus, calculating, working out every possible escape route. But I could see it—see him—the way his mouth tightened, the way his shoulders tensed. The truth hit me like a freight train.

"No," he said, his voice low, deliberate. "You go. Now."

My heart thudded in my chest, a panicked, erratic rhythm that drowned out everything else. "Finn—"

"Go," he repeated, this time with a force that left no room for argument. His eyes, burning with a mixture of love and resolve, held mine in a grip I couldn't break. "I'll be right behind you."

The words felt like a lie, but I knew better than to question him. Not now. The smoke was thickening, swirling around us, making everything feel unreal. My vision blurred again, this time with tears, the sting of them cutting through the haze as I looked at him. His expression was unreadable, but I could feel the weight of his sacrifice in every inch of his posture.

I took a step back, and then another, but my feet felt like they were sinking into the floor, the air so heavy it was like trying to walk through wet cement. "Please don't do this," I whispered, the words barely escaping my lips. "We can make it together. We're in this together, Finn."

He didn't flinch. Didn't even acknowledge my plea. Instead, he turned toward the flames, a sharp intake of breath, as if he could feel them licking at his skin. "You're the one who needs to survive, not me. This is my choice."

I shook my head, but it was useless. There was no breaking through to him. Finn had always been the protector, always the one willing to take the hardest fall for the people he loved. It was who he was, and even knowing that, even in this moment of pure panic, I couldn't seem to accept it.

"You can't just stay—" My voice cracked, the words a broken echo of the reality I didn't want to face.

His eyes softened, just for a moment. He took one last look at me, a fleeting expression that spoke volumes more than his stoic demeanor ever could. Then he took a deep breath and pushed me harder toward the exit, his hands practically shaking with the force of it. "Don't make this harder than it has to be. I'm not asking you to stay. I'm asking you to live."

It hit me then—the weight of it all. This wasn't just a plan gone wrong. This wasn't just fire and smoke and chaos. This was a man, one who had made a choice that had nothing to do with me. This was his sacrifice. His gift.

But I couldn't accept it. Not like this. Not when I had nothing left to give in return.

I stepped forward, determined to reach him, to pull him away from the flames, but as I took that final step, the floor beneath us buckled, sending a shockwave of heat and debris crashing through the room. A large beam fell from above, blocking the doorway and cutting me off from him.

"Finn!" I screamed, my voice raw, desperate.

But he didn't answer.

The beam crashed to the floor with a deafening roar, splintering the air around us as though the building itself were mourning the impending loss. My heart, which had already been racing in time with the flickering flames, now felt like it might explode entirely. A jagged piece of wood slammed into my leg, throwing me off balance, and I tumbled forward, only barely catching myself on the edge of a table. My breath came in shallow gasps as the smoke thickened, curling into my lungs like an unforgiving serpent.

"Finn!" I screamed again, the sound barely escaping, swallowed by the crackling heat and the deafening chaos. It was as though the world had become a suffocating cage, the flames tightening their grip, the smoke swallowing my words before they could ever hope to reach him.

But there was no reply.

I could still feel his presence, like a phantom echo through the haze. My mind played tricks on me as I spun in circles, desperate for any sign that he hadn't vanished into the flames. That the sacrifice he'd made for me hadn't been in vain.

I reached the collapsed doorway where the beam had fallen, the remnants of the fire licking at its edges. But there was no way through. I could hear the distant shouts of others, the chaos of our last-minute escape, but they felt like distant memories rather than the present. The pain in my chest grew unbearable, not just from the fire that threatened to consume the building but from the crushing realization that Finn—my Finn—had stayed behind.

I backed away from the doorway, the heat from the fire battering me like a tangible force. My eyes darted around the room, looking for anything that might help. I needed to get to him. I had to.

I had always thought of myself as a person who was resourceful, someone who could adapt to any situation. But standing there, my legs shaking beneath me, I felt powerless. This wasn't a problem that could be solved with quick thinking or a well-timed punch. This was bigger than me. Bigger than us.

But that didn't mean I was going to give up.

I scanned the room again, my heart pounding with the urgency of every second that passed. The fire was spreading quickly. The walls groaned and cracked, sending showers of sparks into the air, like a million tiny stars.

And then, I saw it.

A fire extinguisher, tucked away in the corner by the broken window. I didn't even think. I just ran. My legs burned with every step as I hurdled over debris, the pain in my body forgotten for the moment. I grabbed the extinguisher and yanked it from its place, my fingers barely able to grip the handle with the sweat that had soaked through my clothes.

I turned back toward the collapsed doorway, feeling the weight of my decision settle over me like a lead blanket. I didn't know if there was any hope of saving him. I didn't even know if Finn was still alive, but I couldn't just leave him. Not after everything.

The air was so thick now, I could barely see, but the fire extinguisher was a beacon of possibility. I took a deep breath, steeling myself for what I had to do. As I approached the doorway again, I slammed the extinguisher into the beam, hoping to break through to the other side. The force of the impact reverberated through my arms, but the beam didn't budge.

I could hear him then—Finn's voice, barely above a whisper, but unmistakable. His groan of pain cut through the roar of the fire, and I froze, my blood going cold and then boiling over with relief.

"Finn!" My voice cracked. I dropped the extinguisher and rushed toward him, only to find my path blocked by more debris, more smoke, more fire.

The sound of his voice, weak and strained, urged me on. I refused to let the flames take him. Not after he had sacrificed everything for me.

I scrambled over the wreckage, crawling on hands and knees, my clothes smoldering, my skin prickling with the burn of heat that followed me every step of the way. I called his name again, louder this time, desperate.

"Finn!"

His voice came again, closer now, a rasping cough that sent another wave of panic through me. My heart thudded as I crawled forward, reaching out with trembling fingers, praying to find his hand.

And then, I did.

His grip was weak, but it was there. His fingers were slick with sweat and blood, his body half-hidden beneath a fallen beam. His chest rose and fell in shallow, labored breaths, his face covered in soot and ash, but when he looked at me, his eyes were still full of that same determination, that same love that had driven him to sacrifice everything to save me.

"You—" His voice was barely audible, but the words were there, heavy with meaning. "I told you to go..."

"No," I whispered, tears stinging my eyes as I cupped his face, wiping away the soot that clung to his skin. "I'm not leaving you. Not now. Not ever."

I didn't care if the building was coming down around us. I didn't care if the flames were creeping closer, licking at the edges of our world. I only cared about Finn. About saving him. Because I couldn't let him be the one to pay for our survival. We had made it this far together, and there was no way I was going to leave without him.

His eyes fluttered closed, exhaustion overcoming him, but I didn't give up. I tugged at the beam, using every ounce of strength I had left. It creaked and groaned, resisting me, but I didn't stop. I kept pulling, kept fighting, knowing I couldn't afford to give in now. Not when we were so close. Not when everything depended on this final, fragile thread of hope.

And then, finally, with one last, desperate heave, the beam shifted enough for me to pull him free.

The moment I freed Finn from the wreckage, I thought we might have a chance. I was wrong. He was still unconscious, his body limp in my arms, but I wasn't going to give up. Not yet. His pulse was there, weak but steady, and I held onto that with everything I had. The building was falling apart around us, the ceiling groaning with every second that passed, the air thickening with more smoke, more heat. But I didn't care. We were going to make it. We had to.

I dragged him toward the door, my hands slick with sweat and the rough material of his shirt as I tried to keep my footing, pushing through the wreckage. The heat was relentless now. I could feel my skin prickling, the sting of the fire licking at my back, but I kept going. One step, then another. The sound of falling debris echoed in my ears, but I focused only on the task at hand—getting Finn out of here.

I wasn't about to let him die. Not like this. Not after everything.

"Come on, Finn. Wake up," I muttered under my breath, more to myself than to him. My voice was barely audible over the crackling flames, but I spoke anyway, willing him to hear me, willing him to wake up. There was no way I was going to do this alone.

The door was within reach now, but it felt like the longest distance I had ever traveled. My muscles screamed in protest, the weight of Finn's body dragging me down, but I couldn't stop. Not now. Not when I was so close.

The doorframe was cracked and splintered, the flames licking at the edges, threatening to collapse at any moment. My breath caught in my throat as I made one final push, my foot slipping slightly on the wet floor beneath me, but I gritted my teeth and forced myself forward.

Just a little further.

Then, the unthinkable happened.

A burst of heat slammed into my back, knocking me forward, the force of it sending me sprawling onto the floor with Finn still in my arms. My face slammed into the cold, charred wood, but I barely felt the pain. My mind was elsewhere, trapped in a whirlwind of thoughts—none of them helpful.

I blinked, disoriented, but the reality of what had happened was quick to set in. The building groaned and cracked, and then—just as I thought I might have a moment of peace—a loud explosion ripped through the air.

I didn't think. I couldn't.

I threw myself forward, dragging Finn with me, praying that we'd make it in time. But the blast threw me back again, the force of it reverberating through the very ground beneath us. The door frame snapped, the beams above us shaking as if the whole structure was about to collapse.

Finn's body went limp in my arms.

"Please...please don't do this to me," I whispered, my voice a mere tremor in the air.

He didn't respond. Of course he didn't. His breathing was shallow, too slow for my comfort. The panic in my chest swelled like a tidal wave, but I fought to control it. I couldn't lose it now. Not when I was so close.

I could hear the crackling of the fire behind me, the sound of wood splintering, the overwhelming stench of burning, but I focused on the path ahead. The exit was right there, just a few feet from me, and with everything I had, I pulled Finn toward it.

The door loomed in front of me. I could see the smoky haze of the outside world beyond it, but the flames that surrounded us were relentless. The walls were burning faster than I could track. We had to get out.

Just as my fingers brushed the edge of the door, I felt a sharp pain in my leg. I glanced down to see a metal beam, half-buried under the wreckage, now pressing down on my ankle. It was heavy, nearly impossible to lift. I couldn't move.

"Damn it," I cursed under my breath, my teeth gritted. The fire was inching closer. I could feel the heat growing, the crackle of flames snapping at my back, but the weight on my leg kept me pinned in place.

I tugged at Finn again, trying to pull him with me, but the effort was futile. He was dead weight in my arms. His skin felt like ice against mine. It didn't matter how much I pulled, how much I tried to drag him forward, the reality was inescapable—this might be the end.

My mind flashed back to the moment when Finn had pushed me toward the exit, his words still ringing in my ears. I had promised him I'd make it. I had promised I would survive. But I couldn't do it without him.

I closed my eyes, summoning every ounce of strength I had left, trying to break free from the weight that pinned me down.

And then, I heard it.

A low, rumbling sound.

At first, I thought it was just the fire, the building shifting under the strain, but no. It was something else—something more deliberate. Something...alive.

My heart skipped a beat.

No. It couldn't be.

The sound grew louder, closer. Something was moving toward us, fast. Too fast for comfort.

"Finn," I whispered, my voice barely audible over the noise of the fire. His eyes were still closed, his body still limp in my arms, but the rumbling continued. And then, through the haze of smoke, a figure appeared. Tall, moving with purpose, a silhouette against the flames.

I couldn't make out their face, but I could see the movement. The determination. And then, the figure spoke.

"You're not alone," the voice called out, steady and calm, cutting through the crackling chaos like a knife.

And then, in the blink of an eye, the ground beneath me trembled once again, and the door... it was no longer there.

Chapter 26: Aftermath of the Heart

The evening air was thick with smoke, lingering like a bad memory, swirling and curling through the broken windows as if it wanted to follow us, to make sure we never escaped its grip. My heart hammered in my chest, a frantic rhythm that wouldn't let me breathe freely, even though the fire was nothing more than a shadow behind us now. Finn was still holding me, his arms wrapped around me tightly, as though he feared I might slip away into the ash-laden wind. His breath was ragged against my ear, a mix of relief and terror. He wasn't entirely unharmed; I could feel the rawness of his palms, the roughness of his clothes as he clung to me. We were both alive, but for how long? The question circled me like the smoke we'd just escaped.

I wanted to cry, to let the tension leave my body, but my pride was stubborn—always had been. So, I squeezed him tighter, hoping he could feel the gratitude that surged through me, even though the words seemed weak and useless in the face of what we'd just endured. "You're okay," I whispered, though my voice felt like it belonged to someone else. Someone who wasn't standing in the wreckage of everything she'd ever known.

Finn pulled back slightly, his face streaked with soot, but his eyes still held that familiar spark. He was here, and that was enough. The fire had threatened to steal so much from us—my past, his future, our chance at something real—but we were still standing. Still breathing. I knew I wasn't ready for the relief to settle, not yet. The aftermath of the fire wasn't something I could put in a neat little box and tuck away. The weight of it sat heavily on my chest, pressing, pushing, making it hard to think of anything other than how badly we had nearly lost everything. How badly I had nearly lost him.

"You're safe," he murmured, brushing a stray strand of hair from my face, his fingers grazing my cheek in a gesture that seemed far too intimate for the moment. But there it was—a tenderness that had somehow survived the chaos, the threat of death, and the madness of that night.

I couldn't help the tears that welled up in my eyes, though I blinked them away furiously. "I was so scared," I said, my voice cracking, revealing the vulnerability I'd been holding back. "I didn't know what would happen. I didn't know if you'd—if we'd—"

His lips were suddenly on mine, silencing me, drowning out the terror that still clung to the air around us. It was a kiss that tasted of smoke and relief, of promises whispered into the dark. It wasn't gentle. It was desperate, urgent, as though he couldn't bear the thought of losing me, and I wasn't about to let him go, either. Not now. Not ever.

When he pulled away, his forehead rested against mine, both of us breathing deeply, finding solace in the rhythm of each other's pulse. "We're not done," he said quietly, a statement more than a question. "This is just the beginning."

I nodded, though the thought of what that meant made my chest tighten again. The arsonist—whoever they were—was behind bars now, but they weren't the only threat we faced. I could feel the tension in the air, the unspoken knowledge that even after the flames were gone, the damage they left behind would be slow to heal. The world wasn't as simple as before. Our world, at least, wasn't.

But there was a flicker of something in me, something I couldn't quite name, a spark of defiance that had never been there before. I couldn't let fear control me. Not anymore. "We've made it through worse," I said, forcing a brave smile, though I knew it didn't quite reach my eyes. "We'll make it through whatever comes next, Finn."

He smiled, but it wasn't the carefree grin I was used to. There was an edge to it now, a knowing that seemed to stretch deeper than either of us wanted to acknowledge. "Maybe," he said, "but we're doing it together. And that makes all the difference."

The sound of sirens grew louder, pulling me back to reality, back to the world where everything was fractured and uncertain. The fire was out, but the wreckage was still there—both around us and within us. As the paramedics and officers approached, I reluctantly let go of Finn, though it felt like a part of me was left behind, tethered to him in ways I couldn't explain.

The officer who approached us was familiar—one I'd seen a few times around town, but never close enough to really know. He looked at me with something between pity and understanding, a look that I wasn't sure I wanted to see. "You alright?" he asked, voice low, the question more about what was inside my head than my physical condition.

"Fine," I replied quickly, brushing my hands over my arms as though I could erase the feeling of being so small in the face of everything that had happened. "We're fine. Just a little shaken up."

He nodded, his eyes flicking over to Finn, who was watching the scene unfold with that detached focus that always made me think he was somehow both in the moment and miles away at the same time. He was a man who carried his burdens without complaint, but I knew the weight of them was getting heavier by the day.

"You're lucky," the officer said, voice growing quieter as he gestured to the building behind us. "Most people wouldn't have made it out."

I met his gaze, swallowing hard. "I know," I whispered, my hand instinctively reaching for Finn's. He gave mine a squeeze, his warmth grounding me in a way that felt both comforting and terrifying.

In the silence that followed, the only sound was the hum of the sirens, the steady presence of the aftermath. But in that moment, amidst the chaos and the fear, I knew one thing for certain: we would fight through it. Whatever was coming, whatever had been left behind in the wake of that fire, we would face it together.

The next few days blurred into one long stretch of exhaustion and disbelief. The fire, the chaos, the fear—it was all still lodged deep in my bones, a constant, gnawing reminder of how close we had come to losing everything. But there was something else, too. A kind of hollow space where things used to be, where peace should have settled but didn't. The house, which had always been a place of comfort, now felt like a stranger's home—too empty, too quiet, as if it had forgotten what it meant to be lived in. I wasn't sure if it was the physical damage, the smoke still hanging in the corners of the rooms, or if it was the emotional wreckage that followed a near-death experience. Either way, the walls felt like they were closing in.

Finn was no better. He moved through the house like a man trying to remember his own name, his eyes distant, his steps slow and deliberate as though every movement required more effort than he had to give. He was here, physically present, but I couldn't shake the feeling that he wasn't entirely with me anymore. Maybe he'd never fully been. I'd always been drawn to the mystery of him, the hidden layers beneath the surface, but now I wondered how many of those layers were just shields he had put up—defenses against the world, against people like me, against the truth he'd never let anyone see.

"I need to get out of here," I said one morning, the heaviness of the house finally forcing my hand. My fingers hovered over the coffee mug, half-tempted to take a sip, but the bitterness of the dark brew suddenly felt like it would choke me.

Finn didn't look up from where he sat on the couch, his head in his hands. "I think we all do," he muttered, a dull edge to his voice that didn't feel like him. He had always been the type to speak in sharp, witty remarks, not the defeated monotone he had slipped into.

I couldn't tell if it was the fire that had broken him or something deeper, something I hadn't quite understood. I wanted to reach out to him, to break through whatever wall he was building, but I wasn't sure if he was still there behind it. Or if I was.

"You can't just shut me out, Finn," I said, my voice harsher than I intended. I hadn't realized how desperate I was for his attention, for him to look at me, really look at me, until the words were already out. I regretted them instantly. It wasn't fair. Not after everything we'd been through. Not when we had barely scraped through the fire alive.

But Finn didn't flinch. He didn't react in that way I had come to expect—sharp, defensive, maybe even teasing. He just sat there, looking at the floor as though the weight of his thoughts was enough to hold him captive.

"I'm not shutting you out," he said quietly, and I almost didn't hear it. His voice was raw, thinner than usual. "I'm just... trying to make sense of all this. Everything. And I'm not sure I can do that right now." He glanced at me, then quickly looked away again, as if my eyes might be too much to bear.

I didn't know what to say to that. What was there to say when the man you loved seemed like a shell of himself, when his body was here, but his heart was somewhere far, far away?

I exhaled a shaky breath, unsure whether I should push, pull back, or give him the space he clearly needed. So, I did the only thing I knew how to do—my usual tactic of doing something, anything, to distract myself from feeling this suffocating distance between us.

"Maybe a change of scenery will help," I suggested, the words already taking shape in my mind. "Get out of the house for a while. Maybe we could go for a walk. Or... you know, drive somewhere. Anything but just sitting here."

Finn didn't respond immediately, and I could feel the pulse of tension between us, thick and uncomfortable. But after a moment, he finally lifted his gaze and met mine. His eyes were stormy, but there was something else there, too. Something like... relief? I wasn't sure, but I clung to it like a lifeline.

"Alright," he said, his voice softer. "I'm not saying no to a drive."

It wasn't much, but it was enough. Enough for me to take a breath, to feel like we weren't completely falling apart. Maybe we weren't exactly fixed, either, but it was a start. And for now, that would have to be enough.

We drove for hours, aimlessly at first, heading out toward the coast. The air was thick with salt and the scent of damp earth as we wound our way through small towns and empty highways. The hum of the tires on the asphalt was the only sound between us, and for once, the silence didn't feel suffocating. It was... comfortable. A strange kind of peace settled in, and for the first time since the fire, I didn't feel like I was drowning in the wreckage of my own life.

"Do you ever just... think about how different everything could be?" I asked, breaking the silence. The question hung there, raw and uncertain, but it felt necessary, like a lifeline I had to throw, even if I wasn't sure if he'd catch it.

Finn glanced at me, his fingers tight on the wheel. "All the time," he said, his tone thoughtful, distant. "But it doesn't matter, does it? What could've been? We've got now, and that's all we can control."

I nodded, though I wasn't sure I fully agreed. The "now" was messy and uncertain, and it wasn't all I wanted. But I didn't press him further. Not then. The way he said it made me realize something I hadn't wanted to admit to myself before: Finn wasn't the only one holding back. I was too.

Somewhere, deep inside, I knew the real work was only just beginning. The fire hadn't destroyed us, but it had exposed things I couldn't ignore. Things I hadn't been ready to face.

The coast was just ahead, the sky darkening to a shade of blue I hadn't seen in years, and I realized that while I wasn't sure what would happen next, maybe that was okay. Maybe all we could do was take the next step. Together.

The next few weeks passed in a haze of mundane yet monumental moments, as if the world was trying to force us back into some semblance of normalcy, but neither Finn nor I were ready to fall into that routine. There were times I would catch him staring out the window, a slight frown pulling at the corners of his mouth, his fingers twitching like he was trying to grasp something just out of reach. I would watch him from the corner of the room, unsure whether I should approach or let him process whatever it was on his own. Sometimes I wished I could do the thinking for both of us, but I knew that was as futile as trying to outrun a storm.

But we had to try.

We had to find a way back to each other, back to ourselves.

"Do you ever feel like we're stuck in the middle of a storm, just waiting for it to pass?" I asked him one evening, the weight of the question heavy on my tongue. We were sitting in the kitchen, a pot of half-brewed coffee cooling between us, and the rain tapping against the windows like a slow, rhythmic reminder that time never stopped, even when it felt like everything else had.

Finn didn't answer immediately. He set down his mug and rubbed his eyes, as if the simple act of blinking could erase the fatigue that seemed etched into his features. "I think we've been in a storm our whole lives," he said finally, his voice a little too calm, a little too resigned. "Maybe we're just learning to wait for it to change direction. Maybe we'll be waiting forever."

I wasn't sure how to respond to that. Part of me wanted to argue, to tell him that waiting forever was no way to live. But another part of me understood what he meant. It wasn't just the fire—the arson, the fear, the aftermath—but the years before, the things we had both carried, hidden beneath the surface. There was more to it. So much more. And if we didn't start digging into it, we'd both suffocate under the weight of things unsaid.

"What if I don't want to wait anymore?" I asked, the words out before I could stop them. They hung in the air, charged and full of the kind of uncertainty that made the room feel smaller, like the walls were leaning in to hear our confessions.

Finn's eyes flicked to mine, and for a brief second, I saw a flicker of something. A spark, maybe, or a recognition of just how fragile this moment was. Then it was gone, buried again behind the cool, measured look he always wore.

"I think we need to talk," he said, his voice quieter now, more serious.

I nodded. "We do. But not just about what happened to us. About everything."

The tension between us thickened, but this time, it didn't feel like a wall I couldn't scale. It felt like a door, cracked open just enough for me to catch a glimpse of the truth. I reached out, my hand resting on the edge of the table, close to his, but not quite touching.

Finn leaned back, his gaze never leaving mine. "What are you so afraid of?" he asked, and his tone was sharp, but there was an edge of something else there—something softer, almost vulnerable, as if he was asking not because he wanted to accuse me, but because he was afraid of what might happen if we didn't face it together.

I swallowed hard, unsure of how to explain the weight I had carried for so long. The fear that had become part of me, so entrenched that it felt like second nature. "I'm afraid we're not enough for each other," I said, the words feeling like they were scraping against my chest as I forced them out. "I'm afraid that no matter how hard we try, we'll never be able to make sense of all the things we've been through. The fire, the things we've never talked about—the people we used to be. I'm afraid we'll break under the weight of it all."

His hand covered mine, warm and steady, grounding me in a way I wasn't used to. "You're not the only one with scars," he said, his voice thick with something I couldn't name. "I'm not perfect, either. But maybe that's what makes us—makes me—want to try, anyway. I don't know what it is about you, but I'm not ready to let you go. Not now. Not when I can see that there's still something here."

For a moment, I just stared at him, a thousand thoughts flashing through my mind. The way he said "here" made it feel like he was talking about something more than just our relationship. Maybe it was hope. Maybe it was the belief that we could survive this. But whatever it was, it made me want to believe it, too.

"Then let's try," I said, my voice trembling with the weight of those words. I wasn't sure what trying would look like—how we would ever get past the things that had broken us, but for the first time in weeks, I felt like we were standing on the same ground. Together.

Before he could respond, a loud knock sounded at the door, followed by the unmistakable voice of a familiar figure. "Finn, we need to talk. It's important."

We both turned, our moment shattered in an instant. I watched as Finn's face shifted from the fragile hope we had just shared to something colder, more guarded. His hand left mine, and I immediately felt the absence of it.

"Who is it?" I asked, already knowing the answer but not wanting to hear it.

He didn't answer, but I could see it in the way his jaw tightened, the way his eyes flickered toward the door with a mix of irritation and something darker—something like dread.

"Stay here," Finn said, his voice firm. "I'll handle this."

But I wasn't about to let him shut me out again. Not now.

"I'm coming with you," I said, rising from my seat before he could stop me.

And as I stepped into the hallway, I knew, deep in my gut, that this would be the moment that changed everything.

Chapter 27: Lingering Embers

It was one of those early mornings, the kind where the sky is a pale blue and the air smells like possibility, yet the earth beneath your feet still carries the scent of rain from the night before. I stood by the kitchen window, watching the last of the fog drift off the hills, leaving behind the faintest trace of dew on the grass. The coffee in my hand was bitter, but necessary, a reminder that the world kept moving even when my thoughts refused to. Finn was in the other room, probably still tangled in his dreams, though he'd told me he hadn't slept well since we'd come back here.

I wondered if the weight of our past was as heavy on him as it was on me. We'd rebuilt the house, rebuilt ourselves, and yet, there was something unsaid, something unresolved that clung to the air like the mist in the valley below. It wasn't enough for me to forget what I had learned—the truth about his secrets, the lies wrapped in half-truths that he'd spun with the ease of someone who'd spent a lifetime perfecting them. It was hard to breathe without feeling that pressure, that whisper in the back of my mind telling me that maybe, just maybe, we weren't done fighting.

I could hear him moving now, the soft creak of floorboards, the rustling of fabric. When he appeared in the doorway, his hair was still disheveled, his eyes bloodshot from lack of sleep. He looked almost sheepish, as if he were waiting for me to say something. Anything. But I didn't. Instead, I focused on the steam rising from my cup, the delicate way it twisted in the morning light.

"I didn't mean to wake you," he said, his voice rough, but there was a softness there too. A hesitation, like he was unsure whether to cross the threshold into my world or retreat to his own.

I finally looked up, my eyes meeting his. He always looked like he carried the weight of the world on his shoulders—dark circles under his eyes, lines etched into his face like cracks in an old stone wall. He had that way about him, where even in silence, you could feel the storm brewing beneath the surface.

"You didn't," I replied, offering him a small smile, though it felt brittle at best. "I was awake long before you."

He stepped closer, his hands in his pockets, his gaze flicking to the cup in my hands. "How's the coffee?"

"Awful," I said, taking another sip. "But it's doing the job."

He laughed, the sound low and familiar, the kind of laugh that once made my heart skip a beat. Now, it just made the ache inside me feel all the sharper. He hadn't changed on the outside, but the inside? That was a different story.

I set the cup down, feeling the weight of the conversation we were avoiding pressing on me again. "We should talk."

Finn froze, his body going still in a way that made me feel like a soldier preparing for battle. He had always been the one to keep the peace, the one to soothe the storm when it threatened to rage out of control. But now, it felt like we were standing on opposite sides of a chasm, both of us too proud to cross the distance.

He exhaled slowly, like he'd been holding his breath since the moment we'd gotten back from the fire. "I know. I just... I don't know where to start."

"How about with the truth?" I said, the words slipping out before I could stop them.

His eyes widened, and for a moment, the air between us crackled with something sharp and unsaid. "You already know the truth."

I tilted my head, studying him. "Do I? Because I'm not so sure anymore."

Finn's gaze faltered, and for the first time, I saw the cracks in his armor. It was only for a second, but it was enough. Enough for me to realize that the man I thought I knew, the man I thought I could trust, was still a stranger in some ways. Maybe we were both strangers now.

"You want the whole truth?" he asked, his voice tight, but there was an edge to it, as if he'd been waiting for me to ask this question all along.

I nodded, not trusting my voice to carry the weight of my thoughts.

He stepped away, running a hand through his hair as if trying to find the right words. "I didn't tell you everything because I was trying to protect you. I didn't think you could handle it, and I was too selfish to let you in. But there's no excuse. You deserve to know it all. You deserve to know who I really am, not just the man I wanted to be for you."

I swallowed, the lump in my throat growing with each word he spoke. But instead of feeling betrayed or angry, I felt something different. Something heavier. The truth was always more complicated than I imagined. It was never as simple as I wanted it to be.

"What are you saying?" I finally asked, my voice barely above a whisper.

"I'm saying that there are parts of me that I buried," he said, his voice softer now, more vulnerable than I had ever heard it. "Parts of my past that I thought I could outrun. But they always come back, don't they? In the end, they always find you."

And just like that, the walls we'd built around ourselves—the ones we'd thought were strong enough to keep everything out—came crumbling down.

I didn't know how to respond to him. My heart was tangled in knots, and each thread felt like it was pulling me in a thousand different directions. His words hung in the air between us, like smoke that wouldn't clear. The things he was saying—about his past, the secrets, the choices he had made—had I ever really known him? Or had I been in love with a version of him that only existed in my imagination?

Finn shifted, his eyes avoiding mine for the first time in what felt like forever. "I didn't want to drag you into my mess," he muttered, voice tight. "You deserved better than that. Than me."

I could feel the heaviness of his words in my chest, the way they settled like stones. How could someone who cared about you—someone who claimed to love you—keep their secrets buried so deep? I had to bite my lip to keep the words from tumbling out. What could I say? What was there to say?

"You don't get to decide what I deserve," I finally said, my voice steadier than I felt. I met his gaze then, locking my eyes with his. "I get to decide that. And I chose you. Even when you weren't honest with me."

He winced, the pain in his expression clear. But it wasn't just regret that flitted across his features. There was something else, something harder to read. "You don't know the half of it."

"Then tell me," I said, my voice sharper than I intended. "Tell me everything."

For a long moment, he didn't say anything. He only stood there, his fists clenched at his sides, his jaw tight. I wanted to reach out, to soothe him, but something held me back. What if the truth didn't come with the kind of redemption I was hoping for? What if it only ripped us apart even further?

"Maybe I don't have the right to tell you," he muttered finally. "Maybe I've done too much damage already."

"Finn," I said, my patience thinning. "You can't fix something if you don't acknowledge what's broken."

I had never seen him look so torn, so defeated. It made my chest ache. Finn had always been the steady one, the one who could handle anything life threw at him. He had always been the one to calm my storms. But now, it felt like the storm had swallowed him whole.

"Let me guess," I continued, crossing my arms, unwilling to back down. "You think I can't handle the truth. But you're wrong. I've been handling it for months. So stop trying to protect me, Finn. Tell me everything."

He exhaled, long and slow, and I thought for a moment that maybe he was going to walk away. Maybe he was going to retreat into whatever dark corner of his mind he had been hiding in for so long. But then he spoke, the words rough, like they were scraping their way up from somewhere deep inside him.

"I used to run with a group," he said, his voice so low that I almost didn't catch it. "A group that wasn't exactly legal. We weren't doing anything that could make the papers, but we weren't exactly law-abiding either. I was good at it. Smart. I kept my head down, did what I was told, and made a lot of money. Then... I got out. I thought I could leave it behind. I thought I could be done with it. But things don't work that way. You don't get to just walk away from that life."

He paused, his eyes drifting to the floor as if he couldn't bear to look at me. "They came for me," he said, his voice quieter now. "And they came for you too, because I let you get too close. I didn't want to drag you into it, but I did anyway."

The silence in the room was thick, oppressive. It felt like the walls were closing in around me, and I could barely breathe. So, this was what he'd been hiding. This was the reason he'd been so distant, so guarded. And I—God, I hadn't even known. I had thought it was something simpler, something I could understand, something I could fix.

"But I'm here now," he continued, his voice strained. "And they're still out there. Watching. Waiting. And I don't know what they want anymore, but I can't keep you safe if they're still looking for me."

I couldn't breathe. Couldn't think. This was all too much—too much to process, too much to take in. My mind was spinning, trying to make sense of the tangled web of lies and half-truths that had been spun around us.

I stepped back, away from him, my hand pressing to my forehead. "You've been living with this? All this time? And you didn't think I deserved to know?"

"I didn't think I could keep you safe if you did," he said, his voice thick with something close to regret. "I didn't think you'd be able to handle it."

The silence stretched on, heavy and suffocating. The weight of his confession hung between us, a barrier I wasn't sure we could ever break through. It was as if the ground beneath us had shifted, and I was no longer standing on solid ground.

I didn't know what to say. I didn't know how to fix this, how to make it right. What could I say? What could I do?

"I'm sorry," he said, the words soft, as if they were a last-ditch attempt to salvage something from the wreckage. "I didn't want any of this. But I've ruined it. Ruined us."

The words stung, but it wasn't just the apology that hurt. It was the realization that we weren't the same people we had been when we first met. We weren't the same people who had danced around our insecurities and laughed at our mistakes. There was too much distance between us now, too much darkness.

And as much as I wanted to bridge that gap, I wasn't sure it was possible. Not anymore.

The next few days passed like slow-moving clouds, neither heavy nor light, just there—looming in the periphery, unremarkable but impossible to ignore. Finn and I moved through our routine, a carefully orchestrated dance that neither of us was truly invested in anymore. I'd learned more than I ever wanted to about the darkness in his past, and the weight of it pressed on me like a stone lodged in my chest. I could see the effort it took for him to act normal, to try to reassure me as if nothing had changed, but I wasn't fooled. We both knew that nothing could go back to the way it was.

By the third morning of this quiet unease, I found myself standing at the window again, my eyes fixed on the hills in the distance, the ones that had once seemed like a comforting presence. Now, they were just mountains, vast and indifferent, much like everything else in my life. The coffee tasted worse than usual, but it was the kind of awful that I didn't mind. The bitterness of it matched the way I felt.

Finn's footsteps came up behind me, light and hesitant. I didn't turn to face him, not yet. It wasn't that I didn't want to see him; I just didn't know what to say. How could I? The truth of what he had shared with me had lodged itself deep inside me, a splinter I couldn't pull out. I had no idea if it was supposed to make things better or worse, but I knew one thing: I couldn't keep pretending I wasn't suffocating.

"Are you alright?" he asked, his voice gentle but with an edge of concern. He had asked that question a thousand times in the past week, always with that same careful tone, as if he were afraid I might break if he spoke too loudly.

I took a long sip of my coffee, feeling the bitter warmth settle in my stomach. "I'm fine," I lied, the word tasting like sand in my mouth. "It's just... I need to go for a walk."

"Now?" His tone was quiet but threaded with surprise, as if he thought walking away from this moment—away from him—was something I shouldn't do.

I turned to face him, leaning against the windowsill. "Yes, now. It's either that or I start ripping up the floorboards in search of buried treasure."

The faintest flicker of amusement passed over his face, but it quickly vanished. He had learned, the hard way, that humor was no longer our safe ground. "I didn't mean to hurt you," he said, the apology heavy in the air between us.

I smiled, but it was small and hollow. "You didn't. Not in the way you think."

He stepped forward, as if he were trying to read me, but it wasn't that simple anymore. "Then why do you look like you've been chewing on a mouthful of glass?"

I didn't answer right away. Instead, I pushed away from the window and grabbed my jacket. The cold outside would help clear my head, I told myself. It would give me space to breathe, to think. Finn didn't follow as I headed out the door, but I could feel his eyes on my back, even though I refused to acknowledge them.

The wind whipped through the trees as I stepped into the yard, sending a chill across my skin. The scent of pine and damp earth filled my lungs, grounding me, pulling me away from the knot in my chest. But no matter how hard I tried to lose myself in the rhythm of my steps, the shadows of our conversation lingered just behind me, like a dark cloud I couldn't outrun.

I found myself at the edge of the property, near the old stone wall that bordered the property line. The stones were worn from years of weather, moss growing in thick patches along their surface. I rested my hands on the cool stone, staring out into the distance. For a moment, I thought about what Finn had said—how the past always found its way back to you, no matter how far you tried to run from it.

I wasn't afraid of the past. I was afraid of what it meant for our future.

The crunch of gravel broke through the silence, and I didn't need to turn around to know who it was. Finn's footsteps were a distinct sound, heavy and deliberate, as if he were carrying more than just his body across the yard.

"You should come back inside," he called out, his voice calm but edged with something I couldn't place.

I shook my head, not ready to face him just yet. "I just need a minute, Finn. A minute to think."

He didn't answer right away, but I could feel him standing there, just a few feet behind me. His presence was a constant, like the air itself. I didn't have to look at him to know that he was still standing there, waiting for me to turn back toward him. But I couldn't. Not yet.

"Did you ever think we could have a normal life?" I asked, the question slipping out before I could stop it.

Finn shifted behind me, the sound of his shoes scraping against the gravel. "I don't know if I ever believed in normal," he said, his voice low. "But I've always believed in us."

His words hung in the air, an echo of something we both wanted but neither of us knew how to reach for anymore. A thought flickered through my mind—something I hadn't let myself entertain until now. Something that terrified me more than anything else.

"What if I can't do this?" I whispered, the words barely audible, swallowed by the wind. "What if... what if we're too broken to fix?"

Finn's voice cracked with a rare vulnerability. "I've never known you to give up before."

But I wasn't sure I was giving up. I wasn't sure what I was doing. I was just standing here, waiting for an answer I wasn't sure was ever going to come.

The hairs on the back of my neck prickled, a chill that had nothing to do with the wind. I turned, my heart pounding in my chest. Something was wrong.

There, just beyond the tree line, a shadow moved.

My breath caught in my throat, my pulse quickening. It was too far to make out any details, but it was there. Someone was watching us. And they weren't supposed to be.

"Finn," I whispered, barely able to form the words. "We're not alone."

Chapter 28: The Haunting

The first time it happened, I was sitting in the living room, feet tucked beneath me, tea cooling beside me on the coffee table. The afternoon sunlight was slanting through the blinds, painting the floor with long, gold-tipped shadows. Everything was still, so still that the soft hum of the refrigerator felt intrusive. I wasn't scared—at least not at first—but a nagging itch at the back of my neck wouldn't leave. I chalked it up to exhaustion, the kind that clings to you after a long week of too many sleepless nights. But then there was the shadow.

It flickered at the corner of my vision, a dark blur outside the window, too quick to be a trick of the light. My breath caught in my throat. I turned, trying to catch a glimpse of whatever it was, but the yard was empty. The trees swayed lazily, their branches creaking as they bent in the wind. No one was out there. No one at all.

I pushed the unease away, forcing my thoughts back to the book in my lap. It was just a shadow, nothing more, a result of the sun hitting the tree at a weird angle. That's what I told myself. But even as I told myself that, the hairs on the back of my neck stood up like they were rebelling against my calm façade. The air in the room felt thick, heavier than it should have been. I glanced at the door, half-expecting it to creak open on its own.

I glanced over at Finn, who was still hunched over his laptop at the kitchen table, absorbed in whatever case files he was working on. He was so focused, so grounded, and part of me wanted to drag him into my nervous whirlwind and make him look out the window, just to see if he noticed anything odd. But I knew what he'd say. "You're imagining things, Liv. It's nothing." He always had a way of calming me with his quiet assurances, his steady presence, even if they never quite erased the anxious tremor in my chest.

But I had to admit, the unease was persistent. It felt like the kind of tension that hovers before a storm. I'd felt it in the pit of my stomach the night we'd found the arsonist, the way the air had been thick with anticipation, charged with an unknown force. But back then, I'd convinced myself it was just the adrenaline. Now? Now, I wasn't so sure.

I stood up, walking over to the window with slow, deliberate steps. The curtains were half-drawn, a thin sliver of light cutting through the gap. I pulled them aside, peering out into the yard. Everything was quiet, the same as before. I even scanned the tree line, just in case someone was hiding in the shadows. Nothing.

Still, the feeling didn't leave me. It was like an itch I couldn't scratch, a hum in the air that didn't belong. My eyes darted over to the driveway. The mailbox. The streetlamp flickering at the end of the road, a faint buzz echoing in the silence. I couldn't shake the thought—what if the arsonist wasn't the only threat? What if there was someone else out there? Someone who hadn't been caught, who was still watching, still lurking.

I shoved my hands into the pockets of my cardigan and turned back to the room, fighting the nagging urge to go out and check the perimeter. I couldn't go outside in broad daylight like some paranoid lunatic. Besides, Finn would just think I was being ridiculous. I wasn't about to risk a lecture on how everything was fine, how the case was over, how I should stop imagining shadows where there were none.

When I dropped back onto the couch, I glanced over at him. He hadn't even noticed my brief moment of anxiety. His brow furrowed as he typed, his focus as sharp as ever. It was comforting, in a way—his constant calmness—but I couldn't help the gnawing feeling that something was wrong. I had to know. I had to make sure that the danger was truly over.

"Finn," I said, my voice softer than I intended, "what if there's more to this? What if we missed something?"

He looked up from his screen, his blue eyes narrowing slightly as he studied me. The concern was there, underneath the quiet, patient understanding. "Liv, we caught the guy. It's done. You're just tired. You've been through a lot."

But there was something in his tone, something that didn't quite match the words. It was that same underlying tension I'd picked up on earlier. I could see it now, the faint furrow of his brow, the way his fingers hesitated above the keyboard. He wasn't as calm as he was letting on.

"I don't know," I said, my voice trembling a little despite myself. "It feels like something's still out there. Something we didn't catch."

Finn sighed and stood, pushing away from the table. He walked over to the window, his broad shoulders casting a long shadow across the floor. I followed him with my eyes as he peered outside, the same way I had just moments ago. He didn't say anything at first, just stood there, his expression unreadable. Then, finally, he turned back to me.

"I'll check the security system," he said, a quiet promise lacing his words. "Make sure everything's locked down. We'll be fine."

He didn't look convinced, but he didn't want to worry me more than I already was. And in that moment, I realized—maybe Finn didn't have the answers either. Maybe we were both just waiting for something to happen, for that next thing to reveal itself.

As he walked over to the door to grab his keys, I noticed the flicker again, out of the corner of my eye. Just a blur, just a shadow, quick and fleeting. I blinked, but when I looked back outside, everything was normal.

That night, I couldn't shake the feeling of being watched. It wasn't the usual paranoia that comes with a bad dream or a horror movie marathon—it was too sharp, too insistent. I lay in bed, the weight of the silence pressing down on me like an invisible hand. Finn was beside me, his steady breathing a soft lullaby that normally would have comforted me. But tonight, the sounds of the house felt alien. The quiet was thick, suffocating, as though the walls themselves were holding their breath, waiting for something to happen.

I pulled the covers tighter around me, trying to convince myself to sleep. But no matter how many times I closed my eyes, the shadows seemed to grow longer, stretching across the room like dark fingers reaching for me. I rolled over, careful not to disturb Finn, and glanced at the clock. 3:17 a.m. No one was awake at this hour—except for me, of course, caught in this web of unease I couldn't explain.

Just then, a noise. A faint scraping sound, coming from the direction of the front door. My heart stopped. I waited, straining to hear any further indication of movement, but all was still. Maybe it was a branch, caught in the wind. Maybe a stray animal brushing against the doorframe. But deep down, I knew better than to dismiss it so easily.

I threw the blankets off with a swift motion, my feet hitting the cool hardwood floor with a soft thud. Finn stirred beside me, a low groan escaping his lips. He was still half asleep, a good thing in this moment, because I wasn't sure what I was about to do. My mind raced—what if I was being foolish, what if it was nothing? But what if it wasn't?

The scraping came again, this time louder. My pulse quickened. I tiptoed to the door, every step feeling like it echoed through the house. I hesitated, my hand on the doorknob, and glanced back at Finn. He was lying on his side, his expression soft and peaceful, blissfully unaware of the threat I felt creeping just outside our walls.

I opened the door a crack, just enough to peek outside. The night air was crisp, biting against my skin, and I could see nothing—just the empty porch, the shadows of the trees stretching across the yard in a way that looked almost unnatural. A cold breeze swept past me, carrying with it the scent of damp earth. It was a night that begged for something to be amiss, a night that promised the impossible, if only you were brave enough to face it.

The scraping stopped.

I stepped outside, the gravel crunching underfoot as I made my way to the edge of the porch. The shadows seemed to shift with me, as though they were aware of my every movement. I scanned the yard once more, the silence now even heavier, the kind of quiet that feels like it could swallow you whole. There was nothing. No sign of movement. No indication that anyone was lurking in the shadows.

I should have gone back inside. I knew it. Every rational part of me screamed to retreat, to leave the strange feeling behind and close the door on whatever it was that had been troubling me. But I couldn't. I stayed there, rooted to the spot, staring into the darkness, waiting for something—anything—to give me an answer.

Then, a flash of movement, so quick it could have been my imagination. A figure darted from behind the tree at the far edge of the yard, vanishing before I could register it fully. My breath hitched. I took a step forward, my eyes trained on the spot where the figure had disappeared, but all I saw were the trees, their branches swaying in the wind.

No. This wasn't right. I wasn't imagining things. There was something—or someone—out there.

I stepped back into the house, my mind racing. The door clicked shut behind me, the soft sound of the latch catching like a sigh of relief. Finn was still asleep, oblivious to the creeping terror that had taken root in my chest. I slid down the door, pressing my back against it, trying to steady my breathing. I should wake him, tell him what I'd seen, but what if it was nothing? What if I was just losing my mind?

The house was still. The world outside was still. But inside, I could feel it—an undercurrent of tension, like a storm waiting to break.

I waited, but nothing happened.

By the time I slipped back into bed, I'd convinced myself that maybe it was just the stress, the lingering effects of everything that had happened. Maybe my nerves were getting the better of me. But as I lay there in the dark, the shadows seemed to grow longer once again, like they were waiting for something.

When I woke the next morning, Finn was already up, making coffee in the kitchen. The warmth of the sunlight streamed through the windows, casting golden beams across the room. The air smelled of freshly brewed coffee and the faint scent of pancakes, a comfort in the otherwise unsettling silence. But even as I moved through my morning routine, the memory of last night's experience clung to me.

I found myself glancing over my shoulder more often than I should have, checking corners I wouldn't normally think twice about. I told myself it was just lingering nerves, the aftermath of the scare. Finn had that effect on me, always knowing when to break through my spiraling thoughts with a soft touch, a gentle reassurance that everything would be fine.

"Liv," he said, turning from the stove with a warm smile, "I was thinking we could take a drive today. Get out of the house for a bit. What do you think?"

I nodded, the idea of a distraction sounding perfect. Maybe getting out of this house would help clear my head, remind me that there was still a world beyond these walls. But I couldn't shake the feeling that no matter how far I went, something was waiting for me. Something I hadn't seen yet, but that was always just out of reach, like a shadow I couldn't outrun.

By the time we hit the road, the weight of the unease still clung to me, like a damp fog that wouldn't lift. Finn had been hopeful that the change of scenery would shake my nerves loose, but I wasn't convinced. The car hummed steadily under us, the world blurring in streaks of green and blue as we passed fields and trees that I'd long since stopped seeing. The rhythmic sway of the road was soothing, but I couldn't stop my eyes from flicking to the rearview mirror, checking the empty expanse behind us. It was irrational, I knew, but the feeling of being followed had become my new constant.

"Liv," Finn said, his voice warm, a touch of concern threading through it. "You okay?"

I glanced at him. He was looking at me, trying to be gentle, but his brow was creased in that way that made me wonder if he was trying to convince himself as much as me that everything was fine. I forced a smile.

"Yeah. Just thinking," I said, voice soft, not wanting to tell him about the thought that had been nagging at me since the night before—what if this feeling was tied to something deeper? What if the arsonist wasn't just a criminal but part of a pattern I couldn't see? What if I had missed something? He had always been my anchor, but right now, I felt like I was drifting, and no amount of calm, measured words could bring me back to shore.

Finn didn't press me, letting the silence stretch between us as we continued down the winding country road. His fingers drummed idly on the steering wheel, lost in thought as well. I wanted to reach out, take his hand, but the distance between us seemed to grow with each passing mile. The quiet was comforting, but it felt off, like something was holding its breath, waiting for us to crack the surface and dive into whatever it was lurking beneath.

We drove for hours, winding deeper into the countryside, where the landscape grew wild and untamed. The green hills rolled on endlessly, dotted with clusters of trees and the occasional farmhouse. The air was fresh, crisp in a way that made me feel alive, but the feeling of being trapped in some unseen web of tension never quite left. It was like walking through a dream—beautiful, yes, but hollow, incomplete.

"I'm glad we're doing this," Finn said, breaking the silence. "I know it's been hard lately. You're not the only one feeling it."

I glanced over at him, my chest tightening slightly. "What do you mean?"

He hesitated, a flicker of uncertainty crossing his face. "I've been... worried. About you. About the whole thing, really. I'm not sure everything's as clear-cut as we thought. I know we caught the guy we were after, but there's something about it all that still doesn't sit right with me."

I swallowed, suddenly feeling the weight of his words sink into me like stones in water. "You think there's more to it? More we haven't uncovered?"

Finn's grip on the wheel tightened, his eyes focusing on the road ahead, but there was a faraway look in his gaze now. "I don't know. But after everything, I don't think we've reached the end of this yet. Something feels off, Liv. Like we've only scratched the surface."

His words hit me harder than I expected, a sharp pang of realization twisting in my stomach. I hadn't wanted to admit it, but the nagging feeling—the one I couldn't shake, no matter how hard I tried—wasn't just paranoia. It was instinct. Something was wrong. But what? And more importantly, why hadn't we noticed it sooner?

We kept driving, the landscape blurring in and out of focus, and I couldn't help but feel like we were chasing something just out of reach, something we couldn't see yet, but it was closing in on us all the same.

Then it happened.

The car jerked violently, throwing me forward against the seatbelt. Finn cursed, quickly regaining control of the wheel, but the steering wheel felt slippery in his hands, almost as if the road itself was conspiring against us. My heart pounded in my chest, my breath coming in quick, shallow bursts. I looked out the window, expecting to see something—anything—that could explain the sudden jolt. But the road was clear, the open fields stretching out on either side, peaceful and still.

"What the hell?" I gasped, trying to steady my nerves.

Finn's knuckles were white on the wheel as he glanced at me. "I don't know. That wasn't just a flat tire, Liv. Something's wrong."

We pulled over, the gravel crunching under the tires as Finn stopped the car at the side of the road. I didn't want to admit it, but a cold sense of dread washed over me as I watched him step out of the car and walk to the front. I stayed inside, staring at the horizon, trying to make sense of the unease that had settled in the pit of my stomach. The sun was dipping lower now, the sky turning a soft lavender as the light began to fade. The air felt thick with tension, like the entire world was holding its breath, waiting.

I glanced back at the rearview mirror, half-expecting to see something—or someone—lurking just beyond the line of sight. But the road behind us was empty, the nothingness stretching out in every direction.

Finn's voice broke through the quiet, sharp with urgency. "Liv. Get out here."

I scrambled out of the car, my heart thudding in my chest. Finn was standing near the front bumper, his expression pale, his eyes wide with disbelief.

"There's nothing wrong with the car," he said slowly, almost as if he couldn't believe the words. "The brakes aren't damaged. No flat. No leaks."

I frowned, stepping closer. "Then what caused the jolt?"

Finn shook his head, his jaw clenched. He didn't have an answer. Neither of us did.

Just then, a rustling sound came from the field to our left. Something moved, something big. I turned instinctively, but there was nothing there. Nothing except the waving grass and the whisper of the wind.

Then, a voice—faint, but unmistakable—whispered across the still air, barely more than a breath.

"Liv..."

My blood turned to ice. I spun around, my heart slamming in my chest, but Finn was already at my side, his face drawn, his expression no longer calm. The wind whispered again, this time louder, closer.

"Liv..." The voice called my name, familiar, like it was coming from right behind me.

But when I turned, there was no one there.

Chapter 29: A Burning Revelation

I was knee-deep in the case files when I saw it. A name, innocuous enough at first glance, but then the details pried their way into my mind like the echo of a distant, haunting memory. It was as if the room around me grew a shade colder, the yellowed edges of the manila folders seeming to shift under my hands. The name was there, simple yet damning: Isabelle Garrett.

I hadn't heard that name in years, and I had certainly never expected it to show up here, in this pile of unsorted chaos. Finn had said her name only once, a passing mention in the midst of a conversation that had been far too casual to raise suspicion. I had filed it away like I did with so many other things, convinced it was a name from a past that he had buried long ago. A name belonging to someone who, like so many others, had drifted in and out of his life, leaving little more than a faint trace.

But this... this was different.

As I read the file more closely, the pieces began to fit together in a way that made my chest tighten with something akin to fear. Isabelle Garrett had been close to Finn, more so than I had ever realized. The kind of close that bordered on dangerous. She had been a part of the very fabric of his life, a shadow weaving in and out of his past like a whisper in the dark.

I ran my fingers over the worn paper, the sensation like dragging my hand through a spider's web, catching every fragile thread of memory. It wasn't just that she had been in his life—it was that she had been in our lives, unbeknownst to me. She had been there, hidden in plain sight, while I had been too blinded by my own naïveté to see the truth.

I leaned back in my chair, the realization seeping into my bones like ice water, and for a moment, I couldn't breathe. The fires, the cryptic threats that had been plaguing us for months—how could I have been so blind? They weren't random. They were part of a plan, a twisted vendetta that stretched further back than either of us had anticipated.

I pulled my phone from my pocket, the weight of it suddenly feeling heavier than it ever had. There was no doubt in my mind now that Finn didn't know the full extent of what was happening. Not yet. But he would. And when he did, it was going to shatter everything.

The thought of him, his unspoken fears, his guarded past... it twisted inside me, pulling at the threads of our relationship that I had so carefully woven together. Could I still trust him? Would he be able to forgive me for not seeing this sooner? The questions gnawed at me, each one louder than the last.

The door creaked open, and Finn stepped inside, his eyes catching mine with an intensity that made my heart race. He didn't say anything at first—he just stood there, taking in the sight of me surrounded by the scattered files, my face pale and drawn. I wasn't sure what he saw, but the tension in the room thickened, a quiet storm brewing between us.

"What's wrong?" he asked, his voice low, guarded.

I met his gaze, the words catching in my throat. How could I explain this? How could I tell him that the woman from his past, the one who had seemed like a footnote in the story of his life, was now the focal point of everything we were fighting against?

Instead of answering him, I did the only thing I could think of. I slid the file across the table toward him, watching as he picked it up, his expression unreadable as he scanned the contents. His jaw tightened, and I could see the shift in his eyes, the way his focus zeroed in on something only he could understand.

"I was hoping you'd be able to explain this to me," I said, my voice barely above a whisper.

Finn didn't respond immediately. He closed the file and sat down across from me, his hands pressed together, the usual confidence in his posture replaced with something much darker.

"Isabelle Garrett," he murmured, the name tasting strange on his tongue. "I never thought I'd hear that name again."

His words, so casual, sent a shiver down my spine. How was it possible that he could speak her name without a flicker of hesitation? As if it didn't matter that the world we had fought so hard to build was now crumbling under the weight of secrets he had buried.

"You know her," I said, the words escaping before I could stop them. It wasn't a question—it was an accusation.

Finn's gaze didn't waver. "I do. But it's not what you think."

The way he said it—soft, measured—made me feel like I was holding a ticking time bomb, a delicate thing that could go off at any moment.

I leaned forward, my hands trembling as I braced myself for whatever came next. "Then explain it to me, Finn. Explain why she's suddenly a part of all of this. The fires, the threats—it's all connected, isn't it?"

He exhaled sharply, leaning back in his chair, his eyes distant. "It's not that simple," he said. "Isabelle... she's part of a chapter of my life I never wanted to reopen. But now, I don't have a choice."

I sat back, my heart pounding in my chest. There it was. The first crack in the armor. The part of Finn's past that had been locked away, deep inside, and now it was threatening to surface with a vengeance.

"You think you're the only one with secrets?" he continued, his voice laced with frustration. "I've spent years running from mine, trying to protect you from the things I couldn't control. But this—this is bigger than us."

I didn't know what to say. There was nothing I could say that would make it right. All I could do was wait, to see just how deep this rabbit hole went. The truth was out there now, and no matter how much we both wished otherwise, we were no longer in control.

Finn leaned forward, his hands still pressed together, the space between us suddenly feeling like miles. "I never wanted to drag you into this," he said, his voice rough, the words tasting like ash in his mouth. "But now it's happening, and I don't know how to protect you anymore."

I couldn't hold his gaze. Not because I didn't want to, but because I was suddenly too aware of the weight of the moment, the gravity of everything hanging between us. I had always known Finn was carrying some kind of burden—a past so tangled, so dark, that it had left him with a permanent shadow on his soul. But this? This was something else.

I ran a hand through my hair, trying to push past the sudden wave of dizziness that overtook me. I had always thought I knew him—really knew him. But now, I realized I had been living in a house of mirrors, seeing only what he allowed me to see. It wasn't his fault, not entirely. I had never pushed him to open up, had always let him keep those layers of himself locked away. Now I regretted that more than I could put into words.

"You said she was part of your past," I finally said, my voice steady, though I wasn't sure how. "But it sounds like she's still part of our present."

Finn didn't answer immediately. He rubbed his hands over his face, his frustration evident. It was rare for him to look so... vulnerable. The Finn I knew was always in control, always a step ahead. But now, he was unraveling before me in a way I hadn't expected.

"I thought I could leave it behind," he muttered, almost to himself. "But it's never really gone. It's always been there, lurking just below the surface. And Isabelle..." He faltered, his gaze flickering to the file I'd pushed toward him. "She's the one who set all of this in motion. All the fires, the threats—it's her. She's been playing this game for longer than I care to admit."

I leaned forward, a chill running down my spine. "What kind of game?"

Finn let out a frustrated breath. "A deadly one. Isabelle was always unpredictable, but I never thought she would go this far." He stood abruptly, pacing the room with a restless energy, as though trying to outrun the weight of his own confession. "She's always had a knack for manipulation, for getting inside people's heads. And she knows how to play dirty. She's not someone you can walk away from without consequences."

I swallowed hard, my mind racing to make sense of everything. Isabelle Garrett, this woman I had barely known about, had been hiding in plain sight, watching us, orchestrating this nightmare. And now, it seemed, she had Finn's past tangled in her fingers, ready to drag him—and me—into whatever hell she was preparing.

"Is she after you?" I asked, my voice tight with something that felt a lot like dread.

He stopped pacing and turned to face me. His expression was hard to read, a mask of anger and guilt. "I don't know," he admitted. "She's always been unpredictable. I never thought I would have to worry about her again, but now... everything she's done, it's all been a message. A warning."

I stood up, my legs shaky as I tried to process the gravity of what he was saying. "And the fires? The threats? They're all connected to her?"

Finn nodded, his eyes darkening. "I think she's trying to get to me through you. She always was... possessive, manipulative. She'll do anything to regain control, to get what she wants." He let out a sharp laugh, but there was no humor in it. "She's like a fire, once it's started, it spreads, and it's nearly impossible to put out."

The room seemed to close in on me, the air thick with the weight of his words. I hadn't signed up for this. I hadn't signed up to be tangled in someone else's twisted vendetta, least of all someone from Finn's past. I had come into his life with the hope of simplicity—of a love that was uncomplicated, free of old ghosts. But now, I could feel them all around us, pressing in, whispering from the shadows.

"I should have known," I said, more to myself than to him. "I should have realized that something was off. But I let my guard down." The bitterness in my voice stung.

"You couldn't have known," Finn said, his tone softer now, almost pleading. "I kept it from you for a reason. I wanted to protect you."

I shook my head. "You think hiding the truth is protecting me? You're wrong, Finn. Keeping secrets, especially the ones that matter, that only makes things worse."

His jaw tightened, and for a moment, I saw the storm brewing behind his eyes. "I didn't want you to see me like this," he said quietly, the words coming out in a rush. "I didn't want you to see the mess that I've made of everything. But now you're in it, too. And I'm sorry. I'm so damn sorry."

There it was—the vulnerability I had been waiting for. The raw truth behind his guarded exterior. It wasn't just the threats that had him on edge; it was the fact that everything was crumbling, and I was right in the middle of it. And yet, despite everything, I couldn't pull away.

"You don't have to protect me, Finn," I said, my voice firmer now, even though the tremor of uncertainty was still there. "I'm not some delicate flower who needs saving. But we need to deal with this. Together."

Finn's eyes softened, a flicker of something passing between us—a silent agreement. "We will," he promised, his voice tight. "I'll do whatever it takes to keep you safe. I just need you to trust me."

It was a dangerous thing, trust. More dangerous now than ever before. But it was all we had left. And if I was going to face whatever Isabelle Garrett had planned for us, I had to believe in him.

I just wasn't sure if I was strong enough to.

The silence between us stretched, thick and suffocating. Finn's face was drawn, his eyes distant, as though he were searching for a way to slip out of the cage his past had built around him. The room was still, the only sound the soft rustling of papers, the occasional scratch of my pen as I tried to make sense of everything that had spiraled out of control.

But no matter how much I tried to focus, one thing kept pulling at me—the glint in Finn's eyes, the flicker of something darker beneath the surface. He was holding something back.

"Finn," I said, the words tumbling from my mouth before I could stop them, "there's more to this, isn't there?"

His gaze snapped to mine, sharp and cutting. He was a master at hiding his thoughts, but not from me—not anymore. I had seen the cracks in his armor, and now, all I could do was push until they shattered completely.

"I told you," he started, his voice low, as though testing the waters, "Isabelle's not someone you want to know. She's dangerous, in ways you can't even begin to understand."

I swallowed hard, the weight of his warning sinking into my bones like stones dropped into deep water. "Then why didn't you tell me about her before? About what she's capable of?" My voice shook, despite myself. "Why keep it all locked away?"

Finn's face hardened, and I saw the briefest flash of pain cross his features. It was gone as quickly as it appeared, but the damage had been done. "Because I thought I could protect you from it," he said, his words clipped, and then softer, "I thought I could keep you safe from all this... chaos. But now? Now, I don't know."

There it was, the raw vulnerability. The very thing I had feared and hoped for all at once.

"Finn, I'm not some fragile thing that you can just shield from the world," I said, my voice steadier than I felt. "I'm not going anywhere, no matter what's in your past. We're in this together now."

He stared at me for a long moment, his eyes like dark pools of turmoil. And then, as if making a decision, he nodded. "You're right. You deserve the truth. All of it."

I took a deep breath, bracing myself for the weight of what was coming. "Then tell me, Finn. Tell me everything."

He exhaled slowly, his hands gripping the edge of the table as though anchoring himself to something solid. "It started years ago, before I met you. Isabelle was... a part of my life I wish I could forget. We were close, in ways I didn't understand at the time. She was brilliant, manipulative, and ruthless. When she wanted something, she didn't care who she had to destroy to get it."

I leaned in, trying to hold on to every word. The pieces were beginning to shift, but I was still missing so many parts of the puzzle. "And the fires? The threats? She's been behind all of it?"

Finn nodded, his expression hardening. "She's been playing a game. A dangerous one. And it's not just about me. It never was. She's always had an eye on you, too."

A cold chill settled in the pit of my stomach. "Me?"

"From the very beginning," Finn replied, his voice edged with a hardness I'd never heard before. "You were always part of her plan.

I should have seen it sooner, but I didn't." His eyes locked on mine. "You're in more danger than you realize."

The words hung in the air, heavy and suffocating. I didn't know what to say to that. I didn't know what to do with the information, the sudden realization that I had been walking into a storm all this time, unaware of the hurricane that had been waiting just outside our door.

"I'm not running, Finn," I said, the words tasting strange on my tongue, but I meant them with every ounce of my being. "Not from you, not from her. We face this head-on. Together."

Finn looked at me, his gaze searching, as though trying to read the depths of my resolve. For a long moment, neither of us spoke, the room thick with tension and unspoken promises. And then, as if realizing something too late, Finn stood abruptly, his hand shooting out to grab my arm.

"Don't move," he whispered, his voice a low command, laced with fear. "She's here."

I froze, my blood running cold at his words. There was no time to process, no time to question. I felt it then, the sudden shift in the air. A presence, like a storm rolling in from the horizon, a weight that settled into the room and pressed down on my chest.

I opened my mouth to say something, but Finn's grip tightened on my arm, his voice urgent, low. "Don't say anything. Don't make a sound."

And then, through the crack in the door, a shadow moved.

I didn't need to be told twice. My heart raced in my chest as I slid to the side, pressing my back against the wall, trying to make myself as small as possible. Finn's hand hovered near the gun at his hip, but he didn't pull it out, his eyes scanning the room with the kind of focus that only came from years of experience.

I could barely breathe, the air thick with the weight of the moment. What the hell was happening?

And then the door creaked open.

I had no time to think, no time to prepare. A silhouette stood in the doorway, a figure I couldn't make out in the dim light. But the voice that followed—sharp, biting, and familiar—sent a tremor through my bones.

"Well, well," she said, her voice dripping with a twisted kind of satisfaction. "It looks like you two have been quite busy."

The room went deathly still, and for a moment, I could have sworn my heart stopped beating altogether.

Isabelle Garrett had arrived.

Chapter 30: The Truth in Flames

I leaned against the doorframe, my arms folded tightly over my chest, feeling the sharp edge of frustration settling in my stomach. Finn stood by the kitchen counter, his hands gripping the edge like it was the only thing holding him up. The room between us felt impossibly wide, the silence thick enough to cut through. The smell of coffee lingered in the air, the bitter scent doing nothing to calm the growing storm inside me. He wasn't looking at me, not really, his gaze fixed somewhere past me, as if the truth would vanish if he simply ignored it long enough.

"So," I said, the word coming out with more force than I intended, "you're telling me you knew this person was a threat all along, and you kept it from me?"

His jaw clenched, the muscles in his neck taut with the weight of unspoken things. He finally turned to meet my eyes, but it wasn't the look of a man who was sorry. No, it was the look of someone caught in a trap of their own making, helpless and stubborn in equal measure.

"I didn't know for sure," he muttered, voice low. "But... I suspected. I saw things, heard things. I thought it was better to keep you out of it. You've been through enough."

My fingers curled into fists at my sides. "I'm not some fragile thing you have to protect. I'm not a child, Finn. You should've told me. We're supposed to be a team."

The tension in his face deepened, and I saw the conflict in his eyes. I wasn't sure if he was struggling to tell me the rest of what he knew or if the guilt was suffocating him. He took a step closer, but I didn't move. I wasn't ready to let him close just yet.

"You don't understand," he said, his voice cracking slightly. "This person... they've been in my life a long time. They know things. Things about me, about us. I couldn't risk dragging you deeper into it."

There it was again—the shadow of a person, their presence like a cloud looming over everything between us. Someone who had the power to unravel us, to expose every crack we'd been trying to patch. But I wasn't interested in his fears anymore.

"No," I said sharply, "you couldn't risk it. That's the problem, isn't it? You were protecting yourself. You let the guilt fester until it became more important than anything else."

I could see the words cut through him, and for a brief moment, I felt a flicker of regret. He wasn't a bad person. He was just... human. But it didn't change the fact that he'd kept me in the dark. He had let me live under the illusion of safety while he knew the truth was far darker than I could have imagined. The betrayal was a cold weight settling heavily on my chest.

"Who is it, Finn?" I demanded, my voice sharp with the need for clarity. "Who have you been hiding from me?"

He hesitated, and I saw the ghost of a name on his lips, but it didn't come out. Instead, he shook his head, looking away.

"I can't just say it like that. You wouldn't understand—"

"Try me," I interrupted, frustration spilling over into impatience. "I've been through enough chaos in my life to know that nothing surprises me anymore. So just say it."

The silence stretched longer, a painful thing between us. His eyes darted around the room, avoiding mine like they were a threat, like the truth would burn him if he said it out loud.

Finally, he spoke, his words barely above a whisper. "It's my brother. Alec."

The name hit me like a slap, like the air had been knocked out of my lungs. Alec. Of course. How had I not seen it before? All the cryptic warnings, the subtle evasions, the way Finn would tense whenever his brother was mentioned. It was there all along, hidden behind layers of denial. Alec had been playing a game that neither of us fully understood, and Finn had been too tangled in his own guilt to pull me in.

I took a deep breath, the reality sinking in like a stone in my stomach. "Your brother," I repeated slowly, as if saying the words aloud might somehow make them less true. "He's the one behind all of this?"

Finn looked away, rubbing his hand over his face, a mixture of shame and helplessness swirling around him. "I didn't know for sure. I thought it was paranoia. But the more I looked into it, the more I saw how deep he was involved. He's been using my past against me. My mistakes. My failures. And now..." He trailed off, glancing at me with a mix of apology and something darker, something I couldn't quite name.

"And now," I echoed, taking a step closer to him, "you're tangled in something you can't get out of. You're afraid to face it because of the damage it'll do. To both of us."

He winced, his shoulders slumping, like the weight of the world had finally found its way onto them. "Exactly."

I shook my head, suddenly feeling a rush of clarity. "You're not alone in this, Finn. You don't have to carry this burden by yourself. But you need to let me in. We need to figure out how to stop him, before he ruins everything we've worked for."

His gaze met mine then, and for the first time in what felt like an eternity, I saw a flicker of hope in his eyes. It was small, fragile, but it was there. And for the first time, I believed that maybe, just maybe, we could face this together.

We stood there for what felt like an eternity, the hum of the refrigerator in the background the only sound breaking the thick silence. It was as if we were both afraid to take the next step, afraid to speak the words that would solidify everything we'd just uncovered. The room felt too small, too confined for what was unfolding between us. The air crackled with an unspoken understanding, a promise that things could never go back to how they were. And yet, despite the heavy weight of the moment, despite the unspeakable things between us, I felt an undeniable pull to stay. To make sense of all of it.

Finn shifted on his feet, the tension in his body still palpable, as if the very act of standing beside me had become unbearable. "I never wanted you to be involved in any of this," he said finally, his voice barely above a whisper, the words rough and jagged like he was forcing them out. "I thought I could handle it. Thought I could fix it without dragging you down with me."

I exhaled slowly, my eyes never leaving his. His words, however well-meaning, only stoked the embers of my frustration. I wanted to scream, to let him know that he didn't get to decide what I could or couldn't handle. But instead, I did something I didn't expect—I took a step toward him.

"No," I said firmly, my voice calm but resolute. "You didn't fix anything by keeping me out of it. You just made it worse."

His eyes widened slightly, a flicker of surprise crossing his face. For a moment, I thought he might apologize again, but the words never came. Instead, he just stared at me, his lips pressed together as if debating whether to say anything more.

The truth hung in the air like an invisible weight, pressing down on us both. I could feel the gravity of it, the enormity of what we were up against. Alec—Finn's brother. The one person who had always seemed like a shadow in our lives, lurking just on the edge of our vision, was suddenly a far more dangerous presence than I'd ever imagined.

"I've been fighting this for so long, trying to outrun him, outrun my own guilt," Finn said, breaking the silence, his voice raw with the confession. "But Alec... he doesn't let go. He keeps pulling me back in."

I could hear the weariness in his tone, the weight of years spent under Alec's thumb. It made sense now, the way Finn had always been so reluctant to talk about his past. Alec had been the constant, the looming threat, the one who knew every secret Finn had buried. The one who could unravel him with a single word, a single whisper in the right ear.

"You don't have to outrun him anymore," I said, my voice steady, though inside, I was barely holding it together. "We'll face him together. You don't have to carry this alone."

Finn's gaze softened for just a moment, but then his eyes darkened again, the worry creeping back in. "I don't know how, Anna," he confessed, the words almost a plea. "He's dangerous. He's always been dangerous, but now... now he's got everything. The leverage. The information. He's cornered me in ways I never thought possible."

I crossed my arms again, my stance firm as I watched him. "Well, we'll just have to change the game then. We'll turn the tables."

Finn let out a short, disbelieving laugh. "And how exactly do you plan on doing that?"

I tilted my head, a sly smile playing at the corners of my lips. "I'm good at digging up dirt, Finn. And you'd be surprised at how many people are willing to talk if you know how to ask the right questions."

Finn stared at me for a beat, his brow furrowing as if weighing my words. He was clearly not used to thinking of me as someone who could take on Alec's dark world. But he was wrong to doubt me. I'd spent too many years buried in the muck of other people's secrets to back down now.

He was about to speak, but I held up a hand to stop him, my gaze sharpening as I cut him off. "No more secrets. No more hiding from the truth. We face it, head on. Together."

His lips parted as though he were going to protest, but then he stopped, as if he'd finally come to the same conclusion I had. He didn't want to fight this alone anymore. And neither did I. The road ahead was treacherous, I could feel it in my bones, but for the first time in a long while, I wasn't afraid.

"I've been trying to protect you," Finn said, his voice rough, like he was trying to find the words to make this all make sense. "But I don't want to keep you in the dark anymore. You deserve to know everything."

"Then tell me," I said, my tone softening, but the resolve was still there. "Tell me what Alec is capable of, and how we can stop him. No more half-truths, Finn. No more lies."

He swallowed hard, his eyes flicking to the floor as if the weight of everything was finally catching up with him. "Alec is ruthless," he said slowly, his voice heavy. "He's always been that way, but lately... it's like he's grown more dangerous. He knows everything about me—about us. He's not just manipulating my guilt anymore. He's trying to control everything. He's got people working for him, people who are close to us, watching us. And I don't know who to trust anymore."

The words hung between us, thick with the dread they carried. Alec had built a network, a shadowy web of influence that reached further than we'd ever imagined. And we were tangled in it, whether we liked it or not.

I felt a surge of determination flood through me. "Then we'll cut that web. One thread at a time."

Finn looked up at me, his expression unreadable, but there was something in his eyes—a flicker of something like hope, like maybe we could actually do this. And for the first time in a long while, I believed it too. Together, we had a chance. But only if we faced Alec head-on, no more hiding, no more running. The truth was out there now, and there was no going back.

The next few hours passed in a blur. Finn and I barely spoke after that conversation, but the weight of it lingered, an oppressive presence that seemed to follow us like a shadow. He paced around the living room, running his fingers through his hair, the rhythm of his movements sharp and anxious. Every so often, his eyes would flick to me, and I could see the struggle written all over his face. I wasn't sure whether he was trying to come to terms with his own guilt or with the fact that we were both standing on the edge of something far more dangerous than either of us had anticipated.

I watched him, waiting for him to say something—anything—but the words never came. The silence stretched long, and I knew that it wasn't just Alec who was keeping secrets. Finn had built a wall around himself, one that was impenetrable unless I found a way to tear it down. But where to start? How to convince him that we were stronger together than apart?

"You can't do this alone, Finn," I finally said, my voice cutting through the heavy quiet like a knife. "You can't keep carrying this burden by yourself."

He stopped in his tracks and turned to face me, his eyes haunted. "I don't know what to do, Anna. I don't know how to stop him."

I crossed the room slowly, stopping just a few feet away from him. "Then let's figure it out. Together."

There was a long pause, and I could feel the conflict swirling in him. He was still holding on to that instinct to protect me, to shield me from whatever Alec was capable of. But that wasn't the person I was anymore. I had come to realize, in the moments we'd spent apart and in the ones we'd spent together, that I wasn't just a bystander in this. I wasn't waiting for a knight in shining armor to come rescue me. I was the one holding the sword now, the one ready to fight.

Finn's eyes softened, but his voice was still rough when he spoke again. "Alec... he won't stop until he's won, Anna. You don't know what he's capable of."

I shook my head, frustration rising in my chest again. "I don't care what he's capable of. We'll find a way to take him down. If we don't, he'll keep doing this to you. He'll keep controlling everything, and I can't let that happen."

Finn didn't say anything, but I could see the slight shift in his expression. It wasn't much, but it was enough to make me believe that maybe, just maybe, he was finally starting to believe in us too.

"How do we start?" he asked quietly, almost as if the words pained him to say.

I stepped closer to him, placing a hand on his arm. "We start by finding out what Alec is really after. What he wants. If we understand that, maybe we can figure out how to stop him. But we need to work fast. Every minute we waste is another minute Alec gains ground."

Finn nodded slowly, his jaw tight. "I'll dig. See what I can find."

"Good," I said, my voice firm. "And I'll start looking into his people. The ones working for him. There's always someone who knows something, Finn. We just have to find them."

The plan felt like a fragile thread between us, but it was something. It was progress.

Finn pulled away from me, his posture still tense but more determined than it had been before. "I'll make some calls," he said, his voice hardening. "We'll find a way to track him down. But Anna..." His voice faltered for a moment, and his gaze dropped to the floor. "If Alec comes for you—"

I didn't let him finish. "He won't," I said, cutting him off. "But if he does, I'll be ready."

There was a flicker of something in Finn's eyes, a brief flash of appreciation, maybe even respect, but it disappeared as quickly as it had come. “Alright. But we need to stay ahead of him. And I’ll need your help.”

I nodded. “I’ll do whatever it takes.”

The sound of my phone ringing broke through the tension in the room, and I instinctively reached for it, my pulse quickening when I saw the name on the screen. It was a number I didn’t recognize, but there was something about it that made my stomach tighten in warning.

“Anna,” Finn said softly, his voice low and tense as he watched me. “Who is it?”

I glanced up at him, my fingers hovering over the phone. “I don’t know. But something tells me I should answer.”

I swiped to accept the call, lifting the phone to my ear, my heart pounding in my chest. “Hello?”

For a long moment, there was only silence on the other end, and I felt a chill run down my spine. Then, the voice that came through was low, almost a whisper, but unmistakable.

“It’s Alec,” he said. “You’ve been asking too many questions, Anna. And that’s a mistake.”

My breath caught in my throat, my body going rigid with shock. It wasn’t just a warning—it was a declaration. He knew what we were doing, and we were no longer in control of the game.

I looked up at Finn, his face pale as he took in the situation. “What does he want?” he asked, his voice barely a whisper.

But I couldn’t speak. Alec’s words had frozen me in place. “You think you can stop me, Anna?” he continued, his voice smooth, almost mocking. “You don’t even know the half of it.”

And then the line went dead.

For a moment, everything around me felt suspended, like the world had stopped turning. Alec’s words echoed in my head, sending a cold shiver down my spine. It was clear now—he was playing a game with no rules, and we were just pawns in his hands.

I took a shaky breath and turned to Finn, my eyes wide with the realization that we had just stepped into something much darker than either of us had imagined. Alec was no longer just a threat; he was a ticking time bomb, and we had no idea when it was going to explode.

"We're out of time," I whispered, my voice barely above a breath.

And before Finn could respond, the sound of a car screeching to a halt outside shattered the silence.

This was it. The storm had come.

Chapter 31: Into the Depths

The air in the office was thick with the smell of freshly brewed coffee and old paper, a scent I had come to associate with late nights and nervous energy. Finn sat across from me, his fingers drumming on the polished wood of the table in an absent rhythm, his gaze fixed somewhere past my shoulder, lost in thought. I had learned not to ask too many questions about his silences—he had a way of retreating into himself, a habit born from years of avoiding the truths that could bring his carefully constructed world down around him.

"Are you sure about this?" I asked, leaning forward, the weight of the moment pressing down on me. I could feel the heat of the room, the claustrophobia of it, but the question lingered in the space between us like a wisp of smoke—there but not really there.

Finn didn't look at me at first. Instead, he kept staring at the papers in front of him, their edges frayed from hours of handling. I knew he was working through his own fears, the kind that lurked in the dark corners of his mind, the kind he didn't like to confront. But this was different. This wasn't just about him anymore. This was about us.

"We don't have a choice," he muttered finally, his voice low, thick with regret. "You know that." He ran a hand through his hair, pushing it back, a nervous gesture I hadn't seen from him in months. It made me want to reach across the table and hold him, but something in the back of my mind told me not to. Not yet. Not until we knew everything.

I let out a slow breath, trying to calm the fluttering anxiety in my chest. It had been building for days, ever since we had started digging into his past. Each interview, each conversation with people who had known him when he was someone else, had left me feeling more unsettled than the last. There was a sense of unease that came with peeling back layers of a person's history, a discomfort that was hard to shake. But I couldn't stop. I wouldn't stop.

"I didn't sign up for this," I said, my voice coming out sharper than I intended. "I didn't sign up for whatever mess you've gotten yourself into." The words hung in the air between us like a challenge, but Finn only sighed, his eyes finally meeting mine, and for a moment, it felt as though the weight of everything pressing down on us had become too much for him to bear alone.

"I never meant for you to be dragged into it." His words were quieter now, but they carried a heaviness that told me more than he meant to admit. "But you are, and so am I. There's no going back now."

I wanted to scream at him, to tell him how much this was all tearing me apart, but instead, I stayed silent, nodding as I felt my heart race. He was right—there was no going back. We had crossed the point of no return the moment we decided to look into his past, the moment we followed the trail of breadcrumbs that had led us to this crumbling web of lies.

The clock on the wall ticked loudly, as if mocking our silence. The room felt colder now, the shadows longer, stretching out from the corners like the tendrils of something dark and unavoidable.

The truth was close. So close, I could almost taste it, like the bitter edge of a drink I had refused to take. But the closer we got, the more I could feel the danger, a sharp prickling sensation crawling up my spine. There was something waiting, just beyond the veil, something I couldn't see yet, but I could feel it. And it was getting closer.

I tried to shake off the creeping dread and focus on the task at hand. "Who do we talk to next?" I asked, shifting in my seat, my eyes scanning the papers in front of me as if they held the answers.

But they didn't. Nothing on paper could prepare me for the way this was going to end.

Finn ran a hand across his jaw, the muscles tight beneath his skin, his thoughts seemingly a million miles away. "I think it's time to talk to Victor," he said, his voice tight. "He'll know something."

The name hit me like a slap. Victor was a man I'd heard about in hushed tones, his reputation a mix of power, mystery, and a touch of fear. He was a name that lingered in the background of every conversation about Finn's past, a shadow that always seemed to be just out of reach. Until now.

"Victor?" I echoed, my throat dry. "Are you sure about that?"

Finn's eyes hardened, the weight of his decision settling over him like a cloak. "I don't have a choice. We need him."

It was the first time I had heard him speak about Victor so openly, and I wasn't sure if I liked it. It made everything feel too real, too inevitable.

"We'll go tonight," he added, pushing away from the table. He stood, as if the decision had already been made for both of us, his body tense with a mix of anticipation and dread. "Get ready."

I stood, my heart hammering in my chest, a knot of fear and excitement tangled in my gut. This was it. The final step toward the truth, and with it, everything I had come to fear about Finn, about myself, about everything we had built. There was no way to know what we were walking into, no way to prepare for what might happen when we faced Victor.

I followed Finn out of the office, my mind racing. My heart was already in freefall, plummeting into unknown territory. There was no going back now, no escaping what was about to unfold. All I could do was hold on and hope that when the dust settled, there would still be something left of us to save.

By the time we arrived at Victor's, the night had grown heavy with a sense of foreboding. The streets, usually bustling with the hum of city life, were quiet—eerily so. There was no one around, not even the usual late-night stragglers who occupied the shadows, looking for whatever distraction the world could offer. Finn's hand, usually steady on the wheel, tightened as he maneuvered through the darkened alleyways. I could feel the tension radiating from him, sharp and palpable, though he said nothing. We both knew that tonight, the past would bleed into the present in a way neither of us could predict.

Victor's building loomed ahead, its dark windows reflecting the moonlight in jagged slivers. It was an old warehouse, the kind that still held secrets in its creaky bones, and I wasn't sure which part of it terrified me more—the man who lived there or the history we were about to unearth.

Finn parked the car with a quiet precision, his movements slow as he turned off the engine. The stillness between us was deafening, and for the first time in a long time, I found myself wondering if we were doing the right thing. But there was no going back. The curiosity that had first drawn me to Finn had evolved into something far more complicated, a mix of dread and determination that had nothing to do with romance and everything to do with the truth.

I slid out of the car, the sharp scent of rain in the air as it threatened to fall, the night pressing in from all sides. My shoes clicked against the concrete as I followed Finn toward the entrance, the silence stretching longer than either of us seemed comfortable with. The coldness of the night seemed to seep into my bones, and I couldn't help but shiver, though it wasn't the chill in the air that made my skin crawl.

Finn knocked on the door three times, the sound of his knuckles rapping against the old wood almost too loud. We waited, the seconds ticking by like hours, before the door creaked open.

And there, standing in the doorway, was Victor. He was everything I had imagined and nothing at all like I had expected.

Victor wasn't tall, but he had a presence that filled the space, his eyes sharp, calculating. His smile, if you could call it that, was all teeth, no warmth, as though he had seen too much of life's darker side to offer anything genuine. He wore a dark coat that looked like it had been tailored just for him, the fabric smooth and sleek, the kind that whispered of wealth and power. His hair, dark as midnight, was cut short and slicked back, giving him an air of precision, as though he was always in control.

"Finn," he said, his voice smooth like honey, but with a touch of something colder beneath it. "And... this must be the brave soul who's decided to tag along." His eyes flicked over me briefly, appraising, before turning back to Finn.

I didn't speak. There was no point in pretending this wasn't about him—about his relationship with Finn, about whatever secrets he was hiding behind that cold smile.

"We need information," Finn said, his voice controlled, but there was an edge to it now, something rough around the edges. "And you're the only one who can help."

Victor stepped back from the door, a silent invitation that spoke volumes. As we entered, the air inside was different—heavier, filled with the scent of old books, leather, and something else I couldn't quite place. The space was dimly lit, the walls lined with shelves that held an assortment of things: books, artifacts, trinkets, all arranged meticulously. It felt more like a museum than a home, and I couldn't help but feel a slight shiver run down my spine as I glanced around. The kind of place where history wasn't just made—it was stored.

Victor led us to a small sitting area, the furniture dark, sleek, and modern, but with an undercurrent of something older, something that didn't quite fit in. He gestured for us to sit, his movements languid and controlled, as though nothing in the world could rush him. Finn sat first, and I followed, taking the seat across from him.

Victor sank into a chair opposite us, his eyes never leaving Finn's face. The silence stretched between us, thick with unspoken things, until Victor finally spoke again.

"You really think you can handle this?" he asked, his voice a quiet drawl. "The past has a way of coming back, Finn. And it doesn't always come back kindly."

Finn's jaw tightened, but he didn't flinch. "I'm not here for a warning, Victor. I'm here for answers."

Victor chuckled, low and knowing, as if he were amused by something I couldn't quite see. "You want answers, but what are you willing to lose to get them?"

I caught Finn's eye, the flicker of something in his gaze telling me more than his words ever would. Whatever Victor was alluding to, it was bigger than what I had imagined. This was no longer just about secrets; it was about survival.

"You think I don't know what I'm risking?" Finn shot back, his voice hardening with each word. "I'm asking you to tell me what happened. What you and I both know happened."

Victor leaned back in his chair, his fingers steepled in front of him, the way a man might if he was toying with someone. "Ah, Finn," he said softly. "You've always had a way of asking the right questions at the wrong time."

I could feel the tension rising, the weight of the words unspoken pressing down on all of us. I shifted uncomfortably in my seat, feeling the weight of history, of choices that had been made long before I had ever known Finn. And in that moment, I realized that we weren't just uncovering a past. We were stepping into a future none of us could yet see, and the path forward was as uncertain as the darkness closing in around us.

Victor's laughter lingered in the air like the echo of a threat, reverberating through the space, cutting into the silence that had fallen over us. His gaze flicked between Finn and me, the amusement in his eyes sharpening with each passing second.

"You still don't get it, do you?" Victor murmured, almost to himself. "You think you can ask questions and expect answers? You think you can waltz in here and expect me to hand you the truth like it's some neatly wrapped gift?" He leaned forward, his elbows resting on his knees, and for a brief moment, the façade of the smooth, untouchable businessman cracked. His eyes darkened, and I caught a glimpse of something cold and dangerous underneath. "Truth isn't something you just find. It finds you."

I glanced at Finn, but his jaw was set, eyes fixed on Victor with the same kind of intensity I had seen when he was determined to get something done, no matter the cost. The tension between them felt almost physical, a standoff that didn't need words to speak volumes. They were two sides of the same coin, both brilliant, both ruthless, and neither willing to let the other win.

"You're wrong," Finn said quietly, his voice almost too calm. "I'm not asking for the truth, Victor. I'm demanding it."

Victor chuckled again, but this time, there was no humor in it—only a kind of resigned acknowledgment. "Demanding? Oh, I do love it when you get like this." He leaned back in his chair, as if settling into a story he knew all too well. "But demanding the truth from me is like trying to trap smoke in your hands. It slips through your fingers, no matter how tightly you hold on."

Finn's fists clenched at his sides, and I could feel the heat radiating off him. But I couldn't help but feel the pull of Victor's words. Was this all a game to him? A twisted form of amusement to watch us struggle, to watch Finn unravel?

I couldn't ignore the feeling gnawing at the back of my mind, a sense that something was off. This wasn't just about finding out what had happened in Finn's past. It wasn't even about what Victor knew. It was about power, control, and the fact that neither of them seemed willing to fully let go of whatever leverage they held.

"What do you want?" I asked before I could stop myself, my voice breaking through the tension. It wasn't a question I had planned, but it felt like the right one to ask. If Victor was going to play games with us, I wanted to know the stakes. What was he really after?

Victor's lips curved into a smile that was as sharp as glass, and for a moment, I thought he might actually answer me. Instead, he gave a small shrug. "What do I want? I suppose I want to see how far you'll go, Finn. How far you'll push before you break. And what, exactly, you're willing to sacrifice to uncover your precious little secrets."

I glanced at Finn, who still hadn't moved. His silence was becoming unbearable, each second stretching between us like an eternity. Was he trying to protect me from whatever came next? Or was he simply trying to protect himself?

"We're not here for a game," Finn said, his voice like steel, but there was a crack in it now, a rawness that hadn't been there before. He stood abruptly, pushing his chair back with a creak of protest. "You're going to tell me what happened, Victor. And you're going to do it now."

Victor's smile widened, and he stood slowly, stretching to his full height. "Or what, Finn? You'll force me?" His voice was full of mockery, but there was a flicker of something deeper—something darker—lurking beneath the surface.

Finn didn't respond, but I could feel the shift in the air, the change in the temperature. He was holding something back, something dangerous, and I wasn't sure if I should be relieved or terrified.

Victor took a step closer, his gaze flicking to me for the briefest of moments before returning to Finn. "You still think you can control everything, don't you?" he said softly. "You think you can just walk away when you've gotten what you wanted? That's the mistake you always make."

Finn's face hardened, the muscles in his jaw working, but he said nothing. Instead, he turned, walking toward the door without a single word. I followed, my heart pounding in my chest, a rush of conflicting emotions flooding me. What had just happened? What had Victor meant by that?

Just as my hand reached for the door, Victor's voice stopped me dead in my tracks. "I'm afraid, Finn, that you'll never get the answers you're looking for. Not unless you're willing to go deeper. You have no idea what you've started."

I froze, my hand hovering over the handle, the weight of his words sinking into my skin like ice. Finn didn't turn, didn't even flinch at the warning. He simply opened the door and stepped out into the dark night.

I followed him, my mind reeling with the implications of what Victor had said. What had we really uncovered? What had we truly walked into?

The air outside was cold, but it did nothing to calm the unease swirling inside me. Finn's pace quickened, his footsteps sharp against the pavement, and I matched his stride, keeping pace even as my heart raced ahead of me.

"Finn," I said, my voice soft but insistent. "What did he mean by that? What do you have to do to get the answers?"

Finn didn't answer right away, and I could feel the weight of the words hanging between us. Finally, he stopped, turning to face me, his expression unreadable. For a long moment, we simply stood there, the world around us growing quieter, darker.

"I don't know," he said finally, his voice low and heavy with something I couldn't place. "But I'm going to find out." He reached for my hand, his grip firm, as if grounding himself. "And I'm not stopping until I do."

The wind shifted, the first raindrops beginning to fall, but it wasn't the rain that made my skin prickle. It was the sound of footsteps—slow, deliberate—coming from behind us.

I turned, my heart lurching in my chest.

We weren't alone anymore.

Chapter 32: The Heart's Inferno

The scent of rain lingered in the air, a fresh, damp promise that clung to the earth as though the world itself were exhaling in relief. The heavy wooden beams of the cottage groaned softly under the weight of the storm as the wind howled outside, sending sheets of water cascading down the windows. Inside, the warmth from the hearth curled through the room like a whispered secret, its flames crackling in rhythm with the thunder.

Finn sat across from me, his elbows resting on his knees, his hands clasped tightly in front of him, like he was trying to hold himself together. His jaw was clenched, the muscles working under his skin as he stared into the fire. He hadn't spoken in hours, not since I'd asked him—no, begged him—to tell me what was wrong. The silence had grown between us, thick and heavy like the storm outside.

I couldn't remember the last time I'd seen him so still, so distant. This was a man who usually moved through the world like it was a dance floor, his every gesture deliberate, yet full of the kind of unspoken energy that set a room alight. But tonight, there was nothing. Just the stillness that settled between us like an insurmountable mountain, each of us on opposite sides of it, unsure of how to cross.

"Finn," I finally whispered, my voice barely louder than the wind. "What's happening to us?"

His fingers twitched, a slight tremor passing through him. He didn't look at me, though. Instead, he exhaled, the sound caught between a growl and a sigh. The muscles in his back tensed, his broad shoulders hunched forward as if trying to make himself smaller, more compact. But there was nothing small about him. Not physically, and certainly not emotionally.

I was so tired of the silence between us, tired of the weight pressing on my chest, making it hard to breathe. I could feel the words boiling up inside me, each one a shard of glass ready to cut through the tension. I leaned forward, my own hands trembling as I reached for him, as if I could somehow bridge the gap with a touch.

"You're pushing me away," I said, my voice raw, trembling with a mix of frustration and fear. "I can feel it. Why won't you just tell me what's going on?"

For a long moment, he didn't speak. He didn't even move. I thought perhaps he was going to ignore me entirely, that maybe I was asking for something he wasn't ready to give. But then he sighed, a deep, shuddering breath, and I saw it—the flicker in his eyes. The same way a storm brews on the horizon before it hits with full force. And when he spoke, his voice was low, almost a whisper, like the words were foreign to him.

"I'm not the man you think I am, Eliza."

His words struck me like a slap to the face. I pulled my hand back, stunned by the sudden force of the confession. My heart hammered in my chest, a frantic rhythm that echoed in the hollow of my throat. I was dizzy, trying to make sense of his words, trying to understand the weight they carried.

"Finn," I breathed, my throat tightening. "What are you talking about?"

He shifted, the tension in his body like a live wire. His eyes met mine, and for the first time, I saw the storm in him. Not the kind that raged outside, but the kind that had been brewing inside of him for years—something dark and seething, something that had festered beneath the surface, hidden from the world. And now, it was all spilling out, a flood that couldn't be contained any longer.

"I've hurt people," he said, each word heavy with a truth I wasn't sure I was ready to hear. "I've made choices, bad ones.

Choices I can't take back. And I'm not sure I even want to anymore."

He shook his head, like he was trying to make sense of it himself, like the admission was as much a surprise to him as it was to me. But there was no denying the truth in his words. It was there, clear as day, written in the way his eyes averted mine, the way his voice broke with each confession.

"I've carried things with me for a long time," Finn continued, his voice trembling now, raw and full of regret. "Things that I thought I could bury. Things I thought I could outrun. But they're still here, Eliza. They've always been here, like a shadow I can't shake. And if I'm being honest with you, I'm afraid that shadow is all I'll ever be."

I opened my mouth, but no words came. I didn't know what to say. What could I say? I wanted to tell him it wasn't true, that he was more than his mistakes. But I couldn't lie to him. I couldn't lie to myself. I could see the truth in the lines of his face, in the way his hands clenched and unclenched as though he were physically holding himself together.

The silence between us thickened, wrapping around us like a shroud, pulling the air from my lungs. But it wasn't just the weight of his confession that suffocated me. It was the knowledge that I was standing on the edge of something I wasn't sure I could survive. This, whatever it was, was bigger than me, bigger than us. And yet, I couldn't seem to pull away.

I should have run. Should have turned my back on him and walked away before it was too late. But I didn't. Because in the deepest part of my heart, I knew something that terrified me: I wasn't ready to let him go.

"You're wrong," I whispered, the words barely audible, but I meant them more than anything I'd ever said. "You're not just your mistakes. You're more than that. And I... I'm not going anywhere."

For a moment, his gaze softened, a flicker of something raw and unguarded flashing across his face. But before either of us could say anything more, the storm outside roared louder, shaking the windows with its fury, drowning out everything else.

And in that moment, I realized something that made my heart shudder in fear: our love—this fragile thing between us—wasn't just a promise. It was a fire, a flame that could either burn us both alive or ignite something that would change us forever. And there was no turning back now.

The room was still, save for the occasional pop and crackle from the fire, which seemed to echo in time with the thudding of my heart. Finn sat there, his gaze trained on the flames, his face a portrait of a man caught between the past and the present. He wasn't looking at me anymore. In fact, he barely seemed to notice that I was still there, like I was a ghost standing beside him in the dark.

I tried to swallow the lump in my throat, but it wasn't working. I was too aware of the tension, too conscious of the unspoken words hanging in the air between us. It had been years since I'd felt this raw, this vulnerable, and I wasn't sure whether I should be angry or grateful that Finn had pulled all the layers off me—layers I didn't even know I had.

I knew there was more, that he hadn't told me everything. He'd given me just enough to crack open a door, but not enough to walk through it. I wanted to be angry with him for that, for keeping things from me, but I understood. Some doors are better left closed, especially when the things behind them have the power to change everything.

I could feel the heat of his presence beside me, even as we sat in silence. The way the air seemed to hum when he was near. The way my own breath seemed to falter in his company, like the mere act of breathing had become an act of defiance. He was like a storm contained in human form—dangerous, beautiful, and unstoppable. But the storm was still raging inside him, and I didn't know how much longer he could keep it contained.

Finally, he moved, shifting his weight in his chair with a sharp, restless motion. It was like he couldn't sit still anymore, couldn't keep pretending that everything was fine when the walls around him were crumbling.

"Do you want to know the worst part?" His voice was low, rough, like he was speaking through a fog. "The thing I regret the most, Eliza?"

I nodded, unable to speak. My throat was tight with emotions I didn't have names for yet. I didn't know if I was ready to hear whatever he was about to say, but at the same time, I couldn't stand the silence between us any longer.

He leaned forward, his elbows resting on his knees, his face cast in shadows. His eyes were bright, too bright, almost feverish as he finally looked at me. "The worst part is that I'm not sure I can change. Not really. Not in the way you think I can."

The words hit me like a slap. They were so simple, yet so heavy with meaning. He wasn't looking for absolution. He wasn't asking for me to forgive him. He wasn't even sure I should.

The heat in the room seemed to double, the air thick with the weight of his confession. I could see the guilt written all over his face, the weariness in his eyes. He wasn't just battling whatever ghosts haunted him; he was battling the man he had become and the man he was terrified he might never escape from.

I wanted to reach for him, to tell him that it wasn't too late, that the pieces of him that felt broken could still be put back together. But I didn't. Not yet.

Instead, I just watched him, searching his face for any sign that he believed the words he was saying, that he could hear what he was telling me. I needed to know if there was still hope in him. If there was hope for us.

"What if I told you," I said, my voice trembling slightly, "that I don't need you to be perfect? That I don't need you to be the man you think you should be? I just need you to be real. To be here."

His gaze flickered, almost imperceptibly, like I had thrown him a lifeline he didn't know how to grab. He looked at me, his eyes searching mine, and for the first time in days, I saw something in him that wasn't just guilt or fear. There was something else—something raw and vulnerable, something that spoke of need. Of longing.

"I don't know if I can be that for you," he whispered, his voice thick with emotion. "I don't know if I'm capable of being anything other than the person I've always been."

I shook my head, leaning closer. "You don't have to be who you were, Finn. Not for me. Not for anyone. You just have to be here. Now. In this moment."

He was quiet, and for a moment, I thought maybe I had said too much. Maybe he needed more time to process, to understand. But then, he reached out, his hand tentative, like he wasn't sure whether I'd let him touch me. His fingers brushed against mine, a tentative caress, but it was enough to make my pulse spike, enough to make my breath catch in my throat.

"I don't deserve this," he murmured, his thumb grazing over my knuckles. "I don't deserve you."

The words were almost too much to bear. My heart twisted painfully in my chest, but I couldn't pull away. I wasn't sure if it was love or something else—something darker, something deeper—but I knew one thing for certain: I couldn't stand to let him go. Not now. Not when we were standing on the edge of something that could be either the end or the beginning.

"You're wrong," I whispered, lifting my gaze to meet his. "You deserve to have someone who believes in you, Finn. You deserve to have someone who sees you, all of you, and still chooses to stay."

The air between us shifted then, the intensity of our connection filling the space until it was almost suffocating. But it wasn't an uncomfortable suffocation—it was a closeness, a heat that I could feel in every fiber of my being. It was the kind of closeness that made the world outside seem irrelevant, made everything else fade into nothingness.

"I don't know how to be what you need," Finn said, his voice thick with emotion. "But I'll try. For you. I'll try."

I wanted to tell him that trying was all I needed. That it was enough to take one step forward, even if it was shaky, even if it was uncertain. But instead, I just nodded, letting the moment settle around us, knowing that whatever happened next, we had taken the first step together.

And in that moment, I realized something terrifying: we were both standing on the edge of a cliff, and there was no way to know whether the fall would be a disaster or the kind of release we had been waiting for.

The fire crackled and popped in the hearth, a constant reminder of the tension swirling between us. Finn's hand still hovered near mine, but I wasn't sure if I should take the next step. The silence was heavy, almost suffocating, as if everything we'd just shared had been too much for the room to contain.

My mind raced with the weight of his confession—those dark, jagged pieces of his past he'd thrown at me, exposing the parts of him that had been buried so deep, I wasn't sure I'd ever fully understand them. But something about the way he looked at me now, so raw and unprotected, made me want to dive in, to explore those hidden crevices, to pull him out of the darkness he seemed to have resigned himself to.

"Finn," I whispered, my voice softer than I'd intended. He looked at me, those storm-tossed eyes of his searching mine like he was looking for something—some kind of assurance, maybe, or maybe just a sign that I wasn't going anywhere. The truth of it was, I didn't know if I could offer him what he needed. I didn't even know if I could give him what he wanted.

But I could give him this: honesty. A willingness to face whatever he was holding inside, no matter how heavy, no matter how dangerous. Because I was beginning to realize that what we had—what we were building together—wasn't just about love. It was about survival. It was about not letting the other person go, no matter how difficult the road became.

"You don't have to be perfect for me," I said, my voice cracking just slightly. "You never did."

He let out a breath, a deep exhale that seemed to relieve some of the tension in his chest. But the moment was fleeting, replaced quickly by the uncertain look in his eyes. The truth was, he didn't believe me. He couldn't, not yet. Not when he was still so trapped in his own demons.

"I'm not sure I can live up to what you need," he muttered, his voice barely above a whisper, but full of the kind of resignation that made my heart ache. "I'm not sure I know how to be the man you want me to be."

My heart twisted at the vulnerability in his words, but there was something else, something I couldn't put my finger on. It wasn't just regret I saw in him. It was fear—fear that no matter what he did, he would never be enough. And I had to decide whether I would stay and prove him wrong, or walk away, leaving him to fight those battles on his own.

"I don't need you to be anyone else, Finn," I said, a small smile tugging at the corners of my mouth. "I just need you to be here. With me. In this moment."

His eyes flickered, his gaze softening for a split second. But then the storm inside him roared back to life. "You don't understand," he muttered, shaking his head. "I don't know how to make peace with what I've done. With the choices I've made. And I don't want you to be dragged into it, Eliza. I don't want you to have to carry that burden with me."

I could feel the weight of his words pressing against me, like a physical force. But it wasn't just his guilt I was hearing—it was his fear that I would leave him. And as much as that fear was laced with the truth, it was also an excuse. He was hiding behind it, keeping me at arm's length because the idea of me walking away was too much for him to bear.

"You're not alone in this, Finn," I said, my voice steadier now. "You're not the only one who's made mistakes. You're not the only one who's carried the weight of the past. I don't expect you to be perfect. But I do expect you to let me in."

The words hung in the air, trembling between us. I wasn't sure if they would be the ones to shatter the barrier between us or if they would push him further away. But I meant every one of them. He didn't have to be perfect. Hell, I wasn't perfect. But I couldn't stand the thought of us, of me, walking away from what we could be.

I reached out, this time more certain, my fingers grazing his. The moment the skin-to-skin contact was made, an electric jolt shot through me, quick and sharp, like the spark before a wildfire. He looked at me, his gaze dark and unreadable, but there was something in it now, something that hadn't been there before.

"I'm not asking for forever," I said, my breath shallow, the words catching in my throat. "But right now... right now, I'm asking for you."

Finn didn't respond immediately. Instead, he looked down at our intertwined fingers, the stillness between us heavy with all the things we hadn't said. I could see the battle waging inside him—the part of him that wanted to pull away, to retreat into his past, and the part that wanted to give in, to let me pull him into the light. His jaw tightened, and for a moment, I thought he was going to walk away.

Then, without a word, he stood up, his hand still holding mine, pulling me gently to my feet. The sudden movement was unexpected, and I stumbled slightly, catching myself on his chest. He didn't let go, though. His arms went around me, enveloping me in a heat that felt both comforting and dangerous at the same time.

"I'm not perfect," he murmured into my hair, his voice rough. "And I don't know if I can ever be what you need. But I can't let go of you, Eliza. Not now. Not when everything feels like it's about to break."

My breath caught in my throat. His words settled into me like a seed, and I knew then that this was no longer just about love. It was about survival. And when I felt his hand move down my back, when I heard the desperate rasp in his voice, I realized that the fire that had been ignited between us wasn't something we could control anymore.

We were both already burned.

And then the door creaked open.

We froze, both of us caught in the tension of the moment, and I felt my heart stop as a shadow filled the doorway, casting a cold darkness over the warmth that had been building between us.

"Finn," a voice said, low and menacing. "I think we need to talk."

Chapter 33: A Trap Unleashed

The night was colder than usual, the kind of sharp chill that sinks into your bones and refuses to let go. It wrapped itself around me, its fingers sliding beneath my jacket, prickling my skin with unease. Finn stood beside me, close but not too close. He had that look on his face—the one that could easily have been mistaken for calm, if you didn't know him better. I knew that look; it was his way of hiding a storm beneath a quiet surface. I could almost hear the crash of waves in his chest, every breath a battle not to shatter the tension between us.

We had set everything in motion hours ago, each step carefully calculated, every detail meticulously planned. The scene we had set was simple: a deserted alley, dim streetlights casting weak, jaundiced pools of light on the cracked pavement. Finn had insisted on being here with me, his presence both a comfort and a reminder of just how much we had to lose. The trap we were waiting for was nothing short of a gamble—a game where the stakes were our very lives.

My gaze flickered to the shadows ahead, the ones that stretched long and menacing under the low glow of the streetlights. The alley was deserted, the night air too still. If we were being watched, they were being patient. We had been for hours, and every minute dragged like a weight in my stomach. I could hear the rapid beat of my heart, feel the pulse of it in my fingertips, my throat tightening as I swallowed against the anxiety rising inside me. Every small noise—the rustle of a rat in the garbage, the distant hum of traffic—felt amplified in the silence.

Finn's voice broke through the stillness, soft but laced with something sharp, something like dread. "You're sure you're ready for this?" His eyes locked on mine, searching for something. I didn't know if he was asking about the trap, or about me—about us. But I answered anyway, as steady as I could manage.

"Ready as I'll ever be."

There was a brief flicker of something in his gaze, something I couldn't quite place, before he nodded. We had made a promise to each other, an unspoken vow to follow this through, no matter where it led. I could almost taste the weight of it in the air, a heaviness that had settled between us and hung there, thick as smoke.

I took a breath, trying to settle the jittery nerves in my chest. My fingers twitched at my side, hovering near the gun tucked into the waistband of my jeans. It wasn't my first time holding a weapon, but tonight felt different. The idea of using it, of pulling the trigger, made something inside me twist and recoil, like a serpent coiling tight around my ribs. But there was no choice. If this worked, we'd have answers. If it didn't... well, that was a future I didn't want to consider.

Minutes passed, each one dragging longer than the last. Finn was silent now, his focus fixed on the alley ahead, his body taut like a drawn bowstring. I envied his ability to stay so calm. My own thoughts were racing, colliding and crumbling against one another like a house of cards caught in a gust of wind. What would I do when they came? Would I be ready? Could I handle it?

And then I saw it.

A movement at the far end of the alley, so subtle I almost missed it. A shift in the shadows, the barest flicker of something—someone—out of place. My heart skipped a beat, the noise of it loud in my ears, but I stayed still, watching, waiting.

Finn's eyes flicked to me, the barest shift of his head. I nodded, just once, and we both tensed, ready for whatever was coming. My breath caught in my throat as I strained my ears, listening to the soft scrape of shoes against pavement, the rustle of fabric as it brushed against something solid. It was them. Whoever they were.

The figure emerged slowly from the darkness, their outline shifting and melting into the dim light. At first, I couldn't make out any defining features, just a silhouette, tall and lean, moving with a fluidity that was almost unsettling. But as they stepped into the full light of the streetlamp, I saw them clearly—and I froze.

There, standing before us, was someone I never thought I'd see again.

Caitlyn.

My stomach lurched, the world tilting on its axis as I stared at her, my mind scrambling to process the sight before me. She looked different—more hardened, her eyes colder, her hair pulled back into a tight ponytail—but it was unmistakably her. The woman who had been my best friend, my confidante, the one person I trusted more than anyone else. And now... now she stood in front of me, a ghost in the flesh, and everything I thought I knew about my life crumbled beneath the weight of the betrayal in her eyes.

She smiled, but it was a hollow thing, sharp and cruel. "You really thought you could outsmart me?" she asked, her voice soft, almost amused, as if this were some kind of game. The question hung in the air, slicing through the tension with a knife's edge.

Finn stepped forward, his jaw tight, his stance wide and ready. "You," he said, his voice low, tight with a kind of fury I hadn't heard from him before. "You're the one behind all of this."

Caitlyn's smile didn't falter. "I didn't expect you to figure it out so quickly. I must admit, I underestimated you both." She tilted her head, eyes glinting in the dim light. "But here we are."

The words hit me like a blow to the chest. I had trusted her. I had shared secrets with her, laughed with her, stood by her through everything. And now, standing here, I could see the lies etched in every line of her face. The betrayal ran deeper than I could have imagined, and my heart—stupid, naive thing—ached with the sharp, bitter taste of it.

Caitlyn's smile deepened, her lips curving with that sharp, dangerous edge that I'd once mistaken for warmth. She stepped closer, her movements slow and deliberate, the kind of controlled grace that betrayed her understanding of power. Power over me, power over all of us. The woman who had once been my ally now stood in front of me as a stranger, a traitor wearing a face I knew too well. The quiet buzzing of the world around us seemed to fade as I processed the weight of her presence.

"You're really going to stand there and pretend this isn't exactly what you expected, aren't you?" Her voice was soft, almost conversational, but every word was laced with venom. "You knew I was always more than what I seemed. It was only a matter of time before you figured it out."

I wanted to scream, to tear into her with everything I had, but the words stuck in my throat like rocks. Instead, I stood frozen, heart hammering against my ribcage as I searched for something to say, anything that could make sense of this moment. But there was nothing. Only a hollow silence, the sting of betrayal coursing through me like a poison.

"You really are as blind as I thought," Caitlyn continued, her eyes narrowing slightly as she studied me, her gaze piercing. "You never saw the cracks, did you? Never noticed the little lies, the ones I let slip through. But you were too busy being the good little hero, weren't you?"

Finn's hand clenched at his side, his jaw clenched tight, but he stayed silent, his anger simmering beneath the surface. I could feel the heat of it radiating off him, his need to act clawing at his restraint. But I knew—knew—that if we rushed into this without a plan, it would all unravel. Caitlyn wasn't stupid. She had her own agenda, and we were just pieces in her game.

"You always were a master manipulator," I finally managed, my voice rough with the weight of the realization. "I didn't want to believe it. I wanted to believe you were still the same Caitlyn—the one who cared, the one who had my back."

Her eyes softened for just a moment, like she was almost pitying me, but then she shrugged, a faint, almost regretful smile tugging at the corners of her mouth. "Caring doesn't get you what you need in this world. You learn that eventually, especially when people start to think they can control you." She tilted her head, a gleam in her eye. "You were always so eager to trust, to give, to be the hero. But the hero never gets what they deserve, do they?"

Her words hung in the air, heavy and bitter, like a poisoned truth I wasn't ready to swallow. I had always thought of Caitlyn as the person who saw through the same cracks I did, the one who understood how the world worked and how to make it bend to our will. But I had been wrong. All along, she'd been playing a different game, one that didn't include me.

Finn took a step forward, his voice low but hard. "You were working with them, weren't you? All this time, while we were fighting this fight, you were pulling the strings behind the scenes."

Caitlyn's eyes flickered with something—surprise, maybe, or just a glint of satisfaction—but she didn't back away. Instead, she held her ground, her smile widening like a cat who had just caught its prey. "You're not as clever as you think, Finn," she said softly. "Did you really think I was just sitting idly by, waiting for someone to tell me what to do? No, I was always making my own choices. And in the end, those choices will be what matter."

Her gaze flickered to me, then back to Finn, as if weighing us both, deciding which one of us was the more interesting threat. She was enjoying this, I realized. She was savoring the unraveling of everything we had believed, the shock in our eyes, the confusion, the disillusionment. This was her victory—no matter how much we tried to fight it.

"You're right about one thing," she said, her tone dropping to something darker, something almost intimate. "You were too busy playing hero. And in doing so, you missed the truth. Missed the signs that would have told you I was never on your side. It was always about control. Always."

"Why?" My voice cracked, and I hated myself for it. "Why, Caitlyn? After everything, after we fought side by side, you could do this?"

She laughed, a cold, brittle sound that didn't reach her eyes. "Oh, sweetie. You've got it all wrong. It's not about you. It never was. This is about power. About taking what's mine. You were just a means to an end, a stepping stone to get where I needed to be."

I wanted to scream, to launch myself at her and tear her apart, but I stayed rooted to the spot, my hands trembling at my sides. How had I been so blind? How had I let her worm her way into my life like this, knowing, deep down, that there was always something off about her?

And then, as if her words weren't enough to shatter what was left of my heart, she stepped closer, leaning in just enough for me to feel the cold edge of her presence. "You're going to be fine," she said, her voice sweetly condescending. "But first, you're going to watch everything burn. And when the smoke clears, I'll be the one standing tall. Not you. Not any of you."

I thought I saw her flinch—just the briefest flicker of hesitation—but then it was gone, replaced with that same, unfathomable mask of cold calculation. Whatever she had planned, she was in control now. And I—well, I was the pawn who had been too late to realize the game had changed.

I could barely process her words, the sharpness of them cutting through me like a knife made of ice. Caitlyn—my best friend, my confidante—standing there, reveling in the destruction of everything I thought I knew about loyalty, friendship, and trust. The world around me seemed to blur, a haze of disbelief clouding my mind, but I had to stay focused. I couldn't let her see how much she'd gotten under my skin. Not yet.

"What happens now, Caitlyn?" Finn's voice sliced through the tension, its low edge dangerous in a way I couldn't ignore. He didn't seem surprised by the reveal, but I knew him well enough to see the simmering rage in his eyes. It was the kind of fury that had the potential to unravel everything.

Caitlyn turned her head slowly, dragging her gaze over to him, and for a moment, I thought I saw a flicker of something familiar—something almost tender—before it was gone, replaced by a coldness so absolute it made my skin crawl. "What happens now?" she repeated, almost savoring the question. "Now, Finn, you get to watch me win."

The words settled over me like a suffocating weight, crushing any remnants of hope I'd been holding onto. I wasn't sure which stung more: the betrayal, or the realization that Caitlyn had been so close this entire time, moving in the shadows while we fought blindly against an enemy we could never understand.

"You really think you're going to win?" Finn's voice was low, threaded with something that wasn't quite a question, but more like a threat.

Caitlyn's lips quirked up at the corners, a smile that could have been beautiful under different circumstances. "Oh, I know I am. You're already in the trap, Finn. You just don't know it yet."

I wanted to ask her to explain—wanted to demand how she'd managed to deceive us so completely, why she'd gone this far—but the words wouldn't come. Instead, my mind spun with a thousand fragmented images: Caitlyn's laughter at late-night dinners, her thoughtful gestures, her reassuring words during moments of doubt. It all felt like a sick joke now.

"What did you want from us?" My voice cracked, but I didn't care. "What was the point of all this?"

She paused, as though considering the question carefully, then shook her head. "You don't get it, do you? It was never about you. It was about taking what I deserve. You were just... convenient." The word rolled off her tongue with such casual disdain that I could feel the sting of it long after she said it. "You were distractions, both of you. In my way. And now, well... Now it's too late."

"Too late for what?" Finn asked, his voice now tight with suspicion.

Caitlyn's eyes danced with a wild, dangerous glint. "For you to stop me. For anyone to stop me."

I glanced at Finn, who looked like he was seconds away from charging at her, but I knew better. The trap was set, and every instinct in me told me to wait. If we rushed at her, we'd be playing right into her hands.

"So, what now?" I asked, my voice steadier than I felt. "Do you think you've won, Caitlyn?"

She laughed, a rich, mocking sound that filled the space between us. "You still don't get it. I don't need to 'win,' not in the way you think. I've already won. Everything you've done, every plan, every move, has been exactly what I needed. You're already on the losing side."

And that's when I saw it—the shift in the shadows behind her. A movement, subtle, almost imperceptible, but it was there. It was coming from a spot I hadn't even thought to check. My heart skipped in my chest as I realized: We weren't alone.

Finn must have sensed it too because he tensed beside me, his gaze flicking to the same darkened corner. There, half-hidden by the thick shadows, were two more figures—figures that hadn't been there before.

"Did you really think we were just going to stand by and let you have all the fun?" Caitlyn's voice was now full of amusement, as though we were just part of some elaborate game, and the rules were already rigged in her favor.

The first figure stepped forward, and I instantly recognized him. Marco. His tall, broad frame loomed out of the darkness, a sly grin spread across his face. But it wasn't the grin that chilled me. It was the gun he casually held at his side, pointed in our direction. My heart leapt into my throat.

"Marco," Finn spat, his voice laced with disbelief. "You're with her?"

Marco shrugged, his expression bored, as though the whole situation was beneath him. "Did you really think I'd let all this fun slip away?" he said with a dismissive wave, his eyes never leaving Finn. "Caitlyn's been more useful than I ever thought. She knows how to play the game. You two? You were just too slow to catch up."

I felt the blood drain from my face, my mind scrambling to keep up with the rapidly shifting events. Marco—another trusted ally, another friend—was in on this from the start. But there was something more. Something darker about his role in all this, something I couldn't yet put my finger on.

And then, as if the revelation wasn't enough, I heard another sound, this one unmistakable. A click. A door opening.

"Looks like the real show's just beginning," Caitlyn said softly, a hint of something dangerous behind her words.

I turned just in time to see a third figure emerge from the shadows, stepping into the faint light from above. This one, I didn't recognize. A man in a dark suit, his face obscured by the brim of a hat that shadowed his features, but I could see the gleam of something in his hand—the glint of metal, sharp and unforgiving.

Before I could react, the man in the suit spoke, his voice calm, controlled, chilling in its cold authority. "I think it's time for you both to finally understand how this ends."

Chapter 34: Trial by Fire

The air was thick with smoke, a choking, acrid miasma that clung to my lungs and made every breath feel like it might be my last. The heat was unbearable, searing through my clothes, lapping at my skin with a violent hunger. I could barely see through the haze, but I didn't need to. The sound of crackling timber, the snap of burning beams, the guttural roar of the fire—it was all I needed to know that we were at its mercy.

Finn was ahead of me, a shadow in the chaos, his movements swift and sure, even in the madness of it all. His hand reached back to me, his fingers brushing mine, a lifeline in the swirling storm of flames. I took it, not even needing to think twice. There was no time for doubt. Not when the world was burning.

"Stay close!" he shouted, his voice barely audible above the inferno, but his grip was firm, pulling me along like I was the most precious thing he'd ever held. Maybe I was. Maybe we both were, in that moment, our survival hinging on the smallest of gestures—his strength, my will, the beat of two hearts pushing through the worst of it together.

The fire was relentless, a beast with a mind of its own, devouring everything in its path. The wooden beams above groaned and cracked, the ceiling buckling under the weight of its own destruction. We couldn't stop, couldn't hesitate. Every step felt like a gamble—each breath a risk. My legs were shaky, the ground beneath my feet uneven, but Finn's presence was an anchor, and I held onto it with everything I had.

I could feel the heat radiating off the walls, feel the scorch of it even through the fabric of my shirt, my hair singed, the scent of burning flesh and wood thick in the air. The fire was a living thing, a chaos of orange and red, twisting through the space with a hunger that could not be sated. It wasn't just the physical heat that was overwhelming; it was the weight of the danger, the reality that we might not make it out of here alive.

We were trapped in the very house that had once seemed so safe. The place that had been my refuge from the world. But now, it was nothing more than a deathtrap. The walls felt like they were closing in, the fire pushing us forward, forcing us into the unknown.

"Move!" Finn's voice cut through the chaos again, sharper now, a warning. I didn't need him to say it twice. I ran, my feet stumbling over the uneven floor, but I didn't care. We had to get out. We had to.

I glanced behind me, the flames twisting up the walls like serpents, and the panic surged in my chest. My breath came faster, my heart hammering in my throat. It felt like the fire was chasing me, licking at my heels, eager to consume me. Every inch forward felt like a mile, each step harder than the last.

Finn was still there, always a few steps ahead, but his hand never faltered in its grasp on mine. Even now, with the world collapsing around us, we were together. And that thought—simple, but essential—was what kept me going. I would follow him anywhere.

We reached the front door, but the sight that greeted us was worse than any of the flames. The fire had already spread to the entrance, the door itself a raging inferno, molten and unyielding. I stopped short, my heart sinking, my mind racing. There was no way out this way.

Finn didn't stop. He didn't even hesitate. His eyes found mine, and in that brief, silent exchange, I saw everything I needed to know. There was no other choice. We had to go through it.

"Trust me," he said, his voice low but firm.

"Do I have a choice?" I shot back, my words harsher than I intended. But the fear was making me snap. My own skin felt like it was being burned, the air so hot it felt like it might sear the very breath from my lungs.

Finn's gaze softened, and for a fleeting second, he looked like he was going to say something else. But instead, he tugged on my hand, pulling me forward. "No turning back now."

We ran straight into the heart of the fire, dodging falling beams, weaving through the smoke, the heat licking at our heels like an animal in pursuit. I could feel the sting of it on my skin, the bite of it in my eyes. But I didn't stop. I couldn't. Every step was a prayer, every breath a plea to survive.

The world was a blur—shapes, sounds, flashes of light—until finally, there was a break in the wall of flames, a gap just wide enough for us to slip through. Finn surged ahead, dragging me through it, and we stumbled out into the yard, collapsing onto the grass with nothing left in us.

I gasped for air, my lungs aching, my body trembling with exhaustion. The fire raged behind us, a towering wall of destruction that seemed to rise higher with every passing second. But here, in this small patch of grass, we were safe. For now.

Finn didn't move right away, his arm still wrapped around me, his chest rising and falling with every ragged breath. We didn't speak at first. There was no need. We both knew what we had just survived.

The night was eerily quiet now, save for the distant crackling of the flames and the pounding of my heartbeat. I could feel his breath against my skin, steady and warm. And for the first time in what felt like forever, I let myself believe we might actually be okay.

The yard was still, but the air felt too thick to breathe. The fire behind us was a monstrous thing, alive and unrelenting, but now there was silence, a chilling stillness that seemed to press against my chest. Finn's arm was still around me, warm and steady, but it was his presence, his grip, that felt like the only solid thing in this ruined world.

I looked at him, really looked at him for the first time in what felt like years, but in reality, it had only been months since we started this insane, whirlwind dance of ours. His face, usually so composed, was smeared with soot and grime, his eyes wide with something I couldn't name. Maybe it was the exhaustion, the disbelief, or maybe, just maybe, it was the fear we'd both been running from, but there it was—raw, unguarded, real. His breath came in ragged gasps, matching mine, but there was something else beneath the panic. Something fragile and fierce, like the ember of a flame that would burn down everything in its path if you dared to get too close.

"Are you hurt?" he asked, his voice low, almost tentative.

I shook my head, though I wasn't entirely sure I was telling the truth. I felt bruised—inside and out—but there was no time to dwell on it. Not when the house I'd called home for so long was still burning to the ground, its fate sealed, and mine tangled up in it.

"You?" I asked, my voice tight. My eyes raked over him—his clothes singed, his hair damp with sweat. The strength and resolve in his jawline were unmistakable, but there was something else, a trace of vulnerability in his eyes that made me pause.

"I'm fine," he said, brushing it off, but even in that single sentence, I heard the lie. There was more to it than that. There had to be. But I couldn't push him on it—not now. I wasn't sure what I'd do with the answer anyway.

The quiet stretched between us, broken only by the distant crackle of fire and the faint, almost rhythmic sound of our breathing. Finn's hand tightened on mine, his thumb tracing circles on my palm, as if the simple touch could pull us both from the wreckage we'd just barely escaped.

"You think it's over?" I asked, my voice barely more than a whisper.

Finn turned toward the still-glowing wreckage behind us, the flames now casting eerie shadows on his face, but his expression remained unreadable. "You've seen enough to know it's never really over."

He was right. There was no fairy tale ending, no moment where everything just stopped. The world had a way of turning things upside down, of throwing in curveballs when you least expected it. Just when you thought you had a grip on something, it slipped right through your fingers. Like the way the fire had crept up on us, hidden behind the illusion of safety until it was too late.

I let out a bitter laugh, the sound hollow. "I should have known," I muttered, glancing over at the smoldering remnants of my life.

Finn didn't reply at first, but then he turned his gaze back to me, his eyes searching mine in a way that made my heart skip a beat. "You didn't know. None of us did."

There was a tenderness in his words, but I could hear the edge, the warning beneath them. He didn't want me to blame myself. It was clear he was trying to protect me from whatever storm was coming next, but I wasn't sure there was much protection left to offer. Not anymore.

Before I could respond, the sound of a distant siren cut through the stillness, sharp and piercing. I glanced toward the horizon, where the flashing lights of emergency vehicles were now visible, like beacons cutting through the night. A strange sense of calm washed over me, even as the reality of the situation started to settle in. We were safe for now, but that was only the beginning. There was no easy way out of this.

"We need to go," Finn said, pulling me away from the burning house, his hand firm around mine. "They'll be here soon, and we need to make sure we're not seen."

I nodded, my legs stiff beneath me, each movement like pushing through molasses. But I didn't ask questions. Not now. Not when everything still felt too fresh, too raw, and I had no idea where to go next.

"Where?" I asked, my voice hoarse.

Finn didn't answer immediately, and I could feel the weight of his hesitation pressing against me. His eyes darted to the shadows that now engulfed us, to the thick forest that bordered the property, and then back to the wreckage of what had once been my life.

"There's a place," he said finally, his words slow and deliberate. "Not far from here. We can lay low until we figure out what to do."

I didn't question him, not for a second. Maybe I should have, but I didn't. Not after everything we had just gone through. The fire was still raging in the distance, an ever-present reminder that nothing would ever be the same again. I couldn't stay here. Not with the charred remnants of my home and everything I'd known. Not when there was still too much at risk.

"Lead the way," I said, my voice barely a whisper.

Finn didn't hesitate. He started walking, pulling me along behind him. The sound of the sirens grew louder, but they were still far off, and I couldn't shake the feeling that we were being hunted. That we hadn't escaped the fire just to run into something worse.

We walked in silence for a while, each of us lost in our thoughts, the weight of the night settling over us like a thick, oppressive fog. I wasn't sure where we were headed, but as long as Finn was by my side, I was willing to follow.

His hand gripped mine tighter, a silent reassurance that I didn't know I needed until I felt it. The road ahead wasn't clear, and I couldn't see what awaited us, but somehow, I knew we would face it together. That thought, small as it was, was enough to keep me moving forward, even when the world felt like it was collapsing at our feet.

The path Finn led me down was little more than a worn trail, tangled in undergrowth, with branches heavy from the weight of rain. The forest around us seemed to pulse with life—an ever-watchful presence, its whispers now more ominous than comforting. The sirens had finally reached the edges of the estate, and though the crackle of radios and the distant murmur of voices echoed in the background, we had long since abandoned any illusion of safety in the open. Our only hope lay deeper in the woods.

Finn was ahead of me, his figure a shadow weaving through the trees, his movements deliberate but fast, as though he could outrun whatever consequences loomed behind us. The air was thick with humidity, the night holding its breath like it was waiting for something to happen. The smell of smoke clung to everything—our clothes, our skin, the air. It was as if the fire had followed us, an unshakable ghost that would never let us forget the cost of survival. I wiped my forehead, the sweat mixing with ash and dirt, and barely registered the sting of a branch slapping my face as I tripped over the uneven ground.

"Stay close," Finn's voice cut through the silence, his tone firm but laced with something I couldn't quite place. Fear, maybe. Or perhaps just the weight of everything that had happened.

I wanted to tell him I was fine, to assure him that I wasn't some damsel to be protected, but the words stuck in my throat. We weren't fine. We were running for our lives, our futures uncertain and slipping further from our grasp with every step. But I followed, because I had no other choice.

We reached a clearing after what felt like hours—though it was likely only minutes—and Finn slowed his pace. He glanced around, his eyes scanning the shadows before turning back to me, his jaw clenched.

"This is the place," he muttered, his hand reaching for the small, weathered cabin just ahead. It sat nestled among the trees like an afterthought, as though it had been abandoned for years, its windows dark and silent. No lights. No signs of life.

I couldn't help the unease that spread through me. The house felt too still, too out of place against the backdrop of the frantic, burning world we'd just escaped. But Finn didn't seem to share my misgivings. He stepped up to the door without hesitation, pulling a set of keys from his pocket, and unlocked it with practiced ease.

"This isn't exactly the Ritz, but it'll do for now," he said, flashing me a half-hearted grin that did nothing to ease the tension in my chest. "Stay low, and don't make a sound. If anyone sees us, we're both as good as dead."

I didn't argue. Inside, the cabin was a dim, musty space. A single lamp flickered weakly from the corner, casting long shadows that danced like ghosts along the walls. The furniture was sparse, covered in dusty sheets. A fireplace sat dormant, and the smell of stale wood and mildew permeated the air.

"What is this place?" I asked, my voice barely above a whisper as I followed him inside.

"An old hunting cabin. Belongs to a friend of mine," Finn replied, tossing the keys onto a wooden table before making his way to the kitchen. "He won't mind us crashing here for a while."

I glanced around, still uneasy, my eyes tracing the small details—frayed rugs, an abandoned coat hanging on a chair, the faint smell of something long forgotten. It was a world away from the life I'd known. It felt like we'd crossed some invisible line, a point of no return where everything was now upended, and nothing would ever feel familiar again.

"Do you always have backup plans for the apocalypse?" I said, my voice a little sharper than I meant. The humor in it felt forced, but it was all I had left. I was fighting to keep the panic at bay, to ignore the fact that our world had just been scorched down to its most basic elements.

Finn paused in the kitchen doorway, looking back at me with a raised eyebrow. "Do you always assume the worst?"

"No," I replied, my gaze flicking to the small window that overlooked the woods, the dark stretching out in all directions. "But sometimes, the worst is all you've got."

He didn't respond immediately, and the silence between us stretched on for what felt like an eternity. I could feel his eyes on me, like he was weighing something in the air between us. But before I could make sense of it, the stillness was shattered by the unmistakable sound of footsteps outside, slow but deliberate, like someone—or something—was approaching.

Finn's eyes narrowed, his hand instantly going to the gun tucked at his waistband. "Get down," he hissed, his voice sharp as a whip crack.

I dropped instinctively, crouching behind the couch as he slipped into the shadows, disappearing as though he were part of the darkness itself. My heart pounded in my chest, my breath shallow, as I waited, trying to steady myself. My mind raced with a thousand thoughts—who was out there? Was it a friend? Or worse, someone looking for us? Someone who had tracked us here?

The footsteps grew louder, closer now. I held my breath, praying for silence, but even the wind seemed to hold its own. The sound stopped just outside the door, and I could hear the faint rustle of fabric, the soft scrape of boots against the ground.

Then, without warning, the door creaked open.

I froze, my entire body locking in place as the faintest whisper of movement came from the other side. A silhouette stood in the doorway, a shadow framed by the pale moonlight. The figure stepped inside, and I couldn't see their face, but the unmistakable feeling of being watched sent a chill down my spine.

And just as quickly as it had come, the door slammed shut behind them.

I didn't dare move. I didn't even breathe. But somewhere, deep inside, I felt the weight of the truth settle on me: We were far from safe.

Chapter 35: After the Smoke

The quiet that followed the flames was almost unbearable. The air, heavy with the scent of charred wood and smoke, seemed to weigh on me in a way that nothing else ever had. Finn's presence beside me was the only thing keeping me tethered to the present, the only thing making the world feel real again. His silence spoke louder than any words could have, a steady reassurance in the chaos of everything else.

We stood on the edge of what had once been a sprawling grove of trees. The charred remnants now stood like ghosts, their jagged outlines reaching toward the sky as if still searching for what they had lost. It was odd, the way the fires had stripped everything down to nothing, and yet the earth below us felt more alive than it had in days. There was a kind of stillness to it, a deep, slow heartbeat that seemed to pulse beneath the ground, urging me to breathe, to remember that life had a way of rising from even the darkest ashes.

I glanced at Finn, whose jaw was clenched in that way he had when he was trying not to show the weight of things. His eyes were fixed on the horizon, distant, as if he were seeing something beyond what was there. The fire had taken so much, but it had also left us with a new kind of clarity. I couldn't deny that. Every night since the flames had receded, the sky seemed just a little clearer, the stars a little brighter. But even that couldn't chase away the tightness in my chest, the dread of what came next.

We didn't speak much in those first days after. Instead, we worked—together and separately. He handled the practical things, sifting through what remained of our supplies, salvaging what he could. I, on the other hand, couldn't bear to do anything that felt too final, so I wandered, picking through the ashes as if searching for some forgotten piece of us that might still be there, hidden beneath the soot. It felt like a strange kind of ritual, one I wasn't sure I believed in but couldn't stop myself from performing. Every scorched branch, every burned-out husk of a plant felt like it held a story I wasn't ready to leave behind.

Finn would occasionally glance at me, his gaze softening when he saw my hands covered in ash, my face drawn tight with the effort of keeping it all together. He never said anything, just offered me his silent understanding. It was both comforting and maddening. Sometimes I wanted him to reach out, to pull me close and tell me everything would be okay. But that wasn't Finn. He was the kind of man who believed that everything was always okay if you just kept moving, kept working. And I hated that he was right.

It was on the third day, when the sun had started to break through the thick, gray clouds that had settled in the wake of the fire, that I found something. A small, burnt journal, its edges curled and singed. I recognized it immediately. It had been my grandmother's—her handwriting so familiar that just seeing it made my chest tighten. I hadn't even realized it had been lost in the flames. But there it was, half-buried beneath a pile of debris. I picked it up carefully, brushing the ash from its surface, feeling the fragile paper beneath my fingers.

"Is it...?" Finn's voice broke through the silence, and I turned to see him standing just a few feet away, his eyes trained on the journal in my hands.

I nodded, my throat tight. "Yeah. It's hers."

He didn't ask any more questions. He didn't need to. His gaze softened, and he turned away, giving me the space to grieve in my own way. I wasn't sure what I expected to find in those pages—maybe answers, or maybe just a piece of my grandmother I hadn't realized I'd lost. But when I opened it, the pages were blank, save for a few faded words in the corner of the first page: After the smoke, there is only the truth.

I ran my fingers over the words, the old ink smudged with time. My heart hammered in my chest, a strange mix of curiosity and dread. What did it mean? After the smoke... what truth? I could feel the weight of those words pressing down on me, like a secret waiting to be uncovered. But there was no more time to linger on it. Finn was already moving, already pushing forward, and I had to follow.

"Let's go," he said, his voice low but determined.

I didn't question him. There was something in his tone that told me we were done with this place for now, ready to move on, to rebuild, to start over. But as we walked away, I couldn't shake the feeling that this was only the beginning, that whatever truth my grandmother had left behind was still waiting for me, buried beneath the ashes of everything we'd lost.

The days blurred into one long stretch of graying light, a hazy rhythm of silence punctuated by the sound of my shoes crunching through the remnants of what had once been vibrant earth. We hadn't spoken much, Finn and I, but there was a language in the spaces between us that needed no words. His presence was constant, like a thread woven through the frayed edges of my thoughts. It wasn't that he hovered; he simply existed beside me, a steady presence that felt both reassuring and unsettling.

Sometimes, in those quiet moments, I wondered if I had been too lost in my own grief to see him for what he really was. It wasn't just that Finn was a man of few words; it was the way he listened, the way he seemed to absorb everything around him with such an intensity that it left little room for anything else. Maybe that's why I found myself retreating more often than not, walking aimlessly through the half-burned remnants of the landscape, as if by wandering I could find something to fix, something to understand. There was always that longing for control, the need to grasp something solid, something tangible that I could hold onto.

But in the aftermath, everything felt so fragile, slipping through my fingers like water.

Finn's eyes followed me from a distance, and even though he said nothing, I could feel the weight of his gaze, a constant pull that anchored me to the present. It was maddening, the way he could be so quiet, and yet somehow more perceptive than anyone else I knew. I didn't want to admit it, but it was beginning to unsettle me.

One afternoon, when the air hung heavy with the scent of damp wood and lingering smoke, I caught him watching me from the edge of the clearing. His expression was unreadable, but there was a tightness around his jaw that told me something was bothering him. I turned, intent on speaking, but before I could get the words out, he was already moving toward me, slow and deliberate, as though he were carefully measuring every step.

"I'm not going to ask you what's going on in your head," he said, his voice quiet, almost amused. "But I'd be lying if I said I didn't wonder."

I raised an eyebrow at him, a dry smile tugging at my lips. "You're the one who's been watching me like a hawk. What's that about?"

He shrugged, a subtle shift of his shoulders that spoke volumes. "Someone has to keep an eye on you."

My smile faltered, and for a moment, I didn't know whether to laugh or to call him out on his quiet intensity. Instead, I opted for something else entirely: silence. We both stood there, side by side, staring out at the twisted remnants of the forest that stretched out before us. The devastation was overwhelming, but somehow, it wasn't the worst thing we had to face. It wasn't even the fire itself that had left me so off-kilter—it was everything else, everything that came after. The uncertainty. The questions that lingered, like smoke still caught in my lungs.

He shifted again, closer this time, and for a moment, I thought he might actually say something more. But instead, his gaze turned to something I hadn't even noticed—an old stone wall, half-collapsed and overrun with weeds. It was a relic from before the fires, a faint reminder of the land's history, and it was here, right in front of me, that something unexpected happened.

Finn's voice broke through the quiet again. "I think that's the place."

I blinked, confused. "The place for what?"

He nodded toward the crumbling structure, his tone thoughtful. "I've been thinking about it. I don't think we're done here yet."

I frowned, my heart skipping a beat. "Done? What do you mean by that?"

"I mean, there's something about this place. Something we missed." His eyes were narrowed, distant again, and I could see the wheels turning behind them, the way his mind was working faster than I could keep up. "I think we need to go there. See what's left."

I wasn't sure what I expected him to say, but it wasn't that. The last thing I wanted was to venture into the heart of this broken world, to poke around in the remnants of something that had burned to the ground. And yet, I felt it—the pull, like gravity, urging me toward it. Finn was right. There was something here, buried beneath the smoke and ash, something I couldn't shake off no matter how hard I tried.

"I don't know," I said, voice tight, my nerves suddenly on edge. "It feels... too much."

He didn't push me, not in the way I'd expected. Instead, he simply looked at me, his expression softening for the first time since we'd started this strange journey together.

"I won't make you do anything," he said quietly. "But you don't have to face it alone."

For a moment, I considered walking away, leaving it all behind, the strange urgency building inside me. But I couldn't. I couldn't walk away from him. Not now, not after everything. I was already too tangled up in him, in the way his presence steadied me and unraveled me all at once. So, with a deep breath, I nodded.

"Let's go," I said, my voice barely more than a whisper, but it felt like the most decisive thing I'd said in days.

Finn didn't say anything else as we walked toward the wall. He simply fell into step beside me, the sound of our boots crunching over the broken earth the only thing that accompanied us. And for the first time in a long while, I allowed myself to hope that whatever came next—whatever secrets lay behind that ancient stone wall—we could face it together.

The wall stood before us, half-consumed by ivy and time, but still resolute, as if it had seen too many seasons to crumble easily. Each stone, worn and faded, had witnessed lives pass by—lives I could only imagine. As I stood there, staring at the remnants of something that had once been grand, I realized I had no idea what I was searching for. There were too many possibilities, too many unanswered questions. What had Finn meant by "something we missed?" I could barely get my head around the mess we were already trying to make sense of, let alone another hidden layer of it.

"Do you think anyone's ever found this before?" I asked, half to myself, half to Finn. My voice was laced with a sarcasm I hadn't expected, a kind of self-defense against the swirling uncertainty.

Finn tilted his head, assessing the stonework with an unreadable expression. "I think that's the point. We're the ones finding it now. Maybe we were meant to."

I rolled my eyes, but not because I didn't agree. No, I rolled my eyes because this was Finn's gift—making everything sound like destiny, like the weight of things was part of a bigger plan. He wasn't wrong. Not really. If there was one thing the past week had taught me, it was that nothing was truly random. The fire, the ashes, the strange comfort in his steady presence—they were all part of some weird, intricate puzzle I couldn't quite grasp.

I crouched down, fingers grazing the cool, moss-covered stones. The texture felt oddly intimate, as if I had slipped into a forgotten corner of history. "What did they use this for?" I murmured.

Finn's eyes were sharp, studying me more than the wall. "I don't know. But it's here for a reason."

"Yeah, well, so are we, right?" I muttered, giving the wall another cautious glance. "Doesn't mean we should start knocking things over."

"I think we should," Finn replied, his voice low but resolute. "The more we leave untouched, the more we risk missing. And we can't afford to miss anything."

I wasn't sure what he meant by that, but something about his words sent a shiver down my spine. I stood, brushing the dirt off my knees, and turned to face him. Finn was already moving forward, fingers trailing along the jagged edge of the stone. For a brief moment, I wondered if he was simply trying to distract me from the weight of everything we'd already been through—his quiet manner had always been a shield, a way of keeping the real pain hidden beneath the surface. But as I watched him now, moving with that same purposeful quiet, I realized something else. He wasn't running from anything. He was leading me somewhere.

"Alright," I said, more to myself than to him. "What's the worst that could happen?"

Finn raised an eyebrow. "I can think of a few things."

I laughed, though it was more nervous than amused. "I should've known better than to ask you for optimism."

Without another word, Finn stepped toward the center of the wall and pressed his palm against the stone, pushing in a deliberate, almost ritualistic manner. The earth seemed to hold its breath for a moment, and I stood frozen, heart pounding, waiting for something—anything—to happen.

At first, I didn't think anything had changed. There was no dramatic shift, no sudden revelation. The wall simply stood there, unchanged, its moss still green, its cracks still gaping. But then, with a sound too soft to be real, a section of the stone shifted. A low grinding noise echoed, and the ground beneath my feet seemed to tremble, as though the earth itself was holding its breath.

I took a hesitant step back, my pulse quickening. Finn, however, didn't budge. He stayed close to the wall, pressing harder, as if the pressure of his touch could coax more than stone from the thing. It wasn't until the stone receded, revealing a narrow, dark passage behind it, that I felt the weight of what we had done.

"Uh," I began, my voice unsteady. "Is that...?"

"Yeah," Finn replied. "It's exactly what it looks like."

I wanted to ask a thousand questions, but none of them seemed to fit the moment. The only thing I could do was stare at the dark void that had opened in front of us, a blackened throat of shadow that beckoned like a siren song.

Finn didn't wait for me to speak. He stepped into the dark space without hesitation, and I, like a fool, followed.

The air inside the passage was thick with dust, a damp, musty smell clinging to the stone walls. My breath echoed too loudly in the confined space, the sound of my heartbeat filling the silence. I squinted against the dark, my eyes straining to make out any details in the narrow corridor. The walls were close, too close, the air heavy with the feeling of being swallowed whole.

"Do you feel that?" Finn's voice was barely a whisper, though his words vibrated in the stillness.

I didn't answer immediately. Instead, I stepped closer to him, my fingers brushing against the rough surface of the stone walls. It felt as though we were walking through a forgotten history, each step carrying us further into something unknown. Something that had been hidden, tucked away for a reason.

"Yeah," I finally muttered, barely able to steady my voice. "I do."

Finn's pace slowed, and I felt his attention shift as he scanned the passage ahead. There was something else now, something I couldn't put my finger on. A presence, maybe? Or maybe it was just the way the air seemed to thicken with each passing second.

And then, just as I thought we had reached the end of the tunnel, I felt it—a sharp, sudden pull in my chest, as if the ground beneath me had shifted in an unexpected direction. Before I could process it, a flicker of light illuminated the walls ahead, revealing something I never could have anticipated.

A figure, standing motionless in the center of the cavernous space.

I froze, the breath caught in my throat, as Finn's hand shot out, catching my arm. "Stay back," he whispered.

But it was already too late.

Chapter 36: The Final Farewell

The smoke from the fire still clung to the air, lingering like a half-remembered dream, a ghost of something that had once threatened to consume everything. Finn stood next to me, his silhouette framed by the soft glow of the morning sun that had started to break through the clouds. There was a subtle weight in the air, the kind that comes after a storm when everything feels heavier, more charged. I didn't need to look at him to know he was deep in thought, his mind wrestling with whatever it was he needed to say. And that was the thing with Finn—he never spoke unless he had something that mattered.

We hadn't spoken much in the days since the case had closed, each of us lost in the tangle of emotions that had come with it. The truth was out now, the person behind the fires finally exposed, and the mystery that had started as a whisper in the dark had been unraveled. There was satisfaction in that, a sense of finality that should have felt like a victory. But standing there in the silence of a world that seemed to have started over, the only thing I could feel was the weight of what had been lost.

I glanced at him, catching the light of the morning on his face, tracing the lines that had deepened over the months. Finn wasn't a man who wore his heart on his sleeve, and yet, now, there was something in his eyes that told me everything. His past had been a shadow, long and unwieldy, and for a long time, it had been too much to escape. But now, with the truth finally out in the open, I could see it—the way he was standing, the slight slump in his shoulders as if the burden had finally been set down. Maybe not completely gone, but certainly lighter.

"Are you ready?" I asked, my voice soft, cautious, not wanting to disturb the fragile quiet that had settled between us.

Finn took a slow breath and turned to face me fully. There was something in his eyes that I hadn't seen before—a kind of peace, a surrender, and maybe even a touch of gratitude. It was the kind of look a man gives when he knows he's been given a second chance, even if he's not entirely sure what to do with it yet.

"I think I am," he said, his voice steady but with a hint of something I couldn't quite place. Maybe relief. Maybe fear. The kind of fear that comes from having to let go of the past, even when it's all you've known.

I nodded, because I understood. I had been holding on to my own ghosts—my own history of disappointments and failures—and it wasn't until I'd been forced to face them, to sift through the ashes of what had burned, that I realized how much of it was still in me, still shaping the way I saw the world. I wasn't so different from him.

"We can go now, you know," I said, taking a step closer to him, close enough to feel the heat radiating from his body. "There's nothing here for us anymore."

He didn't move at first, didn't answer immediately, and I could feel the tension building, the air crackling with the unspoken words that hovered between us. He was still tethered to this place in some way, and I wasn't sure if it was because he felt an obligation, or if there was something else—something I didn't quite understand yet.

"I can't leave like this," he finally said, his voice quieter now, almost lost in the wind that rustled through the trees nearby. "Not without saying goodbye. Not without facing it all."

I swallowed, the lump in my throat making it hard to speak, but I knew he needed this. He needed closure, and so did I. We both did.

"I get it," I said. "We can face it, but it's just a place. The real fight, the real battle, is over now."

His eyes met mine, and I saw something flicker there, something almost vulnerable. “It’s not just a place,” he said, his gaze moving over the landscape as if he were seeing it for the first time. “It’s everything. The fire, the wreckage... it’s been part of me for so long that it’s hard to imagine leaving it behind.”

The words hung between us, thick with the weight of history and the burden of all the things we had both seen and experienced. I knew Finn. And while he was no longer the man I had first met—cynical, angry, guarded—there were still pieces of him that were tied to the past, unwilling to let go. But it was different now. He was ready to let it go. I just needed to remind him that the world beyond this was still worth living for.

“We’ll rebuild,” I said quietly. “We’ll find something new, something better. We’ve already been through the worst of it.”

He didn’t answer, but he didn’t need to. I could see it in the way his shoulders loosened, in the way he took a deep breath and exhaled like he was finally, truly breathing again.

And then, almost as if the words had been a signal, he turned to face the remnants of the place, the charred remnants of what had once been a home. There was a small nod, a silent farewell, and then he turned back to me, his hand reaching for mine, fingers warm and sure. No more words were needed. The past had burned away, and whatever came next was ours to claim.

In that moment, there was nothing left but us and the world we would create together, starting fresh, from the ashes of what had come before. And I believed, more than anything, that it was enough.

We stood there for a moment, hand in hand, the silence between us thick and unyielding. The kind of silence that, rather than offering peace, churns like the quiet before a storm. It wasn’t just the remnants of the fire that left their mark on this place. It was everything—the tension that had built for so long, the ghosts of decisions and missteps that had brought us here. The weight of it all hung over us, and neither one of us was sure what to say next.

Finn shifted, his eyes lingering on the twisted metal and scorched wood, then back to me. "It's funny," he said with a wry half-smile, his voice a low rumble, "how quickly something can change from a dream to a nightmare."

I didn't need him to explain. We had both seen it—the way things can fall apart when you least expect it, the way the promises we make can twist and turn on us like a bad joke. There had been a time, long before any of this had started, when we thought we had it all figured out. A nice house, a future carved out in the world we'd both worked so hard to create. But life, as it tends to do, had other plans. The fire had consumed everything—everything except us. We were still standing, still breathing. And that, I supposed, was enough.

"It's not the place that mattered," I said, not really looking at him but at the remnants of what had once been so full of potential. "It's what we do next."

He gave me a long look, eyes narrowed as if he were trying to piece together a puzzle with missing parts. "What if I don't know what comes next?"

I wasn't sure how to answer that, not because I didn't have my own doubts, but because his words stung with truth. What if we were both so focused on moving forward that we didn't even know what that looked like anymore? Could we rebuild? Could we even trust the ground beneath our feet?

"I guess we'll figure it out," I said, squeezing his hand a little tighter, trying to offer the certainty I didn't feel. "But we'll do it together. No matter what."

His gaze softened at that, and I knew he was searching for the same assurance. A small nod passed between us, an unspoken agreement. We'd make it work, whatever that meant.

The air grew colder as the sun began to dip lower, casting long shadows over the scorched landscape. The fire's remnants still smoldered, sending occasional tendrils of smoke curling into the air, as though the place were reluctant to let go of the past.

"Are you planning to go back to the city?" he asked after a long pause. "After all this, I mean?"

I felt a pang at the thought. The city had always been an escape, a place of anonymity and distraction, a place where I could disappear into the crowd. But it wasn't home, not anymore. Not after everything that had happened. Not after I'd seen what was left of the life I'd built here.

"I don't think so," I said quietly. "Not right away. I think I need something else. Something that feels... real. Maybe a little more... permanent?"

I glanced over at him, watching his face as the words sank in. I wasn't sure what I was asking for—certainty, stability, maybe just a little peace—but I knew that the place I'd left behind was no longer where I belonged. And Finn, in his quiet, unpredictable way, seemed to understand that more than anyone else.

"I'm not sure what I'm doing either," he said, his voice tinged with an honesty that almost made me smile. "But I think I'm tired of running from the things that scare me."

I couldn't help the soft laugh that bubbled up. "Good. Because the last thing we need right now is more running."

Finn's eyes caught mine, the ghost of a smile playing at the corner of his lips. "I guess I'll just have to learn how to face things head-on then, huh?"

"You've got a good start," I said, stepping closer, letting the space between us narrow. "Besides, I've always liked a challenge."

The breeze shifted, carrying with it the scent of earth and ashes, and I realized, not for the first time, how much I had changed in the last few months. It wasn't just the fire or the investigation that had done it. It was Finn, and it was me, and it was everything that had led us to this strange, quiet moment. We were both learning, trying to figure out how to live in the wreckage of what had been, and somehow, despite the fear and uncertainty, I knew we'd find a way to rebuild.

He reached out, brushing a stray lock of hair behind my ear, his touch lingering just a little longer than necessary. "You think we'll ever get used to this? To everything changing all the time?"

I looked up at him, meeting his steady gaze, and for a moment, the world seemed to stop. "Maybe not," I said, my voice steady now. "But maybe that's the point. Maybe change isn't something to fear. Maybe it's just... the only way forward."

He didn't answer at first, but the look on his face said everything. It was a mixture of disbelief and hope, the kind of thing that can only come when you're standing on the precipice of something new, not knowing whether to jump or pull back. But we weren't pulling back—not now, not after everything we had been through.

The sun was almost gone now, leaving behind the last traces of daylight, and as we stood there together, our hands intertwined, I realized something else: there was no map for this, no clear path ahead. But somehow, that made it all feel like the right kind of risk. The kind worth taking.

The night was creeping in now, the last vestiges of sunlight swallowed up by the rising dark, and with it came a kind of peace. I could feel the calm settling around us, as though the earth itself was taking a collective breath after the chaos that had so recently torn through it. Finn and I hadn't spoken for a while, but there was something in the quiet between us that felt more like understanding than tension.

We'd come a long way, both of us—more than we'd given ourselves credit for. I hadn't realized, until this very moment, just how much I had been holding onto: my own insecurities, my need to prove something, my need to escape. And Finn? Well, Finn had his own demons, ones that I couldn't even begin to comprehend. But tonight, standing there beside him, I could sense that we were ready to leave the ghosts of the past where they belonged—behind us.

He tugged at the collar of his jacket, a nervous habit that had become all too familiar over the past few weeks. I hadn't asked about the fire, about the way it had twisted his life. He'd told me what I needed to know, and the rest... the rest was for him to carry or not. I could handle the silence. We both could.

"Is it too late to ask for something crazy?" he finally said, breaking the silence with that half-hearted attempt at a joke that was more Finn than anything else.

I raised an eyebrow, turning to face him fully, curious. "Crazy, like what? You want to get on a plane to Paris and forget everything?"

He chuckled, though it wasn't entirely light. "Not Paris," he said, gaze flicking away for a moment before returning to me. "But something like that. Something... unexpected."

I could hear the vulnerability in his voice, the way he was testing the waters, unsure whether I'd even entertain the idea. But what did we have left if we didn't take chances? I met his gaze, my heartbeat picking up just a fraction.

"Like running away?" I asked, a sly grin playing at the corner of my lips. "Finn, we've both spent far too much time running. Maybe it's time we stopped."

His lips twitched, his gaze narrowing in on me. "Then what do you suggest we do? Because standing here, waiting for some kind of cosmic sign, isn't exactly filling me with confidence."

The wind picked up again, brushing through my hair as I stood there, thinking. Maybe it wasn't Paris or some far-off fantasy.

Maybe it was just... us. Moving forward without looking back, without second-guessing every step we took. Was that crazy? Or was it exactly what we needed?

"I don't know," I said, the words coming out more easily than I'd expected. "But I think we should stop trying to find a way back to something that was never really ours to begin with."

His expression shifted, something softening in his eyes, like he was finally seeing the same thing I was. Maybe the plan had never been the thing that mattered. Maybe it was just the willingness to try, to give this—whatever this was—a shot.

"I guess that's as close to crazy as I'll get for now," he muttered, a smile tugging at the corner of his lips.

I laughed softly. "Good. Because I think that's the kind of crazy I can handle."

But the moment didn't last. Not when the crunch of footsteps suddenly broke the fragile silence. I turned quickly, my hand instinctively moving to the small of my back, where I had gotten used to the weight of a gun. But this wasn't the same thing. This wasn't a confrontation or a last-minute plot twist.

It was her.

Megan.

I froze. The woman I had never expected to see again, not after everything that had happened. Not after what she had done. But there she was, standing just a few yards away, her expression unreadable, her hands stuffed deep into the pockets of her coat.

"Well, this is an unexpected reunion," I said, my voice a little tighter than I intended, but I couldn't help it. There was something in the air now, something heavy that had changed the atmosphere between us.

Finn's jaw clenched beside me, but he didn't say a word. His gaze never left Megan's face, and I could see the mix of anger and confusion there. I didn't know what to say to her, not after everything that had gone down. The fire, the lies, the twisted mess she'd left in her wake. It was hard to reconcile the woman standing in front of me now with the one who had caused so much destruction.

"What do you want?" I asked, keeping my tone as level as possible.

Megan's gaze flicked to Finn, then back to me, her lips tight. "I wanted to make sure you both knew the truth," she said, her voice strangely calm. "The fire... it wasn't just about revenge. It was about a warning."

I frowned. "A warning?" I echoed, my mind racing to catch up with what she was implying.

Finn stiffened beside me, his hand tightening into a fist. "A warning about what?"

She looked between us both, and for a split second, I saw a flicker of something—regret, maybe, or guilt?—before she quickly masked it with that cool, almost clinical expression. "You thought the danger was over," she said. "But it's just beginning."

I opened my mouth, ready to ask her exactly what kind of mess she was dragging us into now, but before I could speak, the ground beneath us seemed to shake, a deep rumbling that vibrated up through my bones.

My eyes darted around, trying to pinpoint the source. "What the hell was that?"

But Megan's face had gone pale, her lips parted in fear. She took a step back, her eyes wide. "You have no idea what you've gotten yourselves into," she whispered.

And then, just as suddenly as it had started, the earth stilled. But the tension, the sense that something much bigger was looming, was unmistakable.

"Finn," I whispered, my heart pounding in my chest. "What's going on?"

He didn't answer. Not immediately. Instead, his gaze locked with mine, and for the first time in what felt like forever, I saw the full extent of the fear in his eyes.

Then, as if on cue, the sound of an engine revving broke the stillness.

We weren't alone anymore.

Chapter 37: Rising from the Ashes

I let the morning sun spill through the window, its golden rays flickering across the floor like tiny, dancing embers. The scent of fresh coffee wafted from the kitchen, filling the house with a comfort I hadn't realized I craved so deeply. Finn was in there, humming softly as he moved around, a cup of coffee in his hand, his shoulders relaxed in a way I hadn't seen before. He'd always carried tension in his body—muscles taut, like a bowstring pulled too tight. But today, the lines of worry seemed to have softened. Maybe it was the quiet of the house, or the fact that we'd finally reached a place where the immediate danger had passed. Or maybe it was just the space to breathe without looking over our shoulders every second.

I leaned against the doorframe, watching him, unable to stop the smile that tugged at my lips. "Did you know you make that sound when you're happy?"

Finn turned, eyebrow arched. "What sound?"

"That little hum." I mimicked it, a soft, almost inaudible noise in the back of my throat. "It's like you're... content. It's a rare thing."

He laughed, a rich, deep sound that made the hairs on the back of my neck stand at attention. "Well, I've got plenty to be happy about these days."

I raised an eyebrow, teasing, "Oh? And what might that be?"

Finn leaned back against the counter, giving me a look that was equal parts amusement and affection. "Maybe because I'm sharing a cup of coffee with a woman who's finally stopped glaring at me like she's about to smack me upside the head."

I rolled my eyes, though I couldn't suppress the warmth spreading through me. "You're lucky I don't throw something at you right now."

He grinned, stepping forward to place the coffee in my hands. The warmth of the mug seeped through my fingers, grounding me in the moment. "You wouldn't dare. I'm a man of infinite patience."

"Uh-huh." I sipped the coffee, my thoughts swirling as I felt the weight of everything that had happened, all of it suddenly crashing into me with the force of a tidal wave. We were free now—finally free from the years of fear, the near constant threat that had hung over us. The danger, the secrets, the lies... they all felt like distant echoes, but they still had the power to make my chest tighten with anxiety.

"Hey," Finn's voice broke through my spiraling thoughts, gentle but insistent. "We're okay, you know?"

I looked up at him, trying to read the sincerity in his eyes. For a moment, it was like I could feel the weight of the past months pressing on his shoulders, too. "Are we?" I asked, my voice barely above a whisper. "Are we really?"

He exhaled slowly, setting his own mug down beside mine, his fingers brushing mine in a simple gesture that meant more than I could say. "We're alive," he said quietly. "That's something, right?"

It was something. It was everything. I knew that. But the truth of it—the brutal truth—was that I wasn't sure what came next. The danger might have passed, but the scars from everything we'd been through were still there, lingering like shadows in the corners of my mind. I wasn't sure how to move forward, how to unearth the version of myself that had been buried under fear for so long.

"I don't know what to do with myself now," I admitted, my voice cracking a little more than I'd intended.

Finn nodded, his expression softening. "You don't have to know. Not yet. We've got time."

Time. The word echoed in my chest. Time felt like a luxury I hadn't known in years, but now, in the stillness of the house, I wasn't sure how to fill it. I looked around, seeing the way the morning light streamed through the windows, how the walls of this house we'd found together seemed to hold us in place, like a promise.

The world outside was moving on, turning and changing, but for the first time, I wasn't sure if I was ready to keep up. There were so many paths ahead, all of them untaken, and the weight of those choices felt like a thousand doors opening at once.

"Do you ever think about what comes next?" I asked, almost afraid of the answer.

Finn's gaze softened as he walked over to the window, looking out at the town beyond. "Every day," he said quietly. "But I'm not in any rush."

I wasn't either, not really. But the uncertainty of it all gnawed at me, a restless presence just beneath the surface. I'd spent so much of my life running, dodging, surviving. Now, I was standing still, and it felt... foreign. I wasn't used to being at peace. It was almost too quiet, too calm, like the world was waiting for something to shatter it.

Finn turned back to me, his expression knowing, like he could read the worry crawling across my face. "We've been through hell and back," he said, his voice steady, his eyes unwavering. "But that's not all there is. There's more to us than the chaos."

I met his gaze, feeling the strength of his words wrap around me like a blanket. Maybe he was right. Maybe it wasn't about knowing what came next, but about allowing ourselves the space to figure it out without the pressure of time, or the fear of the unknown.

"We'll figure it out," I whispered, my heart starting to beat in a new rhythm, one that was slowly but surely replacing the tension that had kept me awake at night.

Finn's smile was slow but genuine, a glimpse of the man who had carried me through so much without hesitation. "I know we will," he said, and for the first time in a long while, I believed him.

The house was quiet again, save for the soft tap of Finn's boots as he paced in the hallway. I could tell by the way he kept glancing at his phone that he was restless, like he couldn't quite shake the feeling that something else was looming—something just out of sight, waiting to make itself known. I didn't want to be the one to ask, but the silence between us had stretched long enough that I finally cleared my throat.

"What's on your mind?" I asked, folding the blanket I'd been sitting under, folding the question into the mundane task.

Finn stopped, fingers brushing against the frame of the door as he leaned against it, his eyes not quite meeting mine. "I'm thinking about the town. About the people. We're safe here, but..." He trailed off, a deep sigh escaping his lips.

"Is this about the donations or the safety patrols? Because I think you can officially cross 'I'm worried about all of them' off your list. They're fine, Finn."

He looked over at me then, his eyes flashing with that stubborn glint that always made me bite back a smile. "You think they're fine? Just because they're safe for now? After everything, I can't help but think that's not enough. I'm not sure it's enough for me, either."

I set the blanket down, crossing the room toward him. "What do you mean? We've made it. You've made it." I reached for his hand, threading my fingers through his, offering him the comfort I wasn't sure I had to give. "You're here. You're here, with me. That's more than enough."

His lips twitched, but his brow furrowed in that way I recognized, the one that always appeared just before he tried to figure out the impossible. "It's not just about us, though. We've been so lucky, Sarah. But I'm not sure we've completely outrun all of it."

I wanted to push him to open up more, but a part of me was starting to recognize the problem. We'd spent too long reacting to the storm, adjusting ourselves to the chaos, that we hadn't actually taken the time to just breathe, to make sense of it all. For me, that felt like one giant mountain I wasn't ready to climb. But the thing about mountains is that they never care if you're ready or not. They just sit there, imposing, daring you to take that first step.

I sighed and leaned my back against the doorframe, watching him pace again. "What if we're finally out of the woods? What if it's over?"

Finn's voice was quieter now, almost a murmur, but it held a weight that pulled at something deep inside me. "What if it's not?"

I didn't know how to respond. The truth was, I didn't have an answer for that. I couldn't be sure whether this uneasy feeling was just the aftermath of what we'd survived, or if there was truly something waiting for us down the road. We had survived the worst of it, sure. But survival, as I'd come to realize, wasn't the same as living.

"I'm just..." Finn started, dragging a hand through his hair, his frustration evident. "I don't know what to do next. It's like I'm standing still, waiting for something to happen. And I hate that."

"I get it," I said, my voice soft but firm. "I really do. It feels like there's a time bomb ticking somewhere in the distance, doesn't it? Like we're waiting for it to go off. But maybe it's just... quiet now. Maybe we can take a breath."

He glanced at me, the weight of his gaze making my chest tighten. "And if it's not? What if I'm wrong about all this?"

I straightened up, the uncertainty between us now hanging heavy in the air. "You're not wrong. You're just... afraid. We both are." I took a step toward him, careful not to crowd him, but offering my presence in the way I knew how. "But there's nothing wrong with that. It's just how we keep going, you know? Fear doesn't mean we stop. It just means we keep moving, even when it's hard."

He smiled then, though it didn't quite reach his eyes. "You're a hell of a lot braver than I am."

I couldn't help but laugh, even though there was an edge of sadness to it. "Brave? I'm just trying to get through the day without falling apart. That's all the bravery I've got left in me."

Finn's smile grew, just a little, and for a moment, the tension that had been building between us seemed to soften. "Well, I'd say you're doing a hell of a job at it."

It was the first time in days that I allowed myself to really look at him—really see him. The way his hair curled slightly around his ears, the hint of a smile that played on his lips, and those eyes that had seen far too much and still, somehow, remained full of tenderness. He was my anchor, my rock, in all this chaos. But he was also human, and I knew that even a rock can wear thin under enough pressure.

I reached up to touch his cheek, my fingers brushing against the stubble there. It had grown a little more than usual, but I liked the way it felt against my skin. "We've got each other. And, for once, we're allowed to just be."

His eyes softened, and I saw something in them—something warm and unspoken. He leaned into my touch, just for a moment, the weight of everything we'd endured pulling us closer.

"You think we're allowed to be happy?" he asked, his voice low, almost tentative.

I thought about it for a moment. It didn't feel right to rush into happiness. Not when there was still so much to figure out. But I also knew that happiness wasn't some distant thing we had to earn.

It was small moments, like this one, when the world felt steady underfoot.

"I think we're allowed to try," I said, my voice steady. "And that's enough for me."

Finn's smile finally reached his eyes, and in that moment, I realized something I hadn't allowed myself to fully grasp until now: we weren't just surviving anymore. We were building. And that was something new. Something real.

The next few weeks passed in a blur of small moments, the kind that seem insignificant in the grand scheme of things, but add up to something far more meaningful. Finn and I settled into the quiet rhythms of a life we never thought we'd have. Mornings filled with coffee and unspoken comfort. Evenings wrapped in the warmth of simple conversation, the kind that didn't feel urgent, just... steady.

The town, too, was finding its footing again. The lingering fear from the past was slowly being replaced by a cautious optimism. It wasn't perfect, but it was better than the tension we'd lived under for so long. I started volunteering at the local community center, offering my time to help organize events, assist with projects. For the first time in a long while, it felt like I belonged somewhere, like I wasn't just passing through. I'd spent so much time running, surviving, that I hadn't truly understood what it meant to be part of something—something lasting, something real.

Finn was still working through his own demons. I could see it in the way his hands would freeze on the wheel when we were driving, like he was bracing for an impact that never came. Or when his gaze would drift to the horizon, and I'd wonder what he was searching for. But we were trying, both of us, to find our way through the wreckage of the past. One day at a time. It was slow, but it was progress.

"Hey," I called from the front door, pulling my jacket tighter around me against the cool evening air. "We're going to be late if we don't leave now."

Finn, who had been in the kitchen, doing who-knows-what with a coffee grinder, paused mid-action, glancing at me with a look that was half-embarrassment, half-amusement. "I'll be there in five."

It had become something of a running joke, this perpetual delay of ours. No matter how many times we planned to leave, Finn always had to finish something, adjust something, double-check something. It was endearing, in a way, but it also meant that we were always rushing at the last minute.

"I swear," I muttered under my breath, "you do this on purpose."

He flashed me a grin as he grabbed his jacket off the hook. "I don't know what you mean. I'm just making sure I don't forget anything."

"Oh, sure. Like last week when you forgot the keys to the car?" I raised an eyebrow, crossing my arms over my chest.

He gave a casual shrug, the corners of his mouth twitching. "Well, you always say you like a little adventure."

I rolled my eyes but couldn't suppress the smile that tugged at my lips. "Adventure, yes. Chaos, no."

We finally made our way to the community center, where a small gathering was being held. It wasn't anything extravagant, just a chance for people to reconnect, share a meal, and enjoy the simple act of being together. I liked those kinds of things. They felt normal. And after everything we'd been through, normal was exactly what we needed.

As we walked into the room, I was greeted by a sea of familiar faces, all smiling and chatting in the way that small towns do. A soft hum of background conversation filled the air, and the smell of homemade dishes—pot roast, fresh bread, the unmistakable aroma of apple pie—wafted in from the kitchen. It was the kind of place where you could forget, for just a moment, about everything else that had happened.

But even here, I couldn't shake the feeling that something was off. It was the odd glance, the whisper just out of earshot, the way people would pause when we walked by, as if unsure of how to act around us now that the dust had settled. Some part of me understood—it wasn't easy to know what to do when someone's survival had been hard-fought. There was a lingering wariness, a hesitance, but it wasn't entirely unkind. It was just... different.

Finn noticed it too. I could see it in the tightness of his jaw, the way his eyes flickered from face to face, searching for signs of something he couldn't quite name. But he didn't say anything. Instead, he wrapped an arm around my waist, pulling me closer, as if to silently remind me that we were a team.

"Let's go get a drink," I suggested, trying to steer us toward something familiar. A simple task, something we could control.

We made our way to the table where a group of people were gathered around, and for a while, it felt like everything was just... fine. Comfortable. But as the evening wore on, that nagging feeling in the back of my mind refused to go away. Every laugh felt a little too forced, every gesture a little too stiff.

Finn, sensing the shift in my mood, leaned in close, his breath warm against my ear. "You okay?"

I nodded, but I wasn't. There was something unsettled in the air, something that I couldn't put my finger on. And just when I thought I could shake it off, I saw him.

Standing at the back of the room, leaning against the doorway like he'd always been part of the crowd, was someone I hadn't expected to see. Someone I thought was long gone.

David.

My heart skipped a beat, my breath catching in my throat as I watched him. His hair was a little longer than I remembered, and there was a weariness about him that hadn't been there before. But it was him, no mistaking it.

I felt the room tilt, like gravity had shifted in the strangest way, and all at once, my mind was rushing to catch up with what I was seeing. Finn noticed my reaction immediately, following my gaze, his eyes narrowing with suspicion.

"What the hell is he doing here?" Finn's voice was low, tight with something I couldn't quite read.

I didn't answer. Because I didn't know.

David took a slow step forward, his eyes locking with mine, and the silence in the room seemed to stretch and bend around us. Everyone had noticed by now. And I couldn't help but wonder, in that moment, what had brought him back.

And why.

Chapter 38: A New Kind of Heat

The sun had barely crested the horizon, its rays breaking through the windows in soft golden slivers, when I felt Finn's breath against the back of my neck. It wasn't the kind of breath that made you squirm in the early hours, unsure if it was too warm or too intrusive. No, his was the kind of warmth that wrapped around me like an old, well-worn blanket, the kind that smelled of rain-soaked earth and cedarwood. It was a comfort, a reassurance that, after everything, we had built something beautiful from the rubble of our past.

I shifted slightly, the soft cotton sheets beneath us rustling with the movement, but it wasn't enough to break the quiet. The world outside was still, and for once, so were we. There was no rush, no ticking clock, just the lingering scent of coffee from the kitchen, the faintest hum of the refrigerator, and the slow beat of his heart against my back. He never spoke in the mornings—not immediately anyway. His way was to greet the dawn with his quiet presence, to let the morning speak for itself.

I loved that about him.

In a world that never seemed to stop, Finn had this way of slowing everything down. He made the chaos feel like a distant echo, barely more than a whisper in the background. When I was with him, I could breathe in full breaths, exhaling slowly, as if I had all the time in the world.

"Morning," he murmured, his lips brushing my shoulder as his hand slid over my waist, drawing lazy circles against my skin. His fingers were warm, a little rough from the work of his hands—calloused but tender. There was a quiet reverence in his touch now, like he'd finally learned to appreciate the softness that had once been foreign to him.

"Morning," I whispered back, my voice still thick with sleep, but I didn't mind. In his arms, sleep felt like a luxury, something to be savored rather than rushed through. I turned in his embrace, my hands curling into the front of his shirt, pulling him closer, not out of need, but out of the certainty that this was where I belonged. The room felt too small to contain us, but I didn't care. There was no other place I wanted to be.

Finn's eyes—those piercing blue eyes that seemed to see straight through to my soul—held mine with an intensity that made my heart skip a beat. He'd always been like this, even when I wasn't sure we had a future. But now, there was no question. No hesitation. The scars we wore, both seen and unseen, had become the story we carried together, a tale of survival, of rebirth. Each mark, each memory, was woven into the fabric of us, not as something to hide but something to be proud of.

"You know, I think I could get used to this," I said, my lips curling into a smile, as I traced the outline of his jaw with my fingertips. "No explosions. No danger. Just... us."

He chuckled softly, the sound deep and rich, vibrating in his chest. It was the kind of laughter that filled me with warmth, the kind that made me feel like I was safe, like I was home. "Is that what you're after now? A peaceful life?"

"Well, yeah. What's wrong with that?" I raised an eyebrow, teasing. "I'm all for some excitement, but I think I've earned a little peace."

Finn's gaze softened, and for a moment, I could see the flicker of something—vulnerability, perhaps? A reminder that, even in the quiet moments, we were still navigating this new chapter together. He placed a gentle kiss on my forehead before resting his cheek against my hair, his arms tightening around me as if to say, I'm not letting go.

"I think I've earned it too," he murmured. "But if you want excitement, I'm happy to oblige." His fingers traced the line of my spine, sending a shiver down my back. His voice dropped, teasing now. "But maybe we could start slow. See how the day goes?"

I laughed, low and amused, pulling back just enough to meet his eyes. "Slow, huh? You're not exactly the slow type."

Finn's lips quirked upward, a playful glint flashing in his eyes. "You're right about that," he admitted with a smirk. "But I've learned that some things are worth savoring."

My heart swelled at the simple honesty in his words, and I couldn't help but lean in for another kiss, one that lingered just long enough to make the rest of the world feel miles away.

When we finally broke apart, I buried my face in the crook of his neck, breathing in the scent of him, of us, of this new life we were building. "I think we're good," I said quietly, almost to myself, feeling the weight of it. "No matter what's next, I think we're good."

He was quiet for a moment, and when he spoke again, his voice was low, sincere. "We are, you know. We've come through hell, and we're still standing. Together."

I pulled back enough to look at him, my hand resting gently against his chest. "Together," I echoed, tasting the word. It felt right. It felt like everything we had worked for—everything we had risked—was finally paying off. We had a future now, one we could shape as we saw fit.

The future was uncertain, as it always was, but for the first time in a long while, I wasn't afraid of it. And neither was Finn.

Later that day, Finn and I took a walk along the shoreline, our shoes leaving footprints in the sand that the waves were quick to erase. There was something meditative about the rhythm of the ocean, how it met the land with unspoken wisdom, a constant reminder that some things in life were beyond our control—like the pull of the tide, or the way we found each other when neither of us had been looking.

The sun was high now, casting long shadows across the sand. The air was salty and thick with the scent of the sea, a heady blend of warmth and fresh water. Finn's hand brushed mine, just a small connection, but enough to make me feel grounded, as though nothing else mattered in that moment but us, here, on this stretch of beach that felt like our private sanctuary.

"I'm glad we're doing this," I said, the words spilling out before I could catch them. I hadn't meant to say it aloud, but there it was, hanging between us like the soft buzz of a new song. "I don't think I realized how much I needed quiet until now."

He glanced at me, that familiar glint in his eyes. The corners of his mouth twitched upward in that little half-smile that always made my heart skip. "You always seem to know exactly what you need... after a little convincing."

I laughed, nudging him with my shoulder. "Convincing, huh? You make it sound like I'm some kind of hard sell."

"I wouldn't say hard," Finn said, his voice low and teasing. "More like... unpredictable. But that's what makes you interesting."

Unpredictable. I wasn't sure I liked the sound of it, though I suspected it was the truth. I had never been one to follow any conventional path, never been content with staying put or letting life unfold without trying to shake things up. But with Finn, it felt different. I was learning to embrace the stillness, to let the world keep moving without needing to chase after it every second of the day.

"What about you?" I asked, stepping over a patch of wet sand. "What's been your idea of peace?"

He took a moment to consider, his eyes narrowing as if he were weighing the answer carefully, but then his lips parted, and he said simply, "I never really knew what peace was. Not until now."

There was something in his tone that made me stop walking. It wasn't sadness, not quite, but it was something deeper—something that spoke of years spent in conflict, both within himself and with the world around him. He wasn't used to letting the quiet in, not when his life had been a constant battle for so long. The fact that he had let me be a part of this slower, gentler version of his life said more than any words could.

I reached out, brushing my fingers over his forearm, the motion light and soft. "I'm glad you're here," I said quietly, trying to convey everything I felt in that single moment. The fear, the uncertainty, the hope that had blossomed between us in the wake of everything.

Finn turned to face me, his expression unreadable for a beat, but then his gaze softened. He leaned down, pressing a kiss to my forehead, the warmth of his lips a promise I didn't need to hear aloud.

"Me too," he murmured, his voice rough with something unspoken. "Me too."

We walked in comfortable silence for a while, the only sounds the rhythmic rush of the ocean and the occasional call of a distant gull. And as we did, I realized something profound: the world around us hadn't changed. The past we had survived was still there, lingering in the shadows, but we had found a new way of living within it. We had made peace, not by erasing the past, but by learning how to coexist with it, to make it a part of the story we were still writing.

Just as I was beginning to lose myself in the quiet of the moment, the sound of a car engine roared to life behind us. I turned to see a dusty, beat-up sedan pulling up to the beach. The engine sputtered before cutting off completely, and I narrowed my eyes. It was an unfamiliar car—too old to be anything impressive, but it looked like the kind of vehicle that had seen better days.

I raised an eyebrow at Finn. "That's... not exactly the most subtle entrance."

Finn chuckled, though it didn't quite reach his eyes. There was a flash of wariness there, something that flickered before disappearing. "Nope. Subtlety's never been its strong suit."

Before I could ask more, the driver's side door creaked open, and a man stepped out, tall and lanky with dark, unkempt hair. His face was weathered, the lines around his eyes deepened by years spent in the sun. His clothes were mismatched, a pair of cargo shorts and a faded T-shirt, and he had a look of someone who was used to being somewhere he wasn't supposed to be.

I frowned, my instincts kicking in immediately. "Who is that?" I asked, keeping my voice low.

Finn's expression hardened, the easy warmth of moments before gone in an instant. He didn't answer right away, his jaw tightening as he watched the man approach us. I felt the tension building between us, the sudden shift from peaceful to something far more charged.

"Finn," I pressed, more insistently now. "Do you know him?"

He didn't answer immediately, his eyes narrowing as the stranger drew closer. There was something about the way Finn stood, that protective stance, that made my heart rate spike.

"I'm about to find out," Finn said, his voice steady but edged with an undercurrent of warning.

And just like that, the peaceful walk along the shore had come to an abrupt, unsettling halt.

I crossed my arms over my chest, the air between Finn and me thick with unspoken questions as the man from the car came closer. His shoes slapped against the sand with an odd rhythm, like he didn't quite belong here. And the more I looked at him, the more I realized that I wasn't sure I wanted him to.

Finn didn't flinch, but I could see the muscle in his jaw working as the stranger came to a halt just a few paces away. The man's eyes flicked between us, pausing a beat too long on me, before settling back on Finn with something like recognition—or maybe it was a challenge.

"You're a hard man to find, Finn," the stranger said, his voice low, rough around the edges.

I tilted my head, studying the way Finn's posture didn't shift, how he was still standing tall, the very picture of control. But beneath that calm, there was something else, something I couldn't name—an undercurrent of tension that crackled in the air between them. The kind of tension that didn't come from small talk.

"I'm sure I've never been easy to find," Finn replied, his voice cool, too calm. I could almost hear the weight of the years between them, the unspoken history they carried. This wasn't a first-time meeting. It was the kind of reunion you wish you could ignore, one you wished you could walk away from without a second glance.

The man smirked, and I could see the way his lips twisted, like he knew a joke Finn wasn't in on. "You always did have a knack for disappearing. Shame, really. Some things should've stayed found."

I glanced at Finn, who was silent for a moment, his gaze fixed on the man with the kind of intensity that suggested there was more here than a simple encounter. And I wanted to ask—what exactly had these two shared? But before I could open my mouth, the stranger shifted, his hand coming up to tug at the hem of his shirt, pulling it higher to reveal a faded scar across his side.

It was nothing compared to the marks Finn bore, but it was enough. Enough to confirm my suspicions: this wasn't just a random guy showing up to ruin our peaceful morning. This was personal.

"Not everything stays buried, Finn," the man said with a bitter edge, and there was something dark in his tone that sent a chill down my spine. "Not even the past."

"Why don't you tell me what you're really after," Finn said, his voice harder now, colder. I could see the way his eyes had hardened, the calm veneer slipping away to reveal the fighter I had come to know. The man I loved wasn't a stranger to confrontation, and if anything, it seemed that his past had prepared him for moments like this.

The stranger didn't answer immediately. Instead, he shifted his weight from one foot to the other, as if he were weighing his next words carefully.

"Do you think you've outrun it?" he asked, almost mockingly, his gaze flicking to the horizon, then back at Finn. "You've been hiding in plain sight long enough. But people don't forget. They never forget."

Finn's lips curled, a flash of something dangerous flickering in his eyes. "I'm not hiding," he said, and though his words were few, they held weight—like a statement of truth, one that couldn't be contested.

The stranger's eyes narrowed at the challenge in Finn's voice. "Maybe not. But I'm sure someone will come looking for you, sooner or later."

I took a step forward, my eyes scanning the man with suspicion. "Who exactly are you?" I demanded, crossing my arms. I wasn't about to sit idly by while this stranger dropped cryptic threats in the middle of our peaceful morning.

The man shifted his stance, his eyes now fully on me, a strange glint dancing in them. "Oh, sweetheart, you don't need to know me. But you'll know my name soon enough." His gaze shifted back to Finn, and a moment of silence passed between them.

I didn't like this. I didn't like the way this encounter was spiraling into something darker, something I couldn't quite understand. But Finn was standing rigidly now, his hands at his sides, his expression unreadable. And I realized that whatever was coming, whatever was being dredged up from their shared past, I wasn't going to be able to stop it.

Finn's gaze flicked to me for the briefest of moments, and the tension in his body loosened just a fraction. He knew. He knew that I was in the dark, and that whatever history he had with this man, I hadn't been prepared for it.

"We'll handle this," Finn said, the words firm, decisive. It was clear that he was trying to reassure me, but I could see through it. I wasn't reassured, not in the slightest.

The man chuckled, but it wasn't the kind of laugh that made me feel comfortable. It was dark, edged with something like warning, and a sense of dread crept into my chest.

"I'm sure you will," he said, his eyes flicking between us once more. "Just remember, Finn, the past has a funny way of catching up. And when it does, there's no outrunning it. No hiding."

I opened my mouth to ask him exactly what he meant, but before I could get the words out, the man turned and walked back to his car, his footsteps leaving deep marks in the sand.

I watched him go, my thoughts racing, but I couldn't shake the feeling that this was far from over. Whatever had been left unresolved between Finn and this man was far from finished. And I had the distinct feeling that we had just walked straight into the beginning of something we weren't ready for.

Finn was still staring at the spot where the man had been, his jaw clenched, his eyes narrowed into something distant, something unreadable.

"I need you to trust me," he said, his voice strained, almost urgent.

And I wanted to, I really did. But there were so many things I didn't know. So many things I needed to understand before I could give him my full trust again.

"Finn," I said, my voice barely a whisper, "what is this? Who was that?"

He took a slow breath, his eyes meeting mine with the weight of the world in them. "You don't want to know."

But as he said it, I realized something. He wasn't just trying to protect me. He was trying to protect us both from something that might break us completely. And in that moment, the ground beneath my feet felt a little less solid.

Chapter 39: Embered Memories

It's funny, isn't it, how we can look at something that once caused us so much pain and, over time, see it differently? Like a scar that starts as something raw and angry but, with the right kind of care, becomes just a mark—still there, still part of the story, but not the story itself. That's how I think of the past now, after everything that happened. The nightmares, the confusion, the loneliness—all of it is still there, tucked into the edges of my mind like an old postcard. I can look at it now and smile, knowing it's not going to swallow me whole anymore.

Finn doesn't know how much it means to me, how every little thing he does makes my world feel less like a battlefield and more like home. The way his fingers brush mine as we walk through the crowded streets of the city, the way he looks at me when I'm rambling on about something, not quite listening, but still there, fully present. It's the little things that build a life, really. The soft hum of his voice in the morning, just waking up, still half-dreaming. The way he teases me about my endless cups of coffee like it's some sort of joke, but I know, deep down, he loves the way I clutch that mug like a lifeline. His hands, calloused from years of hard work, always gentle when they touch me.

But it's not just the softness that binds us. There's an edge to us, too. One born of shared grief, mutual understanding. I can see it in the way he looks at me sometimes, like he's trying to read the lines of my soul, trying to see if I'm still haunted by the things I try to keep buried. He doesn't say anything about it, but I can feel it in the air between us, like the weight of something unspoken hanging there. I'd be lying if I said I didn't sometimes wonder if he sees the cracks I've spent so long trying to cover up, or if he's just too kind to mention them.

I often wonder what it is about him that makes him so different from every other person I've ever known. He's not perfect—far from it—but there's a depth to him, something rare and precious, like a treasure hidden beneath the surface. It's in the way he listens, like I matter more than anything else in that moment. It's in the way he remembers the little things I've said, the things I don't even realize I've mentioned.

We're sitting in the tiny cafe on the corner of Hawthorne Street, where the air smells like cinnamon and fresh-baked bread, and the walls are lined with mismatched chairs and tables that make you feel like you're in someone's living room. I've been here a hundred times, and yet, every time Finn walks in with me, it feels like a first. His hand brushes mine as we sit down, and I can't help but smile at the way he looks at me, like I'm the only person in the room, even though there's a whole crowd of people milling around us.

"So," he says, taking a sip of his coffee and raising an eyebrow at me. "What's next?"

I laugh, a sound that feels foreign to me after all this time. "What do you mean, what's next? I thought we were done with the whole 'what's next' business."

"Oh, I know," he says with that wicked grin of his, the one that always makes my heart skip a beat. "But you have to admit, things have been a little... quiet. And you don't strike me as the type to sit still for long."

I bite my lip, looking around the cafe. He's right, in a way. Life has settled into a strange kind of rhythm, one that I never thought I'd have again. But even in the calm, there's a part of me that itches for something more. I don't know if it's the past that still lingers like a shadow, or if it's just the fact that I'm not quite used to peace, but I can feel it deep inside me—the desire to keep moving, to keep evolving, to keep growing.

"I guess," I say slowly, "I've been thinking about it. About what comes next." I set my coffee cup down and meet his gaze. "It's like... like I'm waiting for something to happen, but I don't know what. Maybe I'm afraid that if I stop, if I let myself get too comfortable, I'll lose everything again."

Finn sets his cup down, his expression softening. He leans across the table, his hand reaching out to touch mine, his thumb brushing over my knuckles. It's a simple gesture, but it feels like everything to me in that moment.

"You won't lose anything," he says, his voice steady. "Not if we're in this together."

I know, in my heart, that he's right. And yet, the fear lingers. The fear that, at any moment, the floor will drop out from beneath me, and I'll be left alone again. But with Finn, with him beside me, I know that no matter what happens next, I'll be okay. We'll be okay.

He smiles at me then, a smile that's both tender and knowing, like he can read the storm brewing inside me, but he's content to let it pass on its own. "Whatever comes next," he says softly, "we face it together. No more running. No more hiding."

I nod, feeling something shift inside me, like a door opening to a future I never thought I'd have. The world outside may be unpredictable, but in this moment, in this place, with him, I feel certain of one thing: we've already won. And whatever comes next, we'll face it with the same strength, the same love that has carried us this far.

I had always thought I would leave certain parts of myself behind when I found someone who could understand the mess of my past, but I was wrong. Some things can't be wiped away, no matter how hard you try. They're like ink stains, settled into the fabric of you, impossible to erase, only to fade with time. I had always imagined that my relationship with Finn would be like a clean slate, a fresh start. And in some ways, it was. But in others, it felt like an extension of the chaos I'd been running from for so long.

We sat on the worn leather couch that had become our refuge, the one Finn had insisted on keeping even after I told him it was too old, too damaged. He had simply shrugged and said, "It has character." I had laughed at the idea of character being synonymous with cracked cushions and stains that didn't wash out, but I had stopped trying to replace it. That couch, the place where we spent so many nights wrapped in blankets, talking or not talking, felt like the one thing in my life that could hold all of me, all of my contradictions. It didn't judge, didn't expect.

Finn stretched out beside me, his hand resting on the back of my neck as I leaned into him, the comfortable silence between us broken only by the occasional sound of the wind tapping against the window. He had this way of being present without feeling like he was waiting for something. He was just there, in the moment, and it was the easiest thing in the world to fall into that space with him. But every now and then, the quiet would feel heavy, and that's when I knew—he was thinking.

"I've been thinking," he said, his voice low, like he was testing the words before they left his mouth. "About what comes next for us."

I turned to look at him, noting the furrow between his brows. "I thought we already decided. We're good. Right?"

He hesitated, a shift in the air, like there was something he wasn't saying. "We are," he said slowly. "But I don't know... there's something that's been bothering me, something I can't quite shake."

I shifted, sitting up a little, feeling a prickle of concern. "What's bothering you?"

Finn let out a breath, running his fingers through his hair. "It's not about us," he said quickly, like he wanted to reassure me. "It's... It's about this whole thing. Us. You know, everything we've been through. I don't know, there's just this feeling. Like we're missing something."

I blinked at him, unsure how to process his words. "Missing something?" I repeated, trying to make sense of it. "What do you mean?"

"I don't know," he said again, rubbing the back of his neck. "Maybe it's because we've been running from the past for so long that we're not really thinking about what happens when the past doesn't catch up to us. We've spent so much time surviving, it's like we forgot how to live."

I frowned. "You're scaring me a little, Finn. What do you mean, we forgot how to live?"

He sat up, his expression hardening as if he were trying to work something out in his mind. "What I'm trying to say is, we've been so focused on making sure we don't fall apart, that we haven't really... dreamed. Not together. Not about the future."

I felt a flutter of unease. "I thought we were building something. Isn't that what we've been doing?"

"We are," Finn said quickly, "but there's a difference between building and living. You know what I mean? I don't want us to be so caught up in surviving that we forget what it's like to truly live. To be... free. To have something more than just this constant vigilance."

I could feel a lump in my throat, the words feeling a little too close to the things I'd been avoiding. The truth of it was, I hadn't let myself dream about the future in a long time. I had buried that part of myself so deep that even I wasn't sure where to find it anymore. Dreams had once been the enemy, because they led to disappointment, to heartbreak, to loss. I had convinced myself that the safest route was to keep my head down, to hold tight to the present, and to never look too far ahead.

But Finn was asking me to do something I wasn't sure I could. He was asking me to trust that the future could be a place worth hoping for, a place that wouldn't crumble under the weight of our past. He was asking me to believe that it could be real, that we could have a real future, beyond the walls we'd built around us.

"I don't know how to do that," I whispered, feeling the fear rise in me.

Finn turned to face me fully, his hand sliding under my chin, lifting my gaze to meet his. "I know you're scared. I know the past still hangs over us like a storm cloud. But we can't let it control us forever. Not if we're going to have something more than just getting through each day."

I swallowed hard, my heart pounding in my chest. "But what if we're just... dreaming too big? What if it all falls apart?"

"Then we rebuild," he said firmly, his voice steady and sure. "But we rebuild together. And no matter what happens, we never stop dreaming."

I wanted to argue, to cling to the comfort of the life we'd carved out, where every day was a quiet victory. But looking at Finn, at the raw honesty in his eyes, I knew I couldn't hide anymore. The future was there, waiting for us, whether I was ready for it or not. And maybe—just maybe—it was time to stop running from it.

It's strange, the way life sometimes throws you a curveball, when you least expect it. You can get so comfortable in the quiet spaces, the ones where nothing feels urgent, nothing feels out of reach. But then—just as you've convinced yourself that you're safe, that nothing could disturb the peace you've fought so hard for—something shifts. And it's small at first, a flicker in the corner of your eye, a change in the air, like a storm brewing on the horizon. You tell yourself it's nothing. You tell yourself that this is just the world shifting slightly out of focus, but deep down, you know better.

Finn and I had built a life together, slowly, steadily. We had started with conversations over late-night coffee and quiet mornings spent watching the sun creep across the sky. It wasn't perfect. It wasn't even close. But it was ours. We had our secrets, our flaws, the things we didn't talk about—but we understood each other in ways no one else ever could. It was supposed to be enough.

But then came the text.

It wasn't even a phone call. It didn't need to be. This was the kind of thing that didn't deserve a voice, a trembling "hello" on the other end of the line. No, this came in the form of a simple, innocuous message that I almost missed because of how mundane it seemed. The number was unfamiliar, the message, at first glance, looked like another spam attempt. But then I read it again.

"Do you remember me?"

That was it. Nothing else. Just those words hanging in the air like a spark waiting to ignite. It wasn't the kind of message you could easily brush aside. It was a question that seemed to carry a thousand different meanings, each one more unsettling than the last. My heart did that annoying skip, the kind it always did when something was off, when the world around me suddenly shifted. I had no idea who it was from, or why they would send such a cryptic message. But I knew—instinctively—that this was no accident.

I sat there for a moment, staring at the screen, wondering if I should respond. I didn't want to. I didn't want to drag whatever it was back into my life, not when we'd finally managed to put the past behind us. But something in me—the part that had always been curious, that always needed to know—made my fingers hover over the keyboard. Before I could stop myself, I typed back.

"Who is this?"

The response came almost immediately. It was like the person had been waiting for me to ask.

"It's been a long time. I've missed you."

I felt a coldness settle in the pit of my stomach. The words didn't belong to anyone I knew. Not anyone who was part of my life now. The message felt... wrong. Off. I stared at it, trying to make sense of it, trying to place the voice I couldn't quite hear through the screen.

It was then that I heard Finn's voice behind me, low and steady as he entered the room. "Everything okay?" he asked, his tone casual, but the question was weighted with the usual concern.

I didn't turn to look at him right away. My fingers still hovered over the phone, but I couldn't bring myself to look away from the message.

"Yeah," I said, trying to sound normal. "Just... just a weird text."

"From who?" Finn asked, stepping closer. He must've noticed the tension in my shoulders, the way my fingers twitched at the phone.

I hesitated for only a second before I showed him the screen, the words still glowing there like a beacon. I could feel Finn's gaze shift, the muscles in his jaw tightening as he read. There was something in his silence that made my stomach flip.

"What's this about?" he asked, his voice tighter than before. It wasn't a question I had an answer for.

"I don't know," I said, shrugging. "It's just some random message. Probably spam."

Finn didn't look convinced. "You don't think it's someone you know?"

I shook my head, but the doubt gnawed at me. The message, the way it was worded, the unsettling sense of familiarity in the words. "I don't know. I can't place it."

Finn sat down beside me, his eyes scanning the message again. He didn't ask any more questions, but I could feel him thinking. He wasn't the type to let things go without understanding them, and I knew better than to think he wouldn't push for answers.

"You should block it," he suggested, reaching for my phone, but I pulled it back before he could.

"I think... I think I need to respond."

Finn froze. "Why?"

"Because," I said slowly, the weight of it sinking in. "Because I need to know who this is. I need to know why they think I would remember them. It's not just a spam message, Finn. I don't know how to explain it, but I feel like this is more than that."

The room was quiet for a beat, and I could hear my own heartbeat thudding in my ears. Finn's expression was unreadable, but I knew him well enough to see the flicker of concern behind his eyes. "What if it's someone from your past?" he asked, his voice quieter now. "Someone you don't want to remember?"

I swallowed hard. The question hung in the air, suspended like a rope I had to either grab onto or let go. I wasn't sure which was scarier.

Before I could respond, my phone buzzed again.

The new message blinked on the screen. My breath caught in my throat as I read it aloud, my voice barely above a whisper.

"Don't you want to know who I really am?"

Chapter 40: Hearts Aglow

I never expected that the smell of freshly baked bread could feel like such a triumph. But there it was, wafting through the air as the sun began to dip below the horizon, casting long shadows over our little gathering. The warm, golden light made everything look more beautiful—Finn's hand on mine, the wildflowers strung together in imperfect but charming bouquets, the laughter of my friends mingling with the clink of wine glasses. It was, in a word, perfect. And not just perfect in that Instagrammable, filtered way—no, this was a perfect that had earned every hard-fought second.

"How's the wine?" I asked, raising an eyebrow at Finn as he sipped from his glass, his face still reflecting that rare, unguarded joy. The kind of joy I'd forgotten existed, something untouched by worry or past mistakes.

He grinned, the corners of his eyes crinkling, and for a moment, it was as though the whole world around us faded to a dull hum. There was only him, only that smile that seemed to say everything I needed to hear. "It's not bad. Could use a little more... oh, I don't know, daring?" He took another sip, his grin widening. "Maybe you should've gone with a red. Something more adventurous."

I snorted, the sound bursting out of me unexpectedly. "Oh sure, because the last thing I need is my friends getting tipsy and revealing embarrassing secrets over a bold Merlot."

Finn's eyes twinkled with mischief. "That's exactly what I'm counting on." He let go of my hand only long enough to pour himself more wine, a glint of playful challenge lighting his face. The man had no idea how to take anything seriously, but I couldn't help but love him for it.

"You're terrible," I teased, nudging him with my elbow. His response was a soft laugh, but one that quickly melted into a sigh when he turned to look at the crowd gathering around the backyard.

It wasn't a large party, not by any stretch. But in that moment, it felt monumental. There was my mother, who, after all these years, finally seemed to be accepting the idea of letting me go—at least in the sense of me having a life of my own, not one dictated by her well-meaning but sometimes suffocating advice. She was talking to Liam, who had somehow survived his awkward teenage years and grown into someone almost—dare I say it—charming. Maybe it was the dimming light, the way it softened everyone's features, but the evening felt like something out of a dream. The hard edges of the past few months seemed to have dulled, leaving behind something tender, something fragile that I was still learning how to hold onto.

Finn caught my eye again, and for a moment, I saw the unspoken question there—about us, about what this new chapter would hold. He'd never been the kind of man to rush. But he was patient with me in a way that left me speechless sometimes. Even now, with everything uncertain, with the weight of the changes we'd both been through, he stood by my side like he always had, steady and unwavering.

"I thought you were the one who was supposed to be nervous," he remarked, his voice low enough that only I could hear.

I arched an eyebrow, feigning ignorance. "Me? Nervous? I'm perfectly fine, thank you very much."

But I wasn't fine. Not exactly. There was a part of me that still couldn't fully believe this was happening. That somehow, after all the missteps and mistakes, the broken pieces that seemed beyond repair, we had ended up here. Not just together, but stronger for everything we'd faced. I wasn't sure when I'd stopped bracing for the next disaster to strike. When did I start to believe that maybe this time, just maybe, it could work?

Finn reached out, brushing a stray lock of hair behind my ear in the slow, deliberate way that made my heart stutter. "I'm not worried," he said softly, his thumb tracing the line of my jaw. "Because no matter what, we've made it this far. We'll keep making it, together."

His words weren't a promise. They were a truth, as solid as the earth beneath our feet. And it hit me then, like a burst of sunlight, that it wasn't just about surviving anymore. It was about living. About choosing to be brave enough to face the unknown, knowing the road ahead would never be perfect, but it would always, always be ours.

I took a deep breath, steadying myself against the wave of emotion that threatened to sweep me away. "You're not getting rid of me that easily, Finn. Not even with your terrible wine suggestions."

He laughed, a rich, deep sound that felt like music to my ears. "Good," he said, squeezing my hand. "Because I wasn't planning on letting you go."

We stood there, for a few moments that stretched into something timeless, just taking in the world around us—the people, the place, the shared history that had brought us here. I realized then that it was all enough. The way the sky bled into dusk, the way the soft murmur of voices wrapped around us, the way Finn's hand fit so perfectly in mine. It was enough. More than I'd ever imagined.

And as I glanced over at the friends and family who had gathered—people who had witnessed our struggles and our triumphs—I knew one thing for sure: this was only the beginning. Whatever came next, we were ready.

I should have known something was coming. Nothing in my life had ever been simple, and just when I thought I'd found a moment of peace, a simple toast and a glass of wine, the universe had other plans.

I was standing beside Finn, the taste of the warm, buttery bread still lingering in my mouth, when I saw her. There, on the edge of the yard, was Vanessa. I would have known her anywhere, even if it had been years since we last crossed paths. She was as striking as ever, her raven-black hair falling in soft waves over her shoulders, her dress hugging her in all the right places—too perfectly, almost like she'd stepped out of some glossy magazine.

I tried not to let my heart drop into my stomach, but the way she glanced around at the people gathered, the cool, calculated look in her eyes as she scanned the scene like she owned the place—it made my skin crawl.

"Who invited her?" I whispered to Finn, trying to keep my voice steady.

He didn't even look at her. I could feel him stiffen next to me, his thumb running absentmindedly over my knuckles. "I didn't."

The words were simple, but they carried weight. Vanessa hadn't been part of our lives in years, not after what happened—the fallout, the distance that had grown between us. But here she was, strolling into my celebration like she was the guest of honor.

Finn cleared his throat, still not looking at her, and I could tell something had shifted in him. I didn't know if it was the past or the pressure of the evening, but something was off.

"She's been like this," he said, finally meeting my gaze. "Always showing up at the wrong moment, like she's got a claim on something that isn't hers."

I nodded, trying not to let the bitterness rise in my throat. "Right. Because a wedding toast and a backyard barbecue scream 'open invitation,'" I muttered, but the words felt brittle in my mouth.

"Don't worry about her," Finn said, squeezing my hand. "She won't ruin this."

But the truth was, I wasn't worried about her ruining the evening. It wasn't that simple. It was the way she had always inserted herself into my life, like a shadow that wouldn't leave. And now she was standing there, staring at Finn the way she used to. It made something cold tighten in my chest. There was no easy way to explain it, but there was always that little thread of doubt she left in the back of my mind, like an itch I could never quite scratch.

I didn't say anything more, but I couldn't tear my gaze away from her as she glided over to our little group. She looked at me, her lips curling in a smile that I had never trusted.

"You look...different," she said, her voice silky, her eyes flickering over me like I was a painting she'd seen in passing, something worthy of a glance but not of real interest. "Happy, I guess."

It wasn't a compliment. And it wasn't a question, either. It was an observation, one that stung more than it should have.

"I'm glad you think so," I said, forcing a smile. "Isn't it a lovely evening?"

Vanessa's smile never wavered, though there was a coldness in her eyes. "I don't know. Haven't really been able to enjoy it, with all the 'new beginnings' floating around. You know how those things go." She glanced at Finn as she said it, and for a brief moment, her gaze softened, just enough to make my stomach drop.

"Is there something I can do for you?" Finn's voice cut through the moment, his tone sharp, uninviting.

Vanessa's eyes flicked back to him, an almost imperceptible glint of amusement in them. "I'm just here to see the show," she replied with a shrug, her fingers idly toying with the glass in her hand. "And to see how long it takes before reality hits."

I wanted to protest, to say something cutting and clever, to tell her she wasn't welcome, but I didn't. Instead, I just took a step closer to Finn, the warmth of his hand a small comfort against the cool tension thickening in the air between us.

Her presence lingered like smoke in a room, and I couldn't shake the feeling that she was watching, waiting for something to break. I knew I had to confront this, whatever it was. Because I had worked so hard to get here—this place of peace, this moment where everything finally felt right—and I wouldn't let her poison it. Not now, not after everything we'd been through.

Finn squeezed my hand again, but this time there was a new tension in his voice, one I hadn't heard before. "Let's get some air," he suggested, his gaze shifting from Vanessa back to me. "Come on."

Before I could even respond, Finn led me away from the group and toward the far corner of the yard, where the shadows were thick and the sounds of the party seemed muffled by the walls of the house. The change of scene gave me a moment to breathe, but it didn't quite shake the feeling of unease that had settled in my chest.

"I don't like this," I admitted, once we were out of earshot.

Finn was silent for a long moment, looking up at the darkening sky. "I don't either. But it's not going to ruin what we've built."

"I just—" I stopped myself, frustration bubbling up. "I don't want her here. She's like a ghost that won't leave."

Finn's eyes softened, and he pulled me closer, wrapping his arms around me like he could shield me from everything else. "I won't let her hurt you. Not again." His voice was low, serious, but the determination in it made my heart ache. "You're everything to me, and no one—no one—gets to change that."

For the first time that evening, I believed him.

The warmth of the evening air wrapped around us like a soft embrace, the flickering light of lanterns casting dancing shadows over the faces of our loved ones. Music swirled in the background, the hum of voices carrying across the garden, each note a promise of joy that hung in the night. It was almost surreal, this moment of peace, as if the storm that had raged for so long had finally settled. We were here. We had made it.

I squeezed Finn's hand, and he turned to me, his smile wide and genuine. The corner of his mouth quirked up in a way that was all his, a silent acknowledgement of the road we'd traveled. The road we were still on, but now, we were walking it together.

"I thought we'd never get here," I murmured, the words slipping out before I could stop them. My voice was soft, laced with something unspoken, something fragile that still lingered between us.

Finn's fingers tightened around mine, his thumb brushing the back of my hand with a tenderness that made my heart beat a little faster. "We're here now," he said, his tone steady, as if to remind me that what had come before was nothing but a stepping stone to this moment.

I took a breath, the weight of the last few months pressing down on me. It hadn't been easy, and there were parts of me that would never be the same. But in his eyes, I found a calmness I hadn't realized I'd been searching for. A peace that anchored me, grounded me in a way that felt more real than anything else in my life.

"Isn't it funny?" I said, tilting my head slightly, watching the way the lantern light caught in his hair. "How we always think we're ready for the next step, but it takes something... big... to make us realize what we're really capable of."

Finn chuckled softly, the sound warm and familiar. "I don't think we ever really know what we're capable of until we're forced to find out. That's the fun part, right? We've got this... whatever this is."

I glanced over at our friends, standing in clusters, laughing, chatting, and sharing in our happiness. Every person here had been a part of our journey, in one way or another. Some had pulled us up when we were too broken to stand on our own. Others had stood beside us in quiet understanding, offering support without ever asking for anything in return. They were the foundation we had built this life on, the ones who had helped shape us into the people we were becoming.

It was a bittersweet realization, that everything we had been through had been necessary. Painful, yes, but it had led us to this moment of connection, of understanding that stretched deeper than just the surface. I could feel it in the way Finn's hand lingered in mine, the way our gazes met, steady and unwavering.

"I never would've thought we'd be here," I said softly, my voice barely above a whisper, but loud enough for him to hear. "If someone had told me, months ago, that this would be our future... I would've laughed."

Finn leaned in closer, his breath warm against my ear. "I would've laughed, too. But I guess the joke's on us, huh?"

I couldn't help but laugh, the sound mingling with the music that played softly in the background. The world felt right, and for the first time in a long while, I wasn't looking over my shoulder, waiting for something to go wrong. Everything that had happened, everything we had been through, had led us here. And somehow, in some inexplicable way, we had survived it all.

As the evening wore on, we found ourselves slipping away from the crowd, walking toward the far end of the garden, where the old oak tree stood—a silent witness to all that had come before. The air smelled of jasmine and fresh earth, the quiet rustling of leaves accompanying our footsteps. Finn's hand never left mine, his fingers tracing patterns along my skin as if he couldn't bear to let go.

"What's on your mind?" he asked, his voice low and thoughtful as we reached the base of the tree.

I paused, looking up at the branches above us, the stars barely visible through the thick canopy. "Just... wondering what's next."

Finn chuckled, stepping closer, his arms wrapping around me. "Next? We keep going. Together."

But there was something in his tone, a quiet tension that I couldn't quite place. He said the words as if they were simple, as if everything about our future was laid out in front of us, clear and certain. But deep down, I knew better. Life wasn't that neat. It wasn't that easy.

Before I could ask him what he meant, a sharp sound broke the stillness—footsteps crunching on the gravel path behind us. We turned, instinctively, our eyes searching the shadows for the source of the noise.

A figure emerged from the darkness, the silhouette familiar but unsettling. My heart skipped a beat, a sudden rush of unease flooding my chest. I couldn't make out the face, but the presence was undeniable. Someone from the past. Someone I hadn't expected to see again.

Finn's grip on me tightened, his body tensing beside me. "Who is it?" he murmured, his voice low and guarded.

I swallowed hard, trying to steady my breath. "I don't know."

But I was already starting to fear I did.

Chapter 41: The Promise

The moon hung low that night, a half-silvered crescent, casting just enough light to make the world feel intimate, like the earth itself was holding its breath. I stood there, barefoot in the cool grass, feeling the earth press up against me like an old friend. Finn's eyes, dark and intense, seemed to drink in the moonlight, his face a sharp silhouette against the velvet sky. The air was thick with promise, as if the universe itself had drawn us into this moment for a reason I couldn't quite put into words.

"Are you sure?" I asked, my voice a whisper that was swallowed by the night. The words felt too heavy, yet they were necessary. This wasn't a question of doubt but of asking for something, anything, to make this moment last. I was already trembling, but I wasn't sure if it was from the cold or the weight of everything we had gone through.

He nodded slowly, a small, crooked smile playing at the corner of his lips. "I've never been more sure of anything in my life." His voice had the kind of warmth that made you believe in impossible things. His hands found mine, rough from work but gentle in their grip. There was no grand gesture, no extravagant promises. Just a simple truth, an unspoken pact that seemed to stretch out beyond the stars themselves.

I let out a breath I hadn't realized I was holding, the tension draining from my body. The grass beneath me felt softer now, as if the earth itself was reassuring me that we were exactly where we needed to be. I closed my eyes for a moment, listening to the steady rhythm of his heartbeat, the sound of our breathing in the stillness. I knew, without a doubt, that I had found something extraordinary in him—something worth every sacrifice, every moment of doubt, every storm we had weathered together.

The night held us in its quiet embrace, and I could feel the heaviness of all the unspoken things between us lift, if only for a fleeting moment. But that moment was enough.

"I don't know what comes next," I said, almost to myself, staring at the stars that seemed to hang there, watching over us like silent witnesses to our quiet vows. "But I'm not afraid of it anymore."

Finn's thumb gently stroked the back of my hand, a small, tender gesture that somehow felt like the most intimate thing in the world. "We don't have to know," he said. "We just have to keep moving forward, together. No matter what."

There was a finality to his words, as though he were wrapping us both up in something unbreakable. But there was a raw honesty there too, a willingness to accept whatever came, no matter how difficult or uncertain. It made me want to believe in the impossible again, to believe that love could be this solid, this enduring, no matter how dark the world might seem.

"I love you," I whispered, and the words felt like a pledge, like something far deeper than mere affection. They were a promise, too, though I didn't need to say that out loud. He knew. Finn always knew.

He leaned in, his lips brushing mine in a soft, slow kiss, as if we were marking the end of something—some chapter, some painful part of our lives—and the beginning of something else. Something new. His kiss deepened, gentle but certain, the taste of him flooding my senses. The kiss was a promise, just as his words had been—a vow that transcended everything we had been through.

"I'll love you, forever," he murmured against my lips, his breath warm against my skin. "And I'll protect you. Always."

The simple power of those words settled over me like a soft blanket, wrapping me in warmth and safety. I knew what it meant to be truly seen now, truly known. I was no longer just a girl caught in the aftermath of a storm. I was someone worthy of this kind of love. His love. I didn't need the stars to tell me that. Finn's touch, his words, the way he looked at me as if I were the most important thing in his world—that was enough.

We pulled back, our foreheads resting together for a moment, both of us breathing in the stillness, as if time had slowed just for us. The world around us seemed to fall away, leaving only the two of us beneath the vast, endless sky.

And in that moment, I didn't fear the future. I didn't fear the unknown. Because I knew that as long as we had each other, we could face anything. No matter how hard, no matter how impossible. Finn's promise wasn't just words. It was a force, something unshakable. Something I could build my entire world on.

He kissed my forehead softly, the gesture both tender and final. "Let's make this our story," he said, his voice quiet but sure.

I smiled, the warmth of his promise filling me from the inside out. "It's already begun."

And somehow, in the quiet dark of that night, I knew it was true. Our story wasn't just a collection of memories or fleeting moments. It was something living, breathing, unfolding with every passing second. It was a promise kept, one that would last far beyond the boundaries of time.

The morning after was no less serene, though the weight of Finn's words hung in the air like a faint, lingering perfume. I could still feel the echoes of the promise in my chest, a rhythm I couldn't shake, no matter how hard I tried to distract myself with the mundane. The coffee pot whistled on the counter, the kitchen bathed in soft light, and I was trying my hardest to make the moment last. To make it something more than just a fleeting chapter in a book I hadn't even begun to understand.

"Morning," Finn called from the doorway, his voice low but still carrying that familiarity that made me feel like we were the only two people in the world. He stood there, leaning against the frame, his sleeves rolled up to the elbows, the fabric of his shirt taut across his chest. There was something quiet about him this morning, a gentleness I hadn't seen before, like a slow breath held for far too long and finally let go.

"Morning," I replied, forcing myself not to stare too intently at him, though I was pretty sure I was failing. I poured my coffee, the rich scent filling the room, as I tried to pretend like my thoughts weren't spinning in circles.

He raised an eyebrow as he walked toward the table, pulling out the chair across from mine. "You look like you've got a hundred thoughts brewing in that head of yours."

I laughed softly, the sound almost a breathless thing. "And you're not wrong." I set the cup down and wiped my palms against the fabric of my jeans. "I've been thinking about everything. About how... well, about how everything feels different now. More real, I guess."

Finn's expression softened, and he leaned forward, his elbows resting on the table. "It is real," he said, his gaze unwavering. "What we have, it's not just a promise. It's a fact."

I could feel the sincerity in his voice, even as it carried that underlying rawness. There was something unspoken between us, something that tugged at my insides. His words were true, but I couldn't shake the nagging question that kept echoing in my mind. What happens when promises are tested? What happens when the world outside starts to unravel?

"What if it gets harder?" I asked before I could stop myself. The words slipped out like a confession, like a hesitation I hadn't even known was there.

Finn's brow furrowed just slightly, and for a brief moment, the lightness that always hung around him seemed to evaporate. He sat back in his chair, his fingers tapping the surface of the table thoughtfully. "Hard doesn't mean impossible," he said, his voice steady, though there was a shadow in his eyes I hadn't seen before. "If it was easy, it wouldn't be worth it."

I bit my lip, the weight of his words landing heavier than I expected. There was something in them that resonated with the small ache in my chest—the nagging, constant whisper of doubt I tried to ignore. It wasn't just the future that was uncertain; it was the path we'd already walked. So much had changed, and it wasn't just the world around us. It was us, too.

"I just..." I hesitated, the words tasting like ashes in my mouth. "I never thought we'd be here. I never thought I'd get to this place, not after everything."

His gaze softened, and he reached across the table, his hand covering mine. "And yet, here we are," he said, his voice a quiet promise in itself. "We've got this, whatever this is. I'm not going anywhere."

I smiled despite myself, the words wrapping around my heart like a shield. But as much as I wanted to believe him, there was a part of me that couldn't quite let go of the worry gnawing at the edges of my mind. The world wasn't as forgiving as Finn was. People weren't always as reliable, and promises, no matter how well intentioned, could easily be broken. But then again, maybe that was just the fear talking—the fear of loss, of the future we couldn't control.

"Hey, we're in this together, right?" Finn's voice broke through my thoughts, grounding me in the present. He squeezed my hand gently, his eyes a steady anchor. "No matter what happens. I've got you."

"I know," I said softly, my heart a tangled mess of gratitude and worry. "And I've got you, too."

The quiet between us settled, but the unease that had bloomed inside me didn't fade. There was something in the air now, something heavier than the ordinary morning chatter. It was a tension, a quiet storm that lingered just out of reach.

"Have you thought about what's next?" Finn asked suddenly, his tone thoughtful as he leaned back in his chair, his fingers drumming softly against the wood.

"Next?" I repeated, still trying to catch up with him.

"Yeah," he said, looking out the window as if the answer might be written on the horizon. "After this. After we figure things out."

I felt the shift in the air again—like the conversation had just gone deeper, even though the surface seemed so calm. "I don't know," I admitted. "It's just... a lot."

Finn didn't push me for an answer, and I appreciated that. Instead, he rose from his chair, moving around the table with an easy grace, his footsteps silent against the floor. He paused beside me, his hand brushing the back of my neck in a soft, comforting touch.

"I don't need you to have the answers right now," he said, his lips close to my ear, his voice warm and steady. "I just need you to be here. With me. That's all."

His words settled over me like a blanket, and for a moment, everything felt manageable again. It was easy to get lost in the idea of forever when you were standing beside someone who made you feel like you could take on the world together. But then, reality always had a way of creeping back in.

"I'm here," I whispered, leaning into the touch, feeling the steady beat of his heart against mine.

And for a fleeting moment, the world outside didn't matter.

The days that followed were a mix of stillness and restlessness, a delicate dance between the peace of knowing that we were in this together, and the nagging uncertainty of a world that seemed to shift beneath our feet every time we took a step forward. Finn and I had settled into a rhythm, easy and familiar, like the echo of two hearts beating in sync. But there was something lurking beneath that quiet—a tension I couldn't shake.

It started with the small things. The way Finn's eyes would sometimes flicker toward the door as if expecting someone to walk in at any moment. The way he'd glance over his shoulder when we were out, like he was checking for someone who wasn't there. It was subtle, so subtle that I almost convinced myself I was imagining it. But the look in his eyes told a different story, one I couldn't ignore.

"I'm going to run some errands," he said one evening, breaking the silence as we sat in the living room, the glow of the fireplace casting long shadows on the walls. He didn't offer any further explanation, just stood up and began to gather his jacket. The way he moved, brisk and purposeful, set off a quiet alarm in my chest.

I watched him for a moment, unsure of what to say. The air between us had grown thicker with unspoken words.

"Do you need me to come with you?" I asked before I could stop myself.

Finn paused at the door, his hand on the handle. His back was turned to me, but I could feel the weight of his thoughts hanging in the space between us. "No," he said quietly. "It's better if I go alone."

There it was again—the distance. A quiet pull that separated us, not physically, but emotionally. I swallowed the words I wanted to say, the questions that hovered on the tip of my tongue. Instead, I nodded, watching him leave. His footsteps grew fainter, and the door clicked shut behind him, leaving me in the silence of the room.

The evening stretched on without him. I could hear the wind pick up outside, rustling the trees and sending a chill through the house. My mind, ever the relentless companion, couldn't stop turning over the image of Finn walking out the door. What was he hiding? What wasn't he telling me? He was so good at making me believe in the simplicity of everything between us, but there were cracks in the façade—ones I had only started to notice. I didn't want to believe it, but the truth felt like a shadow in the corner of the room, waiting for me to acknowledge it.

An hour passed before I heard the sound of a car pulling up outside. I stood, instinctively moving toward the window. Finn's truck was parked in the driveway, but something about his return felt... different. He stepped out of the vehicle with a quick, almost tense movement, his expression unreadable. I couldn't help myself; I watched him through the curtains, my heart skipping in my chest.

As he walked toward the door, I saw it—the briefest flash of something in his eyes. It wasn't fear, not exactly. More like... guilt? Or maybe just the kind of resignation that comes when someone is carrying a burden they can't bear to share.

"Finn?" I called softly as he entered, the question hanging in the air between us before he had even stepped fully into the room.

He looked at me, his face softening just a fraction. "Hey," he said, trying to sound casual, but I heard the underlying strain in his voice. "Everything's fine."

I didn't believe him, not for a second. "What's going on?" I asked, my voice barely above a whisper, though the tension in my chest was anything but quiet. "You've been acting... strange. Like you're keeping something from me."

Finn didn't answer immediately. Instead, he let out a long breath and ran his hand through his hair, a gesture I knew well—one that always came before he had to make a decision, before he had to say something he wasn't ready to admit.

"It's not what you think," he said finally, his words coming out slow and measured. "I've just... been dealing with some stuff. Things that I don't want to drag you into."

"Finn," I said, stepping closer to him, my heart pounding in my ears. "You don't get to say that. Not anymore. Whatever it is, we're in this together. You promised me."

He flinched, just a tiny shift in his posture, but it was enough to make me stop. I hadn't seen him react like that before, and the realization hit me harder than I'd expected. Whatever this was, it wasn't something we were going to walk through hand in hand.

"I know," he said, his voice rough now, the cracks starting to show. "I know I promised. But there are some things that... they don't belong to you. Not yet."

"Finn," I said, reaching for him, my pulse quickening. "You're scaring me."

He took a step back, shaking his head, his jaw clenched tight. "I don't want to scare you," he said, the words low and strained. "But I don't know if I can keep that promise. Not if I don't protect you from this."

"Protect me from what?" I asked, my breath catching in my throat. I was desperate now, the anxiety creeping up my spine like a cold hand. "Finn, what aren't you telling me?"

He looked away, his gaze fixed somewhere beyond me, lost in some private thought. And then, just as I opened my mouth to press him further, the front door swung open with a violent bang.

I froze. My heart stopped in my chest. And before either of us could react, a shadow appeared in the doorway—tall, ominous, and unmistakable.

Finn's face drained of color, and I knew, in that instant, that everything was about to change.

"Who is it?" I whispered, my voice trembling, as I reached for him, my fingers brushing against his sleeve.

But Finn didn't answer.

Chapter 42: Forever in Flame

I couldn't help but watch the fire as it danced, its bright orange tendrils twisting and curling in the cool evening air. The crackling sound was comforting, like the heartbeat of the world itself. Finn sat beside me on the worn wicker chair, the soft light from the flames casting shadows across his face, highlighting the soft lines of his jaw and the gentle curve of his lips. His hand rested on my knee, warm and steady, the kind of warmth that made you feel like you'd been cradled in the earth itself, safe from everything.

For a moment, I allowed myself to breathe, to simply exist in the quiet intimacy we had crafted together. Our world wasn't perfect—what world is?—but in that space, it felt like it could be. It felt like we had created something beautiful, something that could weather any storm. The simple pleasure of watching the fire together, of sitting in the silence that was comfortable and whole, was a luxury I never thought I would get.

It hadn't always been this way. Oh, there had been moments when I thought we wouldn't survive the storms life sent our way—when the shadows of doubt clouded my vision, when the weight of the past threatened to pull us under. But Finn had always been there, his quiet strength the anchor that kept me grounded, even when I wanted to let go and drift away. He had this way of looking at me, like he could see every piece of my soul, every fear, every flaw, and yet he didn't flinch. He didn't turn away.

He made me believe that I was worthy of love, of something real and lasting.

I glanced over at him now, the corner of my lips tugging up as I caught the way his eyes flickered to mine. He was always watching me, studying me, as though there was more to uncover. And I always felt like there was, like there would always be something new between us to discover. He was a mystery, an enigma wrapped in a quiet intensity that I couldn't quite unravel, though I had tried. In his gaze, there was something that reminded me of the wildness in the flames—something untamable, a force that both drew me in and made me want to run.

The sound of a branch cracking in the fire broke the quiet, and I startled slightly, but Finn didn't. He was always so composed, always so steady. The contrast between us used to make me feel unbalanced, like we were two halves of a puzzle that didn't fit. But now, I saw it for what it was—his steadiness was my grounding force, and my restlessness was the spark that kept our world alive, always in motion, always on the edge of something new.

"You're quiet tonight," Finn remarked, his voice soft but sharp enough to slice through the stillness.

I turned my head to look at him, catching the way the firelight flickered in his eyes, a reflection of the storm that sometimes raged beneath his calm exterior.

"I'm just thinking," I replied, my voice almost a whisper.

His brow furrowed slightly, a gesture I'd come to recognize as him trying to navigate my emotions, as though he could read me better than I could read myself. He always had that way about him—able to step into my world, uninvited, but always in the most comforting way. It was as if he could sense when I was struggling, even when I didn't have the words to explain it.

"What are you thinking about?" he asked, his thumb gently brushing over my knee in a rhythm that soothed me more than he probably realized.

I sighed, leaning back into the chair, feeling the worn fabric against my back, the kind of comfort that comes with time and care. "How easy it would be to lose this," I said, the words slipping out before I could stop them. "How easy it would be for us to slip back into the chaos, to let the world tear us apart again."

Finn's fingers stilled for a moment, and I caught the shift in his gaze. His jaw tightened, just a fraction, and I knew the thought had crossed his mind, too. The fragility of everything we had built was never far from either of us. But it was different now.

"We won't," he said firmly, the conviction in his voice cutting through the doubt that tried to settle in my chest.

I looked at him, really looked at him, and saw the strength in his eyes—the kind of strength that came from facing the darkness and surviving it. "But how can you be so sure?" I asked, my voice raw with vulnerability. "How can you be so sure that nothing will come along and destroy it?"

He met my gaze and smiled, that quiet, knowing smile that made me feel both seen and understood, in ways no one else ever could. "Because we've already survived it," he said softly. "Everything that tried to tear us apart... it didn't. And that means nothing can now."

I felt my heart stutter in my chest, a flutter of something I couldn't quite name. But it was enough to make my worries feel smaller, to make the uncertainty in my mind fade just a little. We had fought for this. We had fought for each other. And maybe, just maybe, that meant it was stronger than anything life could throw at us.

I leaned forward, my hand brushing against his, and for the first time in days, I allowed myself to believe it—believe that we were unstoppable, that nothing could extinguish the flame we had started together.

It was a Thursday morning, and the air smelled of coffee, fresh bread, and possibility—the kind of morning that made you feel like something important was just around the corner, waiting to happen. Finn was already up, his easy gait echoing through the kitchen as he prepared breakfast. I could hear the sizzle of eggs, the soft clink of the coffee pot, and the occasional hum of his voice as he sang under his breath. It wasn't much—just the simple act of him being there, of his presence filling the space—but it was enough. Enough to make my heart settle, enough to remind me that all the chaos of the past had, in some way, made this stillness even more precious.

I was still wrapped in the warmth of the bed, the sheets tangled around me like a cocoon, trying to coax the last bits of sleep from my body. But it wasn't happening. Not today. The sun had come up too brightly, the world outside too alive with promise. And there was Finn, as always, moving through the world with quiet purpose, like he was the calm center of everything I had once thought I needed to fix. I had long since stopped trying to figure him out, but sometimes, I still marveled at how easy he made it all seem.

"Morning," I said, my voice thick with sleep as I swung my legs off the bed, bare feet meeting the cool wooden floor.

Finn looked over his shoulder, a smile spreading across his face as he poured coffee into two mugs. "Good morning. How'd you sleep?"

"Better than I deserve." I chuckled, shaking my head. "Though, I'm not sure I'm ready to face the day yet."

He raised an eyebrow, turning back to the stove. "What's the matter? No wild adventures planned for today?"

I padded over to him, my fingers brushing his shoulder as I reached for the coffee. The warmth of the mug seeped into my hands, grounding me. "I'm just tired," I said, my voice softening. "I guess I'm still getting used to this... peace. It feels strange."

Finn glanced at me over his shoulder, his expression more serious now. "You're not used to peace?"

I took a sip of the coffee, the bitterness spreading across my tongue, and I exhaled slowly. "No. Not really." I didn't think I had ever really known peace—not until him, not until this life we were building together. It was like the whole world had been moving at breakneck speed, and only now had I finally come to a stop, trying to catch my breath.

He didn't say anything at first, just set the spatula down and turned to face me. "I know what you mean," he said, his voice low, almost to himself. "Sometimes, I wake up and forget for a second that it's real—that we're real."

I raised an eyebrow, amused. "You think this is a dream?"

Finn gave a quiet laugh, a sound that held both humor and something deeper—something I couldn't quite place. "Sometimes. It's hard to believe after everything we've been through. It's like, how did we get here?"

I leaned against the counter, feeling the weight of his words settle between us. "I don't know," I said, my voice quiet now. "But maybe we're here because we fought like hell for it."

Finn's eyes softened, his hand brushing mine once again. "We did," he agreed. "We both did. But sometimes, I wonder if we've earned it yet. If we're really ready for it."

"Earned it?" I couldn't help but laugh, a little bitterly. "Finn, we've been through hell and back. If we haven't earned it, then what the hell has?"

His face tightened at the edge of my words, and he turned away, focusing on the eggs with an intensity that made me wonder if he was really seeing them or just using them as an excuse to hide behind something familiar. I had learned that look—the way he turned in on himself when something felt too heavy to carry, but he refused to let it spill out.

"Hey," I said, more softly now, moving toward him. I touched his arm, the warmth of his skin grounding me. "We've earned it. All of it. Don't doubt that."

He didn't answer right away. But after a long moment, he set the spatula down again and turned to me, his eyes dark and stormy.

"I know," he said, his voice thick. "I just... don't want to lose it. Not now. Not after everything."

The rawness in his words left me quiet for a long beat, my heart heavy in my chest. There it was again—the fear that had always lingered beneath his calm exterior. The fear that, no matter how much we had fought for this, there was always a chance it could slip through our fingers. A chance that something—anything—could come along and destroy it.

I stepped closer, my hand resting on his chest. I could feel the steady beat of his heart beneath my palm, and for a second, it was like the world stopped spinning. "You won't lose me," I said, my voice firm. "I'm not going anywhere, Finn. Not this time."

He looked down at me, his face softening, but there was still something raw in his eyes, something that made my heart ache. "Promise me," he whispered.

"I promise," I said, my voice steady. "I'm right here. With you."

And I meant it. For the first time in my life, I meant it completely. The world might change, life might throw its curveballs, but nothing could take this from us—not anymore. Not when we had come this far, not when we had built something real. I wasn't about to let go of that, no matter how much it scared us both.

The days began to blur into a sequence of lazy mornings and nights that felt too short, too sweet, as though we were suspended in a bubble. There was a peace to our routine now—one that should have been familiar, yet still startled me, like stepping into a dream and wondering if it would all vanish the moment I woke up. Finn was the grounding force I never knew I needed, and I had grown used to the way his presence was both a comfort and a quiet challenge. We were learning how to navigate this life together, one filled with a gentle rhythm that kept me on my toes.

One evening, as the sky wore the deepening hues of dusk, we were on the porch, each of us lost in our own thoughts. I had a book in hand, but my eyes kept drifting to the horizon, where the last of the sun's light still clung to the edge of the world. Finn was beside me, his focus shifting between the firepit in front of us and the quiet street beyond our home. There was something in his expression tonight—something that I couldn't quite place—that had me watching him more closely than usual.

"Penny for your thoughts?" I asked, my voice light, but the edge of curiosity in my tone was sharp enough to cut through the evening air.

He didn't immediately respond, his fingers tracing the rim of his mug as though he could find the right words if he just held on long enough. "I've been thinking," he said finally, his gaze flicking to mine, "about how fragile this all is. How easily it could all slip away."

I tilted my head, studying him carefully. There it was again—the same fear that had settled between us in the mornings, like a weight pressing down on his chest. "Finn, we've been through worse. A lot worse. And look at us now."

He met my eyes, his jaw tightening. "But what if that's the problem? What if we've already fought too many battles? What if we're just waiting for the next one?"

His words were like an ice-cold splash of water. The unease in his voice seemed to resonate in the space between us, and for a moment, I wasn't sure if I was hearing his doubts or my own fears echoing in my mind.

"Maybe you're right," I said slowly, the words tasting strange on my tongue. "Maybe life is always going to throw something at us. But I'm not afraid of that anymore. I'm not afraid of fighting—because now, I know that no matter what happens, I'm not fighting alone."

His eyes softened, and I saw the flicker of something—some unspoken emotion that I couldn't quite name—before he turned his gaze back to the fire. The crackling flames filled the silence between us, but it wasn't uncomfortable. Not yet.

"You're sure about that?" Finn's voice was quieter now, almost a whisper against the night. "Because I think I'm more afraid of losing you than I am of losing everything else."

There was a weight to his words, one that settled heavily on my chest. His vulnerability was rare, precious, and yet it scared me. Because it meant that, despite everything, despite the love we'd built, there was still something fragile between us.

"I'm not going anywhere," I said softly, even as doubt crept into my own voice. "I'm right here. With you."

But even as I spoke the words, a sense of unease prickled the back of my mind. Could we really be sure of that? Could I guarantee that nothing, not even fate itself, would come between us?

Before I could voice any more doubts, the silence was broken by the distant sound of tires on gravel, the faint rumble of an engine growing louder as it approached. Finn stiffened beside me, his gaze flicking toward the road.

"Who the hell is that?" he muttered under his breath, his eyes narrowing as he leaned forward.

I followed his gaze, and my pulse quickened as I saw the dark silhouette of a car creeping toward us, headlights cutting through the shadows. It wasn't unusual for someone to pass by, but this felt different. The car slowed, then stopped just at the edge of our driveway. My breath caught in my throat as the engine shut off, the night now filled with an eerie stillness.

"Stay here," Finn said, his voice low and steady, his hand gripping mine for just a moment before he stood up and started toward the porch steps.

"No, wait," I called out, my voice betraying the tension that suddenly wrapped itself around my chest. "Don't go. We don't know who it is."

He glanced back at me, his face unreadable, but there was a flicker of something in his eyes. Maybe it was concern. Or maybe something else entirely.

"I'll be right back," he said, his words meant to reassure me, but they only heightened my sense of foreboding.

I watched him step off the porch and make his way toward the car, the crunch of gravel beneath his boots sharp in the still night. A part of me wanted to follow him, to insist that we should wait, but my feet stayed frozen to the spot.

The car door opened slowly, the silhouette of a figure emerging from the shadows. Whoever it was, they moved with a purposeful gait, their steps quick but measured. As they approached Finn, I couldn't make out their features, only the shape of their body, their stance—like someone used to command.

I stood up from my chair, my heartbeat thundering in my ears, as a rush of anxiety swept through me. There was something about this person—about this moment—that felt off. Too off.

Finn's voice carried through the night, too low for me to make out, but the tension in his tone was clear. I could see his posture stiffen, his body language shifting from curiosity to something more guarded, more alert.

I started to move toward them, unable to stay back any longer, when a sharp, sudden noise sliced through the air—the unmistakable sound of a car door slamming shut.

Milton Keynes UK
Ingram Content Group UK Ltd.
UKHW030947261124
451585UK00001B/152

9 798230 775652